THE
EDGE
CHRONICLES

FREEGLADER
BOOK 3 OF THE ROOK SAGA

www.edgechronicles.co.uk

NEW SANCTAPHRAX

OLD UNDERTOWN

THE M...

SCREE TOWN

THE STONE GARDENS

THE DEEP WOODS

THE TWILIGHT WOODS

THE EDGELANDS

The Edge.

THE EDGE CHRONICLES

FREEGLADER
← BOOK 3 OF THE ROOK SAGA →

PAUL STEWART AND CHRIS RIDDELL

CORGI

THE DEEP WOODS SETTLEMENTS

THE FOUNDRY GLADE

THE GOBLIN NATIONS

THE EASTERN ROOST

THE SILVER PASTURES

FREEGLADER
A CORGI BOOK 978 0 552 56971 2

First published in Great Britain by Doubleday,
an imprint of Random House Children's Publishers UK
A Random House Group Company

Doubleday edition published 2004
First Corgi edition published 2005
This Corgi edition published 2014

3 5 7 9 10 8 6 4 2

Penguin Random House is committed to a sustainable future for
our business, our readers and our planet. This book is made from
Forest Stewardship Council® certified paper.

MIX
Paper from
responsible sources
FSC® C018179

Corgi Books are published by Random House Children's Publishers UK,
61–63 Uxbridge Road, London W5 5SA

www.**randomhousechildrens**.co.uk
www.**totallyrandombooks**.co.uk
www.**randomhouse**.co.uk

Addresses for companies within The Random House Group Limited can be
found at: www.randomhouse.co.uk/offices.htm

THE RANDOM HOUSE GROUP Limited Reg. No. 954009

A CIP catalogue record for this book is available from the British Library.

Printed and bound in Great Britain by Clays Ltd, St Ives plc

For Anna, Katy, Jack, Joseph and William

INTRODUCTION

A monstrous pall of swirling cloud hangs over the Edge, obscuring everything below. At its centre, a mighty storm fizzes and crackles with a deadly, destructive energy.

Like some evil demon, this dark maelstrom is devouring its prey, the once great city of Undertown. Yet even as the city crumbles and is washed away by the seething torrent the stormlashed Edgewater River has become, hope lives on in the hearts of the Undertowners – the cloddertrogs, gnokgoblins, lugtrolls and all those others who had once thronged the busy streets – fleeing down the disintegrating Great Mire Road. Led by the Most High Academe, Cowlquape Pentephraxis, and the librarian knights, their tethered skycraft bobbing behind them, they dream of a new life in that beacon of freedom and knowledge nestling in the far-off Deepwoods, the Free Glades.

Ahead of them lies the Mire, a treacherous wasteland of bleached mud and seething blow-holes, which is home to a host of fearsome creatures that prey on the weak and unwary. And then beyond that, beckoning from afar, the Edgelands, a place of swirling mists, where demons, spirits – and even the terrible gloam-glozer – are said to torment those who venture into its barren landscape.

Further still lie the Deepwoods themselves, with their swarms of snickets, packs of wig-wigs, poisonous plants and venomous insects. Bloodoaks that would swallow you whole, and reed-eels that would bleed you dry. Rotsuckers, halitoads, logworms . . . Not to mention the primitive tribes that live there – the skulltrogs and gahtrogs; brutal, speechless creatures that hunt in packs and devour their kill while it is still warm.

But there is no going back. Not now. Every one of the fleeing Undertowners understands this to be true. For many, this is the beginning of the greatest adventure of their lives.

In this, they are not alone, for Undertown is not the only place to be affected by the dark maelstrom. At the far end of the Mire Road, the remnants of the Shryke Sisterhood of the Eastern Roost realize that their lucrative trade with Undertown is over. They, too, must seek a new life, but instead of hope, there is bloodlust and vengeance in their hearts.

News of the great disaster is also reaching the villages of the Goblin Nations, never slow to spot and exploit the weaknesses of others. Talk in the tribal huts, with their heaped skulls and dangling skeletons, is of war and conquest.

And they are not the only ones with grand designs. In the smoky, fiery hell that is the Foundry Glades, Hemuel Spume is hard at work on plans of his own. He is waiting impatiently for his business partner to join him. When he does, Hemuel Spume has a surprise waiting for him. He permits himself a thin smile.

'I'll give them Free Glades,' he mutters scornfully. 'Long live the Slave Glades!'

As the dark maelstrom grows and spreads, the vast multitude of Undertowners struggles on along the Great Mire Road, and all the while driving rain beats against them mercilessly, chilling them to the bone and dampening their spirits.

They are fighting a losing battle. Ahead, sweeping across their path, bordering the Edgelands, are the beguiling yet treacherous Twilight Woods, a place that none but a shryke might journey through unscathed. All round them, the road is collapsing . . .

They must seek help, or perish.

*

The Deepwoods, the Stone Gardens, the Edgewater River. Undertown and Sanctaphrax. Names on a map.

Yet behind each name lie a thousand tales – tales that have been recorded in ancient scrolls, tales that have been passed down the generations by word of mouth – tales which even now are being told.

What follows is but one of those tales.

PART 1

FLIGHT

CHAPTER ONE

THE ARMADA OF
THE DEAD

'What are we going to do?'

Deadbolt Vulpoon turned from the cabin window and glared at the thin quartermaster who had just spoken.

'The storms over Undertown are growing, if anything,' said a cloddertrog in a bleached muglumpskin coat.

The other sky pirates at the long table all nodded.

'And there's nothing moving on the Mire Road,' he added. 'All trade has stopped dead.'

The nodding turned to troubled muttering.

'Gentlemen, gentlemen,' said Deadbolt, resuming his seat at the head of the table. 'We are sky pirates, remember. Our ships might no longer fly, but we are *still* sky pirates. Proud and free.' His heavy hand slammed down on the table so hard, the tankard of woodale in front of him leaped up in the air. 'And no storm – dark maelstrom or not – is going to defeat us!'

'I repeat my question,' said the thin quartermaster with a supercilious sniff. 'What are we going to do? There are over thirty crews in the armada. That's three hundred mouths to feed, three hundred backs to clothe, three hundred purses to fill. If there is no trade on the Mire Road, then what shall we live on? Oozefish and mire water?' He sniffed again.

'No trading, no raiding,' said the cloddertrog.

Again, the assembled sky pirates nodded in agreement.

Deadbolt Vulpoon grasped the tankard and raised it to his lips. He needed to collect his thoughts.

For weeks, the dark clouds had gathered on the far horizon at the Undertown end of the Great Mire Road. Then, two days ago, the huge anvil formations of cloud had merged into the unmistakable menacing swirl of a dark maelstrom.

Sky help those caught underneath, he'd thought at the time.

Now Undertown was lost from view and the Mire Road was deserted. A great shryke battle-flock had disappeared in the direction of Undertown just before the storm struck, and then the remaining shrykes from the tally-huts had retreated back to the Eastern Roost . . .

Deadbolt took a deep draught from the tankard and slammed it back on the table. 'I have sent out another raiding party,' he announced with a confidence he didn't feel. 'And until we get to the bottom of this, I for one don't intend to panic.'

'Raiding party!' snorted the thin quartermaster, pushing his chair noisily back and climbing to his feet. 'To raid what?' He paused. 'I hear there's opportunities opening up in the Foundry Glades, and that's where my crew are headed. And you're all welcome to join us!'

He strode from the cabin.

'Gentlemen, *please*,' said Deadbolt, raising a hand and motioning to the others to remain seated. 'Don't be hasty. Think of what we've built up here in the Armada. Don't throw it all away. Wait until the raiding party returns.'

'Until the party returns,' said the cloddertrog as the sky pirates got up to leave. 'And not a moment longer.'

As they trooped out, Deadbolt Vulpoon climbed to his feet and returned to the window. He looked out through the heavy leaded panes at the Armada of the Dead beyond.

What exactly *had* they built up here? he wondered bitterly.

When stone-sickness had begun to spread through the flight-rocks of the sky ships, he and the other sky pirates had read the writing on the wall. They came together and scuppered their vessels, rather than letting sky-sickness pick them off one by one.

The hulks of the sky ships had formed an encampment in the bleak Mire, and a base from which to raid the lucrative trade along the Great Mire Road. It wasn't sky piracy, but it was the closest thing to it in these plagued times. And sometimes, when the mists rolled in and the wind got up, he would stand on his quarterdeck and imagine he was high up in Open Sky, as free as a snowbird . . .

Vulpoon looked at the grounded vessels, their masts pointing up so yearningly towards the sky, and a lump formed in his throat. The ships still bore their original names, the letters picked out in fading gold paint. *Windspinner, Mistmarcher, Fogscythe, Cloudeater* . . . His own ship – the *Skyraider* – was a battered and bleached ghost of her former glory. She would rot away to nothing eventually if she didn't raise herself out of the white mire mud.

But that, of course, could never happen, for the flight-rock itself at the centre of the great ship was rotten. Unless a cure for stone-sickness was discovered, then neither the *Skyraider*, nor the *Windspinner*, nor the *Mistmarcher*, nor any of the other sky pirate ships would ever fly again.

Thick, sucking mud anchored the great hulls in place, turning the once spectacular sky vessels into odd-shaped buildings, made all the more peculiar by the additional rooms which had been constructed, ruining the lines of the decks and clinging to the sides of the ships like giant sky-limpets.

What future lay ahead for him? he wondered. What future was there for any of the those who called the Armada of the Dead home?

Deadbolt reached for the telescope that hung from his breast-plate. He put it to his eye and focused on the distant horizon.

He could see nothing through the impenetrable black

clouds – either of Under-town or of the Great Mire Road. Even the distant Stone Gardens, normally silhouetted against the sky, were covered with a heavy pall that obscured them completely.

Deadbolt Vulpoon sighed. He lowered the eye-glass and was about to turn away when something caught his eye. He returned the tele-scope to his eye and focused the lens a second time. This time his efforts were rewarded with a clear picture of seven, eight . . . nine individuals tramping towards him. It was the raiding party.

Back so soon? he won-dered, a nagging feeling of disappointment settling in the pit of his stomach.

Two of the sky pirates were holding up poles, at the top of which was a large brazier-cage. The burning lufwood charcoal it contained blazed with a bright purple light which illuminated the treacherous Mire, ensuring that no one inadvertently stumbled into a patch of sinking-sand, stepped on an erupting blow-hole, or stumbled into a fearsome muglump . . .

As the raiding party came closer, Vulpoon leaned out of his cabin window. 'Any luck?' he bellowed.

Yet even as he cried out he knew the answer. The sacks slung across their shoulders were empty. The raid had yielded nothing.

'There's nothing to be had at all,' a tall mobgnome with an eye-patch shouted back.

'The road's deserted,' added another. 'The shrykes must have headed back for the Eastern Roost.'

'We found these two halfway across the Mire,' said a third, a lanky flat-head with a large ring through his nose. 'Claimed they were on their way to see us. Nothing but a few trinkets on either of them.'

Deadbolt Vulpoon noticed for the first time the two strangers in their midst. Both were young. One of them was dressed in librarian garb, the hood of his cloak pulled up against the cold Mire wind. The other – taller, tougher-looking – was clothed in bleached muglump skins. He raised his head and returned Vulpoon's gaze boldly.

'What can we do for you, lad?' said Vulpoon.

'My name is Felix Lodd,' came the reply. 'As for my business, that is between me and the leader of the great Armada of the Dead.'

For a moment Vulpoon hesitated. The youth was

impudent. He could have him locked up until he learned a few manners – and yet he had spoken admiringly of the Armada . . .

'Bring them up,' he ordered.

'And there was a battle, you say?' said Deadbolt Vulpoon.

They were in the captain's cabin, the assembled sky pirates seated at the long table. The youth in the muglump skins stood before them, his hooded companion behind him.

'Yes, a great and terrible battle,' said Felix, nodding. 'Vox Verlix . . .'

'Vox Verlix, ruler of Undertown!' interrupted the thin quartermaster who, on hearing of the raiding party's return, had delayed his departure. 'Is that slimy skyslug still around? Swindled me out of a whole consignment of bloodoak timber once, he did. He was busy building that tower of his on the Sanctaphrax rock. Swore I'd get my revenge!'

Deadbolt raised his hand to silence him. He turned back to Felix. 'What about Vox Verlix?' he asked.

'Organized the whole thing, by all accounts,' said Felix. 'Tricked the goblins and the shrykes into going down into the library sewers, then triggered a storm to drown the lot of them.'

'So *he's* responsible for the dark maelstrom!' Deadbolt shook his head. 'I might have known. Typical academic – always meddling with the sky.'

'Yet it was also to be his undoing,' said Felix.

'You mean he's dead?'

'Almost certainly,' said Felix. 'I saw his palace collapse as the maelstrom closed in.'

'Pity,' said the quartermaster, his teeth glinting unpleasantly in the yellow lamplight. 'I've been looking forward to slitting his gizzard.' His right hand, poised as if holding a dagger, slashed through the air. 'Like so,' he said and his cruel laughter, echoing round the cabin, was joined by the others seated about the table.

'Undertown is destroyed,' said Felix, and the laughter stopped abruptly. 'Utterly destroyed. We managed to escape . . .'

'Who is "we"?' asked Deadbolt, leaning forward in his chair.

'Undertowners, young and old; librarians from the Great Library in the sewers, and . . .' He paused. 'And those I command – the Ghosts of Screetown.'

A low murmur went round the table. Suddenly the youth's confident, almost impudent, manner made sense. Even out here in the Mire they had heard of the Ghosts of Screetown – so called because of their bleached white, ghostly appearance – who were a band of fearless hunters and fighters from the worst part of Undertown.

'So, you're the leader of the ghosts,' said Vulpoon, trying to disguise the awe in his voice.

'Since when does a ghost need help?' interrupted the quartermaster in a sneering voice. 'I mean, after Screetown, surely the Mire can hold no terrors for you – if you *are* who you say you are.'

Felix took a step towards the quartermaster, his eyes

blazing. 'I do not ask help for the ghosts,' he said. 'I ask it for the Undertowners and the librarians who, even as we speak, are back there in the black mists of the Mire Road. They cannot return. They must go on, but the way is perilous.' He took a long, slow breath. 'But you know the Mire,' he said. 'By going through the Edgelands, we can avoid the Twilight Woods. But first, we must get across the Mire. For that, we need your help . . .'

'And if we do help you,' said Vulpoon, 'what's in it for us?'

Felix smiled. 'Spoken like a true sky pirate,' he said impudently.

Deadbolt Vulpoon felt himself redden with sudden anger. 'What's left for you here?' the youth continued. 'Without Undertown and the Mire Road trade, you'll rot away here like these precious ships of yours. Join us, and you can build a new life in the Free Glades . . .'

'And what's to stop us simply raiding you?' Vulpoon interrupted gruffly.

'Try that,' said Felix hotly, 'and the Ghosts of Screetown will cut you down, and the mire mud will run thick with treacherous sky pirate blood.'

'You march in here, insulting sky pirates and our sky ships,' said Vulpoon, his eyes blazing and fists clenching. '*And you expect us to help you!*'

The librarian stepped forward and lowered his hood for the first time. The others fell still and looked at him.

'Once, Deadbolt Vulpoon, *you* needed help,' he said, his voice low, the words quick. 'You were locked up in one of the roadside shryke cages. I gave you food to eat and water to drink. Do you not remember? You *said* you would never forget,' he added softly.

The sky pirate captain looked stunned for a moment before breaking into a huge grin that made his face wrinkle up and his eyes disappear.

'You!' he boomed, striding across the cabin. 'That was *you!*' Roaring with laughter, he clapped Rook on the back warmly. 'Barkwater, isn't it?'

'Yes, sir. Rook Barkwater,' he said. 'And now it is my turn to ask for help from you.'

'Rook Barkwater,' Vulpoon repeated, shaking his head in amazement. 'Of all people!' He turned to the other sky pirates. 'This lad saved my life,' he said. 'I cannot refuse him what he asks. We shall help the Undertowners.'

'He didn't save *my* life,' snorted the thin quartermaster.

Deadbolt's face darkened. He reached out and grasped the quartermaster by the collar with a huge hand, and twisted. 'You were ready enough to quit the Armada before,' he roared. 'This way, you get to enjoy the Free Glades rather than the filth of the Foundry Glades. Say "no", and I'll snap your scrawny neck, Quillet Pleeme, by Sky I will!'

'There'll be no need for that, will there, Quillet?' said the cloddertrog in the bleached muglumpskin coat, loosening Deadbolt's grip.

The quartermaster shook his head weakly.

'The ghost is right,' the cloddertrog said. 'The Armada is finished. There's nothing for us here. We're with you, Captain.'

'To the Free Glades!' roared Deadbolt, releasing the quartermaster and clapping Rook on the shoulder once more.

Rook smiled. 'To the Free Glades!' he replied.

CHAPTER TWO

EXODUS

'**B**y Sky, lad,' gasped Deadbolt Vulpoon, pausing at the top of the mud dune to catch his breath, 'that's a dark maelstrom all right. The darkest, blackest, most accursed I've ever seen, and no mistake.'

Rook scrambled up beside him, the claggy white mud pulling at his mud-shoes and mire-poles like hungry oozefish. 'And it seems . . .' he panted, 'to be spreading.'

Deadbolt hawked and spat with disgust. 'This is what you get when you tamper with nature,' he growled. 'Cursed, meddlesome academics! They can't leave anything alone!'

In front of them, a thick, dense line of low mesanumbic cloud – flat at the top and with great billowing forms beneath – was advancing from the direction of Undertown and steadily engulfing the Great Mire Road, like a huge logworm swallowing its prey.

Felix appeared at Rook's shoulder, his pale face stained purple by the lufwood light of the brazier he was carrying. 'We can rest later,' he said tersely. 'Time is

29

running out.' He shook his head. 'I only hope they'll have the sense to get off the Mire Road before the storm catches them.'

There were purple braziers all around them now as the sky pirates of the Armada breasted the ridge and gazed down at the white plains below. Far ahead, the Great Mire Road loomed out of the boiling cloudbank and wound its way across the wilderness on spindly legs like a half-swallowed thousandfoot.

'Allowing for heavy carts and young'uns,' said Deadbolt Vulpoon, scanning the horizon, 'these Undertowners of yours should be approaching the Twilight Woods tally-huts, give or take a span or two. That's half a day's hard mud-marching from here. Judging by the speed of that storm we should reach them just before it does!'

'Well, what are we waiting for?' said Felix, clapping Deadbolt on the back and smiling for what, to Rook, seemed the first time in days. 'I'll take a mud-march over a stroll in Screetown any time.'

Deadbolt's eyes twinkled. 'We'll see, my lad,' he chuckled, 'we'll see.' He turned to the sky pirates. 'Armada, advance!' he bellowed, his voice booming across the tops of the dunes. 'And look lively about it!'

Each crew raised its brazier-cage in assent, and the great mass of sky pirates slipped and slithered down the far side of the dunes and strode out across the sucking mud towards the imperilled Mire Road.

Rook would never forget that march across the vast Mire plain. Each crew tramped on in single file, following

the brazier-carrier at its head, chanting in unison, a dirge-like marching song.

'*One 'n two 'n three 'n four; mud in the eye to old Muleclaw!*'

The slap of mud-shoes on mire mud beat out the rhythm.

'*Five 'n six 'n seven 'n eight; chase her back to the Mire Gate!*'

Before long, Rook found himself joining in, his eyes fixed on Deadbolt's brazier-cage in front of him. Soon his breathing was harsh and heavy, and sweat was running down his face. But the steady beat of the mud-shoes and unwavering rhythmic chant drove him on.

He was dimly aware of the cawing of white ravens swirling in angry flocks overhead, and occasionally the shuddering thud of a nearby blow-hole exploding, sending a tall, glistening column high into the air and spattering the entire party in hot, clinging mud. After the third such shower, Rook, like the sky pirates in front of him, didn't even flinch, but trudged mechanically on. The mud clung to his boots, weighing them down and making every step he took more difficult than the one before. Up ahead, he heard Deadbolt's booming commands.

'Bear west, you mudlubbers! Close up the line, *Windjammer*! Hold steady, *Fogscythe*!'

As he closed his eyes and willed himself on, Rook began to imagine that he was part of a real armada, up there in the wide open sky, high above the cloying mire mud, and that Deadbolt Vulpoon was back on the quarterdeck of his sky ship, marshalling his sky pirate fleet.

It wasn't long though before this daydream was drowned out by the sound of his own rasping breath and the blood hammering in his temples. His legs felt like hull weights, his head seemed lighter than air and, as he stared ahead, Deadbolt's brazier light swam before his eyes as if under water. On and on they marched, the pace never flagging.

'One 'n two 'n three 'n four; Tytugg's goblins at the door . . .'

Rook stumbled and felt the rope secured round his middle jerk him upright.

'Five 'n six 'n seven 'n eight; leave that hammerhead to his fate . . .'

Rook stumbled again, this time falling to the ground and sprawling in the soft mud.

'Halt!' came Deadbolt's command. 'Loose the ropes!'

Rook felt hands untying the rope. He tried to get to his feet. How long had they been marching? Hours? Days?

'I'm . . . sorry . . .' he gasped. 'I . . . can't . . .'

'Sorry, lad?' Deadbolt's voice boomed at his ear. 'There's no need to be sorry. Look.' Rook raised his head and wiped the caked mud from his eyes.

There, in front of them, towering above the mire mists, was the Great Mire Road, beyond it the jagged treeline of the Twilight Woods. Gathered at the balustrades above the sky pirates, the Mire Road teemed with a vast multitude of Undertowners, cheering and brandishing flaming torches.

It was getting dark – and not only because night was approaching, Rook realized with a jolt. The vast billowing form of the dark maelstrom was on the far horizon to the east, and looming ever closer.

The Undertowners must have noticed it too, for as Rook gazed back, too exhausted to move, he saw them climbing over the balustrades and clambering down the ironwood-pine struts of the Mire Road onto the mud below. All around, the bustle of feverish activity became more desperate, and the air grew thick with urgent cries and screeched demands. He scanned the balustrades for any sign of his friends, the banderbears, but it was impossible to pick them out in the milling throng.

The librarians were busy manhandling great crates, stuffed with barkscrolls and treatises, off the precarious walkway and down onto the mud below. The Undertowners, too, were hurriedly evacuating the Mire Road, with those still up on the wooden structure lowering bundles of belongings and livestock and cradles bearing mewling young'uns carefully down into the upstretched arms of those far below. And all the while, the Ghosts of Screetown – distinctive in their white muglumpskins and bone-armour – hurried between them all, marshalling, corralling, shouting commands and offering help wherever it was needed.

Groups of lugtrolls and woodtrolls were working together on makeshift shelters and tents. A band of cloddertrogs were securing their bundles of belongings to long stakes, driven into the mire mud, whilst beside them, librarian knights expertly tethered their bobbing skycraft to heavy mooring-poles. Directly ahead, a large family of gnokgoblins was helping one another down from the road, their meagre possessions strapped to their backs.

Rook felt a hand under his arm lifting him to his feet, and found himself looking into Felix's smiling face.

'Not bad mud-marching for a librarian!' he laughed, though from the way he looked – mud-spattered and red-faced – Felix was just as exhausted as Rook himself. 'Looks like we got here just in time,' he added, pointing to the storm that was coming closer with each passing minute. 'But if they don't get down off the road in double-quick time, we might as well not have bothered.'

'So those are your Ghosts of Screetown,' said Deadbolt, standing hands on hips and whistling through his teeth. 'Mighty fine bunch, and that's the truth. Handy with those ropes as well.'

'They could do with some help,' said Felix, turning to the sky pirate captain, 'if your crews are up for it after our little stroll.'

'By Sky, you're an impudent young pup!' laughed Deadbolt, and flourished his brazier-cage. 'Armada!' he barked. 'To the Mire Road! Let's get this rabble out into the Mire and hunkered down. There's a storm abrewing, or hadn't you mudlubbers noticed?'

The sky pirates instantly sprang forwards and began clambering up the struts of the Mire Road, slinging ropes and grappling-hooks up to those above, and attaching pulleys and slings to their tether-ropes. Soon, a steady flow of Undertowners was descending safely to the mud, and a vast encampment began to form all round Rook.

'Get clear of the road!' came Felix's clear voice. 'You don't want to be under it when the storm strikes!'

'Secure those prowlgrins!' Deadbolt's voice thundered. 'And overturn those carts for shelter!'

Even as he spoke, a heavy gust of wind snatched his words and carried them off. Rook looked about him. He must find the librarians and make his report. Unlike Felix, he was a librarian knight, and under orders from the Most High Academe, Cowlquape Pentephraxis.

As he started to make his way through the bustling throng of Undertowners, pitching tents and overturning carts, and even digging shallow holes in the mire mud,

Rook felt a wave of exhaustion break over him. He was about to join a cloddertrog family under a hammelhorn cart when a familiar voice called out.

'Master Rook. I trust you have done the library a good service.' Fenbrus Lodd strode towards him, his bushy beard bristling in the growing wind. 'The sky pirates have agreed to guide our Great Library across this desolate wasteland?'

Rook nodded. 'Yes, High Librarian,' he replied. 'Captain Vulpoon . . .'

'And that son of mine, why is he not with you?' interrupted Fenbrus, irritatedly.

'He's . . .' began Rook.

'I'm here, Father,' said Felix appearing, flanked by two of his ghosts.

'So you are,' said Fenbrus haughtily. 'So you are. Now, Felix, I want you and those ghosts of yours to secure the Great Library over there.' He pointed with his staff to a large throng of librarians who were hauling several huge carts, complete with protesting hammelhorns, into a rough circle. 'There are still a number of library carts on the road and time is running short. We must not lose them.'

Felix smiled grimly. 'There are still Undertowners up

on the road, father,' he said.
'My ghosts are helping them
first . . .'

'But the Great
Library!' blustered
Fenbrus, growing red in the
face. 'I must insist that you . . .'

'I don't take orders
from you!' thundered Felix,
sounding to Rook's ears not
unlike his father.

A crowd was gathering
round, listening in to the
heated words between the father and son.

'The library carts must be secured,' said Fenbrus Lodd
stubbornly, his eyes blazing. 'Not a single scroll must be
lost.'

'Nor must a single Undertowner perish!' countered
Felix hotly.

'Now, now,' came a quavering yet authoritative voice,
and Cowlquape himself stepped between them. 'If we all
work together, we shall be able to ensure the safety of
both the library *and* the Undertowners,' he said.

From behind him, there came a loud snort and everyone turned to see Deadbolt Vulpoon standing there, his
hands on his hips and a scornful look on his face.

'That's the last of the Undertowners off the road,' he
said grimly, 'but how you expect *any* of this rabble to
make it across the Mire with you lot bickering like this is
beyond me.'

'We were rather hoping,' said Cowlquape, approaching the sky pirate and bowing his head in greeting, 'that you might be able to help us, Captain . . . err . . .'

'Vulpoon,' said Deadbolt. 'Captain Vulpoon.'

A trace of a smile flickered across Cowlquape's face. 'Ah, yes. Captain Vulpoon. I met your father once a very long time ago – and in circumstances quite as perilous as these, if my memory serves me right.'

'You must tell me about it sometime,' said Deadbolt, returning his smile. 'But right now, you all need to get everything and everyone secured if this here storm is to be weathered.' He nodded towards the huge flat-topped cloud formation boiling up overhead. 'After that' – he was shouting now, to be heard above the roaring wind – 'we can talk about getting across the Mire.' He smiled darkly. 'That is if there's any of us left *to* get across.'

Felix stepped forward. 'You heard the captain!' he roared. 'Jump to it!'

The crowd dispersed, battening everything down and hurriedly disappearing into holes and tents, and under the upturned carts.

'Secure those hammelhorns!' Deadbolt bellowed, striding off towards a group of slaughterers. 'We'll have need of them soon enough!'

Fenbrus rushed after him. 'The library carts, Captain. Don't forget the library carts!'

As the High Librarian's voice was swallowed up by the rising howl of the wind, Cowlquape turned back to Felix and Rook. 'You've done very well,' he said. 'Both of you. I was unsure whether you'd be successful. After all,

I've come across enough sky pirates in my time to know how stubborn and wilful they can be . . .'

'Sounds like someone I know,' said Felix with a sigh.

Cowlquape nodded understandingly. 'You must try and understand your father,' he said. 'His dream is to recreate the Great Library in the Free Glades . . .'

'I know that,' said Felix, and again Rook heard the mixture of emotions in his voice. 'Him and his accursed barkscrolls! And what are they anyway? Bits of paper and parchment. It is the Undertowners – the *Freegladers* – who are important.'

'Of course, Felix,' said Rook, the wind almost drowning out his voice. 'But we are librarians. The barkscrolls are like living things to us.'

Felix didn't seem to hear him. 'I must see to the ghosts,' he said, turning on his heels and striding away.

Rook shrugged sheepishly at Cowlquape, and was about to run after Felix when he felt a tap on his shoulder. He turned, to see two of his best friends, Xanth and Magda, standing there, huge grins spread across their faces.

'It *is* you, Rook!' Magda exclaimed. 'We hardly recognized you under all that mud!'

Rook smiled back. 'Am I glad to see you two!' he said.

The heavy rain started as darkness fell, whipped into lashing sheets by the driving wind. Huge hailstones followed, and heart-stopping crashes of thunder. The Mire Road writhed, creaking and groaning like a dying monster as its timbers gave way, one by one. From inside their makeshift shelter, Rook huddled between Xanth and Magda.

'Do you think it's ever going to stop?' he said miserably.

Magda sighed. 'I wonder if the weather's ever going to be the same again.'

The shelter had been fashioned from an upturned cart and heavy bales of straw, covered with a tarpaulin staked down in place. So far it had kept the worst of the storm out, but at any moment Rook expected the terrible wind to rip the cart from over their heads and scatter the bales.

'So you're to fly with the Professor of Light,' said Rook, trying to keep his mind on something else. The librarian knights were masters of flying their delicate, wooden skycraft, made of buoyant sumpwood and powered by huge spidersilk sails. Since stone-sickness had put paid to the great sky ships, these tiny craft were the sole means of flight in the Edge.

'Yes,' said Magda, managing to smile. A crack of thunder broke overhead. The ground trembled. 'The plan is for Varis Lodd and her flight to head directly to the Free Glades to summon help, while the Professor of Darkness leads a flight high over the Twilight Woods section of the Mire Road in case shrykes are massing there to attack.'

'And you?'

Magda tried to sound brave. 'The Professor of Light is to lead us to the Eastern Roost to check on the shrykes there,' she said. 'There are rumours of a Hatching.'

Rook shivered. The words 'Eastern Roost' brought back such terrible memories. 'Aren't you afraid of going back to . . . that place?' he asked.

'We've got no choice,' said Magda simply. 'But at least this time I'll have *Woodmoth* with me – and the Professor of Light. He's one of the best librarian knights we have.'

'I wish I had *Stormhornet*,' said Rook with a sigh, remembering his lost skycraft, wrecked in a crash in Screetown. 'Then I could go with you, instead of having to stay with the footsloggers.'

'If it's good enough for Felix Lodd, it's good enough for you and that's a fact,' said Magda, trying to make light of it, but Rook could tell she, too, was upset by the fact that they wouldn't be flying together.

'*I'm* not even welcome amongst the footsloggers,' said Xanth darkly.

'What do you mean?' said Rook.

'I'm a traitor, Rook,' said Xanth, 'or had you forgotten? I served the Guardians of Night. I plotted and spied. Because of me, brave librarian knights were murdered. Because of me, *you* almost perished in the Foundry Glades.'

'All that's behind us now. The Guardians of Night are no more,' said Rook, 'destroyed by the dark maelstrom back in Undertown. And besides, you've changed, Xanth. *I* know. And I'll tell anyone else who wants to know as much.'

'And so will I,' said Magda. 'You rescued me from the Guardians, Xanth. I'll never forget that.' She tried to smile encouragingly.

Far above their heads, the storm seemed to be reaching a new intensity.

'You don't see the look in the librarians' eyes,' said Xanth bitterly. 'The look of distrust, the look of hatred. They look at me and see a traitor and a spy.'

Magda put an arm round Xanth. 'But inside, Xanth, your friends can see plainly . . .' she said softly, 'you have a good heart.'

Outside, a huge thunderclap broke and the little cart shook until its wheels rattled.

·CHAPTER THREE·

MUD-MARCH

Shortly before dawn, with feathers of light dancing on the horizon, the wind died down, the torrential rain eased off at last and an eerie silence descended over the mudflats of the Mire. Rook rubbed his eyes and looked round blearily, as disturbed by the unearthly stillness as he had been by the tumultuous storm that had raged through the night.

He rolled over and, leaving Xanth and Magda to sleep on, crawled to the edge of the shelter and attempted to push the tarpaulin back. But it was stuck fast, held in place by something pressing against it from outside. Grunting with effort, Rook pushed hard. There was a soft *flummp!* and the tarpaulin abruptly flapped free. Rook poked his head out of the gap he had created.

'Earth and Sky,' he murmured.

The vast encampment, with its upturned carts, battened-down tents and hastily constructed shelters, was now just a series of gently undulating mud-dunes stretching off into the distance as far as the eye could see.

Here and there, one of these dunes would erupt into life as its occupants dug their way out – just as Rook had – only to pause and look around with the same bemused expression on their faces.

'Rook?' Magda's sleepy voice called out. 'Is it over? Has the storm passed?'

'Come and see for yourself,' Rook called over his shoulder. 'It's incredible.'

Magda's head appeared next to his own, followed by Xanth's. They peered out across the bleached plains, shocked and bewildered.

'Look!' Rook exclaimed, pointing at the flat, muddy horizon.

'What?' said Magda, who was already scooping handfuls of mud aside and squeezing out of the hole on all fours. 'I can't see anything.'

'Exactly!' said Rook, following her. 'The Great Mire Road! It's gone!'

Xanth scrambled after them. All around, other mud-dunes were coming to life as the Undertowners emerged from their shelters into the blinding light of the white mud and early morning sky.

'You're right,' gasped Xanth, following Rook's gaze.

Where the Mire Road had towered over them the night before, now there was only a low ridge of mud, punctured here and there by splintered beams and pylons, like the ribs of a giant oozefish. Wreaths of acrid smoke began to coil up into the sky as braziers and cooking-fires were lit, and the air filled with the sounds of scraping and scratching as everyone struggled to rid themselves and their belongings of the clinging mud.

Xanth and Magda seized a couple of pieces of broken wood and began shovelling at the drifted mud-dune surrounding the hammelhorn cart. But it was hard going, with the wet mud constantly sliding back into the areas they had cleared.

'Come on, Rook,' Xanth panted. 'We could do with a hand here.'

But Rook did not hear him. He was staring at the remains of the once impressive feat of engineering, lost in his thoughts. So, this was the end of the Great Mire Road; a road he, Rook, had travelled as an apprentice librarian . . .

The image of Vox Verlix's fat face hovered before him – Vox Verlix, the greatest architect and builder the Edge had ever seen. The Great Mire Road had been his masterpiece, the greatest of all his mighty projects. But, like the Tower of Night and the Sanctaphrax Forest, it too had been wrested from him by others, leaving the former Most High Academe angry and bitter. And so, like a petulant child breaking its toys, he had brought down the power of the dark maelstrom on Undertown and destroyed his precious creations – and destroyed himself in the process.

Rook shook his head and turned away. Vox Verlix, Undertown, the Great Mire Road – they were all in the past. There was no turning back. Now, the homeless Undertowners and librarians had to look to the future, Rook realized, a future that lay far away across this desolate wasteland . . .

'Head in the clouds as usual!'

The sound of the voice snapped Rook out of his reverie. In front of him stood Varis Lodd, Captain of the Librarian Knights, resplendent in her green flight-suit. Rook bowed his head in salute.

'Captain,' he greeted her.

Varis laid a hand on his shoulder. 'I wish you could come with us, Rook,' she said kindly. 'But our loss is the library's gain. Keep the barkscrolls safe until our return, Rook, and you'll have completed a task every bit as important as ours.'

Rook nodded and tried to return her smile.

'Now, where's that friend of yours?' Varis looked past Rook and, as her gaze fell on Xanth, Rook noticed her jaw tighten and her eyes glaze over.

Xanth looked up and must have seen her expression too, for he stopped shovelling mud and stared down dejectedly at his boots.

'Xanth!' Magda laughed, still shovelling furiously. 'Don't give up! You're as bad as Rook . . .' She stopped when she saw Varis and straightened, bowing her head. 'Captain,' she said.

'The flight awaits, Magda,' said Varis, pointedly ignoring Xanth. 'Say goodbye to . . . your friends, and report for duty.'

Magda nodded solemnly. She turned and hugged Rook, then Xanth. 'Take care of each other,' she said

urgently. 'Promise me.'

They promised. Xanth's face was ashen white; his voice, barely more than a whisper.

'It'll be all right, Xanth,' said Magda. 'Rook and I will speak up for you in the Free Glades, won't we, Rook?'

Rook nodded earnestly.

'Now, come and see me off,' she said, trying to sound cheerful.

'I'll stay here,' said Xanth. 'You go, Rook. I'll finish digging the cart out.'

Magda gave him another hug, then turned to Rook. 'Here goes,' she said, and strode off after the Captain of the Librarian Knights.

Rook followed them through the gathering crowds, the buzzing hum of excitement in the air growing louder as they neared the tethering-posts. Heavy stakes had been driven down into the mud and the skycraft lashed securely to them. Now they were being untied, and the great flocks of skycraft were bobbing about in the early-morning air. Two squadrons were already prepared, with scores of young librarian knights seated astride their skycraft and waiting for the signal to depart.

Rook watched Magda climb onto her *Woodmoth*, unfurl the loft and nether-sails, realign the balance-weights and unhitch the flight-ropes. At the sight of her, he felt a heavy weight pressing down on his chest, turning to a dull ache. He swallowed hard, but the pain remained. Beyond the excited crowd he spotted Varis Lodd and the Professors of Light and Darkness, the three of them already hovering in the air, one at the head of each squadron.

As the last librarian knight climbed aboard his skycraft, Varis Lodd flew up higher, bringing the *Windhawk* round. She raised an arm and gave a signal.

Free Glades Flight, depart, she motioned in the signalled language of the librarian knights.

At her command, and as silently as snowbirds, some three hundred or so skycraft soared up into the sky as one. They hovered expertly overhead, securing and setting their sails, and adjusting the flight-weights that

hung beneath each craft like
jewelled tails.

Twilight Woods Flight, depart. The
Professor of Darkness silently gave
the command, and the three hundred hovering craft were joined by three hundred more.

Eastern Roost Flight, depart. It was the Professor of
Light's turn to give the signal; a right arm crossed to the
left shoulder, three fingers outstretched. The air seemed
to tremble as the squadron of librarian knights under his
command – including Magda herself – rose up from the
ground.

Like a vast and silent array of exquisite insects, nine
hundred skycraft filled the sky above Rook's head.

'Oh, *Stormhornet*,' he murmured, his heart breaking.
'How I miss you.'

A sudden gust of wind seemed to galvanize the skycraft as, one by one, their sails filled like blossoming
flowers and they moved off.

Rook followed their path, his mouth dry, his chest aching, as the skycraft caught the stronger currents high in the sky and began to gather speed. All around him cheers went up as the Undertowners and librarians saluted the librarian knights.

But as the skycraft grew ever more distant, the cheers fell away and the mood of the crowd changed. They were on their own now, out here in the vast muddy wilderness. Rook sighed. He felt the same.

Of course, he knew that the skycraft would be no use in the swirling, howling winds of the Edgelands that awaited them. He knew it made sense for the librarian knights to go on ahead to scout for danger and bring help from the Free Glades. He knew they all planned to meet up again at the Ironwood Stands. He knew all of this – but still, he couldn't shake off the feeling of having been abandoned.

In the distance, high above the Twilight Woods, the vast flock split up into three; one section swooping off to the north, one to the south, and the third continuing due west in the direction of the Deepwoods. Soon they were lost from view and, with a low murmur, the crowd began to disperse.

Rook turned and made his way back to Xanth as, all through the encampment, the Undertowners began to prepare for the long march ahead. From his left he heard commands being issued and he spotted Deadbolt Vulpoon striding through the encampment, barking into a raised megaphone.

'Mud-shoes and mire-poles for everyone!' he instructed. 'And eye-shields. Those without should improvise. There's plenty of timber to be had from the old Mire Road.'

There was a feverish scramble for scraps of wood and, all over the encampment, trogs and trolls, goblins, ghosts and librarians – all aided by the sky pirates – began lashing lengths of wood to the soles of their boots, cutting down sticks to the right length and fashioning eye-shields that would, they hoped, protect them from the dreaded mire-blindness.

'Batten down all crates and boxes!' Deadbolt's amplified voice continued. 'Charge your brazier-cages with lufwood, and fix runners to the bottoms of every cart and carriage!'

Again, there was a scramble for wood, and the air was soon echoing with the sounds of chopping and sawing and hammering as every vehicle had its wheels removed and stowed, to be replaced with long, curved runners which, Earth and Sky willing, would glide effortlessly over the treacherous mud.

'Those with prowlgrins, put them in harness!' Deadbolt's voiced boomed as he continued marching through the bustling encampment. 'Those without will

have to strap themselves in. Always pull! Never push!'
He caught sight of a herd of hammelhorns standing
forlornly in a shallow pool. 'And hammelhorns may *not*,
I repeat, *not* be used for pulling the sledges. They'll only
sink. They must be tethered together and led.' He
paused and stood looking round, his hands on his hips.
'*And get a move on!*' he roared. '*We depart at midday!*'

Rook found Xanth sitting on the remains of the
hammelhorn cart, which had been completely stripped
of wood for mud-shoes. He was surrounded by four
huge mountains of shaggy, mud-caked fur, and smiling
broadly.

'I can't understand a
word they're saying,'
he laughed as Rook
ran up.

'Wumeru!' Rook
shouted out in delight.

The banderbear
turned. 'Wurrah-lurra!
Uralowa leera-wuh!'
she roared, her words
accompanied by arm
movements, curiously

delicate for one so large. *Greetings, Rook, he who took the
poison-stick. It is good you are back with us.*

'Wuh-wuh!' Rook replied, his hand lightly touching
his chest. It was good to hear his banderbear name again.
'Wurra-weeg, weleera lowah.' *Greetings, friend. Together
we shall face the journey ahead.*

'Wurra-weeg, wurra-wuh!' the other banderbears joined in, clustering around Rook in an excited group. There was Wuralo, who he'd rescued from the Foundry Glade; Weeg, with his great, angry scar across one shoulder, and old Molleen, her single tusk glinting in the low sunlight as she tossed her head animatedly about.

'What are they saying? What are they saying?' said Xanth excitedly, joining the throng.

'They're saying,' laughed Rook, 'that they've been searching the camp and have been trying to ask you if you'd heard of me – but you didn't seem to understand a word they said. Molleen here thinks you seem rather stupid, but that it isn't your fault – it's because your hair's so short!'

Xanth burst into laughter, and the banderbears yodelled in unison.

'Tell her,' said Xanth, 'that I'll grow my hair just for her.'

As the sun rose higher in the milky sky, the chaos of the Mire encampment gradually took on a semblance of order. Every cart was laden, every backpack stuffed full; at Fenbrus Lodd's command, the prowlgrins had been harnessed up to the sledges carrying the precious library crates.

An hour earlier, following Deadbolt Vulpoon's orders, the Undertowners had started to rope themselves together in groups of twelve. Now, they were all taking up the positions allocated to them by the sky pirates in a huge column, with the family groups and the Great Library at the centre, the sky pirates themselves at the head and the Ghosts of Screetown bringing up the rear. Roped together, Rook, Xanth and the banderbears were just behind the last of the huge library sledges, its jostling, slavering team of fifty prowlgrins raring to go.

Felix called to them from towards the back of the column. 'Good luck, Rook! Make sure those great shaggy friends of yours don't step on any prowlgrin tails!' His laughter boomed out across the Mire.

Rook smiled. He wished he could be as brave and cheerful as Felix.

Just then, Deadbolt Vulpoon strode past, his sword held high and the megaphone clamped to his mouth. Rook raised his scarf to shield his eyes from the dazzling whiteness ahead, his stomach turning somersaults. High above his head, a great flock of white ravens circled noisily, the furious cawing echoing off across the endless Mire, and reminding Rook just how far they had to go.

'ADVANCE!!' Deadbolt Vulpoon's voice boomed as he strode out ahead.

The column began to shuffle forward – front first, then further and further back down the lines, until every single individual in the vast multitude was in motion. Rook fell into step, Xanth and the banderbears marching beside him. Up ahead, families of gnokgoblins and lugtrolls marched, their makeshift mud-shoes slapping on the mud, keeping them from sinking.

Yet the going was tough for all that.

Soon, many were struggling – from frail old'uns, their aged limbs protesting, to young'uns, thin and under-nourished, yet too big to be carried. Behind them came the library sledges, with Fenbrus Lodd and Cowlquape Pentephraxis walking alongside them, the High Librarian anxiously checking and rechecking the ropes, the runners, the prowlgrin harnesses . . .

'Nothing must be lost,' he was muttering. 'Not a tome, not a treatise, not a barkscroll.'

They all tramped on resolutely through the afternoon and into the evening. Dark clouds gathered overhead once more, and Rook pulled his collar up against the rising wind.

From up ahead, Deadbolt's voice boomed. 'Keep marching! There can be no stopping, you mudlubbers! Close up the gaps!'

It was almost completely dark when the rain first started – big, fat drops that spattered down on the mud-flats. Within seconds, it had become torrential, bucketing down on the Undertowners for the third time in as many nights.

'We keep on!' Deadbolt's voice called out above the hiss and thunder of the howling wind and battering rain.

His words were passed back down through the lines of the drenched multitude, growing more despondent with every repetition.

'We keep on?' muttered a gnokgoblin matron desperately, glancing back at her family, roped behind her, barely able to keep going.

A cloddertrog to her left, bathed in purple light from the brazier-cage he was carrying, nodded grimly. 'We keep on,' he said.

Rook himself was struggling. He was hungry, and

the icy rain had chilled him to the bones. On either side of him, the banderbears panted noisily, while behind him – pulling on the tether-rope that bound them together – Xanth slipped and slid on his unfamiliar mud-shoes.

A curious numbness seemed to grip both Rook's body and his mind. He was no longer thinking of where he was going. The future no longer existed; nor did the past. There was only this, here, now. One step after the other, trudging across the endless reaches of the Mire.

One step. Then another, and another . . .

The night passed in a stupor of mud, sweat and shivers, and a cold grey light began to dawn. Despite Deadbolt's best efforts, the pace had slowed to a painful crawl, with small pockets of stragglers beginning to fall behind. If this continued, he knew the column would soon cease to be a column at all, and become instead a disorganized rabble, impossible to lead.

At last there came the command everyone had been waiting for.

'HALT!' bellowed Deadbolt. 'We rest for one hour! No more! Any longer and we'll all be muglump bait – that is, if the mud-flows don't get us first.'

With a collective sigh, the column stopped marching, and the long lines of Undertowners broke up into small groups, huddled together against the biting wind. Sitting between Molleen and Wumeru, Rook and Xanth escaped the worst of it – but were still both chilled to the bone.

'I never thought I'd say this,' said Xanth, smiling

weakly, 'but I almost miss Undertown. How can anybody call this desolate waste home?'

Rook didn't answer. He was gazing past Xanth at the
treeline in the distance.

'The Twilight Woods,' he murmured.

From the cold, icy mud of the Mire, the twinkling light
of the Twilight Woods was hypnotic. Warm, inviting
glades sparkled, fabulous clearings shimmered; nooks
and crannies, sheltered from the bitter winds, beckoned
seductively.

Xanth put his arm on Rook's shoulder. 'Don't even
think about it,' he said sternly. 'That path leads to death
. . . A *living* death.'

Rook looked away and shook his head. 'I know, I
know,' he said. The Twilight Woods! That beautiful,
seductive, terrible place that robbed you of your mind
but not your life, condemning you to live on for ever as
your body decayed. 'It's just that . . . it looks so . . .'

'Inviting,' Xanth said grimly. 'I know that.' He
shivered as a blast of icy wind hit him. The next
instant he was up on his feet and waving wildly.

'Molleen! No!' he cried out. 'Molleen! *Come back!*'

Rook leaped up. The old banderbear had torn free of her tether and was stumbling across the mudflats, her eyes fixed on the Twilight Woods ahead.

'Weeg-worraleeg! Weera wuh-wuh!' Rook shouted desperately. *Come back, old friend, that is death calling you!*

Wumeru, Wuralo and Weeg's anguished yodels rang out. *Come back, old friend! Come back!*

But the old banderbear ignored them. And she wasn't alone. Up and down the column, individuals were cutting the ropes that bound them to their groups and dashing towards the alluring glades of the Twilight Woods.

Deadbolt's voice boomed from the front of the line. 'Column fall in, and advance if you want to see another dawn! Advance, I say! And keep your eyes looking up front, you mangy curs!'

Ahead of them, the library sledges lumbered forwards. Rook, Xanth and the banderbears broke ranks as one, and made after Molleen, only to be jerked back by the rope that secured them to their sledge. Rook tore at the rope feverishly.

'Molleen, wait!' he shouted. 'We're coming to get you!

'Fall back in line!' roared a voice in Rook's ear. Deadbolt Vulpoon, his face like thunder, loomed over him. 'Fall back in line or I'll run you through!' He brandished a serrated-edge sabre menacingly. 'And don't think I won't!'

Rook stopped, tears stinging his eyes. 'But Molleen,' he said, his voice breaking. 'She's our friend, we must . . .'

'You follow her and you'll all be lost,' said Deadbolt firmly. 'There's no saving her, believe me, lad.'

The library sledge pulled the rope taut as Rook fell back into line. The others followed, the banderbears moaning softly, Xanth shaking his shaven head.

'Sky curse it!' Deadbolt thundered. 'This is all my fault. I took us too close to the treeline, then took pity on you mudlubbers and allowed you to stop. Well, there'll be no more of it. We march on! Or we die!'

With that he was off, striding back down the column, barking orders left and right. Rook shut his eyes, and concentrated on putting one foot in front of the other. The plaintive yodels of the banderbears rang out across the white mudflats as, in the distance, the shuffling figure of Molleen disappeared into the Twilight Woods.

They marched on all through that dismal grey morning and on into a rain-sodden afternoon. Few spoke; even the chants of the sky pirates up in front tailed off, and the only sounds were the barks and yelps of the prowlgrins and the relentless *slap, slap, slap* of mud-shoes on mire mud.

The grey afternoon gave way to the dim half-light of evening, and the wind grew stronger once more, pelting them with heavy rain that stung their faces and soaked them to the skin.

'That's the Edgeland wind,' called back the librarian on the library sledge. 'We must be getting close!' He cracked the whip and urged the yelping prowlgrins on.

The rope round Rook's middle jerked taut, forcing him to quicken his pace. All round him, the air was filled with curses and moans as the marchers struggled to keep up.

Suddenly, rising above it all, there came the noise of squelching mud, and a curious *plaff-plaff* sound. Rook looked up. To the left of the column, a cluster of low mud-dunes seemed to be approaching, rising and falling in a slippery rhythm as they did so.

'MUGLUMPS!'

The cry went up from the back of the column, where the Ghosts of Screetown had obviously spotted the danger.

The rope suddenly tugged Rook violently to the right as the librarian on the library sledge battled to control the panicking prowlgrins. Ahead, the four other sledges were in equal trouble. The low shapes were gathering and, from their path, it was obvious that the closely harnessed packs of prowlgrins were their intended prey.

Felix and his ghosts appeared out of the gloom on all sides. Fenbrus Lodd, Cowlquape beside him, shouted desperately to his son.

'The library sledges! Felix!' he screamed. 'They're after the sledges!'

Rook was running now, with Xanth and the banderbears dragged behind him, as the library sledge careered across the mud.

'Cut yourselves loose!' shouted Felix to Rook and the other librarians. 'And follow the braziers of the sky pirates!'

With a grunt, Rook tore at the knotted rope round his middle and slid to a halt as it fell free.

'There!' shouted Xanth, beside him. He pointed.

Ahead, Deadbolt stood on a mud-dune, waving a flaming purple brazier over his head as if possessed. 'Rally to me, Undertowners!' he roared. 'Rally!'

The huge library sledges slewed and skidded away to the right, the yelping screams of the prowlgrin teams drowning out the cries of their drivers. The muddunes seethed and boiled with the low, flapping shapes of the half-hidden muglumps in pursuit.

Panting, Rook reached Deadbolt, who was now surrounded by a huge crowd of mud-spattered and bewildered Undertowners. Xanth and the banderbears came lumbering up behind him.

'There lie the Edgelands, Sky help us! We'll regroup there!' shouted Deadbolt above the howling winds, and pointing to a low, grey ridge in the middle distance. 'Mothers and young'uns first!'

The Undertowners surged forwards across the glistening wind-flattened expanse of mud ahead, all eyes fixed on the distant ridge. Every one of them was driven by a desperate, half-mad frenzy to get out of the clinging mire mud and onto dry land. Rook was jostled and bumped as Undertowner after Undertowner barged past.

'You heard him!' Xanth shouted. 'Come on. We're nearly there, Rook!'

But Rook shook his head. 'I'm a librarian knight,' he said in a low voice, his words almost lost in the gusting wind. 'My place is with the library.'

He turned back towards the library sledges. Xanth and the banderbears hesitated. It was obvious from their eyes that they shared the Undertowners' mire-madness. Every fibre of their beings longed to be rid of the terrible white mud.

'And our place is with you,' said Xanth.

They turned and fought their way through the crowd, and back out into the Mire. The library sledges, like huge lumbering beasts, were away to the right, and had halted their mad dash. Now they seemed marooned, their tops bristling with librarians like hairs on a hammelhorn. As they approached, Rook could see why.

Felix and the ghosts were busy cutting the traces that harnessed the prowlgrin teams, while his father waved his hands in the air wildly, from on top of one of the sledges.

'Stop! Stop!' he was bellowing, but Felix ignored him as he cut through another tilderleather strap.

The slithering mounds had congregated in a flapping, slurping reef round the sledges, kept at bay for the moment by brazier-wielding ghosts – but inching closer by the second.

Rook stopped. If they went any further, they risked straying into the midst of the muglump pack. He shook his head miserably. There was nothing they could do; they were helpless spectators. He sank to his knees in the cold white mud. How he hated the oozing filth that seemed to cling so, pulling you down, smothering the life out of you, until you were so weary you just didn't care any more . . .

All at once, the mire mud erupted in front of him. Felix had cut the last harness and given the signal. With piercing screams, the prowlgrins – all two hundred and fifty of them – stampeded out across the mudflats.

The mounds closed in around them. Up out of the mud, the muglumps reared, in plain sight at last. Rook stared, transfixed with horror. The last time he'd seen a muglump was with Felix, in the sewers of old Undertown – but that sewer-dweller seemed tame compared to these monsters. The size of a bull hammelhorn, with six thick-set limbs and a long whiplash tail, each muglump slithered through the soft mire mud just below

the surface, breathing through flapped nostrils.

Now, with a bone-scraping screech, they pounced on the hapless prowlgrins and, in a frenzy, tore them limb from limb with their razor-sharp claws. Soon, the mire mud was drenched in prowlgrin blood as the muglumps feasted.

'Let's save this library of yours!'

Felix's booming voice pulled Rook away from the horror. He was helping the librarians down from the sledges, organizing them into teams and picking up the traces.

'We don't have much time,' said Felix, motioning to the ghosts to join them. 'They'll be back for us soon.'

'Come, librarians!' Cowlquape's voice rang out. 'We must all pull together!'

Rook, Xanth and the banderbears ran over the mud to join the librarians who, when they saw the huge figures of Wuralo, Weeg and Wumeru, gave a cheer.

'Thank Sky we've got you,' said the prowlgrin-driver, greeting them. 'If you and your friends here could set the pace, we'll try to keep up!'

They picked up the traces and tether-ropes, and each sledge, drawn by a team of ghosts and librarians, resumed its journey across the wastes towards the thin grey ridge in the distance, now twinkling with purple lights. Behind in the gathering dusk, the snarls and grunts of the muglump feast spurred them on.

One step after the other, Rook thought grimly. One step. Then another, and another . . .

·CHAPTER FOUR·

THE EDGELANDS

It was dark as the exhausted librarians dragged the last library sledge up out of the Mire and onto the flat, rocky pavement of the Edgelands. They were greeted by Undertowners, young and old, who held out flasks of warming oakapple brandy and bowls of broth. There were small braziers ablaze, groups huddled round them for warmth, and clusters of muddy-cloaked Undertowners who'd simply lain down and fallen asleep where they'd stopped.

Rook rubbed his eyes and looked about him. To the south were the Twilight Woods, their hypnotic golden glow bright and enticing in the darkness. To the north, the Edge fell abruptly away into the bottomless void. Trapped between the two, the vast multitude of Undertowners, librarians, sky pirates and ghosts prepared to sleep, while all around them miasmic mists writhed and swirled – now thinning to show the full moon glinting on the rocky pavement, now thickening and obliterating everything from view.

Rook accepted a bowl of warm broth from a gnok-goblin matron, and stumbled over to a brazier where the banderbears were being patted on the back by some library scroll-scribes and lectern-tenders. Xanth hung back with that unhappy look in his eyes that Rook noticed whenever his friend was near librarians.

All around them, the night was throbbing with activity as the Undertowners pitched their tents, raised their wind-breaks and got their stock-pots bubbling. Food was bartered; meat for bread, woodale for water. Young'uns were settled down for the night. And while they slept, their elders worked on, preparing themselves for an early start the following morning – and post-poning the moment when they too would have to turn in for the night.

It was reassuring working together; safety in numbers, so to speak. They all knew that when asleep, every single one of them would be alone. That was when the Edgelands was at its most dangerous, when the misty phantasms filtered into their dreams and nightmares . . .

The fires were stoked and restoked, and the brazier-cages were filled to the brim with their supplies of lufwood. Hammelhorns were fed and watered. The mud-clogged runners were removed from the sledges and the wheels returned to their axles. And amidst it all, Rook noticed, a brisk trade in good-luck charms was establishing itself, with the trolls, trogs and goblins vying for business.

'Amulets! Get your bloodoak amulets here!' a stocky woodtroll was calling, a bunch of carved red medallions on thongs clasped in his stubby fingers. 'Guaranteed to repel every dark-spirit and empty-soul!'

'Leather charms!' shouted a slaughterer. 'Bone talismans. Ward off wraiths and spectres. Keep the gloamglozer himself at bay.'

'Bristleweed and . . . *slurp, slurp* . . . charlock pomanders,' cried a gabtroll, her long tongue lapping at her swaying eyeballs. 'Bristleweed . . . *slurp, slurp* . . . and charlock pomanders.'

'I don't think we'd have made it without your friends here,' said a sprightly-looking under-librarian by the name of Garulus Lexis, clapping Rook on the back.

Rook smiled and passed on the librarian's thanks.

'Wug-weeghla, loora-weela-wuh,' said Wumeru. *His words warm my heart, but my stomach remains empty*.

'Well, we'll soon see to that,' laughed Garulus when Rook had translated, and he bustled off, returning a few moments later with a sack of hyleberries and a large pot of oak-honey. 'Enjoy!' he said, as the banderbears tucked delightedly into their feast.

Xanth sat down quietly next to Rook and drew his cloak about him.

'Does your ... er ... friend need anything?' said Garulus, nodding at Xanth, a look of mild contempt on his face.

'Nothing, thank you,' said Xanth.

The other librarians round the brazier exchanged glances.

Rook gave Xanth his bowl. 'Here, finish this, Xanth,' he said. 'I've had my fill. Go on, it's good.'

Xanth accepted the bowl with a thin smile and drained its contents. The librarians ignored him.

'Well, *now* what are we to do?' Ambris Loppix, an assistant lectern-tender asked. 'Without the prowlgrins, the library carts are all but useless.'

'I don't know about you,' said Queltus Petrix, an under-librarian, 'but I just about broke my back pulling the blasted thing through the Mire even *with* the help of young Rook's friends here.'

They all nodded.

'We can't take it with us, and we can't leave it behind,' said Garulus, shaking his head sadly. 'After all, what are librarians without a library?'

'There *is* something you could do,' said Xanth quietly. The librarians all looked at him. 'A way to get every barkscroll across the Edgelands and to the Free Glades,' he went on.

Ambris snorted and Queltus turned away. Garulus pushed his half-moon spectacles back onto the bridge of his long nose. 'And what, pray, is that?' he said, contempt dripping from every word.

'Every Undertowner could carry a scroll. There are thirty thousand scrolls, aren't there?'

'Yes,' said Garulus uncertainly.

'And there are at least thirty thousand of us – Undertowners, ghosts, sky pirates, librarians . . .'

'And one Guardian of Night,' said Garulus, fixing Xanth with an icy stare.

'No, listen . . .' Rook began, jumping to his feet. But before he could speak further, the gaunt figure of Cowlquape, Most High Academe, stepped into the brazier light, flanked by Felix and Fenbrus Lodd, doing the rounds of the librarian camp fires.

'It is a *brilliant* idea,' he said with a gesture of the hand that they should all remain seated. 'If we entrust one scroll to each one of us, librarian and Undertowner alike, then we all become a *living* library, and we can cast off these cumbersome carts.'

'But the lecterns . . .' began Fenbrus.

'We can build more lecterns, my friend,' said Cowlquape. 'It is the barkscrolls, and the knowledge they contain, that is precious. Xanth, here, has remembered that, when some of us have been in danger of forgetting it.'

Fenbrus coughed loudly, and his face reddened. Felix beamed and winked slyly at Rook.

'We shall unload the carts at dawn and distribute the library. Felix, can you and your ghosts supervise?'

Felix nodded.

'Now,' said Cowlquape sternly, looking round. 'Fenbrus has something to say to you. Please listen carefully, and pass it on. It could mean the difference between life and death to us out here in the Edgelands.'

Fenbrus stepped forwards, coughed again, and cleared his throat. 'Tomorrow, we venture through the Edgelands,' he began, 'and as your High Librarian, I have consulted the barkscrolls to learn what I can of what lies ahead. Make no mistake,' he said gravely, looking at each of them in turn, 'we are about to enter a region of phantasms and apparitions, where your ears and eyes will deceive you. Out there on the barren rocks, the Twilight Woods are on one side and the Edge itself on the other. If the wind blows in from the Edge side, we shall be travelling through heavy cloud and fog. The danger then is of losing our sense of direction and plunging over the Edge and into the void.'

Rook shuddered. All eyes were glued to Fenbrus.

'On the other hand, if the wind changes and blows in from the Twilight Woods, then the madness of that place will infect the Edgelands and, most likely, will infect us too.'

'And if that happens?' asked Garulus.

'Hopefully,' said Fenbrus, 'it will not last long, but our only defence is to rope ourselves together in pairs, and to talk to each other. For the great danger is to sink into a waking dream without even realizing it. If your partner falls silent, you must wake him instantly, or the phantasms will take hold and he will be lost for ever.' He paused. 'I intend to partner my son, Felix, here.'

He coughed again, and Felix smiled.

'And I was hoping,' said Cowlquape, 'that you, Garulus, would do me the honour . . ?'

Garulus nodded. Rook felt a hand on his shoulder.

'Would you, Rook . . ?' Xanth mumbled as the other librarians left to spread the news.

'I'd be honoured,' said Rook, smiling.

'And then, Xanth?' said Rook. 'What happened then? We've got to keep talking, remember.'

'I know, I know,' said Xanth wearily. 'But I'm so tired.' He sighed. 'And then I became his assistant. Me, assistant to the High Guardian of Night himself, Orbix Xaxis! It all seems like a dream to me now . . .'

No one had slept well that night on the rocky pavement. The ground beneath them was too hard, and it was cold, with the howling wind slicing through the air like ice-scythes. Long before the sun had even risen, everybody in the vast multitude had already packed up their belongings and tethered themselves together in lines, ready for the daunting journey ahead. Felix and the Ghosts of Screetown had ushered them to the five great library carts and, as they'd walked past, each in turn had been handed a barkscroll, a treatise, a tome; one tiny part of the whole library.

Now, as the sun rose slowly – creamy-white behind the dense, swirling mist – they were marching on, their elongated shadows stretched out in front of them. A low babble of voices echoed above the clatter of cartwheels as the pairs of Undertowners indulged in feverish conversations, anxious that none of them should fall prey to the Edgelands' phantasms.

In their midst, the librarians marched, with Rook and Xanth still deep in their own conversation.

'And that metal muzzle he wore,' said Rook, chuckling. 'What was all that about?'

Xanth smiled weakly. 'Orbix Xaxis was a creature of many superstitions,' he said. 'He only bathed by the full moon. He never ate tilder if there was an "r" in the month. And he believed that the air was still full of the "vile contagion" which had brought stone-sickness to the Edge.'

'He blamed the librarians for stone-sickness, didn't he?' Rook added. 'Believed we'd brought it back from the Deepwoods. Is that why he killed so many of us?'

'He was mad, I realize that now,' said Xanth, his face drawn and tense. He shuddered. 'Oh, those accursed Purification Ceremonies of his. I dread to think how many Undertowners and librarians were sacrificed to the rock demons. And for what?' He shook his head, leaving the question hanging in mid air. 'Orbix Xaxis was mad all right, Sky curse his wicked soul . . .'

'Xanth,' Rook gasped, looking round uneasily, half expecting to see the spirit of the High Guardian himself emerging from the mists. 'Careful what you say, here of all places.'

The wind that had been howling continuously since they first stepped on to the rocky pavement had now died down, and a heavy swirling fog had descended like a white blanket.

'This reminds me of when I was a young'un,' said Rook, still endeavouring to keep talking, despite the cold, suffocating mist that tightened about them. 'There was this old forgotten cistern in the sewers. I'd lower myself into it, pull the top shut over my head and spend hours there, tucked up and hidden, with only a lantern and a smuggled treatise for company . . .' He frowned. 'Xanth?' he said, concerned that his friend was letting his mind stray. 'Are you listening?'

'Oh, yes,' said Xanth, his voice dull.

Behind them, Ambris Loppix's voice could clearly

be heard. 'They say he hand-picked the captured librarians for that master of his.'

'I heard that he actually enjoyed listening to their screams. Called it "singing", he did,' replied his partner.

'Do you know how they celebrate Wodgiss Night in a woodtroll village?' said Rook, trying to drown out the sound of the librarians' conversation. 'It's in my barkscroll, *Customs and Practices Encountered in Deepwoods Villages*.' Rook patted his knapsack, where the barkscroll he'd been entrusted with was safely packed.

Xanth made no response.

'First of all, there's this huge procession,' said Rook, 'with drums and trumpets, and everyone wears these fantastic exotic head-dresses . . .'

'And then he became a spy . . .' Ambris was saying.

'And the young'uns all get their faces painted,' said Rook. 'Like animals. Some are fromps, some are lemkins, and there is even one done up like a vulpoon, in a feathered suit and a strap-on beak . . .'

'Betrayed *hundreds* of apprentice librarians on their way to the Free Glades, apparently . . .'

Rook turned and glowered at the librarians – though tethered as he was, there was little he could do to shut them up.

'Execution's too good for him, that's what I say,' replied Ambris's partner.

'They'll know what to do with him in the Free Glades, the stinking traitor . . .'

'Don't listen to them, Xanth. They don't know what

they're talking about,' said Rook, still glowering at the librarians.

'I'm sorry, Rook, I just can't stand it any more,' Xanth said tremulously. 'They're right. I'm no good. I'm rotten . . .' His voice trailed away.

Rook turned back to his friend. 'You're *not* rotten, Xanth. You're . . . Xanth? What are you doing? Xanth! *Xanth!*'

His friend had vanished, the rope that bound him hanging limply from the main tether.

'No, Xanth,' Rook shouted, struggling to loosen his own binding. The rope fell away behind him as he dashed off after his friend. 'Xanth. Xanth, wait! Come back!'

Behind him, Rook heard the banderbears yodelling in alarm, and the librarians bellowing at him to come back. But he couldn't abandon his friend. He just couldn't.

Up ahead, he caught a glimpse of a misty figure through the thickening fog – but almost at once, it was gone again. Like a snowbird in an ice-storm, the shaven-headed youth had disappeared.

'XANTH!' Rook roared.

But there was no reply save his own muffled echo.

'XAAAAANTH!!'

As the desperate cry faded away, Rook realized that he could hear nothing. Nothing at all. It was as if the vast multitude of Undertowners, librarians, ghosts and sky pirates had simply vanished along with his friend. Suddenly, he was alone, lost in the swirling mists of the Edgelands, the treacherous Twilight Woods on one side, the Edge on the other – and no one to talk to.

The wind began to pick up again, but it had changed. Now, instead of lifting the fog, it swirled into eddies and ripples. And as Rook stumbled on over the greasy stone, trying his best not to twist his ankles in the cracks and fissures, he began to hear voices.

Lots of voices. Wailing and keening and whispering softly.

'Sweet dreams, Master Rook,' they seemed be saying, the innocent words belied by the cold, menacing hiss. 'Sweet dreams . . .'

·CHAPTER FIVE·

THE SEPIA STORM

Rook stumbled on, sweaty and scared, trying hard to shut out the whispering voices – but it wasn't easy. No matter how hard he pressed his hands to his ears, how loudly he hummed, how vigorously he tried to engage in conversation with himself, they would not be silenced. They would not be still.

'Xanth!' he cried out, his own voice carried off on the warm wind sweeping in from the Twilight Woods. 'Xanth, where *are* you?' He paused, removed his hands from his ears and cocked his head to one side, hoping against hope that this time his friend would reply. The air echoed with a thousand voices; high, low, angry and sad – every voice in the world it seemed but the one he longed to hear.

'Oh, Xanth,' he murmured. 'Not all librarians are like Ambris Loppix. Why did you listen to him?'

'Once a Guardian, always a Guardian!' the voices seemed to hiss back at him. 'He betrayed others. Now he's betrayed you.'

'It's not true!' Rook shouted back at the swirling, sparkling air. 'Xanth's changed. He's one of us now!'

'One of us, one of us,' taunted the chorus of voices, and Rook glimpsed a black shape out of the corner of his eye. He spun round, to be confronted by a tall figure in a black gown and a metal muzzle.

'Orbix? Orbix Xaxis?' Rook gasped, his conversation with Xanth flooding back to him. 'No, it can't be, I must be . . .'

'Dreaming?' a cold, cruel voice hissed through the muzzle. The white gloamglozer emblazoned on the black gown fluttered in front of him.

'You're not real,' said Rook, backing away, his feet slipping on the greasy rock.

'Aren't we, young librarian knight?' hissed the

voice. 'Are you quite certain of that?' The gowned figure cackled with laughter, and waved a bony claw-like hand.

As if in response, spectres and phantasms loomed out of the shadows, each one with a gloamglozer of its own emblazoned across its chest. They doubled in number, and doubled again, and again and again, until all around him, everywhere he looked, they were all Rook could see. It was as if he'd wandered into a mighty army of Guardians of Night.

'We are real enough,' the voices sounded about him, mocking, jeering. 'As real as your blackest thoughts!'

'As real as your darkest fears!'

'As your deepest nightmares!'

The countless images of the gloamglozers smiled as one, their great fangs glinting savagely, their eyes flashing. The muzzled figure raised his clawed hand and beckoned slowly.

Rook felt a terrible, numbing fear welling up deep inside him. It spread out from his chest, along his arms and into his fingertips; it coursed down his legs, making his knees tremble, and sinking to his toes. He tried hard to fight it, but it was no good. Like a lemkin, held by the murderous stare of a predatory halitoad, he was paralysed. There was nothing he could do. Even his face seemed frozen as the fear travelled up his spine, over his scalp . . .

'No, no, no,' Rook muttered, unable even to blink. 'Remember what Fenbrus said. This is one of those waking dreams. But that's all it is. A dream, that's all . . .'

'That's all! That's all! That's all!' jeered a thousand cackling voices.

Rook could bear it no longer. He threw back his head and screamed like a wounded animal.

'Xanth! Xanth! *Xanth!*'

His cries drowned out the jeering voices and, for an instant, the black figures seemed to shrink back into the swirling mists. At the same moment, the fear that held him released its grip and, without a second's thought, Rook was up and running across the slippery pavement as fast as his legs could carry him.

'I've got to get out of here! I've got to get out of here!' he shouted, as he ran blindly through the swirling mist.

'Out of here! Out of here!' cackled voices behind him, driving him on.

This way and that Rook ran, slipping and stumbling, terrified of falling yet too frightened to stop, until – imperceptibly at first – the thick grey mist seemed to thin out and take on a golden tinge.

All at once, Rook came to an abrupt halt. Ahead of him, the jagged skyline of the Twilight Woods crackled with electric blue filaments as, high in the air above, boiling black clouds swirled in a gathering whirlwind. The glow from between the trees brightened and faded as a warm, slightly sickly mist blew in from the woods and into his face.

Was he awake or asleep? Was it dreams or illusions that surrounded him? Could he even be sure that it was the Twilight Woods he could see before him now, and not simply something else his feverish imagination had conjured up. Certainly, it *looked* like the Twilight Woods, and with the seductive whispers and wheedling cries floating in on the rising wind, it *sounded* like it too. What was more, it had never seemed more inviting.

Rook took a step forward, and then stopped. 'That way lies death,' he reminded himself. 'Living death.'

He was about to turn and go back into the swirling mists of the Edgelands Pavement when, high above the gold-drenched trees, the sky tore itself apart with a deafening *crack*, and the air blazed dazzlingly bright. Rook looked up to see a huge, zigzag lightning bolt break off from the base of the dark, spinning cloud and hurtle down into the woods below.

He gasped as a blast of scalding air hit him full in the face. The air filled with the scent of toasted wood-almonds. Eyes wide open, mouth agape, Rook watched the blinding lightning turn to crystal as it pierced the glow of the woods, solidifying in an instant to a zigzag crystal spear which continued down behind the trees to the earth below. He shivered, awestruck by the in-credible sight. A Great Storm, born of the dark maelstrom and drawn to the Twilight Woods like a moth to a flame, had discharged its colossal electric charge in the form of a mighty lightning bolt, deep at its centre.

'Stormphrax,' Rook breathed.

There was a distant echoing *thud* as the point of the frozen lightning bolt plunged deep into the twilit ground. The rock beneath Rook's feet trembled and he fell to the ground. It was as if the Twilight Woods – itself astonished by the lightning strike – had taken a sudden

intake of breath, sucking back the mist it had previously been blowing out across the Edgelands. And, as the mist disappeared into the Twilight Woods, Rook found himself being sucked after it and had to claw at the rocky pavement to prevent himself toppling head over heels into the deadly glades in front of him.

The next moment, and as abruptly as it had begun, everything suddenly fell still. Rook released his grip on the rock surface and climbed gingerly to his feet. As he looked round he saw that, for the first time since he'd set foot in the Edgelands, the thick, swirling mist had gone and he could see the pavement of rock stretching away into the distance on either side and in front.

There was no sign of the Undertowners . . .

But wait! Rook's heart missed a beat. Yes! There, in the distance, by a great rocky crag, was a figure, waving frantically.

'Rook!' Xanth's voice echoed across the flat, rocky expanse. 'Rook! Look out!'

'Xanth!' Rook shouted joyfully, and began running towards the far-off figure.

'Look out!' came Xanth's voice again. 'Behind you!'

Rook glanced back over his shoulder, from where there came a rumbling, rolling sound that was growing louder by the second. The next instant, a great, boiling blanket of sepia dust – rushing and roaring like a torrent of floodwater – burst out of the Twilight Woods and spread across the rockland.

It was heading straight for him. Even as he went to turn away, Rook knew that there was no point trying to flee. He could never outrun the oncoming storm. Having breathed in, the Twilight Woods was now expelling the full force of the lightning that had just struck it, in one mighty roar. Transfixed, Rook stared at the sepia-coloured storm surging across the rock towards him; closer, ever closer . . .

'*Aaaiiii!*' Rook cried out as it scythed his legs out from under him, sending him crashing to the ground and jarring his elbow painfully as he landed.

The turbulence tightened its grip around him, roaring and whistling and tugging at his clothes. He found himself being blown over and over, unable to stop, as – like a great, glowing tidal wave – the storm swept him across the rocky pavement towards the Edge itself.

All round him as he rolled, the dust sparkled brightly, like a maelstrom of tiny stars. It filled his eyes, his ears, it seeped in through the pores of his skin and, every time he inhaled, he breathed the glittering fragments and particles deep down into his lungs.

'Must . . . stop . . . myself . . .' he groaned, flinging his arms and legs out, trying in vain to stop the storm sweeping him on any further. But it was no good. The rock was too slippery, and the storm too strong.

All the while, the Edge was coming closer, flashing before his eyes as he continued to roll, a gaping nothingness where the rocky pavement simply stopped and the Edgelands fell away into the bottomless void beyond.

Bruised and battered, Rook was losing the battle. He was dizzy, he was dazed. Ahead of him, as he was driven on inexorably towards the Edge, he thought he

glimpsed the gloamglozer
– and not some fancy emblem stitched
to the front of a robe either. This was the
real thing. Huge. Imposing . . .

Yes, there it was again, looming out of the glittering dust-storm ahead, its great horned head raised in evil triumph. It was as if the terrible creature had come to gloat; to stand at the very Edge itself and watch him, Rook Barkwater, tumbling helplessly into the empty nothingness.

Rook knew then that he was done for.

'Rook! Rook!'

Rook trembled. It even knew his name.

'ROOK!'

Beneath him now, the last few strides of rocky pavement were rolling past. In front, the void yawned. Rook clamped his eyes shut and hugged his arms to his chest. There was nothing, nothing, that he could do to save himself.

With a lurch, and a gasp, he felt the rock suddenly disappear from beneath him.

Falling. He was falling. This was it. He'd tumbled over the Edge and . . .

'*Unkhh!*'

With a heavy jolt, his fall was broken. Something tightened round his middle, pinning his arms to his side and leaving him gasping for breath. Bewildered, Rook looked down, to see a rope! He was dangling from a rope above the endless emptiness beneath, with the torrent of dust-filled air cascading over the Edge to his left like a mighty waterfall.

The next moment, he felt himself being yanked upwards, backwards through the air. His back slammed hard against the rock. Hands seized him by the shoulders, rolled him round and dragged him up over the lip of rock and onto solid ground. Then they released him.

Wriggling round awkwardly, Rook managed to loosen the rope and slip free. He climbed shakily to his feet, his stomach churning, his ears ringing. Looking up, he found himself standing in the shelter of a great angular crag of rock, carved and weathered by the Edgeland winds into a monstrous hunched form.

'The gloamglozer,' Rook whispered.

The brightly glowing sepia storm was swirling round it on both sides as it poured out over the Edge. Xanth, he saw, was standing beside him, bent double and panting noisily. Straightening up slowly, he put his hands on his hips and took a long, deep breath.

'Thank Sky the mist cleared when it did,' he said at length, 'or I'd never have spotted you.' His face clouded over. 'Oh, Rook, I'm so sorry I ran off . . .'

Rook silenced him with a wave of his hand. 'Just thank Sky you were top of the class at ropecraft,' he said. 'And that this rock was here to shelter behind . . .' His voice faded away. He was feeling increasingly light-headed, and his arms and legs were beginning to ache. 'It's strange,' he said softly, 'but I think I know this place.'

The pair of them looked out. Even as they had been speaking, the great waves of dust-laden storm-ripples were losing their power, the sepia storm exhausted. And as the roaring softened, the torrent shrank to a trickle and the sparkling light grew dim.

'Come on,' said Xanth quickly. 'There's still a chance we can catch up with the others . . .'

He stopped and stared at Rook, who had dropped to his knees and was peering cautiously down over the cliff-edge.

The wind had abruptly changed direction, and was driving in from beyond the Edge once more, icy cold and heavy with moisture. From below, there came eerie sounds of chains clanking and something *tap-tap-tapping* against the rock-face, while behind, the northerly winds howled through the cracks and crevices of the huge, monstrous-shaped rock.

Despite the dull pain behind his eyes that made it so difficult for him to focus, Rook was more certain than ever that he knew where he was. He leaned over a little further and . . .

Yes, there they were; the great mooring-rings driven

into the rock that he
remembered seeing
once before. Most
were empty, some
bore ropes or
chains, while
from others,
there hung the
shattered
remains of
sky pirate
ships that had
been destroyed
where they were
moored, swaying in the storm
winds like great, bleached skeletons.

'I do know this place, Xanth,' he called back hoarsely. 'Wilderness Lair, it's called. The mighty sky pirate fleets used to take refuge here, clinging to the cliff-face like rock-limpets.'

Xanth made no reply.

'It's the place where the *Skyraider* was moored,' Rook went on. He was finding it difficult to catch his breath. 'You remember the *Skyraider*?' he added, turning to see whether Xanth was paying attention.

His friend was staring at him, his eyes wide.

'Captain Twig's sky pirate ship,' Rook said slowly, softly. 'The one that launched the attack on the Tower of . . .' His voice faded away completely. 'Xanth?' he said. 'Xanth, what is it?'

'It . . . it's . . .' Xanth faltered. He looked Rook up and down. 'You're . . .'

Rook gasped. He could see for himself now. Climbing shakily to his feet, he raised a hand to his face. Then the other. Both were glowing. As were his arms, and his chest, his body, his legs . . .

'Xanth,' he breathed, as the glowing grew more intense, 'what's happening to me?' His head was spinning. His legs turned to jelly. 'Xanth . . .'

He saw his friend running towards him, his arms outstretched, his face creased with concern. Inside and outside, the light grew brighter; dazzling him, blinding him, till he could take no more.

'Help me,' he whispered, his last words as he crumpled to the ground in a curled and glowing heap.

Xanth crouched down and put an ear tentatively to Rook's chest. His heartbeat was so faint, Xanth could hardly hear it.

'I'm so, so sorry, old friend,' he said, scooping Rook up in his arms and heaving himself to his feet. 'This is all my fault.'

He turned and began the long, arduous journey across the Edgelands rock, the heavy burden weighing him down and making every step an ordeal.

'By Earth and Sky, Rook,' he swore, stumbling on across the rocky pavement, 'enough brave librarian knights have died because of me. I shan't let *you* become one of them.'

·CHAPTER SIX·

DUSK

i

The Palace of the Furnace Masters

Hemuel Spume rubbed his spidery fingered hands together and smiled a thin-lipped smile. He always enjoyed this time of day.

The furnace fires had been freshly stoked for the night shift and the tall chimney stacks were belching out thick clouds of acrid smoke that stained the early evening sky a brilliant red. Exhausted lines of workers were tramping off to the low open-sided huts to snatch a few hours of much-needed sleep amid the unceasing din of the drills and hammers coming from the metal-working shops. An undercurrent of low, muttered complaints filled the air as the night workers jostled each other to reach their benches and forges.

The Foundry Master was standing in the upper gallery of the Counting House, a tall, solid wooden tower at the western end of the magnificently carved

Palace of the Furnace Masters. The mullioned windows were grimy with soot, both inside and out, yet this did little to mar the splendour of the view outside.

As far as the eye could see, the rows of blackened chimneys pointed like accusing fingers up at the blood-red sky. Beneath them, the glowing furnaces seemed to stare back at Hemuel, like the eyes of a thousand forest demons, throwing grotesque shadows across the huge timber stacks that fed them. Everywhere there was noise, bustle and industry, just the way he liked it – and never more so than now, as dusk was falling. With the changing of the shifts, the clamour of activity in the Foundry Glades was reaching a crescendo, before settling into the night-time cacophony of hammer-blow, foundry-clatter and furnace-blast.

Hemuel traced a bony finger through the soot on the window, and pushed his steel-rimmed glasses up his long nose. It hadn't always been like this. Oh, no. When he – Hemuel Maccabee Spume – had first come to the Deepwoods all those years ago, the Foundry Glade had been an insignificant forest forge, turning out trinkets and cooking pots for itinerant goblin tribes and the odd band of wandering shrykes. The ambitious young leaguesmen back in Undertown had said he was mad to bury himself out here in the Deepwoods, but Hemuel knew better . . .

The corners of his eyes crinkled with amusement as he thought back to those early days. So much had changed since then, and almost all for the better – at least, for him.

Stone-sickness had put an end to sky-flight, changing

the patterns of trade in the Edge for ever. No longer could the heavily-laden league ships transport the manufactured goods of the Undertown workshops out to the Deepwoods and return with precious timber and raw materials; no longer could the sky pirates prey upon the wealthy merchants and traders. After stone-sickness had struck, *all* cargo had to travel overland. And that – as Hemuel Spume had taken note – was a costly enterprise.

Once the shrykes had taken control of the Great Mire Road, the Undertown leagues had been forced to pay them high taxes for the right to trade with the Deepwoods. Costs of their products had soared and, as a result, the Undertowners had priced themselves out of business. Hemuel Spume had seized the opportunity to fill the gap in the market. The Foundry Glade – independent of the shrykes' greedy influence – had grown and prospered.

Soon it wasn't just one glade but many, spreading through the boundless Deepwoods like a fungus. Its influence increased. Why, without the success of the Foundry Glades, the Goblin Nations themselves would never have grown to their present size. And what's more, whether they liked it or not, they were now totally dependent on the knowledge and skills of Hemuel Spume's Furnace Masters.

Yes, times were good, Hemuel Spume had to admit, but you couldn't stand still. On no, not for a moment. Once you did that, you became complacent.

After all, look what had happened to the shrykes at the Eastern Roost. They'd sat back and grown rich on the

Undertown trade, putting all their eggs in one basket, so to speak. And now, if the reports he had received from his business partner were to be believed, they, along with Undertown itself, were finished.

As Foundry Master, Hemuel Spume wasn't about to stand still. He had great plans, monumental plans; plans that would change the face of the Deepwoods settlements for ever. Territory, riches, power: he wanted it all.

He turned and surveyed the ordered rows of leadwood desks stretching off before him down the dark hall. At each one, hunched over and spattered with black ink, sat a scribe. There were mobgnomes, lugtrolls and all manner of goblins, all furiously scribbling, accounting for firewood quotas, ore extraction, smelting rates and workshop output. The air buzzed and hissed with a sound like mating woodcrickets as five hundred quills scratched and scraped at five hundred pieces of coarse parchment.

The sound was punctuated by the dry rasping cough peculiar to the Foundry Glades. Foundry-croup, it was called. Most who breathed the filthy, smoke-filled air suffered from it. The scribes, up in the Counting House gallery, got off relatively lightly – unlike the slaves who worked the foundries. Two years they lasted on average, before their lungs gave out.

Hemuel Spume made it a habit always to wear a gauze mask when he inspected the foundries. At other times, he kept to the high towers and upper halls of the palace, where the air was considerably cleaner. Nonetheless, even he was prone to the occasional coughing fit. It simply couldn't be helped. Feeling a tell-tale tickle in his throat, he reached into a pocket of his gown and pulled out a small bottle, which he unstoppered with his spidery fingers and put to his lips.

As the pungent syrup slipped over his tongue and down his throat, the tickling stopped. He returned the stoppered bottle to his pocket, removed his glasses and polished them fussily with a large handkerchief.

Thank goodness for Deepwoods medicines and the gabtrolls who dispensed them, he thought. He, personally, had ten of the stalk-eyed apothecaresses at his sole disposal. How his sickly business partner would enjoy that, he mused.

'Excuse me, Foundry Master, sir?' came a tentative voice.

Spume looked up, replacing his glasses as he did so. An aged clerk, Pinwick Krum, stood before him, an anxious frown on his pinched face.

'Yes, yes,' Spume
snapped impatiently.
'What do you want?'

'The latest consign-
ment of workers has
arrived from Hemtuft
Battleaxe,' Krum replied.

Spume's eyes narrowed.
'Yes?'

'I'm afraid there's only
five dozen of them,' came
the reply. 'And they're
all lop-ear goblins ...'

'Lop-ears!' Spume
cried, his face redden-
ing and a coughing fit
threatening to explode at any moment.
'How many times do I have to tell him? It's hammerheads we need, or flat-heads – goblins with a bit of life
in them – why, those lop-ears are nothing but slack-
jawed plough-pushers!' He poked his clerk in the chest.
'Battleaxe is not to be paid until we've tried them out. If
they're no good, he doesn't get a single trading-credit,
do you understand?'

'Yes, sir,' said Krum, his voice laden with weariness.

Hemuel Spume turned, rubbed a hand over the sooty
window and peered out into the darkness. Below him
were five chained columns of abject goblins, their heads
bowed and bare feet shuffling, being led by guards
through the filthy encampment, one after the other.

Lop-ears they certainly were, the curious tilt of their crooked ears accentuated by the number of heavy gold rings which hung from them – but Spume was relieved to see that the majority were pink-eyed and scaly goblins, fierce in battle and hard workers, rather than the indolent low-bellies that Battleaxe had tried to fob him off with before.

'*Humph!* Better than the last lot, I suppose,' he said peevishly. 'But nowhere near enough.'

'I know, sir,' said Pinwick Krum, wringing his hands together ingratiatingly. 'But what is one to do?'

Spume slammed his fist down on his desk, causing the great mass of scribes to look up as one, consternation on their brows and nervous coughs in their throats.

'This is intolerable,' he shouted. 'Absolutely intolerable. The furnaces have to be fed! Now, more than ever. I will not allow everything we have built up here to be jeopardized by a lack of labour. Doesn't *anyone* want to work these days?' He poked the shrunken clerk hard in the chest again. 'I want three hundred new workers,' he said. '*Good* workers! *Hard* workers! And I want them by this time next week at the latest. Do you hear me?'

'Yes, sir. But . . .'

'Hammelhorns butt, *Mister* Krum,' Spume interrupted. 'You are not a hammelhorn, are you?'

'No, sir. B . . .'

'If Hemtuft Battleaxe wants our goods, then he has to pay for them!' he shouted. 'And our price is goblin labour! And it's just gone up, tell him. Now, get out!'

Pinwick Krum turned and left, muttering quietly

under his breath as he went back down the lines of coughing, quill-scratching scribes, and over to the side door. Hemuel Spume watched him going, an unpleasant smile playing over his thin lips.

'Three hundred, Krum. Don't disappoint me,' he called after him. 'Or I'll have you put on double stoking-duty in the leadwood foundry. You won't last five minutes.'

As Krum shut the door quietly behind him, Hemuel Spume returned his attention to the window. Although the sun had only just set, the thick pall of smoke that hung permanently overhead had already thrown the Foundry Glades into darkness. The tail-end of the column of lop-ears was being checked in at the slave-huts.

'Sixty measly goblins,' he muttered. It was barely enough for five foundries, and he had *twenty*-five to fill.

Hemuel Spume shook his head. With the projected rate of expansion, even if Pinwick did manage to secure a deal for three hundred goblins, a month later they would need another three hundred, and three hundred more the month after that . . . It was simply unsustainable.

He raised his head, and stared off past the great Foundry Glades to where the distant Deepwoods lay. There, far off to the north, lay the Free Glades. Hemuel Spume smiled, his small, pointed teeth glinting in the lampglow.

'The Free Glades,' he purred. 'That so-called beacon of light and hope . . .' His lips twisted into a sneer. 'And a limitless supply of slaves.'

ii

The Great Clan-Hut of the Long-Haired Goblins

'So that's the great Hemtuft Battleaxe, is it?' Lob asked, peering over the heads of the goblins in front of him, struggling to get a good view.

'Doesn't he look fine in that shryke-feather cloak of his!' commented his brother, Lummel. 'They say he plucked each feather himself from a different shryke-sister.'

'Shut up, back there,' a voice hissed angrily. 'Some of us are trying to listen.'

Lob and Lummel fell silent. As a rule, their older brothers would have attended such an important assembly, but all six of them had recently been dispatched to the Foundry Glade as slave-labour, and what with harvest-time fast approaching and all, there had been no one else to send to report back. The last thing either of them wanted to do was get on the wrong side of a hefty great hammerhead at their very first Meeting of the Clans.

'Sorry, Master.' Lob touched his bonnet deferentially and nudged his brother to do the same.

The hammerhead ignored them.

Lob and Lummel Grope were low-bellied goblins of the lop-ear clan. In their straw harvest-bonnets and characteristic belly-slings, they stood out amongst the warlike goblins all around them, and both felt more than a little overawed.

They were standing at the centre of a vast crowd that had assembled outside the great open-sided clan-hut of the long-hairs; a crowd packed with goblins of every description, all crushed together so tightly it was difficult even to breathe. Flat-heads and hammerheads, pink-eyed and scaly goblins; long-haired and tufted goblins, snag-toothed, saw-toothed and underbiter goblins; all were represented.

Inside the clan-hut, on a raised stage, sat Hemtuft Battleaxe of the long-hair goblin clan, leader of the Goblin Nations. Preening his shryke-feather cloak, the grey-haired Battleaxe looked down from his carved wooden throne, placed as it was on top of a pile of skulls of deceased clan elders. On the platform before him stood the leaders of the four other clans, their heads bowed in supplication.

Rootrott Underbiter, clan chief of the tusked goblins, was the first to look up, his two massive canines glinting, his yellow eyes impassive. As leader of one of the larger clans, there was a look of sullen insolence on his face, despite his thin, twitching smile.

Next to him stood Lytugg, leader of the hammerhead clan, and granddaughter of the old mercenary, General Tytugg of Undertown. For one so young, she boasted an impressive array of battle scars as befitted the leader of the most warlike of all the goblin nations.

Beside her, sat the old, hunched figure of Meegmewl the Grey, clan chief of the lop-ears, as sharp-witted as he was ancient. Although the least warlike of the major clans, the lop-ears were the most numerous by far, and Meegmewl was not to be underestimated.

Nor, for that matter, was Grossmother Nectarsweet the Second, clan chief of the symbites. She spoke for the gyle, tree, webfooted and gnokgoblins of the nations – the symbites who were responsible for such a rich array of products, everything from gyle-honey and dew-milk, to teasewood rope and lullabee grubs. Her five chins wobbled in a languid ripple as she raised her huge head and met Hemtuft's gaze levelly.

Hemtuft Battleaxe waved a hairy hand. As leader of the long-hairs and most senior of the goblin clans, his word was law. He knew though that, without the support of the other clans, the Goblin Nations would disintegrate and return to the roving, warring tribes they had been before. And that was something no one wanted.

'I understand, of course I do,' he said, as the crowd around the clan-hut jostled closer, trying to catch every word. 'Your lop-ear clan has paid a heavy price in supplying the labour to the Foundry Glades, and yet it is a price we must pay for the spears, the ploughs, the cooking-pots, and everything else that none of us would do without.'

'Say the word, and my hammerhead war bands could overrun the Foundry Glades like that,' said Lytugg, with a snap of her bony fingers.

Hemtuft shook his head. 'Lytugg, Lytugg. How many times must we go over this?' he said wearily. 'It is point-less to use force against the Foundry Glades. Hemuel Spume and the Furnace Masters would die before they revealed the secrets of their forges and workshops to us. And then where would we be? In charge of a lot of use-less machinery that none of us could operate. No, if we are to succeed, we must pay the price the Foundry Master demands of us . . .'

The skeletons of the old clan chief's predecessors, hanging from the rafters of the huge thatched roof, clinked like bone wind-chimes in the breeze.

'But why must *we* pay it alone,' Meegmewl the Grey croaked, turning his milky eyes to the ceiling.

'Because there are so many of you,' retorted Rootrott Underbiter nastily.

'. . . And not a single hammerhead or flat-head shall stoke a furnace!' Lytugg snarled fiercely. 'We are war-riors!'

Around Lob and Lummel, the hammerhead and flat-head goblins cheered and brandished their hefty clubs and spears.

'But things can't go on like this!' Grossmother Nectarsweet's big, wobbly voice proclaimed, silencing the cheering.

'And nor shall they!' Hemtuft roared, getting to his feet and spreading his arms wide, until, in his feathered cloak, he resembled a large bird of prey. 'For if we attack the Free Glades and enslave them, then never again will goblins have to be sent to work the foundries.

*Slave*gladers will go in their stead!'

Lob and Lummel turned to one another, eyebrows raised. All round them, the crowd exploded with noise, and a chant got up.

'Slave Glades! Slave Glades! Slave Glades!'

'There has never been a better time for this, our greatest battle!' General Lytugg's voice rang out above it all. 'The shrykes are all but done for! Undertown is no more! With help from our friends in the Foundry Glades, we shall launch an attack on the Free Glades while they are vulnerable and in disarray; an attack the like of which the Edge has never known. No one will withstand the might of the Goblin Nations.'

Lob shrugged. Lummel lowered his eyes. They both knew that it hadn't been Freegladers who had sent their brothers to be worked to death in the Foundry Glades: Hemtuft Battleaxe and the other clan chiefs had seen to that.

'We shall be victorious!' bellowed Lytugg, and a mighty roar echoed round the great hall.

Lob and Lummel were feeling increasingly out of place in the midst of all the grimacing faces and frenzied cries. What was wrong with farming? That was what they wanted to know. After all, everyone had to eat. Instead, all their neighbours seemed to have but one thing on their minds the whole time. War!

Flaming torches were lit and waved in the warm evening air as the crowd began to break off and return to their villages.

'To victory!' roared Hemtuft Battleaxe after them. 'And the Slave Glades!'

iii

The Hatching Nurseries of the Eastern Roost

'Look at the little darlings! Always hungry!' hissed portly Matron Featherhorn to her gaunt companion, the elderly Sister Drab. The pair of them were making their way along the central aisle of the great hatching-hut, inspecting the nursing pens as they went.

As they passed them by, the shryke juveniles in each enclosure scuttled towards the barred gates and craned their necks towards the two elders, screeching loudly for food. Only two days had passed since they had hatched out from their eggs, yet already they were more than half their fully-grown size.

'They certainly are, my dear,' Sister Drab replied, nodding approvingly. Her eyes narrowed and glinted coldly. 'It won't be long now.'

The pair of them reached the end of the hall, where a complicated wood and rope construction of cogs, pulleys and connecting-rods was anchored. The penned shrykes grew louder. Matron Featherhorn jumped up and seized a heavy lever which, with the weight of her swinging body, slowly lowered. There was a hiss overhead as tank-valves opened and a torrent of warm prowlgrin entrails poured down into the feeding pipes.

All round, the hatching-hut exploded with frantic scratching and squawking as the juveniles scurried across the pens – crashing into one another in their greed – clamped their beaks round the feeding pipes and waited impatiently, their eyes rolling and stubby wings flapping.

Matron Featherhorn turned her attention to the winching-wheel, and there was a loud *clunk* as she seized it tightly, pulled it sharply to the right and released the entrails down the pipes. The juveniles sat back on their haunches – their eyes instantly glazed with contentment – as the meat sluiced down their necks and into their stomachs.

Matron Featherhorn watched their bellies swell. 'That should do for now,' she said at last, tugging the wheel back the other way.

The flow of entrails abruptly ceased. The bloated shrykes flopped to the floor on their backs and closed their eyes.

'That's it, my pretties,' Sister Drab hissed. 'Sleep well; grow tall and strong and fierce.' She turned to Matron Featherhorn. 'Soon we shall have a new battle-flock to feast on the entrails of our enemies.' She shook her head. 'And a new Sisterhood and roost-mother in fine plumage!'

The old matron fiddled with her mob-cap uncertainly. 'I only hope you're right, Sister Drab,' she said. 'With Mother Muleclaw and the Sisterhood lost in Undertown, we are sorely in need of new flock leaders.' She clucked unhappily. 'After all, we're getting too long in the beak to take *that* responsibility on, eh, sister?'

Sister Drab sighed. With her eyes dim and her tawny feathers grizzled with grey and white, she had thought her days of decisions and responsibility were long since past. In her prime, High Sister Drab had been an important figure in the Shryke Sisterhood, second only to the roost-mother herself. Yet, when they had moved to the Eastern Roost, she had been happy to relinquish power, unable as she was to adjust to the new permanent settlement.

Now, everything had changed again. With the battle-flocks, the entire High Sisterhood *and* Mother Muleclaw herself, all massacred in the sewers of Undertown, apart from a shifty gathering of useless shryke males, there was no one left in the Eastern Roost but a small flock of hatchery matrons and a handful of venerable elder sisters like herself. It had been left to them to tend to the mighty clutch of eggs – their future battle-flocks, high sisters and roost-mother.

They had stayed up through the stormy night, assiduously adding and removing layers of straw and down to the great nests, ensuring that the eggs remained at a constant temperature. They had slaughtered and gutted the prowlgrins and filled the feeding-tanks ready. And when the time had come for the great Hatching itself, they had raised their voices as tradition decreed and screeched their greetings to the newly-born fledglings;

'From shell to air,
From yolk to feather;
Gorge and grow strong!'

The hatchlings had lost their downy fluff within hours of being born, and were fully fledged by their third meal. There was every type of plumage, from striped and speckled beiges and browns, to the gaudiest of purples, reds, blues and oranges – the feathers pointing to the future mapped out before them all, be it forming warlike battle-flocks or creating a new High Sisterhood. Now, with the new flock growing taller and stronger as they slept, even as she watched, it was indeed – as Matron Featherhorn had just reminded her – left to her to start making decisions once again.

'Ah, sister,' Sister Drab replied at length. 'It is as I always suspected. We shrykes are nomads, wanderers. We were never meant to settle down in one place.'

'But the Eastern Roost . . .' Matron Featherhorn began.

'The Eastern Roost is unnatural,' Sister Drab inter-rupted. 'A shryke nest should never be settled. She paused. 'Oh, I concede it worked well enough when we could control the traffic on the Great Mire Road. But now that the road has been destroyed, and Undertown with it, there is no longer any reason for our great city to exist.'

Matron Featherhorn's beak dropped open.

'Yes, sister,' the gaunt shryke elder continued. 'I know my words come as a shock, but the time has come for us to leave the Eastern Roost. We have become soft here, pampered and indolent. We must pack everything away, saddle up the prowlgrins and return to the treetops. We must go back to our old slaving ways – after all, such a way of life saw us prosper for hundreds of years.' She flapped an arm towards the future battle-flocks. 'And with these little darlings, we shall soon prosper once more, sister, and for hundreds of years yet to come.'

The grizzled matron shivered, and tightened the shawl around her shoulders. 'Slaving, you say,' she said. 'Slaving's no longer the easy life it once was. Times have changed, venerable sister. The Deepwoods tribes have organized themselves. There are the Goblin Nations, made strong by their alliance with the Foundry Glades. And then, the Free Glades . . . They stand and fight together, not like the old days when scattered villages were easy prey. Are you suggesting we attack any of these?'

Sister Drab tutted and shook her head. 'No,' she replied. 'At least, not yet, cautious sister,' she replied. 'We are too few in number. But there is another target. A moving target, many of leg and soft of underbelly, flee-ing this way from a ruined city . . .'

'The Undertowners!' Matron Featherhorn shrieked excitedly.

'The very same,' came the reply. 'I have spies out searching for news of their progress, and have high hopes . . .'

Just then, there came the sound of furious squawking from outside the hatching-hut. Sister Drab and Matron Featherhorn exchanged glances before scurrying back down the aisle, past the slumbering juveniles, and out onto the jutting balcony outside.

High above their heads, the air was filled with hundreds of insect-like craft, slowly circling the Eastern Roost. Mother Featherhorn looked up. 'Librarian patrol,' she muttered.

Sister Drab nodded. 'It seems we are not the only ones to have sent out spies.' She leaned over the balustrade.

Far below her, at the foot of the rows of hatching-huts, a gathering of aged sisters, greying matrons and scrawny shryke males were standing round the central platform, pointing up at the sky and chattering nervously. Beside them, at the battlements, the Eastern Roost's defences stood idle.

'Don't just stand there!' Sister Drab shrieked furiously. 'Do something!'

The shrykes sprang instantly into action; priming the air-catapults, aligning the sights, setting the lufwood balls ablaze . . .

At least, that is what they were attempting. But the tasks were as unfamiliar as they were testing. This was guard work; work that, in the past, all of those gathered on the platform had either been excused or excluded from. Now, however, the guards were gone, and with no one to defend them, it was up to the so-called 'roost-minders' to defend themselves, and more importantly, their precious charges in the hatching-huts.

'FIRE!' Sister Drab screeched – and threw herself to the ground as a purple fireball whistled past her head, singeing her ear-feathers as it went.

It was not the only fireball to be misfired. Half a dozen of them slipped ignominiously from their firing-bowls and had to be doused with water before they set fire to the walkways and platforms themselves. Others flew feebly out in a low arc before flopping down into the forest beyond.

Yet there were some – not many, but a few – that were perfectly launched.

'Yes, yes, yes!' Sister Drab hissed excitedly as, looking up from the floor, she saw four, five . . . six of the flaming purple fireballs speeding up into the sky and hurtling into the swirl of distant librarian skycraft.

There was a loud *bang* and an explosion of sparks as one, then two more of the skycraft were struck and began spiralling down, down, through the sky. Two of them fluttered off towards the Deepwoods. The third, however, out of control, was heading straight for the Roost.

Sister Drab climbed to her feet and rubbed her taloned hands together in anticipation. 'Come on, my lovely,' she whispered. 'Come to Sister Drab.'

Like a wounded snowbird, the skycraft flapped and fluttered down to the ground and landed with a soft clatter on the boards of the central platform. Its rider struggled – but the tangle of tethers and ropes which had prevented the hapless librarian from ejecting over the relative safety of the Deepwoods, continued to bind fast. The shrykes gathered round in a circle, lances prodding and flails swinging.

'Careful!' shrieked Sister Drab. 'Don't kill it!'

Squawking with disappointment, two of the shrykes sliced through the ropes and dragged the librarian from the ground.

'And the rest of you, resume firing!' Sister Drab screeched.

Matron Featherhorn turned to her. 'It seems we might not need to rely on those spies of yours after all,' she said.

'True, true, sister,' said Sister Drab, her neck ruff rising menacingly. 'First we shall pluck this librarian, then we shall skin it slowly, until *all* of our questions have been answered. For I tell you this, Matron Featherhorn,' she said, her voice rising to a screech, 'the Undertowners' whereabouts will be revealed – even if I have to read the prisoner's steaming entrails to find them!'

CHAPTER SEVEN

THE IRONWOOD STANDS

Rook noticed the breathing first. It was slow and regular. In and out, it went. In and out. In and out . . . Then he became aware of soft, moss-scented fur pressed against his cheek and the loamy odour of warm breath in his face. He felt great muscular arms enfolding him, cradling him gently.

This is a dream, Rook told himself. An old familiar dream – a dream from my childhood.

He was a young'un, little more than a toddler, and he was being rocked to sleep by a crooning banderbear, safe and secure in her Deepwoods' nest. The air was filled with the sound of a familiar lulling voice that rose and fell as he rocked softly back and forth, back and forth . . .

It was a beautiful dream. Rook felt safe and protected. His head ached and his limbs felt dull and heavy, but the nest was warm and the yodelled song was soothing. He didn't want to wake up. He wanted to lie there for ever, his body warm and his head empty, yet even as he had this thought, he knew the dream couldn't last. He'd have to wake up and face . . .

What, exactly? With a jolt, Rook realized he didn't know. He struggled to collect his thoughts.

There was Undertown, and the dark maelstrom pouring down, flooding the streets, washing everything away . . . The Mire Gates, the Undertowners fleeing, and then . . .

And then . . .

Nothing. His mind was a blank. The banderbear's soft yodel filled his head, and the gentle rocking continued. Slowly, Rook opened his eyes.

Moss-stuffed leafy boughs, curved and secured above his head, forming a familiar shelter.

It was a *banderbear* nest.

'Can it be real? Or am I still dreaming?' Rook croaked, his throat feeling as dry as dust.

'Ssh-wuh-ssh,' came a voice.

Rook's eyes focused on the kindly face of a banderbear. 'Wumeru,' he whispered, as he recognized his oldest banderbear friend. 'Is that you?'

'Wurra-wooh. Uralowa, wuh-wuh!' the banderbear whispered, gently stroking his temple with her thumb. *This is no dream. You are safe now, friend who took the poison-stick. But you need to rest.*

'Meera-weega-wuh,' Rook replied, his hand movements languid and slow, before stabbing at the air. 'Wuh! Loora-weer? Wellah-wuh?' *But how did I get here? I can remember nothing!*

Wumeru's ears fluttered as she replied, her voice gentle, her gestures animated. *The stubble-headed one says he saved you from an Edgeland storm and brought you back to us, here in the Deepwoods . . .*

'Deepwoods?' Rook murmured uncertainly, his voice faltering. 'Stubble-headed one . . ?'

Wumeru nodded over her shoulder and Rook became aware of another figure, hanging back in the shadows of the nest. The banderbear grunted and the figure came forward and crouched beside them. It was a youth. He looked concerned. His skin was sallow, his eyes sunken, his hair shaven close to the skull.

'Rook! Are you all right?' he asked, staring anxiously into Rook's oddly pale – almost glowing – eyes.

Rook stared back, his mouth open, bewilderment flickering in his eyes.

'Rook, it's *me*,' said the youth. 'Xanth. We've made it to the Deepwoods, old friend.'

Rook frowned, and racked his brains. 'Xanth?' he said at last, a memory flickering at the back of his mind. 'Xanth Filatine? I . . . I haven't seen you since we trained together in the Free Glades . . . You ran away . . . They . . . they said you were a spy, Xanth; a traitor . . .'

Rook's head began to spin, and with it, the shaven-headed youth's face seemed to fade back into the shadows. Wumeru resumed her gentle rocking as Rook's head slumped against her soft fur and he drifted into a dreamless sleep.

The banderbear waved a huge paw at Xanth, who had hesitated by the nest's entrance. 'Wuh!' she grunted, and though Xanth could speak not a word of the curious banderbear language, he was left in no doubt that his presence in the nest was not wanted.

Then again, his presence was not wanted outside either, he thought bitterly.

He crawled out of the banderbear nest, which was expertly camouflaged on the forest floor with mosses and ferns, and straightened up. All around him, the massive trunks of the Ironwood Stands rose up, their uppermost branches lost in the clouds blowing in from the Edgelands close by. On their lower branches – each one as wide as the Mire Road and heavy with pine-cones the size of hammelhorns – the Undertowners were setting up camp.

Xanth had been lucky to find them, he knew that. Carrying Rook on his back, he'd stumbled across the Edgeland Pavement through the thick swirling air. Just when he thought he could go no further, the mists had thinned and he'd glimpsed the tops of the mighty iron-wood pines, dark giants looming out of the fog. With one last gigantic effort, he'd forced himself to continue and had dropped down from the hard rock of the pavement onto the soft, springy floor of the Deepwoods themselves.

When he stumbled into the camp, already forming in the Ironwood Stands, the banderbears had taken Rook away and he'd been left to face the stony faces of the librarians, who whispered behind their hands. Snubbed by them and uncertain what to do for the best, Xanth had turned away and sought out the banderbears. They had allowed him to help them construct their nest, but begrudgingly – and he could tell by their whispered grunts that they, too, blamed him for luring their friend into danger back in the Edgelands.

And now, evening was falling here on the edge of the mighty Deepwoods. Unwilling to stray far from the banderbear nest, Xanth sat himself down heavily on a rock close by. He leaned forwards, his shoulders hunched, his head held in his hands.

'Sky above and Earth below,' Xanth groaned miser-ably, the palms of his hands rubbing over his rough, stubbly scalp. 'What *am* I to do?'

'Now, now,' came a voice, and Xanth felt a bony hand clapping him on the shoulder. 'What are you doing down here on the ground, eh? You should be up in the trees, getting yourself ready for the long night ahead.'

Xanth looked up to see Cowlquape Pentephraxis smiling down at him kindly.

'Cheer up, lad,' said Cowlquape. 'Things are never quite so bad as they seem.'

Xanth winced. He knew the old professor meant well, but the words stung. 'Aren't they?' he said glumly.

Cowlquape's gaunt face creased with concern. 'The Edgeland mists can cause madness, Xanth,' he said. 'You can't be blamed for that. And besides,' he added, nodding towards the concealed nest, 'you did a brave thing carrying young Rook to safety.'

Xanth's eyes welled with tears. 'Try telling *him* that,' he said. 'There's something wrong. The storm's changed him. He hardly seems to know me. He called me a spy . . . a traitor . . .'

Cowlquape squeezed Xanth's shoulder reassuringly, and sat himself down next to the youth. 'Give him time,' he said. 'He needs to rest.'

'But his eyes . . .' Xanth blurted out. 'They were dazzling, and such a strangely piercing blue . . . And his skin; his whole body – it was *glowing* . . .'

'I know, I know,' said Cowlquape. 'The treetops are buzzing with talk of it. Caught in a sepia storm, I believe you said?'

Xanth nodded.

'I, myself, once saw something similar,' the High Academe mused.

'You did?' said Xanth.

Cowlquape nodded. 'The ways of the Sky are strange indeed,' he said. 'I was a young apprentice in old Sanctaphrax, when I met a young sky pirate captain who'd been caught by a great storm. He was found in the Stone Gardens, glowing every bit as brightly as young Rook there.'

'What happened? Did he recover?' Xanth asked.

'The glow died away after a few days,' said Cowlquape reassuringly. 'His strength returned and, eventually, one stormy night high on a balustrade in old Sanctaphrax, he got his memory back.' He shook his head. 'We can only hope that the same is true for Rook.'

Xanth gasped. 'You mean he might *never* properly remember who I am?' he said anxiously.

'What the Sky inflicts,' said Cowlquape, spreading his arms wide as he climbed to his feet, to indicate the Deepwoods around them, 'the Earth can often heal.' He smiled. 'Come on, now. You can't spend the night down here on the ground. It's far too dangerous . . .'

Xanth shrugged miserably.

'I've got my hanging-stove going,' Cowlquape continued. 'We could share a spot of supper together. What do you say?'

Xanth glanced round at the banderbear nest, then back at Cowlquape. He smiled. 'Thank you,' he said. 'I'd like that very much.'

*

The Ironwood Stands – where the vast multitude of fleeing Undertowners had set up camp – stood out from the
surrounding trees, their angular tops plunging through
the rest of the forest canopy like arrowheads.

Once, the stands had been a familiar landmark both to
league ship masters and sky pirate captains. These days,
following the arrival of stone-sickness and the
subsequent scuppering of all those old vessels, it had
become just as familiar a sight to the brave young
librarian knights who had mastered flight in their small,
wooden skycraft – which was why it was the obvious
place for the Undertowners to wait for the return of the
librarian knight squadrons.

The ragtag army of Undertowners, librarians, sky
pirates and ghosts could then proceed to the Free
Glades, with the librarian knights flying protectively
overhead.

'Keep up,' Cowlquape said urgently as he and Xanth made their way across the bouncy forest floor to the base of a huge ironwood tree. 'Night is falling, and it's not safe for us down here on the ground.'

They passed a herd of hammelhorn, clustered in a large circle – tails touching, horns facing outwards – to form an impregnable wall. They were sound asleep. Cowlquape reached for a dangling rope-ladder that was secured to a huge branch above and began to climb. Xanth quickly followed him.

Covered lamps and hanging-lanterns were attached to the trees all around them, illuminating the broad, sweeping branches. The air was filled with shouts and whistles. Ropes and pulleys were being used to hoist the boxes, bags and chests up from the ground. Hammocks and cooking-braziers swung from overhead hooks; and the huge branches bristled with sleeping bodies, four, five, sometimes six abreast.

As he continued up the tree after Cowlquape, Xanth was a little dismayed to find that he was surrounded by librarians. Earth and Sky forgive him, but he would have preferred to be in one of the neighbouring trees where others were setting up camp. Families of amiable mobgnomes, gnokgoblins and woodtrolls; gangs of rowdy cloddertrogs, parties of good-natured slaughterers – all of them taking help and instruction from the gruff sky pirates and the energetic ghosts, who were leaping between them from branch to branch, tree to tree, their rope lassoes and grappling-hooks never still.

Xanth could feel accusing glares boring into his back, and hear hateful whispers. And when they arrived at the Most High Academe's hanging-stove, Xanth's heart sank.

'How's it coming along, Garulus?' said Cowlquape.

The under-librarian looked up. 'Almost done, sir,' he said. He stirred the stew, raised the wooden spoon to his lips and sipped. '*Mmm*,' he murmured thoughtfully, 'tad more salt, perhaps.' He held the spoon out to Cowlquape. 'What do *you* think, sir?'

'I'm sure it's marvellous,' said Cowlquape. He ushered Xanth forward. 'Let the lad try a bit.'

Garulus's eyes narrowed. He dipped the spoon into the bubbling stew, filled it and held it out. Then, just as Xanth was about to take a sip, Garulus tipped the spoon forward, spilling the stew all down Xanth's tunic.

'Oh, dear. How *clumsy* of me,' Garulus muttered.

'Why, you . . .' Xanth stormed, his eyes blazing, his fists clenched. This was the final insult.

Garulus trembled and leaped behind Cowlquape. 'High Academe! You saw, it was an accident!' he appealed from behind Cowlquape's back.

Xanth glared back at Garulus, his teeth bared, his dark eyes black.

'Look at him, High Academe. He's an animal – a wild animal!' Garulus's voice was high-pitched and quavery.

'Now, now,' said Cowlquape calmly, laying a restraining hand on Xanth's shoulder and dabbing at his tunic with a handkerchief. 'You've had a hard day, Xanth. You're tired. And look, no harm done.'

'Once a Guardian of Night, always a Guardian,' hissed Garulus, growing bolder. 'It'll all come out at the Reckoning, you wait and see.'

'That'll be all, thank you, Garulus,' said Cowlquape, fixing the under-librarian with a cold stare.

Garulus tutted and shrugged his shoulders. 'As you wish, High Academe, but I'd be careful if I was you . . .'

'Yes, yes,' said Cowlquape, waving him away to a rope ladder. 'Don't you worry, Garulus. Xanth and I are old friends, aren't we, Xanth?'

Glancing over his shoulder, the under-librarian left them, and Cowlquape crossed to the hanging-stove and dished up two bowls of steaming stew.

'Old friends?' said Xanth, when they were seated cross-legged on blankets beside the warm hanging-stove, eating. 'You mean I was your jailer in the Tower of Night.'

Cowlquape smiled. 'You might have been a Guardian, Xanth, but even back then in that terrible prison, I could tell you had a good heart. You visited me, took the trouble to talk to me, to learn all you could of the Deepwoods and the knowledge they contain . . .'

'But I was still your jailer,' said Xanth bitterly, putting down the bowl, his stew untouched. 'And I spied for the High Guardian of Night. The librarians know that, and will never accept me.'

'You must wait for the Reckoning,' said Cowlquape, 'in the Free Glades.'

'The Reckoning?' said Xanth, his dark eyes troubled.

'At the Reckoning, someone must speak up for you,'

said Cowlquape, finishing his stew and placing the bowl aside. 'I only wish that "someone" could be me,' he added, 'but even though I know you have a good heart, I only knew you as a Guardian, so my testimony would do you more harm than good, I'm afraid. No, you need someone who has witnessed you doing good . . .' He looked up and smiled. 'Now, finish your stew. Look, you've hardly touched it.'

'I'm not hungry,' said Xanth. It was true. At the mention of the Reckoning awaiting him at the Free Glades, his appetite had left him.

'Then get to your hammock, lad,' Cowlquape told him. 'You look exhausted.'

'I am,' said Xanth, turning to go.

'And don't worry,' Cowlquape called after him. 'Everything will look brighter after a night's sleep.'

Xanth nodded, but made no reply. That was easy for the Most High Academe to say. And as he lay in his hammock, staring up through the branches above his head at the marker-beacons blazing at the tops of the trees, he couldn't help worrying. What if Rook never regained his memory? And where *was* Magda? He turned over and pulled the blankets round him. Perhaps the Most High Academe was right, he thought as he drifted off to sleep; things *would* look better in the morning.

Xanth slept lightly through the night, his dreams punctuated by the night-noises of the Deepwoods. The shriek of razorflits, the squeal of quarms, the distant yodelling of banderbears communicating with those nesting below him on the forest floor. At sun-up, he was roused by the raucous chattering of a flock of bloodsucking hacker-bats, vicious creatures with large, violet eyes and tube-like proboscises, roosting upside down in a nearby tree – along with the cries of the cloddertrogs and flat-heads who were beating sticks and shouting in an attempt to scare them off . . .

Xanth rolled over in his hammock, and looked round at the curious tree-encampment, strung out in the high branches of the ironwood pines. The sun, dappled against the rough bark and pine-needles, was bright and warm after the previous day's overcast gloom. Xanth smiled. Tomorrow had indeed turned out to be a brighter day, just as Cowlquape had said it would. Perhaps it would also be a better day . . .

'Skycraft approaching from the east!' bellowed a voice high above him, as one of the look-outs spotted an incoming squadron.

All about him, as Xanth climbed from the hammock, the Ironwood Stands abruptly exploded into activity, with all eyes turning to inspect the sky.

'They're coming from the Twilight Woods,' someone shouted.

'It must be the Professor of Darkness,' bellowed some-one else.

On a branch some way above Xanth, Fenbrus Lodd passed Cowlquape his telescope. 'They're right,' Xanth overheard him saying. 'It's Tallus all right. Let's hope he brings good news.'

Shielding his eyes against the sun, Xanth watched the

distant rash of dots grow larger. Closer they came, the
light blazing on their bulging sails and swinging
weights, turning expertly as they swooped down
through the air, preparing to land. Soon, across the entire
Ironwood Stands, the uppermost branches filled with
skycraft – sending the hackerbats flitting off at last,
screeching with fear and indignation.

'Over here!' Fenbrus called across to the Professor of
Darkness, who had manoeuvred his own skycraft down
low amongst the trees and was looking for a place
to land. 'And welcome back, Tallus!
What news do you bring?'

'Nothing,' came the reply as the
Professor of Darkness touched
down. He dismounted. 'Whatever
the shrykes are doing, they're not
in the Twilight Woods.'

Fenbrus frowned. 'Curious,'
he said, rubbing his beard
thoughtfully. 'Being immune to
its effects, I was quite convinced
that they would launch an attack
from there . . .'

'Maybe they sensed that a Great
Storm was on its way,' said the professor. 'You know how sensitive the
bird-creatures are to the weather.
And I'll tell you this, Fenbrus,
nothing – not even the shryke-
sisters – could have survived the

after-shocks of that terrible explosion of lightning as it struck.'

'You saw it happen?' said Cowlquape.

The Professor of Darkness nodded. 'Everything,' he said. 'From the advancing swirl of cloud, to the release of the bolt of stormphrax lightning. Quite awesome,' he said, 'though nothing compared with what came afterwards. A gigantic, glittering sepia storm that pulsed outwards in all directions, through the Twilight Woods . . .'

Cowlquape shook his head sagely. 'And poor Rook, unsheltered on the rocky pavement of the Edgelands, must have taken its full force,' he said softly. 'It's a miracle he survived.'

Xanth, who was standing on a ledge to the right, busying himself with the rolling up of his hammock and packing of his bags, listened carefully. If it was as bad as they were suggesting, then maybe Rook would *never* fully recover.

'A truly remarkable experience,' the professor went on. 'It was only a shame that Ulbus wasn't there to witness it for himself. As Professor of Light, he would have found it uniquely interesting . . .'

'Skycraft approaching from the south!' two look-outs bellowed in unison, and all around them, Undertowners and librarians began to wave and cheer.

'Perhaps that's him now,' said Fenbrus, raising his telescope and focusing in on the second squadron of skycraft approaching the Ironwood Stands. He frowned a moment later. 'No it isn't,' he said. 'It's my daughter.'

Three hundred more skycraft swooped down into the

branches to be greeted with a rising swell of cheers and cries and whoops of delight. As Varis came closer, heading straight for the tallest tree in the Ironwood Stands, where Cowlquape, Fenbrus and Tallus Penitax were all assembled, Xanth swung his belongings onto his back and started down to the forest floor. Perhaps Rook had woken up feeling better this new day . . .

'Good news,' Varis Lodd announced excitedly, as she jumped down from the *Windhawk*. 'Greetings, Most High Academe.' She bowed her head. 'Greetings, High Librarian.'

'Yes, yes, daughter,' Fenbrus frowned. 'Forget the formalities. What *is* the news?'

'Help is at hand,' she said. 'Even as we speak, the Freeglade Lancers are on their way!'

'But this is tremendous news,' said Cowlquape, excitedly.

'Excellent, Varis,' added Fenbrus. 'You have done well. Very well, indeed. The Freeglade Lancers – finest fighters in the Deepwoods!'

'Finest, until now, father,' came a voice, and Fenbrus and the others turned to see the muglumpskin-clad figure of Felix on a branch of the next tree. He was standing with his hands on his hips, surrounded by the Ghosts of Screetown.

'Oh, Felix,' said Varis. 'This isn't a competition.'

Felix glanced at his sister, and then at his father. Fenbrus coughed awkwardly and looked away. Felix smiled ruefully. 'Isn't it?' he said. He turned to his companions. 'Ghosts!' he called out. 'Help the

Undertowners down from the trees and spread the good news.' He glanced back at his father. 'The Freeglade Lancers are coming! We're saved!' he added sarcastically, and then was gone.

Down on the forest floor, Xanth was searching for the banderbear nest. It was so cleverly camouflaged that, even now in the daylight, he was having trouble spotting it. Suddenly, from behind him, a few strides away, there came a yodel and Xanth spun round to see Wumeru emerging from a thicket with Rook in her arms. Barely able to contain himself, Xanth rushed up to them.

'Rook! Rook!' he began.

Rook opened his eyes and stared at Xanth. The startling blue intensity of his gaze chilled Xanth to the bone.

'Xanth Filatine,' Rook mumbled. 'I remember now. You betrayed librarian knights on their way to the Free Glades, then ran away to the Tower of Night before you were unmasked . . .'

Xanth hung his head, tears stinging his eyes.

'Oh, Xanth, you were my friend. How could you have done it? How *could* you . . .'

Rook's eyes closed again. Xanth stretched out a hand, but Wumeru shook her great head, and he stepped back to let her pass. What now? Xanth thought.

Just then, high above, fresh cheers broke out. Xanth's heart gave a leap. The third squadron of librarian knights – those who had set off under the leadership of the Professor of Light, Ulbus Vespius – must be returning from their foray to the Eastern Roost. Xanth craned his neck back and searched the skies.

Of course, Magda should be amongst them. Magda would speak up for him, even if Rook couldn't!

Soon, the air around the crowded Ironwood Stands was buzzing as the last three hundred skycraft hovered round, searching for landing spaces. High up near the top of the trees, the Professor of Light dismounted and strode towards the waiting welcoming-committee, all eager for his news. Bowing in turn to Fenbrus, Tallus and Varis Lodd – and Deadbolt Vulpoon and Felix Lodd, who had joined them – he addressed himself directly to Cowlquape.

'I bring bad news,' he said grimly.

'From the Eastern Roost?' said Cowlquape.

'Yes, sir,' said the professor. 'There has been a great Hatching – the biggest battle-flock I've ever seen!

Thousands of them, flooding out of the hatching-huts, and heading this way. They're young, but fully-grown, sleek of feather and sharp of beak and claw – and with a frenzy of blood-vengeance in their hearts.' He shook his head. 'I've never seen anything like it.'

'And how far off are they?' asked Cowlquape.

The Professor of Light shrugged. 'Half a day on prowlgrin-back,' he said. 'Maybe more, maybe less . . .'

Cowlquape took a deep intake of breath. He turned to Fenbrus. 'We can't risk breaking camp,' he said. 'The Undertowners must remain up in the trees.'

Fenbrus frowned. 'Are you sure?' he said. 'If they're heading for the Ironwood Stands, shouldn't we get as far away from here as we can?'

'On foot, we wouldn't stand a chance,' said Cowlquape. 'There are too many old'uns and young'uns among us. Why, we'd be picked off like the ripe fruits of a woodsap tree. No, our only hope is to wait for the Freeglade Lancers.'

'But what if the shrykes get here first?' asked Fenbrus.

'Then we must defend ourselves,' said Varis. 'There are the librarian knights, the ghosts, the sky pirates . . .'

Deadbolt nodded in agreement. 'We're well used to

combat with the scraggy bird-creatures,' he chuckled, and gripped the handle of the great curving sword at his side. 'It'll be a pleasure to dispatch a few more.'

'All right,' said Fenbrus Lodd, at last. 'But no fighter must carry a barkscroll. They must hand them over to a librarian or an Undertowner up in the trees for safe-keeping – until after the battle. Not a single item from the sacred Great Library must be risked in combat.'

'You and your barkscrolls!' snorted Felix, turning away. 'If we lose this battle, father, there will be no barkscrolls, no Great Library! And the shrykes will make slaves of all those they don't slaughter!'

As news of the battle-flock spread through the Ironwood stands, a numb panic gripped the Under-towners, one and all, as their thoughts turned to the awful possibility of their having to come face to face with the cold, bloodthirsty bird-creatures.

Xanth, still anxiously searching the skies, left the forest floor and climbed up into the trees once more. High into the upper branches he went and, as the pilots of the Eastern Roost flight landed, one after the other, he rushed after them, grabbed them by the arms and asked them all the same question.

'Have you seen Magda Burlix? Have you seen Magda Burlix?'

Most of the librarians merely shook their heads. Either they hadn't seen her or, more often, they had no idea who she was. Xanth was becoming increasingly desperate.

Then, seeing a rather rotund individual landing his

skycraft on a branch of the next tree along to his right, he leaped across the yawning gap – with no thought of the danger. The librarian looked at him curiously.

'Magda?' said Xanth breathlessly as he climbed to his feet.

The librarian finished tethering his skycraft. ''Fraid not,' he said. 'The name's Portix.'

Xanth frowned impatiently. 'Have you *seen* her?' he said. 'Magda. Magda Burlix.'

The librarian shook his head and turned away. Xanth was about to leave when a gaunt individual appeared from the shadows, the tethers of his own moth-shaped skycraft wrapped round his hand.

'Magda Burlix, you say,' he said. 'Are you a friend of hers?'

Xanth nodded keenly. 'I am,' he said. 'We were in Undertown together.'

The gaunt librarian stepped forwards and clapped his free hand on Xanth's shoulder. 'Bad news, I'm afraid, young fellow,' he said. 'She was shot down over the Eastern Roost. I'm sorry to have to tell you, she hasn't made it.'

CHAPTER EIGHT

BLOOD FRENZY

In the forest clearing, a grazing tilder doe looked up, startled, ears twitching. Her fleshy pink nostrils sniffed nervously at the air. She could sense something approaching – something dangerous.

All around her, other Deepwoods creatures were similarly uneasy. Up in the branches, fromps coughed their warning alarm while roosting hackerbats and snowbirds chattered and chirruped. A panic-filled family of lemkins, trembling in the long grass, tried hard to remain still and not give themselves away. But it was no use. Abruptly, terror got the better of one of the nervy youngsters.

'Waa-iiii – kha-kha-kha-kha-kha . . .' it shrieked, breaking cover and bolting across the forest floor in a streak of blue, followed quickly by all the rest.

The fromps followed suit, leaping away from tree to tree. The hackerbats and snowbirds took to the sky. Halitoads and razorflits, woodboar and weezits, and all the other creatures that had been poised, ready to run, scurry, slither or flap off at the first sign of danger – they each erupted from their hiding-places and fled.

For a moment, the forest clearing was a frantic, screeching, snorting, dust-filled place; a noisy blur of panic. Out of it sprang the tilder doe, her legs like coiled springs as she bounded through the air and skidded off into the surrounding forest. The next moment, the clearing fell still.

It was quiet, empty and hushed like the moment of tranquillity at the end of a storm, or that instance of stillness just before dawn. The air was motionless. Nothing stirred . . .

The next moment everything changed, as a single shryke exploded from the vegetation, the sunlight in the clearing flashing down on her tawny feathers and glinting on her bone-flail. Then another. And another. Then thousands as, like a great wall of fire driven on by hurricane winds, the vast shryke battle-flock sped past on powerful legs.

Some were brown, some were grey, some were a drab mixture of the two; some were striped, some were spotted, some mottled, some flecked; some had neck-ruffs, some had crests. All of them had razor-sharp beaks and rapier claws – and, as if these were not enough to strike fear into the hearts of their enemies, the shrykes also carried fearsome weapons: lances, maces, pikes and flails, curved scythes, serrated swords . . .

'Kaaar-kaaar! Kut-kut-kut!' a piercing call sounded from the treetops as a shryke-sister with red and purple plumage appeared, leaping from branch to branch on the back of a prowlgrin.

'Keer-keer-keer!' Her call was answered by her sisters in the treetops all round.

Like a swarm of snickets, the battle-flock veered off in answer to the treetop calls, never easing up for a moment as they thundered on through the forest. High above, clinging on tightly to the prowlgrin-reins, the noble Shryke Sisterhood – several hundred strong, with gaudy plumage and flamboyant battledress – guided the battle-flock towards their distant goal.

At their head, resplendent in tooled gold armour, the young roost-mother – Mother Muleclaw III – threw back her fearsome head and gave a piercing shriek.

'Kut-kut-kut-kaaaar!'

Red and yellow, purple and blue, her luxuriant plumage gleamed in the early morning sun, her neck-ruff and tail-feathers flapping as the grey prowlgrin she sat astride leaped on through the forest. Below her, the battle-flock increased its pace.

Some way behind her, also on prowlgrinback, Sister Drab, Matron Featherhorn and the shryke elders trotted across the clearing, pulling a large group of tethered shryke-mates behind them.

'It's good to be on the move again,' squawked Matron Featherhorn.

'Indeed, sister,' agreed Sister Drab, giving a vicious tug on the leashes in her clawed hand. 'See how the Deepwoods tremble before us! Nothing can stand in the way of a battle-flock with its blood up!'

'The little darlings!' clucked Matron Featherhorn. 'Hard to believe they were hatchlings such a short while ago. Oh, and look at Mother Muleclaw!' She cooed with pride.

Sister Drab nodded. 'A natural roost-mother,' she said. 'I knew it the moment she hatched. Why, she'd killed and eaten the others in her clutch before her shell was even cold. Magnificent!'

'I can't wait to see her in battle,' said Matron Featherhorn.

'Patience, sister,' replied Sister Drab. 'We shall be there soon enough and, if the librarian knight spoke correctly, the Undertowners will be at our mercy!' She closed her eyes and smiled with pleasure.

Oh, how that captured librarian knight had screamed and shouted and begged for death, writhing beneath her probing talons as she'd extracted every last bit of information. Then, when she'd got everything she wanted, how the hapless creature had turned tack, begging for mercy instead.

And she *had* been merciful, she remembered. Rather than linger over the flayed, tortured body longer than she'd needed, she had torn out the heart with a single stab of her beak and swallowed it while it was still beating. Delicious! The librarian had lived just long enough to see it.

Sister Drab looked up ahead as she cantered on and, as the forest thinned for a moment, she glimpsed the unmistakable shape of the mighty Ironwood Stands, rising up out of the forest canopy and silhouetted – dark and imposing – against the pinky-yellow sky in the distance.

'Not far now,' Sister Drab clucked contentedly. 'Not far. I can almost taste the blood on my tongue!'

Preparations had been made and now an eerie silence hung in the air. High up at the very top of the tallest ironwood pine, Felix Lodd and Deadbolt Vulpoon were deep in conversation.

'Do you think it'll work?' said Felix.

'It's *got* to work,' said Deadbolt, 'or we're dead meat, the lot of us, and that's a fact!'

'Dead, or slaves,' said Felix bitterly.

'Oh, if the shrykes triumph, there'll be very few slaves, believe me,' said Deadbolt, ruefully stroking his beard.

Felix raised an eyebrow.

'It's a young battle-flock, according to your Professor of Light,' the sky pirate said.

'He's not *my* Professor of Light,' said Felix.

'Maybe not, lad,' he said, 'but that doesn't alter the

fact that these shrykes are newly hatched. They're ill-disciplined and inexperienced. Once they go into battle, they'll get the blood frenzy, and the only way to stop them will be to kill them. You mark my words.'

Deadbolt raised his telescope and looked back across the Deepwoods for any trace of the approaching shryke battalions.

'See anything?' Felix asked.

The sky pirate captain shook his head and snapped his telescope shut. 'Not yet,' he said darkly, 'but they're on their way.' His eyes narrowed, and his nostrils twitched. 'I can *smell* the scurvy creatures . . .'

Far below, on the forest floor, Xanth felt a heavy hand on his shoulder and turned to see a cloddertrog sky pirate looming over him. The pirate wore a muglumpskin coat and carried a heavy poleaxe.

'Librarian, is it?' he asked, scrutinizing Xanth. 'You lot are with the Undertowners at the lufwood mount. The shrykes are on their way – or hadn't you heard?' he added sarcastically.

'I was looking for my friend, Rook Barkwater . . .' said Xanth, nodding towards the empty banderbear nests in front of them. 'But he seems to have left.'

'Rook Barkwater?' said the cloddertrog. 'Isn't he that librarian knight who got caught in the sepia storm?'

'Yes,' said Xanth. 'The banderbears were tending to him in this nest . . .'

'If he's with banderbears then he'll be safe enough,' said the cloddertrog. 'It's yourself you ought to be worried about, out here in the open with a shryke battle-flock due at any moment. You should be with your librarian friends.'

Xanth shook his head sadly. 'The librarians aren't my friends,' he said. 'In fact, I don't seem to *have* any friends.' With a sigh, he slumped down on the forest floor.

'Well, you can't sit round here feeling sorry for your-self,' said the cloddertrog. 'Here, you can join me if you like,' he added, and held out a massive hand. 'Henkel's the name. Captain Henkel of the *Fogscythe* – currently without a crew, on account of them having run off to seek their fortunes in the Foundry Glades with a scurvy cur by the name of Quillet Pleeme. *Pah!* But that's another story . . . Come on, if you're coming.'

Xanth smiled, and was about to reach up and take

Henkel's hand, when he noticed an oil-cloth bundle resting against the moss-covered side of the abandoned nest. He reached over and picked it up.

'What have you got there?' asked Henkel, peering down as Xanth carefully unwrapped the package.

'It's . . . it's a sword,' said Xanth.

'And a mighty fine one at that. Can't leave it lying around here,' said Henkel, as Xanth got to his feet. 'Best hold on to it for now, lad. You can look for its owner later. Anyway, if you stick with me, you'll have need of it . . .' he stuck out his massive hand again '. . . friend.'

This time Xanth clasped it and shook it warmly. 'Friend!' he replied.

'Keer-keer-kaaaaarrr!' screamed Mother Muleclaw, spurring her prowlgrin on through the branches.

Below her, the shryke battle-flock surged forwards, shrieking and screeching in reply. Ahead of them stood the Ironwood Stands, their branches heavy with the hunched figures of Undertowners huddled round burning stoves. It was almost too good to be true. They were at her mercy, and she, Muleclaw – beautiful, strong, hungry Muleclaw – would show them none!

Foam flecked her long, curved black beak. She opened

it, threw back her head and spat a trailing arc of bile high into the air. Her bright yellow eyes flashed, their dark pupils fully dilated. A mist was descending in front of them; a red mist.

She must taste blood! She must taste it now, and gorge! And gorge! And gorge . . .

From below her, a volley of flaming arrows flew up from the bows of the jostling flock and into the tops of the massive ironwood pines. One by one, the resinous tips of the huge trees caught fire and blazed like gigantic torches. Below, on the branches, the Undertowners remained motionless, as if rooted to the spot, their hanging-stoves twinkling in the fading afternoon light.

With a grunt, the roost-mother's prowlgrin launched itself from the topmost bough of a copperwood and onto the end of one of the massive branches of an ironwood pine. She was followed by her roost-sisters, shrieking with savage glee.

'Kut-kut-kut-kaaaaar!'

'Keer-keer!'

'Kut-kut-kut-kaaaaarrr!'

Below, the main body of the battle-flock flowed round the massive trunks of the Ironwood Stands in a screech-ing feathered flood. Thousands of piercing yellow eyes turned upwards in eager anticipation.

They didn't have long to wait. Mother Muleclaw and the shryke-sisters were spreading out through the branches, slashing and swiping with their claws and bone-flails from astride their leaping prowlgrins. The bodies of the Undertowners fell like ripe fruit, down into the seething mass below.

'Kaaar! Kaaaar! K-k-k... Ki? Ki? Ki-i-i-i-i!'

The expectant shrieks of the battle-flock changed abruptly to indignant, high-pitched whistles. What was this? Not flesh and blood, entrails and guts, but ... Wood ... Cloth ... Bundles of moss and sacking!

The shrykes tore at the stuffed effigies in frustration. Mother Muleclaw pulled up her prowlgrin with a vicious tug on its reins and seized a figure slumped beside a hanging-stove.

'Kiii-kiii-i-ai-ai!' she screamed as she recognized it for what it was; a stuffed dummy in a woollen shawl, its hastily carved wooden head grinning back at her mockingly.

Suddenly, on the branch above, a shryke-sister gave a strangled scream and plunged past Muleclaw, her throat skewered by a crossbow bolt. The roost-mother's eyes swivelled round. They were under attack!

'KAAAAAR!' shrieked Mother Muleclaw in a frenzy of rage and frustration as, the next moment, the sky around the Ironwood Stands filled with librarian skycraft.

They swooped in close, firing blazing arrows and heavy bolts, before swerving away. The shryke-sisters were easy targets and fell in twos and threes, then fours and fives, and then dozens, as the skycraft swarmed about the ironwoods like angry woodhornets. Down on the forest floor, the battle-flock erupted into a frenzy as the bodies rained down and they began gorging themselves on their fallen sisters.

And still the librarian knights swooped in, loading, firing and reloading, until not a single prowlgrin-mounted shryke-sister remained in the blazing Ironwood Stands.

Below, the frenzied battle-flock seethed. They had tasted blood at last – but not nearly enough. Suddenly, clambering down the massive trunk of an ironwood tree like a gaudy feathered beetle, Mother Muleclaw appeared. Her prowlgrin dead, her armour battered and her gaudy silks singed, she halted above the heads of her flock, with her talons embedded in the rough bark.

'Kut-kut-kaaaaii!' she shrieked, and all eyes turned to her.

She waved a claw towards the forest where a trail, marked by discarded bundles of belongings, led away. Her yellow eyes flashed. Above them, the skycraft soared up and away over the trees.

'Kaaaar!' Mother Muleclaw screamed. '*KAAAAAARR!*'

*

'It's gone quiet,' Gilda whispered to her companions. 'What do you think's happening now?'

Turntail, an elderly mobgnome, squeezed her hand warmly. 'The lull before the storm,' he said, his voice soft and wheezy. 'By Sky, if I were only fifty years younger, I'd show those disgusting bird-creatures a thing or two. I'd crack their skulls and split their gaudy gizzards open, so I would. I'd . . . I'd . . .' He collapsed in a fit of hacking coughs.

'Quiet, back there!' came an urgent voice.

The mobgnome pulled away and tried to stifle the cough with his hands. Gilda patted him on the back. Rogg, a grizzled, one-armed flat-head who was sitting with them, pulled a bottle from his belt, unstoppered and wiped it, and handed it across.

'Sup that,' he said gruffly.

Turntail held it to his lips, slurped, swallowed – and gasped for breath, his eyes streaming. 'What . . . is . . . it . . ?' he rasped.

'Firejuice,' said Rogg. 'Like it?'

'It's . . . it's . . .' the mobgnome began. 'The most disgusting drink ever to have passed my lips.'

Rogg snorted. 'Stopped you coughing though, dinnit?'

Behind them, a high-pitched voice spoke up. 'I wouldn't mind a drop of firejuice myself,' he said. The others turned to see a wizened old lugtroll, pale and trembling, wrapped up in a tattered scrap of blanket. He smiled toothlessly. 'Warm these palsied bones of mine a tad,' he said.

Rogg passed the bottle back. 'Just a drop, mind,' he said. 'Don't want you keeling over.'

Gilda nodded. Although the journey from the Ironwood Stands to the lufwood mount had been little more than a few hundred strides, it had severely tested several in their small party. Gilda had had to support Turntail the whole way, while Rogg had ended up carrying the lugtroll under one arm, and a portly gabtroll and her babe-daughter under the other.

Still, at least Gilda hadn't had to carry the sword any longer. Wrapped in its oil-skin cloth, it had been an awkward bundle – though she'd kept it safe all the same, carrying it all the way from Undertown and into the Deepwoods. It was the least she could do for the brave young librarian who had lost it when he'd rescued her from slavers in old Undertown. She'd feared he was dead, but she'd kept the sword with her all the same, just in case . . . And then she'd spotted him! She could hardly believe it.

Oh, he'd changed all right. He was sick, she could see that clearly. He was carried right past her in the arms of a huge banderbear. His eyes were closed and he was moaning softly, but it was definitely him; *her* brave young librarian.

The banderbear had disappeared inside a nest with him, and Gilda had been too frightened to follow. The creature had looked so big and fierce, and the poor librarian so ill. She decided it would be best not to disturb him, so she'd propped the precious bundle by the entrance where they'd be sure to find it. She'd planned to go back to make sure – but then news of the shryke attack had broken and everyone was suddenly

running around in a terrible panic, gathering up everything they could carry . . .

That was just this morning. Gilda looked around at
her companions. Together, like all the other
Undertowners – old and young, rich and poor – they
had struggled gamely on, heading westwards, away
from the ironwood pines and on through the dense
Deepwood forest.

Twice, they had come to places where the trees had
been felled by teams of ghosts and sky pirates – two vast
concentric circles which ringed the lufwood-covered
crag – and had had to pick their way over the jumble of
fallen branches and logs. Finally, they had arrived at the
top of the mount; tired, weak and frightened.

They'd made camp there, along with the thousands of
other Undertowners. Below them, the lufwood-covered
mount had soon echoed with the sound of sawing and
chopping as the ghosts and sky pirates erected makeshift
barricades to protect them. Then, as the afternoon light
had begun to fail, the librarian knights had taken off and
flown back towards the Ironwood Stands.

Gilda had marvelled at the sight. How proud and
brave they'd looked! Then, along with the others, and
hardly daring to breathe, she had listened for the tell-tale
sounds of battle.

When the first furious shryke scream had echoed
through the trees, everyone had fallen silent, and as the
mighty battle had raged at the Ironwood Stands, they
had all listened carefully to every crack, every cry, every
distant screech, scream and wail. The more suspicious

among them had stroked their amulets and whispered prayers and incantations that the brave librarian knights would prevail and that the Undertowners, in their concealed fastness, might survive.

Now it was quiet again, with the stillness more terrifying even than the noisy battle. As the sun set, the librarian knights arrived back, and as the moon rose, the sky glowed red in the distance where the Ironwood Stands blazed. The librarians, ghosts and sky pirates took to the barricades in the darkness below the lufwood mount.

Slowly, whispered rumours of the slaughter of the shryke roost-sisters filtered up to the Undertowners, and low murmurs filled the night air. A battle had been won, so it seemed, yet the roost-mother lived on. The battle-flock still had a leader and, having regrouped, was heading towards them.

Gilda pulled her cloak around her and shivered. It was going to be a long night.

*

Xanth was glad he was standing next to Henkel. With the whole shryke army on its way, he felt better knowing that the hefty, battle-scarred cloddertrog was at his side, mighty poleaxe in hand. Xanth looked down at the sword in his own hand. It was certainly magnificent, with a polished pommel, an ornate handle and a blade so sharp it could split a hair lengthways.

He looked up at the cloddertrog, his eyes gleaming. 'It's fantastic, isn't it?' he said.

'Certainly is,' said Henkel. 'Some kind of ceremonial sword by the look of it. Though I daresay that won't stop it slicing a shryke or two in twain.' He laughed throatily. 'Try it out, lad.'

Xanth parried and lunged and swung the sword round in wide sweeps, before jabbing at the air in a succession of short sharp movements. It was so well-shaped and perfectly balanced that it seemed almost to move by itself, slicing through the air like an agile ratbird in flight.

'Excellent, excellent,' said Henkel. 'It could have been made for you. And I'll tell you this, lad, if . . .'

The cloddertrog stopped and his eyes narrowed. Around him, the sky pirates stopped talking and scanned the treeline. They were behind the second ring of barricades, constructed from the trees cut down in front of them.

'Open ground,' Deadbolt had growled. 'It'll stop them coming at us from the treetops.'

Ahead of Xanth, across the cleared forest, he could see

the first ring of barricades. These were being defended by Felix and the ghosts. He could just make out the helmeted figure of the leader of the ghosts as he signalled to his companions to prepare for the onslaught they all knew was coming.

Xanth heard Henkel's gruff voice. 'Hold your ground, lad,' he told him.

Xanth gripped the handle of his sword and prayed that he might be brave. The night air was still, the only sound, the odd cough or muttered curse from the ranks of sky pirates lining the log barricade. All eyes were focused on the ghosts at the first barricade across the clearing.

Then Xanth heard it. A blood-curdling scream that sent shivers coursing down his spine. It was followed by another and another from the dark shadows of the treeline.

'Here they come,' muttered Henkel. 'Sky protect us.'

Suddenly, a huge wave of screaming bird-creatures, crested with a glittering array of pikes, war hammers and bone-flails, broke through the trees and smashed into the first barricade. Xanth gasped. Everywhere, the ranks of ghosts splintered into individual fights as first in one place, then another, shrykes broke through their defences. The whiplash cracks of ropes cutting through the air and wrapping themselves round feathered necks sounded all down the line as the ghosts fought desperately to hold back the tide.

But it was hopeless, Xanth could see that, and his stomach gave a sickening lurch. There were just too many of the shrieking, frenzied shrykes.

Every instinct told him to turn and run away, now, before the evil flood of feathers and fury swept *him* away. Henkel must have seen the look on his face, for he turned to Xanth and laid a huge hand on his shoulder.

'Steady, lad. This is the hardest part, waiting for the storm of battle to break. Trust in that sword and stay close.'

Xanth nodded and tightened his grip on the handle of the sword. Sharp and bright as it looked, could it really stop one of those evil shrieking bird-creatures? He was about to find out.

'Fall back, Ghosts!'

Felix's shouted command sounded above the din of battle, and suddenly the air filled with whipcracks as ropes shot over Xanth's and the sky pirates' heads and wrapped themselves round tree branches behind them. In an instant, hundreds of white-armoured ghosts launched themselves out of the midst of the thrashing, flailing shrykes and flew through the night air, landing behind the second barricade.

Xanth gasped. He'd never seen anything so spectacular.

'Very pretty,' Henkel growled. 'Now the real fighting begins!'

At the first barricade, the battle-flock screeched with frustration as the shrykes saw their enemy escape from their clutches. They swarmed over the log wall and surged forward across the cleared ground.

Xanth could see the eyes of the approaching bird-creatures flashing, bright yellow, their sharp beaks and talons glinting in the moonlight.

'*Fire!*' came Deadbolt Vulpoon's booming command, and a deadly volley of crossbow bolts spat from the ranks all around Xanth.

The first wave of shrykes screamed and fell beneath the clawed feet of those following, but the huge battle-flock hardly checked its pace.

'*Fire!*' came the command again. '*Fire!*'

Each volley of missiles cut swathes through the feathered ranks – but still the shrykes continued towards them.

'Here they come!' bellowed Henkel as the wave of shrykes threw themselves on the barricades. Xanth gagged as the stale odour of rancid entrails and shryke waste tainted the air. All round him, the terrible feathered creatures burst over the barricade and fell upon the sky pirates, their eyes blazing, their beaks gaping. Beside him, Henkel swung his poleaxe in a low, horizontal sweep, decapitating three screaming shryke guards. Xanth thrust his sword out in front of him and felt a jolt run through his arm as first one shryke, then another, ran onto the point and skewered themselves through their hearts.

'Well done, lad, well done,' Xanth heard Henkel shouting across to him as he withdrew his sword, sticky with shryke blood. There was a roaring in his ears and he felt as if his heart was about to explode. 'Watch out!' Henkel roared. 'Behind you!'

Xanth turned, to be confronted with a huge, muscular

shryke, with flecked brown and cream plumage, swinging a spiked ball the size of his own head through the air towards him.

He leaped back, ducking as he went, and brought the sword round in a sharp uppercut, severing the shryke's arm, sending the ball and chain spinning back through the air before embedding itself in the creature's neck. Thick, dark blood gushed down her front as she fell, gurgling and twitching, to the ground.

He had scarcely a moment to catch his breath when three orange-feathered shrykes with scythes came at him. Desperately, Xanth parried their blows and ducked out of the way of stabbing beaks and claws. Sweat was pouring down his face as he gasped noisily, his lungs burning and his limbs aching.

'*Urrghh!*' he cried out as a claw-hammer glanced off his shoulder and he fell to one knee.

Suddenly, the shrykes in front of him exploded in a shower of blood and orange feathers and Xanth looked up to see Henkel, bloodied poleaxe in hand, looming over him.

'Run!' he roared.

Xanth didn't need telling twice. He leaped to his feet and dashed after the cloddertrog, who cleared the way with massive swings of his poleaxe. They were joined on all sides by bloodied, feather-spattered sky pirates, as they dashed up the steep wooded slopes of the lufwood mount towards the summit. Behind them, the ghosts covered their retreat by swinging through the trees and raining down burning lufwood darts into the battle-flock's path.

At the summit, they were greeted by the ashen faces of thousands of Undertowners, huddled together in abject terror. Around them, the librarian knights had spread a thin defensive line, their skycraft firmly anchored to the rocky crag. It was clear by the grim looks on their faces, that this was where they were going to stand and fight.

Xanth saw the imposing figure of Fenbrus Lodd standing, arms folded defiantly, next to the stooped Most High Academe, Cowlquape. Varis Lodd and the Professors of Light and Darkness stood guard round them, their crossbow quivers bristling and their swords unsheathed.

Deadbolt Vulpoon came stamping up to them, his beard red with shryke blood, and his greatcoat cut to ribbons. 'We held them as long as we could,' he growled, bowing his head to Cowlquape. 'And that son of yours and his ghosts are making them pay for every step of the mount they climb,' he added, turning to Fenbrus. 'He's a good 'un, and no mistake.'

Fenbrus Lodd looked grave. 'This is where we make our stand,' he said. 'If the Great Library is to perish, let it be here on the lufwood mount over our dead bodies.'

'It most likely will be,' said Deadbolt darkly. 'For they're in a blood frenzy now, just as I feared.'

Xanth sat down on a rock next to Henkel and tried to catch his breath. A pale moon shone down and bathed everything in silvery light. All round, there was the sound of quiet sobbing and stifled moans.

'You did well back there, lad,' said Henkel, wiping his bloodied poleaxe on his muglumpskin coat. 'I was glad to have you by my side, friend.'

'And I you, friend,' said Xanth, managing a smile.

'Come,' said the cloddertrog. 'The night is not over yet.'

The sky pirates joined the librarian knights defending the summit of the lufwood mount, and before long, the white figures of the ghosts came whistling through the trees on their long ropes and added to their number. Dark clouds drifted across the moon and a chill wind got up as an eerie silence fell over the crowded mountain top.

'What are they waiting for? Why don't they attack?' whispered Xanth.

They could hear the shrieks and calls of the battle-flock in the trees below them. 'They're gorging on the dead,' said Henkel simply. 'And when they've fin-ished . . .' he surveyed the treeline with weary eyes 'then they'll come for us.'

They hadn't long to wait. The calls of the shrykes abruptly grew louder, with one piercing shrieked cry loudest of all.

'KAAAAR-KAAAAR-KAAAAR!!'

It sounded through the lufwood trees of the mount.

'Kut-kut-keer-keer!' came answering shrieks from all around.

Suddenly, the air was alive with feathered arrows whistling out of the trees and into the defenders. One grazed Xanth's cheek and sent him cowering to the ground. When he looked up, the battle-flock had broken cover and was advancing towards them.

They no longer swarmed in a shrieking, surging tide, but instead, were walking slowly and deliberately up the rocky slope. Their feathers dripped with blood; their claws and beaks were crimson and their eyes glowed a deep, throbbing red.

Xanth stared at the bloody spectacle, mesmerized. There was nothing anyone could do to stop this terrible onslaught, he realized miserably. They were all doomed.

As the huge circle of shrykes closed in on the Undertowners and their defenders, the piercing call sounded again.

'KAAAAR-KAAAAR-KAAAAR!!'

The huge shryke roost-mother pushed through the flock and raised a dripping claw. This was it! The final gorging!

Then all at once, there came the clear, sweet sound of a tilderhorn calling out from the forest below, followed by a low rumbling like distant thunder. The roost-mother paused, her claw still raised high. What was this?

'Kiii-kiii-kiii.' Small, yelping cries spread through the battle-flock behind her, which changed to shrieking calls of panic a moment later.

From behind them, out of the forest, a great, bristling, writhing creature was attacking and driving the startled shryke battle-flock into a confused jostling heap. As Muleclaw turned, the creature seemed to split up into hundreds of individuals, each with a spike, stabbing and goading the shrykes from every angle.

Xanth looked up. Around him, all eyes had turned

towards the sounds of distress coming from the back of the battle-flock. Suddenly, an armoured lancer on an orange prowlgrin burst through the shrykes, followed by twenty more. Green and white chequerboard pennants fluttered from their lances; red banderbear badges emblazoned their white tunics.

'The Freeglade Lancers!' the shout went up.

Soon, everywhere Xanth looked, lancers on prowl-grins were breaking through the shrykes and scattering them in confusion.

'KAAAAR-KAAAAR-KAAAAR!' shrieked Mother Muleclaw as she saw her battle-flock disintegrate and fall back in a frenzied, flapping panic.

Behind her, Xanth gripped the magnificent, razor-sharp sword, took a deep breath and swung it through the air.

'KAAAAR-KAA . . . K . . . *urrgh!*'

The roost-mother was dead before she hit the ground, her magnificent plumed head with its curved black beak separated from her gold armoured body.

'Henkel! Henkel!' Xanth cried, turning back in triumph. 'I did it! I got her! I killed . . .'

He stopped and fell to his knees. Henkel stared back at him with unseeing eyes, a thin trickle of blood dripping from the corner of his mouth, his body slumped forward in a half-sitting, half-crouching position and a barbed, feather-flighted shryke arrow protruding from his chest.

'Hey, you there! Yes, you!' came an angry voice. Xanth turned, to see Felix Lodd standing over him, his eyes blazing. 'Where did you get that sword?'

Sister Drab and Matron Featherhorn tramped back through the forest, their shryke-males still on leashes clasped in their shaking hands. It was dark and cold, with the moon lost behind rain-drenched clouds that had swept in from the north.

'Our darlings!' wept Matron Featherhorn. 'So young, so inexperienced. They couldn't help themselves . . .'

'It was the blood frenzy,' said Sister Drab, shaking her head. 'That I should have lived to see the day a battle-flock turned on itself, and shryke gorged on shryke.'

'There was nothing you could do, sister,' said Matron Featherhorn, her eyes streaking. 'Nothing *any* of us could have done. Their blood was up. They couldn't help themselves. With Mother Muleclaw dead up there on that accursed mount, there was no one left to control them.'

'Curse the Undertowners!' spat Sister Drab. 'And curse the Freeglade Lancers! To think we had victory within our grasp . . .'

'What is there for us now?' asked Matron Featherhorn. Behind her, the males warbled and twittered feebly.

Sister Drab turned and looked at her companion, her gaze cold and unblinking.

'Our finest battle-flocks destroyed in Undertown. Now our fledgling army killed in the Deepwoods. We have nothing left, dear Matron Featherhorn,' she said bitterly. 'The age of the shrykes is over.'

PART 2

RECKONING

·CHAPTER NINE·

NEW UNDERTOWN

The sun shone down on the Free Glades. Never before had the streets of New Undertown thronged with quite so many revellers as that evening in late summer, when the new turned out to celebrate the arrival of the old. After their long and dangerous journey, the vast multitude from old Undertown marvelled at their new surroundings.

Every ornately carved building on every thorough-fare, from grand avenue to narrow alley, was festooned with flags and streamers, and multi-coloured bunting criss-crossed overhead. Long lines of twinkling lanterns – yellow, pink and white – had been strung up through-out the town, from the elegant Lufwood Tower at its centre to the cowl-shaped Hive Huts to the south. They zigzagged along each street, they lined the bridges, they ringed the squares; down to Lakeside they went, gleam-ing and glinting from every market stall and reflected in the deep, still waters of North Lake.

As the golden light of the setting sun dimmed, the

lanterns seemed to glow brighter than ever, flickering on the happy faces of the Undertowners, new *and* old. Some were laughing, some were singing, some were dancing – everything from whirling goblin jigs and rowdy trog stomps, to a hopping lugtroll line that snaked its way through the streets. A band of musicians played alongside it on pipes, drums and a vast stringed instrument carried by four and played by three more. Through the centre the winding chain of dancers went, past the Lufwood Tower and down to Lakeside, where the street-stalls were overflowing with food and drink.

'Woodale! Get your woodale here!' bellowed a ruddy-faced mobgnome from behind a trestle table which bowed in the middle under the weight of a large and heavy barrel.

'Goblets of winesap!' called a gnokgoblin matron from a neighbouring stall.

A group of lugtrolls – young and old, and all weary after their long journey from old Undertown – compared what was on offer, before pausing in front of a gabtroll's barrow. One of them – a young male in a ragged cloak – leaned over a steaming vat and breathed in deeply.

''Tis oakmead, sir,' said the gabtroll softly. 'Spiced and honeyed, with just a hint of nibblick.' She picked up a tankard and a ladle and poured a little of the warm liquid out. 'Would you care to try some?' she said.

The lugtroll took the tankard and sipped. It was delicious. 'How much?' he asked cautiously.

'How much?' the gabtroll replied, her eyeballs bouncing about on their stalks in amusement. 'This is the Free Glades. All for one, and one for all.' She swept her arms round in a wide arc. '*Everything's* free. All that you poor, dear old Undertowners can eat and drink.'

The lugtrolls looked at one another, smiles breaking out on their faces. Back in the filth and misery of old Undertown, they'd had to scratch a living hauling firewood for the leagues' forges. The work was hard and the days were long, and the only payment was a meagre supper of grey gruel and black bread. Yet here in New Undertown, the air was sweet and everywhere they looked they were greeted by happy, smiling faces.

'Thank you, mistress gabtroll,' the young lugtroll proclaimed gratefully. 'Thank you a thousandfold.'

'So it's oakmead all round, is it?' the gabtroll said, her tongue slurping noisily over her eyeballs as she ladled out the drinks. 'To your very good health!' she announced. 'And welcome! Welcome one and all.'

In every part of the throbbing town, as was happening throughout the Free Glades, from the southern meadow-lands to the northern fringes, from the eastern woodtroll villages to the western shores of the Great Lake, the new-comers were being greeted and feted like long-lost friends and relations.

'Toasted pine-nuts,' cried a mobgnome from a kiosk close to the waterside as she spooned the salted delicacies into barkpaper cones. 'Candied woodsaps, jellied dellberries . . .'

'Tilder sausages and black bread,' shouted a slaughterer nearby. 'As much as you can eat.'

As the sun sank and the moon rose, the streets grew fuller and fuller. Groups of colourfully dressed clodder-trogs streamed in from the cliffside caves in the south-east to greet their ragged, weary compatriots newly arrived from the over-crowded, rundown boom-docks of old Undertown, and it wasn't long before they were all carousing noisily, drunk on traditional tripweed beer.

Columns of woodtrolls and slaughterers trooped

northwards together to New Undertown to join in the festivities, joined on their way by gaggles of gyle goblins, sweeping in from the east. And they all came together, old Undertowners, New Undertowners, grinning and bowing, slapping one another on the backs and shaking each other's hands. They talked and they sang and they shared what they had, from tales of their pasts to plates of tilder sausages. And the cry went up in every single corner of the town, a thousand times or more.

'Welcome to the Free Glades! Welcome, indeed!'

Down on a small wooden jetty jutting into North Lake, two flat-head goblins were sitting close to one another, idly flicking bits of gravel into the water and watching the ripples spread and interlock.

'I never thought I'd ever see you again, Gorl,' said one, her eyes filling up with tears.

'Nor I you, Reda,' came the reply, as he squeezed her hand tightly.

'When they took you away . . .' she sobbed. 'When they chained you up and marched you off to the Sanctaphrax Forest, there was nothing left for me in old Undertown. So I came here and made a new life for myself. But I never forgot you. I always . . .'

'I understand,' said Gorl, 'but that was *old* Undertown. It's all in the past. The important thing is that we're together again.' He looked round. Far to his left, the Ironwood Glade stood out against the starry sky. Behind, the glow of the lights, the smells of the food and drink, the sounds of music and dancing and laughter continued, all reminding him of where they now were. He smiled and pulled her close. 'And we're Freegladers, now.'

Reda remained still, smiling to herself as she felt his strong arms wrapping themselves around her.

Back at the Lufwood Tower, a small procession was making its way through the cheering crowds to the foot of the grand sweeping staircase that led up to the first-floor platform, which was bedecked with garlands of flowers and forest fruits. There, waiting patiently, stood the Free Glade Council, all three of them.

Parsimmon, High Master of Lake Landing, a short gnokgoblin in shabby robes, peered over a large bunch of woodlilies, a huge smile on his wizened face. Next to him, on a high stool of carved lufwood,

Cancaresse of Waif Glen stood on tiptoe, her huge translucent ears quivering expectantly. Next to them, Hebb Lub-drub, the mayor of New Undertown – a low-belly goblin – looked huge, his embroidered belly-sling festooned with a gleaming chain of office.

As the procession drew closer, the prowlgrins' feathered collars fluttered and the ceremonial bells attached to their harnesses jangled loudly as the carriage they were drawing jerked to a halt at the foot of the stairs. The door opened and the stooped figure of Cowlquape Pentephraxis climbed out, followed by Fenbrus Lodd and his daughter, Varis. With each new appearance, the crowd cheered. Last to emerge from the carriage were the Professors of Light and Darkness, their gowns – one black and one white – flapping in the rising breeze.

As the five of them climbed the steps, one after the other, towards the garlanded platform, so the gathered crowd clapped their hands and stamped their feet and roared with approval. At the top, Cancaresse held out a tiny hand to Cowlquape in greeting. Her soft melodious voice sounded in the minds of everyone watching.

'Welcome, friends. The Council of Three has become the Council of Eight. It is time for all of us to rejoice – as Freegladers!'

'Freegladers!' roared a red-faced cloddertrog to a nightwaif, throwing his beefy arm around the weedy creature's narrow shoulders. 'There's no such thing as *old* Undertowners and *new* Undertowners, any more. We're all Freegladers now!'

'Indeed,' chirped the nightwaif. 'Freegladers, one and all – and,' he added, his huge, batlike ears fluttering and swivelling to the left, 'if I'm not very much mistaken, the New Bloodoak Tavern has just broken open a fresh batch of woodale barrels to celebrate!'

'It has?' said the cloddertrog, hoisting his new friend up onto his shoulders. 'Then let us go and share a tankard or two, you and I.'

They had indeed broken open a fresh batch of woodale at the New Bloodoak Tavern. They'd needed to. Mother Bluegizzard, the old shryke matron who ran the place, had been so busy that she had been forced to assist her serving-goblins as they rushed round topping up tankards and keeping the drinking-troughs full. With the ale flowing so freely, the atmosphere was rowdier than normal, with laughter and singing and clapping and the *clatter-clomp-crash* of dancing on the tables echoing from every window.

'More woodale, gentle sirs?' Mother Bluegizzard asked – a laden tray balanced on the crook of her arm and her spectacular blue throat feathers fluffed up with exertion – as she squeezed her way through the swaying crowd to the table where a group of new arrivals was sitting.

'A friendly shryke with foaming woodale?' said Felix Lodd, swapping his empty tankard for a full one. 'The Free Glades is truly a wondrous place!'

'Wondrous indeed!' said Deadbolt Vulpoon, following suit. 'Thank you, gracious madam. This old sky pirate will be forever in your debt!'

At the other side of the table, Wumeru, Wuralo and Weeg were given fresh beakers of frothing dellberry and woodsap juice. Although there was nothing in their refreshments to affect their mood, the three of them had already got so caught up in the atmosphere of the place that whenever a song went up, they yodelled along with the rest, swaying from side to side, their great hairy arms raised above their heads.

Mother Bluegizzard looked at them all benevolently. They were an interesting bunch, these old Under-towners; the confident young ghost with his twinkling eyes and shock of blond hair, and the grizzled old sky pirate, with his charming manners. And those bander-bears! They'd alarmed her when they'd first lumbered in, but they were so gentle and good-natured, the old bird-creature had quite taken to them. And then there was the quiet young librarian with the startling blue eyes, who was smiling at her now as she offered him the tray. He seemed a little lost, and didn't say much, and the banderbears fussed over him as if he was their cub.

The librarian took a tankard of woodale from the tray, and Mother Bluegizzard turned away to check on her other customers.

In the corner, Bikkle, her scraggy shryke-mate, was collecting the tankards and sweeping up. He was a drab little creature, but he was *her* drab little creature and she loved him.

'Two more tankards over here,' a voice whispered in Mother Bluegizzard's head. She looked across the crowded room and saw the tavern waif flapping his huge ears at her. She winked back at him and approached the two drinkers he was pointing to with his long, spidery fingers.

'Mother Bluegizzard, you're a marvel!' laughed Zett Blackeye, a small tufted-eared goblin, as she took his empty tankard and replaced it with a full one.

His hefty sidekick, Grome, a cloddertrog in a battered leather cap, grunted his approval as she handed him his drink. 'No one ever goes thirsty at the New Bloodoak, eh, Mother?' he boomed.

'Our trough's getting low!' came a chorus of voices behind Mother Bluegizzard, and she turned to see her regulars, Meggutt, Beggutt and Deg – comrades from General Tytugg's army, who had deserted together and made the perilous journey to the Free Glades – beckoning to her.

'If you fine sirs will excuse me,' she clucked to Zett and Grome, and bustled over to where the three goblins squatted at their drinking trough. 'Same again, lads?'

The three goblins nodded eagerly and Mother Bluegizzard rolled a fresh barrel across the floor and leaned it against the rim of the trough.

'Ready?' she asked.

Three heads nodded and she pierced the wooden barrel with a razor-sharp talon, releasing a foaming stream of ale into the trough. The three heads went down and the air filled with the sound of heavy slurping.

'You're welcome,' said Mother Bluegizzard cheerfully, wiping her claw on her apron. 'Now, how about another tot of woodgrog, Captain?' she chuckled, turning to a tall, gaunt figure with a thick matted beard.

He was another one of her regulars. The Mire Pirate, they called him, but as he never spoke, no one knew his real name. He'd turned up in New Undertown more than a dozen years earlier and had soon found his way to the Bloodoak, where he had been a regular ever since. Certainly he looked like a sky pirate and from his

bleached skin, it was clear he'd spent much time in the Mire, hence his nickname. And yet, to Mother Bluegizzard, it was his eyes that were the most mysterious thing about him.

Misty and unblinking, those pale, staring eyes somehow managed to give the impression that they had seen sights that no one should ever witness – though, since she'd never heard him utter a single word, it was impossible to tell for sure.

Over in the other corner, the festivities were livening up.

'A toast!' cried Deadbolt Vulpoon, rising a little unsteadily to his feet. 'To us!' he proclaimed, raising his tankard. 'Free-gladersh!'

'Freegladers!' cried Felix.

'Fr-uh-gl-uh-wuh!' yodelled the banderbears.

Deadbolt turned to them as he fell back into his seat, his eyes twinkling mischievously. '*Wuh-wuh-wuh*,' he grunted. 'I can't unnerstan' a wor' you say!'

Wuralo and Weeg chortled to themselves. Wumeru nodded and gave an airy wave of her left arm. 'Weelawuh, wurra-yoola-wuh,' she murmured.

'Wha' she say? Wha' she say?' said Deadbolt, turning to Rook.

Rook smiled, his eyes softly glowing. 'She said, "The woodale has loosened old Tanglebeard's tongue. Soon he will be yodelling!"'

The sky pirate roared with laughter. 'Why not,' he said. 'It don't seem too hard.' Throwing back his head, he bellowed out loud, 'Wuh-uh-uh-wuh-ooooo!'

Felix turned to him, his hands clamped over his ears. 'What on earth was *that*?' he said.

'Wasn't it obvious?' said Deadbolt, pointing into his empty tankard. 'I'm thirsty!'

Felix laughed. 'Woodale all round! And more squashed fruit for our hairy friends here!' he added, winking over at Fevercule, the tavern waif.

Deadbolt got to his feet and pulled each banderbear in turn to theirs. 'Now, here's a language we can all share!' he laughed, and began dancing an unsteady jig.

Rumbling with deep laughter, the banderbears joined in.

Felix turned to Rook, his eyes twinkling, and frowned. 'Rook?' he said. 'Are you all right?'

His friend was pale and the rings beneath his eyes were darker than ever.

'It's just that I get so tired,' Rook said, sitting back in his chair. 'And yet I can hardly sleep. Thoughts and half-remembered images race through my mind in a jumble. I can remember some things as if they happened yesterday, but others are a complete blank . . .'

'Do you remember this?' asked Felix, pulling a sword out from beneath his cloak.

'My sword . . .' said Rook slowly, frowning as a lost thought hovered at the edge of his memory. 'But it's . . . it's the one you gave me,' he said, 'all that time ago. Back in the underground library. I remember losing it in old Undertown . . .'

'And yet I found it in the Deepwoods,' said Felix, 'in the possession of one Xanth Filatine – the same Xanth

Filatine who led you astray in the Edgelands. Claims he found it.' He snorted. 'A likely story! He and his Guardian of Night friends probably looted it, and he's too ashamed to admit it.' He shook his head. 'He's a bad lot, that one, and no mistake,' he said. 'Didn't I tell you to watch out for him?'

'Xanth Filatine,' Rook repeated. 'I remember him from our time together at Lake Landing . . . He was unmasked as an agent of the Guardians of Night . . . But after that . . . nothing.' He looked up at Felix. 'Where is he now?'

'Don't worry about him,' said Felix gruffly. 'He's being taken care of.'

'I don't understand,' said Rook.

'He's being held in the Gardens of Light beneath the Ironwood Glade,' said Felix. 'And that's where he's going to stay until his Reckoning. And from what I hear, there are plenty who intend to speak out against him when the time comes, myself included . . .'

'Rook Barkwater!' exclaimed a voice. 'As I live and breathe. Rook Barkwater!'

Felix and Rook turned to see a stout individual standing behind them, his hands on his hips and a huge grin on his face.

'Don't tell me you don't know who I am!' he said, sounding hurt. 'It's me, Stob. Stob Lummus.'

'Stob Lummus,' Rook repeated thoughtfully.

'They told me at Lake Landing that I'd find you here,' he said, 'and here you are!' He leaned forwards and pumped Rook's arm up and down. 'It's so good to see you.'

'It's good to see *you*, too,' said Rook, struggling to make sense of the jumble of memories clattering about in his head. 'Lake Landing ... We were apprentices together, weren't we? You, me, Magda, and Xanth ...'

The smile faded from Stob's face. 'They told me of your trouble, Rook,' he said. 'A sepia storm. Is it true that that traitor, Xanth Filatine, led you into it on purpose?'

'I ... I ...' said Rook. 'My memory, it's ...'

'I understand, old friend,' said Stob, patting him on the back. 'A good dose of pure Free Glade air and you'll soon be on the mend ...'

'Hammelhorn,' Rook blurted out. 'You carved your skycraft in the shape of a hammelhorn.'

'That's right,' said Stob, nodding enthusiastically. 'Mine was a hammelhorn, Magda's was a woodmoth and yours was a stormhornet.' He frowned. 'And Xanth's was a ...'

'A ratbird,' said Rook.

Felix snorted. 'That figures,' he said darkly.

They were joined by the banderbears, who now supported a sleeping Deadbolt Vulpoon between them. Stob shook their paws, one after the other. 'Welcome to the Free Glades. Welcome, indeed!' he said to each in turn, pausing when he came to Deadbolt. He looked questioningly at Rook.

'Don't mind him,' laughed Felix, getting up. 'He's been warmly welcomed enough for one evening. Come, we'll find cosy hammocks waiting for us in the Hive Huts.'

Just then, the entrance doors flew in. Everyone inside the tavern fell still, the chaotic hubbub of loud voices and raucous song instantly replaced by the sonorous chanting of low voices.

'Ooh-maah, oomalaah. Ooh-maah, oomalaah. Ooh-maah, oomalaah . . .'

All eyes fell on the line of oakelves – seven in all – as they marched in, and wound their way round the crowded room. Their turquoise hooded robes were stained by the juice of lullabee trees and rustled slightly as they walked.

'The Oakelf Brotherhood of Lullabee Island,' Fevercule's whisper sounded in Mother Bluegizzard's head.

The one at the front swung an incense-burner on chains to and fro, to and fro, filling the air with sweet aromatic smoke, while at the back the last oakelf in the line rang a heavy bell, over and over, like the tolling of a death-knell.

'Ooh-maah, oomalaah. Ooh-maah . . .'

'To what do we owe this unexpected pleasure?' clucked Mother Bluegizzard, trying to disguise the peevishness in her voice. These oakelves certainly knew how to spoil a party.

The procession brushed past her and made for the corner of the room. The Mire Pirate's unblinking eyes followed it. All at once, the oakelf leading the small procession stopped in front of Rook Barkwater and lowered his hood. His face was as brown and gnarled as the trees the creatures had taken their names from. The chanting softened to a low, ululating drone. Above it, the oakelf spoke.

'We come in search of the one who was touched by the sepia storm,' he said, his voice frail and cracked.

He reached out with the censer and swung it, sending wreaths of smoke coiling round Rook's head. The young librarian knight's pale blue eyes gleamed more brightly than ever.

'Come with us,' said the oakelf, as the chanting grew louder once more. 'To Lullabee Island.'

·CHAPTER TEN·

LULLABEE ISLAND

'Lullabee Island?' said Rook, taking the oakelf's outstretched hand and finding himself looking into eyes so black that it was like staring into the depths of open sky itself. Twinkling there were lights, as bright as the stars, as full as the moon; yet as he looked more closely, he realized that it was his own eyes – eerily glowing – which were reflecting back at him.

'You are tired, yet cannot sleep?' asked the oakelf.

'Yes,' said Rook.

'Your head is full of thoughts and memories,' the oakelf continued, 'and yet you can find no peace?'

'Yes,' said Rook, his eyes glowing more brightly than ever.

'Then come with us to Lullabee Island. My name is Grailsooth, and these . . .' He waved a hand to indicate the others, and Rook was aware of the disconcerting gaze of six more pairs of dark eyes. 'These are my fellow brothers from the lullabee grove there. We have dreamed of you, Rook Barkwater, and have come to offer you what help we can.'

The silence in the tavern was broken by the clatter of a beaker of woodgrog as it slipped from the old Mire Pirate's hand and clattered to the floor.

'I'll come with you,' Rook said, his voice hardly more than a whisper.

He stood up and the oakelves turned to go. Felix jumped to his feet, followed by the banderbears on either side of him, low growls in their throats.

Deadbolt slid to the floor and began to snore softly.

'Rook!' Felix's voice was imploring. 'You're not well. You can't just disappear off to some grove on some island in the middle of the night...'

'Calm yourself, gentle sir,' clucked Mother Blue-gizzard, laying a restraining talon on Felix's arm. 'These are the Oakelf Brotherhood. They spread peace and heal-ing throughout the Free Glades.' All round the tavern, heads nodded. 'Their ways might seem strange to you and me, but no harm will come to your young friend in their care, I can promise you that.'

The banderbears looked at each other, their ears flut-tering, then stepped aside and bowed their heads. The oakelves' turquoise robes rustled as they shuffled in single file towards the door, Rook following after.

'You don't have to go with them,' Felix called out as his friend reached the door to the tavern. 'Just say the word and...'

Rook turned and smiled. 'It's all right, Felix,' he said, his voice weary and hoarse-sounding. His pale blue eyes were glowing so brightly that Felix gasped. 'Perhaps they can help me.'

'Would you like us to come with you?' Felix persisted, starting towards him. 'We can if you want.'

Mother Bluegizzard's ruff sprang up around her throat and she shook her beak at Felix. 'No, no, gentle sir, that just won't do. Only those invited can set foot on Lullabee Island. Everybody knows that. Now why don't you all have another drink, and let them take care of your friend?'

Wumeru took Felix gently by the arm and guided him back to his chair. 'Wuh-wuh,' she muttered softly.

Felix stopped. He couldn't understand the great lumbering beast, but he knew that she, as Rook's oldest, most trusted banderbear friend, would not allow anything bad to happen to him. If her instincts were to trust these oakelves, then who was he to disagree? He looked back. At the far side of the room, the door to the New Bloodoak Tavern swung open, the column of oakelves – Rook among them – walked out, and the door slammed shut behind them.

In the corner, the Mire Pirate, who had climbed from his seat and was watching the young librarian knight intently, a puzzled frown lining his brow, abruptly sat down once more.

The next moment, as if nothing at all had happened, all round the New Bloodoak Tavern, the revellers at every table took up where they had left off – every table, that is, expect for the one where Rook's friends had been sitting.

'Well, if we can't go with him to this Lullabee Island,' Felix murmured, as Deadbolt let out a loud snore, 'then the least we can do is go down to the lake shore and wait for him to return.' He shook his head. 'Though something tells me it's going to be a long night.'

In the corner, the Mire Pirate stared at the Ghost of Screetown as Mother Bluegizzard flapped towards him, a beaker of woodgrog in her claws.

Outside on the busy street, Rook Barkwater found himself being encircled by the group of oakelves, all chanting softly once more as they made their way slowly through the town. Down the bustling side-alleys they went, towards North Lake. Being so much taller than the oakelf brothers, he could see all round. They were surrounded still by the vast celebrating crowds of goblins, trogs, trolls and waifs, all dancing, singing, laughing and joking – and yet, as he continued, Rook noticed something strange.

Although he could see the revellers' lips moving, he could hear neither their song nor their laughter; their whoops, their yells, their happy cries. Only the low, ullulating chant of the oakelves reached his ears, filling his head with its deep, dark sounds.

'*Ooh-maah, oomalaah. Ooh-maah, oomalaah. Ooh-maah, oomalaah . . .*'

He paused for a moment where he stood, and shook his head, trying to clear it of the hypnotic chant – only to be gently urged on by the ring of oakelves around him. Down to the water's edge they went, turning right onto a lamp-lined path that hugged the lake, the dark, slightly ruffled surface of the water to his side. Past the jetties they continued, lines of pink and yellow lanterns strung out along them; past the fishing cabins and reed-stalls; past reunited families and friends, and couples strolling arm in arm along the waterside promenade.

And gradually, as they continued, the twinkling lights of New Undertown receded behind them. In their place, reflected in the water – sometimes crystal clear, sometimes blurred and fuzzy, as the wind rose and fell – was a sprinkling of stars and the huge, silver face of the full moon. The number of individuals out walking diminished and the amount of woodland and shrubbery increased until the empty path, no more than a small track now, disappeared into the trees.

Dark and overgrown, with the moonlight blocked out by the dense overhead canopy, the only light in the forest came from the circle of oakelves' robes as they glowed about him, a soft, luminous turquoise. And still the oakelves went on, picking their way through

the woods, before cutting down through the undergrowth to the lake.

Rook was entranced. The soft chanting, the fragrance
of the incense and delicate blue-green shade all seemed
to wash over him, through him, outside and inside. And
as they approached the water's edge, the full moon laid
out across its velvety black surface like a huge piece of
silver, Rook realized that he was growing increasingly
sleepy. His legs felt like lead and he could barely keep
his eyes open.

'Step lightly, Master Rook,' said the oakelf with the
swaying censer. 'I shall hold the side steady for you.'

For a moment Rook was confused. Then, looking
down, he saw the small coracle which had been lashed
to a twist of knotted root just above the surface of the
water. The bobbing vessel was small, almost round,
made of a plaited frame of woodwillow and sallowdrop,
and clad in pitch-sealed tilderskin.

Once he, the largest of the group, had stepped across
and settled himself down on the bench at the blunt end
of the coracle, the others climbed in after him. It was a
tight fit, and Rook was aware of the warmth of the
bodies pressed in about him as the oakelves picked up
their paddles, pushed off from the bank, and began
propelling the little boat slowly across the moonlit lake.

The water splashed softly, the coracle dipped and
swayed, and all the while the oakelves kept up their low,
sonorous chanting. It was only as they drew close to
Lullabee Island that Rook realized it wasn't the only
music he could hear. Ahead of him, coming from

somewhere in the centre of the island, was more music – similar to that of the chanting oakelves, though a thousand times sweeter.

Rook's eyes closed and his head began to nod.

'Not yet, Rook Barkwater,' Grailsooth's voice sounded in his ear. 'Not just yet.'

Suddenly he heard a grating noise as the bottom of the coracle scraped against the loose gravel below them. He shook his head groggily and stifled a yawn. The oakelves abruptly stopped their chanting, and six of them jumped down into the water and began dragging the little boat up onto the shore.

Grailsooth took Rook gently by the arm. 'This way, Rook Barkwater,' he said.

Together, they headed away from the banks of the lake. The undergrowth grew thicker, the number of trees increased and between the trunks and branches, Rook noticed a pale turquoise light glowing in the distance and lightening the sky.

'Not far now,' Grailsooth murmured, turning and smiling at him.

Rook smiled sleepily. As he went further into the woods, the sapwoods and various willows began to give way to lullabee trees – massive specimens, with broad, bulbous trunks, spreading branches and huge leaves. Music filled the air – plangent chords and interweaving harmonies – as a warm wind passed lightly through the air. And, as the full moon shone down upon them, the leaves gave off a fine, glowing mist that cast the whole forest in a pool of deepest turquoise.

'It's so ... so beautiful,' Rook murmured softly.

'It is welcoming us,' said Grailsooth.

'Welcoming us?'

'The lullabee groves are the most ancient and mysterious places in all the Deepwoods,' he said. 'And the grove here on Lullabee Island is the most ancient and most mysterious of them all.' He smiled and placed a hand on the young librarian knight's shoulder. 'And it is welcoming you, Rook Barkwater, for here you shall find rest.'

'But ... but why *me*?' Rook muttered, as all round him, the music switched to soft glissandos, which rippled through the shifting shades of turquoise light.

'The Brotherhood dreamed of you,' said Grailsooth. 'You have suffered much.'

'The sepia storm?' said Rook, frowning, as the memories came back to him. 'In the Edgelands?'

'That, too, was in our dreams,' Grailsooth nodded. 'You were touched by the passing storm, as others have been touched before you ...'

'And you can help me?' asked Rook, a tremor of unease tingling inside his skull.

The oakelf glanced round at him. 'That, Rook Barkwater, is for you to discover,' he said.

They continued through the lullabee grove towards the centre, where the oakelves gathered in a circle. Rook looked round him at the curious clearing in the trees. High above his head, the leaves glowed and hummed, filling the air with the most glorious chorus of musical sounds. And there, as the wind parted the great leaves, he saw several dusty-grey sacklike objects hanging from the branches, glittering slightly, dangling down into the misty turquoise air, and turning slowly. Although he had never seen one before in real life, he recognized them at once from his studies in the Great Library of the underground sewers.

'Caterbird cocoons,' he gasped.

'Indeed,' said Grailsooth. 'The caterbirds have been hatching here for longer than any of us can imagine. Why, some of these cocoons are thousands of years old. While others,' he added, and pointed to a cocoon dangling from a branch to his left, 'are still to hatch.'

Rook's jaw dropped in amazement. 'You mean, that's a caterbird about to hatch?' he said.

'Perhaps,' said Grailsooth. 'But probably not in

my lifetime or, who knows? Not in yours either . . .' He shook his head sagely. 'A caterbird hatching is a rare thing indeed, Rook Barkwater, witnessed but once in a hundred years, perhaps longer. And yet, in this place, as you can see, it has occurred many, many times.'

Rook looked about him, awestruck. There was so much to take in; the entrancing music, the unearthly light, the sparkling cocoons which had been added to, one after the other, down the centuries.

The branches and the huge leaves glowed a shimmering turquoise and swayed gently to and fro as if in a breeze, yet to Rook, the air seemed unnaturally still. Grailsooth's huge dark eyes followed Rook's gaze, and he smiled.

'The caterworms are feeding on the lullabee leaves, filling the grove with their music,' he said.

Rook frowned. 'Caterworms? Where?'

'They are in the trees – all around us, Rook Barkwater. They are glisters. You see them only as light. It is they who weave themselves into cocoons and emerge as . . .'

'Caterbirds!' breathed Rook.

'Indeed,' said Grailsooth, and nodded to his companions, who melted away into the trees. 'And now, the time has come . . .'

All around, the music of the lullabee trees grew to a rousing crescendo.

The time for what? Rook wondered, suddenly feeling the weariness overwhelm him once more.

As if reading his thoughts, Grailsooth took him by the arm and pointed up into the trees to one of the caterbird cocoons. 'Time,' he said, 'to sleep in a cocoon. You will dream the dreams of the all-knowing caterbirds. You will see yourself through their eyes and, Sky willing, find peace . . .'

Rook realized he was trembling. See himself? Find peace?

'Go now,' said Grailsooth gently. 'Climb the lullabee and crawl into the caterbird cocoon. There, sleep will come to you and you will rest.'

As Grailsooth looked on, Rook did as he was told. He climbed the great knobbly trunk of the lullabee tree, shinned his way along a broad branch and lowered himself into the cocoon. It was soft and downy, giving slightly beneath his weight as he curled up inside it. Within seconds, he felt his arms and legs relax and his breathing became regular and heavy.

His eyes flickered for a moment as he realized that he was about to fall asleep in the cocoon of a caterbird. How strange, and yet how natural it felt. His eyes flickered again before shutting completely.

A soft, rasping snore mingled with the music of the glade as Rook drifted into a deep, dream-filled sleep.

CHAPTER ELEVEN

COCOON DREAMS

Rook was standing in a magnificent chamber, its walls decorated with murals and rich tapestries; the floor, a swirl of delicate mosaics. There was a fire roaring in the grate. Huge ironwood logs, nestling in a crimson bed of glowing embers, crackled and hissed as the yellow and lilac-white flames danced over them. And as they burned, so they shifted, and bright orange ash showered down.

Before the fireplace, the firelight flickering in their faces, were four boys. They had short, dark, wavy hair. One wore glasses. All of them shared the same fine, angular features and bright, darting eyes. They were laughing. The youngest was telling the others of some exploit or other, while they gently teased him.

As Rook watched them, his heart seemed to effervesce with happiness, as though thousands of tiny bubbles were filtering through it. So this was what it felt like to be part of a large family, surrounded by brothers.

There were two other boys in the chamber – older and

taller – practising their sword skills with tipped foils. A woman in an ornate gown and lace collar sat in an armchair to the right of the fireplace, the expression on her face as she surveyed her brood a mixture of amusement and pride; while on the far side of the room, a tall, dark-haired sky pirate stood by the window staring out. His beard was plaited and his moustache waxed. He wore a breast-plate of gleaming black, and a heavy sabre hung at his side. How imposing he looked, Rook thought – and strangely familiar, as if he'd seen him somewhere before.

As the fire crackled, the swords clashed and the laughter continued, Rook looked about him. To his left, the wall was covered with a spectacular mural. It was a townscape, with tall, elegant towers and magnificent palaces, and a river running through it all. In the sky above was a swirling flock of ratbirds, a sky pirate ship, and a great caterbird flapping endlessly across the shimmering blue heavens; while in the foreground, staring ahead, were eight figures. A mother and father; six brothers.

Rook took a few steps towards the wall and raised a hand to touch its painted surface. As he did so, the paint seemed to blister and boil, the colours turning dark and the image of the family disappearing before his eyes.

Smoke – suddenly, there was thick dark smoke coiling up from the floor.

Rook could hear terrified screams and calls for help. He turned and ran blindly across the tiled floor, desperately searching for a way out amidst the thick blanket of choking smoke.

The next moment, everything was in flames – the rugs, the tapestries, the curtains, the chairs. And the smoke grew denser, and the heat more intense.

Rook was shouting now, with all his might, but no sound came out. He sank to his knees, the acrid smell of the smoke in his nostrils and the roar of the flames in his ears. Sadness overwhelmed him, like raindrops pouring down a window-pane. It was as if he could touch it, smell it. He was racked by silent sobs.

Then everything went black . . .

Rook's body felt light, like a fragment of soot or a burnt ember. He was being blown away on a cool wind, a speck amongst the ashes of the terrible fire which had now burned itself out. He was floating, high above the roofs, towers and minarets of a great city. He peered down.

Far below, there was someone on a rooftop amidst the smoking buildings. It was one of the brothers. The youngest one. Crouched beside a shattered skylight, tears streaming down his cheeks, he hugged his knees closely to his chest and rocked slowly to and fro, to and fro . . .

Rook flew on, light as air, in and out of huge tumbling clouds. And as he did so, he felt an elation growing; a wild, exhilarating excitement!

Suddenly, he was on a sky ship in full sail, its deck rolling and bucking as the mighty ship sliced through the clouds. He clutched the stout lufwood mast to steady himself and looked up at the aft-deck.

There, standing proudly in the elegant clothes of a sky

pirate, was a lad with dark wavy hair. Beside him stood the sky pirate captain with the plaited beard and waxed moustache. He was leaning over the youth, guiding and advising him, as the lad – his eyes gleaming and his mouth smiling – steered the sky ship, turning the wheel and adjusting the flight-levers.

As he watched, Rook felt the father's love for his son, and the bond between the two. A heavy lump swelled in his throat and his eyes misted with tears . . .

Rook shivered. He was no longer on the sky ship in Open Sky, but inside a tall, draughty building. Looking up, he saw a long, curved staircase, twisting away into dark shadows. Halfway up – a tray clasped in its front claws – a huge, translucent spindlebug slowly climbed the stairs. Rook could see the blood pumping through its veins, the three bulbous lungs rising and falling, the two hearts slowly beating as, eventually, the creature reached a landing and approached a large ironwood door.

It knocked and waited – one, two, three, four, five seconds; Rook counted them – before seizing the handle and entering.

A girl with dark plaits and large green eyes looked up and smiled as the spindlebug approached with its tray. She was at a table, making a vast mosaic picture out of thousands of pieces of coloured crystal. Standing beside her, looking out of place and ill at ease, was a young sky pirate of about Rook's age, with dark wavy hair. He kept glancing over towards the balcony windows, where Rook glimpsed the backs of a sky pirate captain and a tall academic, the two of them deep in conversation.

Out beyond them, past the ornate balcony balustrade, Rook could see a magnificent skyline. To the left, a dome-shaped building with a huge bowl at its top, rose up from the rows of spiky towers around it, whilst in the distance, a mighty viaduct set upon a series of gigantic arched supports snaked through the city. To the right, twin towers, their upper ramparts topped with curious spinning, net-like minarets, stood out black against the billowing clouds.

'The mist-sifting towers of the School of Mist,' breathed Rook.

There was no doubt about it. He'd seen them in the ancient barkscrolls. Somehow, he was standing looking out over old Sanctaphrax . . .

Rook shivered again, this time violently. It was suddenly icy cold, and he was in a great circular space, buildings towering above him on all sides. Snow was falling. It fluttered down in large feathery flakes, covering every walkway, every rooftop, every road. Giant icicles hung from the eaves and sills. Looking up, Rook saw the youth again, at the top of what seemed to be the tallest tower of them all, so high above the ground it made Rook reel with dizziness just to watch him.

With one hand he gripped the balustrade; with the other, the hand of a girl as she dangled precariously over the edge. Clouds of condensation billowed from her lips, as she screamed and Rook could see her mouth forming three little words, over and over.

'Save yourself, Quint!'

But the snow got thicker and heavier, a great white blinding blizzard, until all at once it obliterated everything from sight . . .

Then Rook heard sobbing. Quiet, muffled sobbing. The dappled sunlight dazzled him for a moment but, as he shielded his eyes and looked around him, Rook realized that he was in the Deepwoods, and that the sobbing was coming from a stooped figure on a path, just ahead of him.

His instinct was to approach and ask what the matter was. But something made him hang back. The figure seemed so distraught, so inconsolable as it hugged a small bundle and swayed backwards and forwards, its heavy hooded cloak flapping. Just then, a tall sky pirate brushed past him and approached the figure. Rook heard sharp words and urgent whispers, and the sobbing grew louder.

Suddenly, the sobbing figure knelt down, and placed the bundle gently at the foot of a tree, before straightening up. Its hood fell back and Rook glimpsed a gaunt, dark-eyed face. The sobbing stopped. The sky pirate held out a hand and the cloaked figure took it and, as Rook watched, they walked silently away, not once looking back. Curious, Rook approached the foot of the tree and looked down at the bundle. He gasped.

It was a baby! A small baby, wrapped up in square of cloth, intricately embroidered with the picture of a lullabee tree. Its dark eyes stared back at him.

A sound made Rook look up, and with a jolt of surprise, he noticed a wooden cabin nestling in the branches of the tree above. Its circular door was opening. In the trees all around him, other small, rounded cabins were secured to the upper branches, purple smoke coiling from pipe-chimneys, and lights appearing at windows.

A stocky woodtroll-matron emerged from the door and climbed down the lufwood tree, huffing and puffing. Reaching the ground, she let out a shriek of surprise, before picking the bundle up. Rook felt a warm surge of love replace the icy chill in his chest. Before him, the woodtroll mother cradled the foundling, whispering sweet lullabies and tickling him under his chin. The baby cooed with delight . . .

The light faded and Rook was in the depths of the Deepwoods once more, tramping on through the night, his legs aching and his feet hurting. He was alone and without hope.

Suddenly, he felt a hand on his shoulder, and he found himself looking up into a kind, gentle face. It was the cloaked figure, but instead of the sky pirate with her, she was surrounded by young'uns of every description. Mobgnomes, cloddertrogs and red-haired individuals who hadn't yet turned termagant; woodtrolls, lugtrolls, gabtrolls and goblin young'uns from each major tribe; hammerhead and long-haired, lop-eared and tusked.

They were happy, and so was she, her eyes burning with joy. Rook found himself laughing and dancing in the sunlight in the midst of the throng of young'uns. They were beside a lake – one of three, stretched out in a line – with a towering cave-studded cliff behind them and a tall, imposing ironwood glade far to their left. And as they danced in a big circle – laughing and singing – the cloaked figure looked on, a huge spindlebug by her side . . .

The sounds of laughter faded and were replaced by beautiful music and turquoise light.

He was in a lullabee grove, not in a cocoon high in the branches, but on the forest floor. Suddenly, all round him, he could hear thrashing and tearing and muffled cries. And he looked up to see a majestic bird standing on one of the branches, high above his head. Beside it, the cocoon from which it had just hatched swayed emptily in the gentle breeze.

It was a caterbird.

It preened its violet-black feathers and scratched at its snowy white chest with long, jagged talons for a moment. Then, turning its head to one side, it looked down, and fixed him with a long, unblinking stare.

Rook stared back at it and felt his head begin to spin under its hypnotic gaze . . .

The next moment, Rook became conscious of beating wings, and the air whistling past. To his right and left, huge black wings pumped up and down, up and down, driving him on through the air. Below him, the forest canopy flashed past – greens, blues, yellows – an ocean of foliage.

He was a caterbird! It was *his* wings beating; *his* beak open wide and *his* strange echoing cry.

Looking back over his shoulder, he saw a sky ship, with its billowing sails and sparkling varnished masts and hull soaring through the air behind him. And no wonder, he realized a moment later, for it was attached to a rope tied around his middle.

He was pulling the magnificent sky ship across the sky!

He opened his beak and gave another triumphant cry. The young sky pirate captain at the helm waved and shouted in reply. Rook turned back and flapped his wings, soaring ahead, resplendent against the sparkling sky.

But wait! What was that up ahead? A vast, swirling vortex of cloud and wind was hurtling towards him, and there was nothing he could do. He and the sky ship were heading straight for it.

The next instant, the vortex enfolded them and Rook felt himself falling, no longer a bird, but a librarian knight once more, his arms flapping uselessly in the rushing air. Down, down he fell; down into inky darkness . . .

Flames flickered around him. Lamps gleamed. He was sitting at a long table, spiky, red-haired slaughterers jostling him from either side, and a huge brazier of burning leadwood in front of him. The table groaned with tilder sausages, hammelhorn steaks, latticed tarts and huge, dripping pies. Tankards of woodale were raised and toasts loudly proposed. The warm air was full of delicious smells and hearty laughter. A sky pirate was getting married to a pretty slaughterer lass, and this was their wedding feast.

Rook slapped the table delightedly and joined in the singing. The woodale was delicious and the brazier fire wonderfully warm, and Rook felt his head begin to swim . . .

The sounds of merry-making faded. It was quiet in the slaughterer village, the hammocks overhead bulging with sleeping bodies. On the other side of the clearing, Rook could see the sky pirate captain pacing outside one of the leadwood cabins.

All at once, the thick hammelhornskin which hung across the doorway was swept apart, and a slaughterer matron emerged, her shock of red hair damp and sticking to her forehead. In her arms, she held a small baby, which she handed gently to the waiting captain.

'Your daughter, Captain,' she said, smiling.

And as the sky pirate captain raised the child high up in the air, waves of joy flooded Rook's heart.

He wanted to shout and dance and jump in the air! But the village was so quiet, he was afraid he'd wake the sleepers overhead. He was about to get up to run over to the captain – but the trees abruptly faded and the light turned from the crisp blue of dawn to the golden glow of dusk . . .

Rook was back in the Free Glades, on the edge of New Undertown, the Lufwood Tower dark against the glowing sky. A young couple with a young'un beside them were seated at the front of a prowlgrin-drawn cart, their belongings at the back, secured beneath a bulging tarpaulin.

A sky pirate stood beside them; a tall, heavily-built individual with a thick beard and dark, doleful eyes. Clearly agitated, the pirate was waving his arms around, remonstrating with the young couple, trying to stop them from leaving the Free Glades and setting out on their journey. He seemed desperate.

'It isn't safe,' he kept saying. 'The slavers are out.'

But they wouldn't listen. Instead, the young couple smiled indulgently, bounced the young'un on their knees and told him to 'kiss goodbye to Great Uncle Tem'.

As they rode away into the sunset, the sky pirate stared after them, tears streaming down his face – a face Rook was sure he'd seen somewhere before.

The sun set and the moon rose, and Rook felt his stomach give a sickening lurch . . .

It was the old dream, the nightmare that had recurred all through his childhood from as long ago as he could remember. Now, it was back again – and with all its familiar horror.

First came the wolves – always the wolves. White-collared, bristling and baying, their terrible yellow eyes flashing in the dark forest.

His father was shouting for him to hide; his mother was screaming. Rook didn't know what to do. He was running this way, that way. Everywhere were flashing yellow eyes and the sharp, barked commands of the slave-takers.

Rook whimpered. He knew what came next, and it was worse – far worse.

He was alone in the dark woods. The howling of the

slavers' wolf-packs was receding into the distance. Alone in the vastness of the Deepwoods – and something was coming towards him. Something huge . . .

Suddenly Rook felt the panic and terror leave him, to be replaced by a feeling of peace. He was in the huge, soft, moss-scented arms of a great banderbear, who hugged him to herself and yodelled gently in his ear . . .

Rook opened his eyes, the warm, safe feeling of the banderbear's enfolding arms lingering. He was inside the caterbird cocoon, the soft woven fibres holding him as securely as the rescuing creature of his dreams.

Sitting up, he felt wonderful. His head was clear and, for the first time in weeks, he felt fully rested; charged with a strength and energy he could feel coursing through his body. As he crawled towards the opening in the cocoon and stuck his head out, the images were already fading away, like water slipping between his fingers. He struggled to make sense of them as he looked around.

An early morning mist hung over the grove as Rook climbed down the gnarled trunk of the lullabee tree. On the ground, he stretched luxuriantly.

'I trust you slept well, Rook Barkwater,' Grailsooth's voice sounded beside him.

'Better,' said Rook, smiling back at the oakelf, his eyes no longer glowing unnaturally blue, 'than I have ever slept before!'

CHAPTER TWELVE

PASSWORDS

i

The Foundry Glades

As the sun sank low in the sky, a ragged band of sky pirates struggled to the crest of yet another densely forested ridge. Their leader, a weasel-faced quartermaster in a torn and muddied greatcoat, unhooked a telescope from his belt and put it to his eye. In front of him, the endless Deepwoods stretched away to the golden, cloud-flecked horizon.

You might as well put your telescope away, Quillet Pleeme, a quiet, sibilant voice sounded in the quartermaster's head. *It might have served you well in the Mire, but it is almost useless here in the Deepwoods.*

The quartermaster turned, anger plain on his thin, sharp features. Beside him, gasping for breath, stood a huge matron – a cloddertrog – with a small, frail-looking ghost-waif strapped to her back. The waif's barbels quivered as he fixed the quartermaster with an unblinking stare.

'If you have something to say, Amberfuce,' said Quillet Pleeme, 'then say it out loud, instead of sneaking into my head.' Ever since he and his sky pirates had hooked up with the sickly waif and his huge nurse back in the throng of Undertowners in the Mire, the odious creature had been listening in to his thoughts.

'Apologies,' whispered Amberfuce meekly. 'But I simply wanted to point out that sight is less important than the other senses here in the Deepwoods.'

The other sky pirates joined them on the ridge, sweating profusely and blowing hard from the long climb. There was a heavily tattooed flat-head goblin, three thin, ill-looking gnokgoblins, a long-haired goblin and a couple of mob gnomes, all of them wearing heavy sky pirate coats festooned with weapons, canteens and grappling-irons. Together they had formed the crew of the *Fogscythe* before they had deserted their captain – a cloddertrog in a muglumpskin coat – and followed Quillet Pleeme.

Amberfuce, the waif, had promised them all riches beyond their wildest dreams, for they – every last one of them – were going to be Furnace Masters in the Foundry Glades. Amberfuce had promised them, and he would deliver on his promise because he knew someone; a very important someone.

That someone was Hemuel Spume, the head of the whole Foundry Glades. All they had to do, Amberfuce had explained, his eyes twinkling, was to escort him and his nurse to the Foundry Glades and then sit back and reap the rewards from a grateful Hemuel Spume.

How difficult could that be?

The sky pirates had soon found out. Sneaking away from the multitude of Undertowners as they trudged through the Mire had been easy. Even with Flambusia Flodfox, Amberfuce's nurse, carrying the ghostwaif on her back, complaining loudly and slowing them down, they'd made good progress. They were used to the Mire and mud-marching, and once they'd crossed back over the shattered Mire Road, they'd arrived at the southern Edgelands in less than a day.

The Edgelands had been unpleasant, and all of them were plagued with visions and nightmarish apparitions – especially the ghostwaif, before Flambusia had given him some of her special medicine. But again they'd made good progress, and the journey really did seem to be as straightforward as Amberfuce had said it would be. And then they had entered the Deepwoods.

They'd lost Brazerigg to a logworm almost at once, and the gnokgoblins had come down with pond-fever soon after, forcing them to pitch camp for a week. Now their provisions were running out, and the way ahead lay over endless forest ridges which stretched off as far as the eye could see.

'There must be an easier route,' Myzewell the flat-head had moaned on the third day of hard climbing and bone-jolting descents.

The way to riches is never easy, my friend, Amberfuce's sibilant whisper had sounded in his head.

Now, on the fourth day, here they all stood, tired and hungry, at the top of yet another ridge with the Foundry Glades still nowhere in sight.

'Where now?' Quillet Pleeme snarled, snapping his telescope shut.

The ghostwaif closed his eyes and sniffed the air, his huge, paper-thin ears quivering. 'I can hear clinking and clanking,' he whispered. 'Grinding and hissing, hammering and howling. I smell molten metal and furnace smoke.' He stretched out a long thin finger. 'Over there, just beyond the next ridge, my friends . . .' His hand trembled, and a harsh cough racked his tiny body.

'That's what you said two days ago,' snarled Myzewell the flat-head.

'There, there, Amby, dear,' fussed Flambusia, throwing a blanket over her shoulder. 'You wrap up warm, and don't go getting into a bother.'

Quillet shrugged and turned to the other sky pirates. 'We've come this far. What's another hill or two, between friends? Come on, you scurvy curs! Look lively!'

Cursing beneath their breath, the sky pirates began the long descent into the growing dusk. As Myzewell started after them, Quillet pulled him back and, glancing up ahead at the figure of Flambusia disappearing down the slope, whispered in his ear.

'I've had enough of this. I, for one, think the waif's lost. One more ridge. If we get to the top and we don't see furnace chimneys, then we cut our losses and return to the Mire.'

'But what about the waif and his nurse?' growled Myzewell.

'We ditch them. We'll travel more quickly, and there'll be two less mouths to feed.' The quartermaster drew a hand across his throat in a cutting motion. 'Wait for me to give the word,' he whispered. 'And mind you keep your thoughts clear, or the waif'll suspect something.'

'And the word?' said Myzewell, giving a sharp-toothed grin.

'"Goodbye",' said Quillet quietly.

Five, hard, scrambling, bone-jarring hours later, the sky pirates wearily approached the crest of the next ridge. The slope had been heavily forested, with sharp thickets of razorthorns amid dense stands of greyoaks and flametrees. Several times, as the thorns ripped their coats and the branches scratched their faces, Quillet and Myzewell exchanged dark looks. At last they reached the top, and Quillet's mouth dropped open.

It was the smell that hit them first. Thick, acrid and choking smoke, mixed with a sulphurous metallic stench. Then the low insistent roar of the furnaces and the sound of thousands of hammers on metal. Looking down, Quillet could see the glowing fires of the Foundry Glades twinkling through the drifting wreaths of smoke.

Amberfuce turned to the open-mouthed quarter-master, a slyly knowing look on his face. *You have something to say, perhaps?* he asked, his sibilant voice hissing in Quillet's head. *No? Well then, let us make our way to my good friend Hemuel Spume's palace without delay.*

As they made their way down the hill towards the glades below, the noise and smell and choking smoke grew more and more intense. Ahead of them, the trees thinned until they found themselves picking their way through a forest of tree-stumps. The air grew hot and sooty, and instead of tall forest trees, the glowing metal foundry chimneys towered over them, belching out smoke.

Amberfuce pulled his scarf up over his mouth. His breath was coming fast and wheezy. Flambusia fussed with him anxiously, reaching up every few steps to pop a cough-lozenge into his mouth.

They approached the first furnace they came to, and Quillet's beady eyes narrowed. A long line of workers snaked from the huge timber stacks on one side of the furnace to its open fiery mouth on the other. With heavy groans of exertion, they fed the flames with an endless supply of logs passed by hand down the line, while overseers patrolled, cracking heavy tilderleather whips. The sky pirates looked at one another.

'Poor creatures,' muttered Stegrewl, the long-haired goblin.

'Oi! You, there!' came a rough voice. 'Stop right there!'

They turned to see a phalanx of burly flat-head goblin guards bearing down on them, a large, battle-scarred captain at their head.

Amberfuce tapped Flambusia on the shoulder, motioning her forward, but before he could speak, Quillet Pleeme had pushed past her and addressed the captain face to face.

'Greetings!' he said, bowing his head in salute. 'We are sky pirates who have risked our lives to escort Chancellor Amberfuce of old Undertown safely to the Foundry Glades . . .'

The captain delivered a swift blow to the quartermaster's midriff that sent him tumbling to the ground, doubled up and gasping for breath. 'Silence, scum!' he roared, raising his sword.

My dear captain . . . er . . . Hegghuft, is it? Amberfuce's honeyed tones sounded inside the guard's head. *I can tell you are a warrior of great distinction. One of my great friend Hemuel Spume's most trusted captains. He will be pleased when I tell him of your . . . er . . . diligence.*

The waif pulled his scarf down to reveal a sickly, ingratiating smile.

The goblin stared back at him and slowly lowered his sword.

'Now if you would be so kind as to take me to your master . . .' Amberfuce said out loud, fighting to stifle the cough rising in his throat.

The captain nodded slowly, then turned to his guards. 'Take their weapons,' he ordered, indicating the sky pirates before turning back to the waif. 'This way, Chancellor,' he growled.

They made their way through the Foundry Glades, past furnaces bigger and more terrible than the first, barging through scurrying workers and their bullying guards, until at last ahead of them, the palace loomed into view. They hurried across the front courtyard, in through the gates and – still accompanied by the goblin guards – up a broad staircase to the third floor. In front of them, a huge metal-plated door swung slowly open and a stooped individual with steel-rimmed glasses and long side-whiskers appeared, flanked on either side by palace guards.

'Amberfuce! Amberfuce!' he cried, peering up at the ghostwaif slumped on Flambusia's back. Can it really be you? After all these years!'

'Hemuel, my dear friend,' said Amberfuce, looking down. He pursed his lips with irritation. 'Get me down, Flambusia,' he said. 'Now!'

The nurse reached up, lifted her charge out of the sling on her back and plonked him down with just a touch more vigour than was absolutely necessary. 'There,' she said, smiling sweetly.

Amberfuce collected himself. 'It's been far too long, Hemuel,' he said, breathlessly.

'Indeed,' said Spume. 'But I've made great progress here in the Foundry Glades while you've been holed up in Undertown.' He smiled, revealing a row of jagged yellow teeth, and rubbed a forefinger and thumb together. 'Your investments have done very well. We're expanding, Amberfuce, expanding beyond our wildest dreams. I've got the goblins just where I want them, and the Free Glades in my sights. And now you're here, Amberfuce, old friend, to share in this great venture.'

'Wild prowlgrins couldn't have kept me away,' said Amberfuce excitedly, his barbels quivering. 'We must speak in private, right away.' He tapped the box clutched to his chest. His voice dropped. 'I think you'll find what I have here of interest.'

'Oh, but of course,' said Hemuel Spume. 'Follow me.'

He turned away. Amberfuce followed, Flambusia stooping over him, mopping his sweaty brow with her handkerchief as she went.

'What about us?' said Quillet Pleeme, peevishly. 'Aren't you forgetting something? You promised that your friend here would make us Furnace Masters . . .'

Hemuel Spume stopped and spun round on his heel. 'Furnace Masters?' he said, a ghost of a smile playing on his thin lips. He looked at the ghostwaif, who smiled back at him. 'Oh, Amberfuce, you naughty old thing! Sky pirates as Furnace Masters? Whatever next! You knew I'd never agree.'

Amberfuce nodded. 'Yes,' he whispered, 'but *they* didn't know that.'

'You said you'd have a word!' Quillet Pleeme pleaded, his voice a thin whine. 'A word, you said. A word . . .'

'Oh, I have a word,' said Amberfuce nastily. 'Perhaps you recognize it?'

Quillet, Myzewell and the sky pirates stared back at the ghostwaif as the guards seized them by the arms.

'Goodbye!'

Hemuel Spume smiled. 'Some do very well here,' he said, 'if they work hard. Guards, take them away!'

As the cursing and moaning faded behind them, Hemuel Spume led Amberfuce and Flambusia to the back of the great hall. He paused by a small door, and waved Flambusia away.

'If you'd be kind enough to leave us, my dear,' he said.

'But . . . But . . .' cried Flambusia outraged. 'His medicines! His embrocations! His . . .'

'Flambusia *never* leaves my side,' said Amberfuce, his barbels quivering with agitation.

Hemuel flashed the same thin-lipped, yellow-toothed smile as he turned the handle, pushed Amberfuce inside the ante-chamber and slammed the door in Flambusia

Flodfox's pink, indignant face. Locking it, he turned to
Amberfuce.

'First things first,' he said. 'You wanted to speak to me
in private . . .'

'Yes, yes,' said Amberfuce. 'But I didn't mean without
Flambusia . . .'

Hemuel steered the ghostwaif over to a small table.
'Forget the nurse for a moment,' he said, 'and show me
what's in that box!'

Amberfuce laid the box down, pulled a key from
around his neck and opened it. Inside, there were
wads of folded paper. He pulled

one out at ran-
dom, opened it
up and spread it
out on the table.
He cleared his
throat.

'As the right-
hand waif to Vox
Verlix, the most
brilliant mind in old
Undertown, I had access
to his private chambers.
When I sent word
to you that I was
coming, I prom-
ised I'd bring
s o m e t h i n g
special with me.'

'Indeed you did. But just *how* special?' said Hemuel Spume, his eyes glinting.

'This,' said Amberfuce with a little chuckle, 'is one of Vox Verlix's blueprints. Everyone knows the Sanctaphrax Forest, the Tower of Night, the Great Mire Road . . .' He shrugged. 'Yet they were but a few of his ideas. He worked on others, too. Many others.' He removed a second blueprint and spread it out over the first; then a third . . . 'Catapults, log-launchers, flaming slings . . . His mind was never still. And this . . .' He took a fourth blueprint from the box and spread it out carefully on top of the others. 'This is the finest of the lot.'

'So I can see,' said Hemuel, his eyes glinting wildly as he pawed over the detailed design. 'Wonderful! Wonderful!' he breathed.

'I knew you'd be pleased,' said Amberfuce.

'I couldn't be more pleased,' said Hemuel. 'And now, in return, I have a little surprise for you.'

'A surprise?' said Amberfuce, coughing with excitement. 'What . . . sort of . . . sur . . .' The coughing grew worse. 'Oh, Flambusia!' he gasped. 'I need Flambusia!'

From behind them, there came a muffled hammering on the door and the sound of Flambusia's outraged voice, demanding to be let in.

'You don't need her, believe me,' said Spume with a smile, as he led the frail ghostwaif over to the far side of the ante-chamber, and opened a second door.

Amberfuce looked through into the room on the other side. His eyes widened, his cheeks coloured – and his cough magically melted away. 'Hemuel,' he gasped.

'Have I died and gone to the Eternal Glen?'

The Foundry Master chuckled as he ushered the waif inside the room, where a score of gabtroll apothecaresses immediately surrounded him, each one bearing kneading-rods, birchwood-twigs, rough flannels and spicy, aromatic massage-oils.

'I'm putting my own personal attendants at your disposal. Enjoy!'

'Amby?' Flambusia wailed bleakly.

The ghostwaif was gently laid out on a raised table.

'*Amby?*'

But Amberfuce didn't reply. Doused in oils and ointments, unguents and salves; rubbed, kneaded and stroked, a radiant smile spread across his face. His eyelids fluttered for a moment, then closed.

'*AM-BY!*'

'Not now, Flambusia,' he purred happily, as he submitted to the wonderfully rough, firm hands. 'Not now.'

ii
The Goblin Nations

'But why must the lop-ear clan always bear the heaviest burden?' Meegmewl cried out indignantly.

The old grey goblin had heard some things in his life, but to demand a consignment of a thousand goblins a month was outrageous, even for Hemuel Spume. With the harvest not yet in, it would mean hunger in the clan's villages at the very least.

'Because, old goblin, my flat-heads and hammerheads are warriors,' said Lytugg fiercely. 'They're willing to act as guards, but as for operating the foundries and furnaces . . .'

'And that goes for my lot, too,' snarled Rootrott Underbiter. 'We tusked goblins are prepared to make sacrifices, don't get me wrong.' He drained his tankard and slammed it heavily down on the table. 'We're ready to fight, of course we are, but as for those accursed Foundry Glades, enough is enough!'

Hemtuft Battleaxe shifted forward in his chair, adjusted his feathered cloak and cleared his throat. 'We need those "accursed Foundry Glades", as you put it,' he said, fixing the tusked clan chief with a cold stare. 'I don't believe we have any choice in the matter.' His eyes darkened. 'Now, more than ever before, it is vital to keep them well supplied with labour.' He looked round. 'I take it we're all agreed on that, at least.'

The other clan chiefs nodded cautiously.

Sensing that his hastily convened closed-meeting was shifting in his direction at last, Hemtuft seized the advantage. He looked sternly at the clan chiefs, one after the other: Lytugg the hammerhead, her red eyes blazing; Rootrott Underbiter the tusked goblin, scowling; Grossmother Nectarsweet the symbite, her huge chins glistening with drops of woodale, and Meegmewl the Grey, shrunken and frail, yet defiant even now . . .

'There are great plans afoot in the Foundry Glades,' Hemtuft said. 'Plans that will bring the clans untold wealth and prosperity in the future – if only we are

prepared to make a sacrifice now . . .'

As he spoke, a dumpy black-eared goblin matron went round the table, topping up the goblets. Knowing how challenging the meeting would be, Hemtuft had got in extra woodale specially. The five of them present were already on their second barrel.

'What are these plans you speak of?' Meegmewl asked. 'Plans that demand so much of my clan brothers.'

Hemtuft Battleaxe looked grave. 'You must trust me, Meegmewl the Grey,' he said. He looked askance at the black-eared goblin matron retreating from the chamber. 'There are Free Glade spies everywhere! We must be careful. All I can say is that Hemuel Spume is working on something big; something that will take a huge workforce to bring to fruition, but something that will guarantee us victory! He calls it "the glade-eater".'

For a while, no one spoke. The only sounds were those of sipping and slurping, and the hammering down of pewter tankards on the ironwood tabletop. It was Rootrott Underbiter who first broke the silence.

'Glade-eater, eh?' he said. 'I like the sound of that.' He smiled unpleasantly. 'I'll give you old'uns, the sick and the lame, and that's my final offer. As for my finest tufteds and black-ears, they're needed for battle. The Furnace Masters aren't getting their sooty hands on *them*!'

A murmur of agreement went round the table. Hemtuft nodded sagely. 'I'll send our third-borns,' he said. 'They never make the finest warriors anyway.'

'No hammerheads, but I can spare some flat-heads,' said Lytugg. 'Strictly for guard-duty, you understand.'

'Good,' smiled Hemtuft. 'How about you, Nectarsweet?'

'I suppose I can spare a colony or two of gnokgoblins,' she replied, the rolls of fat beneath her chins bouncing about as she spoke. 'But I need my gyle goblins, every one of them. They're my babies . . .' Tears sprang to her tiny eyes.

'Yes, yes,' said Hemtuft, turning to Meegmewl. 'You heard the sacrifices the other clans are prepared to make,' he said sternly. 'Now it is the turn of the lop-ear clan.'

Meegmewl sighed. 'I've already sacrificed too many a pink-eye and grey,' he said. He shook his head. 'The mood in the clan villages is turning ugly . . .'

'Pah!' said Lytugg scornfully. 'Is the great clan chief, Meegmewl the Grey, frightened of his own goblins?'

Meegmewl looked down at the table. Hemtuft laid a hand on his shoulder.

'What about your low-bellies, old friend?' he said, smiling. 'They're a good-natured, docile lot – and there's plenty of them. I'm sure Lytugg can lend you some of her flat-heads to round them up.'

Lytugg nodded.

'Ah, yes, the low-bellies,' said Meegmewl quietly. He sighed again. 'I suppose you're right, though I don't like it. I don't like it at all. Good-natured, docile creatures they may be, but even a low-belly can be pushed too far.'

Hemtuft raised his goblet. 'To the glade-eater!' he roared.

*

'Now, friends of the harvest, let us gather round the table and each say our piece.'

'It's not a table!' someone shouted. 'It's a hay-cart!'

'Move over!'

'Who are you pushing?'

Lob and Lummel Grope were attempting to bring a meeting of their own to order. Having attended Hemtuft Battleaxe's great assembly of the clans in the long-hairs' open-sided clan hut, they knew more or less what to do. The trouble was, no one else did.

'Friends,' said Lob, in a loud whisper. 'Please! If we all speak at once, no one will be heard.'

'S'not fair, so it isn't and that's a fact,' said an old low-belly, scratching his swollen stomach through the grubby fabric of his belly-sling.

'S'always us,' another piped up, his straw bonnet jiggling about on his head. 'An' I for one have had enough of it.'

'I've lost a father, two brothers, eight cousins . . .' broke in a third heatedly.

'No one cares a jot about us . . .'

The babble of voices rose, with everyone trying to speak at the same time and no one able to hear anyone else. It was punctuated by occasional knocks on the barn-door, as others arrived to join the meeting. Lummel raised his hand to restore order. The last thing they wanted was to get into a shouting match and attract the attention of a flat-head patrol. But feelings were running high.

Word of Hemuel Spume's latest demands had gone round the Goblin Nations like wildfire, and it wasn't only the lop-ears in the western farmlands who were protesting. Goblins from all over were covertly whispering, one to the other, that enough was enough, and the meeting in the old wicker barn was getting larger and more unwieldy all the time.

'Who goes there?' bellowed a low-belly with a stubbly chin and a pitchfork, menacingly raised as yet another visitor knocked on the door.

'A friend of the harvest,' came the hissed reply. 'Let me in.'

The door was unbolted and pulled back. The new-comer – a young tufted goblin with a jagged-toothed sabre and an ironwood shield – poked his head inside.

'Enter, friend,' the low-belly guard said. 'But leave your weapon outside.'

The tufted goblin did as he was told and went in. A moment later, the guard was admitting a sick-looking tusked goblin, and a trio of garrulous gnokgoblins.

'Friends . . .' Lob shouted, his call lost among the rising cacophony of voices.

'I mean, we've only got half the harvest in,' someone was complaining. 'Are we expected to leave the rest in the fields to rot?'

'It just don't seem to occur to them that we all gotta eat!'

'War, war, war – tha's all they ever seem to talk about.'

'Friends, one and all!' Lummel called out. 'We must band together . . .'

But no one heard him. Of course, it didn't help that each and every one of the gathered goblins was tucking in to the woodapple cider that they had discovered was being stored in the barn. In the end, it was an old tusked goblin who took it upon himself to impose some kind of order on the proceedings. He strode to the front, where Lob and Lummel were now standing on top of the hay cart, and bellowed for quiet, before collapsing and calling for a swig of cider.

Shocked, the gathering of goblins fell silent. All eyes turned to the front.

'Thank you, friends,' said Lob, humbly. He turned to face the expectant crowd. 'We have all lost loved ones to the Foundry Glades,' he began.

'And soon the flat-head guards will come for us,' Lummel continued. 'Low-belly, gnokgoblin, long-hair and tusked, young and old, frail and sick!'

The crowd murmured, heads nodding. 'But what can we do?' called out a gnokgoblin.

'We must work together,' said Lob.

'We must help each other,' said Lummel.

A muttering got up in the crowd as the two brothers' words sank in. They made sense, and the goblins started offering help to one another, suggesting places where those who were on the lists for the Foundry Glades might safely be concealed. As the noise began to rise once more, Lummel raised his hand for quiet.

'We all know what this is about,' said Lob, as the noise abated. 'The clan chiefs want a war against the Free Glades, a war that'll make them rich. That much is clear. But why should *we* fight the Freegladers? Do not all of us have friends and relations who live among them?'

A murmur of assent went round.

'What quarrel have the Goblin Nations with the Free Glades?' Lummel added. 'Why, their mayor is a goblin. A low-belly goblin! Hebb Lub-drub is his name.' He paused, to let the words sink in. 'A low-belly goblin, mayor of New Undertown.' He shook his head. 'Do any of us here want to help destroy such a place?'

For a moment there was silence. Then, tentatively at first, but with growing conviction, voices from all round the old wicker barn answered.

'No . . .'

'No . . .'

'No!'

Lob and Lummel looked at one another and grinned. It was a start. A good start.

iii
New Undertown

As darkness fell, Mother Bluegizzard – fresh from her afternoon nap – flapped round the tavern, a long flaming taper in her claws, lighting the lamps and greeting her faithful old regulars as she went. It was only when she got to the far corner that she realized one of them was missing.

She nodded towards the empty table. 'No Mire Pirate again tonight?' she asked.

Zett shrugged. 'Doesn't look like it,' he said.

'Haven't seen him all week,' added Grome, scratching his great hairy chest with all fingers as he spoke.

Mother Bluegizzard frowned, her neck ruff trembling. 'Most peculiar,' she commented. 'I wonder where he's got to.'

Meggutt, Beggutt and Deg poked their heads up out of their drinking trough, one after the other.

'We ain't seen him, neither,' they said. 'Not hide nor hair.'

The old bird-creature lit the last lantern and blew out the taper. 'I hope he's all right,' she said. 'Place doesn't seem the same without him.'

The others all nodded. None of them had ever heard the old Mire Pirate utter so much as a word, yet his empty table seemed to make the tavern even quieter than usual. Even Fevercule had no idea. They returned to their drinks.

In fact, if any of the regulars had bothered to look,

they'd have discovered that
the Mire Pirate wasn't far
from the Bloodoak Tavern
at all. The dishevelled old
sky pirate, with his great
bushy beard and haunted
eyes, was standing on a
small hill screened by
lufwood trees, but with a
clear view of the North
Lake jetty below. He'd been
coming to this exact same
spot for a week now, standing and staring, as silent as
a statue, through the long
moonless nights until dawn
broke above Lullabee
Island. Then, each morning,
he'd turn and trudge
silently away, only to return
the next night.

This night was no excep-
tion. The Mire Pirate stood
on the secluded hill top and
stared over at the island in
the lake and waited. He
waited as the moon rose,
clouds drifted across the
sky and the hawkowls
hooted. He waited as the

235

moon sank and another dawn broke. He was just about to turn away and trudge back to New Undertown once more, when a distant splash made him hesitate.

As he watched, a small coracle bobbing on the water made its way from the island to the jetty. He raised a hand to his mouth, as if stifling a cry, and was about to descend the hill when he noticed a small group hurrying towards the North Lake jetty below.

The Mire Pirate checked himself and waited.

'There he is!' shouted a youth in a bleached muglump-skin jacket, and the three banderbears beside him yodelled out across the water.

The *splash-splash* of the paddles increased as the coracle approached the shore. With the help of its crew of turquoise-clad oakelves, a librarian climbed from the little boat and onto the jetty.

'Rook!' Felix exclaimed. 'At last! There you are!'

'Good morning, Felix!' Rook smiled, clasping his friend's hand and shaking it vigorously.

The banderbears yodelled and gesticulated in delight. The oakelves smiled and, without saying a word, pushed off from the jetty and began the journey back to Lullabee Island.

'All week, we've been waiting,' said Felix. 'All week! I was beginning to wonder if you were *ever* going to return! But, my word!' He let go of Rook's hand and stared into his face. 'It seems to have done you the power of good, by the look of you, Rook!'

'A week?' said Rook, shaking his head in disbelief. 'I've been asleep in the caterbird cocoon for a whole week!'

'Caterbird cocoon?' said Felix. It was his turn to look amazed. 'So that was the miracle cure, was it? Why, those clever old oakelves. We were right to trust them after all, weren't we, fellas?'

The banderbears yodelled their agreement.

'Now, we're wanted at Lake Landing, Rook,' said Felix, clapping him on the back. 'Absolute hive of activity it is. But you'll see what I mean when we get there.' He laughed and pulled Rook after him. 'Come, it's a fine morning for a stroll and you can tell us all about the dreams you had in this caterbird nest of yours – a whole week's worth!'

As the small group made off, the old sky pirate emerged from behind the lufwood trees. He watched them for a moment, his pale eyes misted with tears. His lips moved and in a voice deep and gravelly from lack of use, he whispered one word.

'Barkwater.'

·CHAPTER THIRTEEN·

TEA WITH A SPINDLEBUG

Despite the early hour, the Gardens of Light were far from still. Spindlebug gardeners with long rakes and stubby hoes patrolled the walkways between the fungus fields, tending to the pink, glowing toadstools. Milchgrubs, their huge udder-sacs sloshing and slewing with pink liquid, grazed contentedly. Slime-moles snuffled round their pits, trying to find any uneaten scraps from their last feed; while all round the illuminated caverns, crystal spiders and venomous firemoths strove to keep out of one another's way.

Up above, in the Ironwood Glade, there was no moon and the sun had not yet risen. Apart from the occasional snorts and cries of the prowlgrins roosting in the branches of the tall trees, the place was silent. The fromps and quarms were sleeping, and the predatory razorflits had not yet returned from a night of hunting.

Suddenly, breaking the stillness and illuminating a

patch of dark forest floor with light, a column of several dozen gyle goblins appeared. They were fresh from a successful foraging trip collecting moon-mangoes – large, pink-blushed fruits that ripened at night and had to be picked immediately if their succulent flesh was not to turn sour. Walking in single file, the gyle goblins made their way to the centre of the Ironwood Glade where a well-like hole in the ground was situated. They stopped, swung the baskets down and, one after the other, tipped their contents down the hole.

'That's the gardens fed. Now let's fill our milch-pails and take them back to the colony,' one of them commented.

'Honey for breakfast, deeee-licious!' said another, her heavy eyelids fluttering.

Far underground, as the first load of moon-mangoes landed on the giant compost heap below, a gaunt youth glanced over from the raised ledge he was ambling along. The glowing light played on his short cropped hair. A second load tumbled down through the air, followed by a third and a fourth. The youth looked up and focused wistfully on the long tube they were emerging from, high up and inaccessible in the domed ceiling, far above his head. As he watched, half a dozen firemoths fluttered round the bottom of the tube, and disappeared in, heading for the forest outside.

'I wish *I* could leave,' he murmured.

But that was not possible. There was only one way in and out of the Gardens of Light large enough for those who dwelt underground – and that was guarded at all times. He had no choice but to remain under the ground, roaming the paths and ledges, always bathed in the same unchanging pink light. Close to three weeks he had spent down there already, yet he'd only seen a fraction of the sprawling Gardens of Light, with their winding labyrinth of walkways and glowing tunnels, stalagmites and stalactites, fungus beds and drop-ponds.

Crossing a small bridge of opalescent rock, he heard the sound of steady chomping and looked down to see a brace of slime-moles in a steep-sided pit below him, chewing contentedly on fan-shaped fungi. A couple of glassy spindlebugs – heavy trugs swaying from their fore-arms – were passing along the walkways, dropping food down into the pits. One of them paused for a moment.

'That's right. Tuck in, my beauty!' it said, as one of the slime-moles below wobbled over and began devouring the fungus. 'Will you look at that.' The spindlebug nudged his companion. 'Her slime-ducts are bulging!'

'Just as well,' replied its neighbour. 'The rate those young apprentices get through mole-glue! Filling their varnish pots every few minutes . . .'

'I know, I know,' said the first one, tutting. 'It's not as though we're made of the stuff.'

'No, but *they* are!' said the second one – and the pair of them looked down at the slime-moles as they squirmed about, leaving trails of gleaming, sticky goo in their wake, and trilled with amusement.

The youth walked on. A herd of huge, lumbering milchgrubs being herded down to the great honey-pits for milking crossed his path. Shortly after that, a librarian apprentice – his eyelids puffy with lack of sleep – came hurrying towards him, an empty bucket clutched in his hand.

'Run out of mole-glue, eh?' the youth asked.

'Uh-huh,' came the gruff reply, and the librarian knight scurried past, his head down and eyes averted.

The youth sighed. Everyone knew who he was and why he was there – and no one, it seemed, wanted to be caught talking to him.

He climbed higher, up a bumpy ramp and onto a narrow ledge which hugged the arched wall. There were caves leading off it. Some were empty, some were being used for storage; from one, there came the soft murmur of voices.

Scratching his stubbly head, the youth paused for a moment and looked in. Half a dozen young librarian knights were sitting on low stools, each one bent over a pot balanced on a small burner, stirring vigorously. There was a familiar smell, like singed feathers and burnt treacle. One of them noticed him, looked up, frowned and looked away.

The youth turned, and headed sadly off. No one wanted anything to do with him.

Then, just as he was rounding a jutting rock, he caught sight of an old spindlebug tap-tap-tapping its way along a broad ledge on an upper level. The creature was huge – far bigger than any of those who were tending to the fungus beds or slime-moles. In one of its front arms it carried a tray. In the other, a walking stick to help support its immense weight. Both the size and the yellow tinge to the outer casing indicated that the spindlebug was ancient.

As the two walkways converged, the creature came closer, the glasses and tea-urn on the tray clinking together softly. 'Up so early,' it said as it approached, its voice high and quavery.

The youth shrugged and pulled a face. 'I can't sleep well down here,' he said. 'It's always so light. I never know whether it's day or night . . .' He sighed miserably. 'I miss the sky, the clouds, the wind on my face . . .'

The spindlebug stopped before him, and nodded. 'You're here to prepare for your Reckoning,' it said. 'Use this time to reflect on your life, to contemplate your deeds and . . .' It coughed lightly. 'And your *mis*deeds. The time to leave will come all too soon.'

'Not soon enough for me,' the youth snorted. 'Stuck down here in this prison . . .'

'Prison, Xanth?' the great, transparent creature interrupted. 'You, of all people, speak of prisons!'

Xanth visibly shrank at the spindlebug's words, and when he spoke, his voice had lost its arrogant bravado. 'You're right,' he said quietly. 'And I'm sorry. I know I can't compare this place to the Tower of Night . . .' He shook his head miserably. 'Oh, Tweezel, when I think of the years I spent serving the Guardians of Night; the evil I did, the misery I caused . . .'

Tweezel nodded. 'Come now,' he said gently. 'Let us go and share a spot of tea together, you and I. Just like we used to do. Remember?'

Xanth's looked up into the spindlebug's face and saw his own reflected in the creature's huge eyes. Yes, he remembered the times he'd spent drinking tea and listening to the spindlebug's stories as a librarian knight apprentice. How he'd loved those quiet moments they'd shared, but his memories of them were poisoned by the knowledge that even as he'd smiled and sipped the fragrant brew, he'd been an imposter.

'Are you sure?' he said.

'Certainly I'm sure,' said Tweezel, his antennae trilling. 'Follow me.'

Keeping close to the ancient spindlebug, and ignoring the muttered comments and angry glares from the apprentices they passed, Xanth followed him down the ledge and in through a narrow opening in the wall. Beyond the doorway, the space opened up to reveal a cosy, if rather cramped, chamber, furnished with a squat table and low benches. Tweezel ushered Xanth to sit down and placed the tray down on the table in front of him, knocking his arms and elbows on the walls as he did so.

'My, my,' the ancient creature commented. 'I swear this place gets smaller every day.'

Xanth smiled. Clearly it was Tweezel who had grown rather than the tea-chamber which had shrunk, and Xanth found himself wondering just how old the spindlebug actually was.

Quietly, methodically, the spindlebug placed one of the glasses under the spigot of the ornate wooden tea-urn and turned the tap. Hot, steaming, amber liquid poured out, filling first one, then the other glass. Next, he added crystals of honey with a set of silver tongs, and a sprig of hyleberry blossom. As Xanth watched the familiar ritual, remorse and guilt welled up within him.

Tweezel noticed his tortured expression. 'You are not the first to have felt guilt,' he said. 'And you certainly will not be the last.'

'I know, I know,' said Xanth, fighting back the tears. 'It's just that . . .'

'You wish you could undo the things you have done?' said Tweezel as, with a slight incline of his head, he handed Xanth the glass of tea. 'Change the decisions of the past? Put things right? Lift the heavy weight of guilt that is pressing down on your chest?' He fell still. 'Try your tea, Master Xanth,' he said.

Xanth sipped at the tea, and as the warm, sweet, aromatic liquid slipped down his throat, he began to feel a little better. He set the glass aside.

'Guilt is a terrible thing if you hide from it,' the spindlebug said. 'But if you face it, Xanth, accept it, then perhaps you can start to ease the pain you are in.'

'But how, Tweezel?' said Xanth despairingly. 'How can I face up to the terrible things I've done?'

The spindlebug crouched down on his hind quarters, and sipped at his own tea. He didn't speak for a long time, and when at last he did, his voice was croaky with emotion. 'Once, a long, long time ago,' he said, 'there was a couple – a lovely young couple – who were very close to me. *They* had to do a terrible thing . . .'

Xanth listened closely.

The spindlebug's eyes were half-closed, and he rocked backwards and forwards very slightly as he remembered a distant time.

'It all began in old

Sanctaphrax, when I was a butler in the Palace of Shadows to the Most High Academe himself. Linius Pallitax was his name, and he had a daughter, Maris. Delightful young thing she was,' he said, his eyes staring dreamily into the middle distance. 'Heavy plaits, green eyes, turned-up nose, and the most serious of expressions you ever did see on the face of a young'un . . .'

He paused and sipped at his own tea. 'Hmm, a touch more honey, I think,' he murmured. 'What do you think, Xanth?'

'It's delicious,' said Xanth, and drank a little more.

Tweezel frowned. 'One day, a sky pirate ship arrived,' he said. 'The *Galerider*, it was called, captained by a fine, if somewhat unpredictable, sky pirate by the name of Wind Jackal. I remember coming to inform my master of his imminent arrival, only to discover that he – and his son – were already there.'

'His son?' said Xanth, who was beginning to wonder where exactly the story was going.

'Aye, his son,' said Tweezel. 'Quint was his name. I remember the very first time I clapped eyes on him.' He frowned again and fixed Xanth with a long, steady gaze. 'In some ways, he was not unlike you,' he said. 'The same guilty tics plucking at his face; the same haunted look in his eyes . . .'

Xanth hung on his every word.

'Of course,' Tweezel went on, 'it all came out later. He told me the whole story,' he added, and smiled. 'I've a good ear for listening.'

'So what happened?' said Xanth.

'What happened?' Tweezel repeated. 'Oh, how cruel life can be. It transpired that, apart from his father who had been away at the time, the poor lad had lost all his family in a great and terrible fire. His mother, his five brothers, even his nanny – they had all perished in the flames. Somehow, being the youngest and smallest, he had managed to squeeze through a tight hole and had fled across the rooftops to safety.' He paused. 'He was full of guilt for being the only one to survive.'

'But he'd done nothing wrong!' Xanth blurted out.

'That's exactly what I told him,' said Tweezel. 'But I don't think he was ever able to accept it – which possibly explains what happened later . . .'

'What?' said Xanth.

'I'm coming to that,' said Tweezel calmly. 'Time passed, and Quint and Maris became friends.' He smiled. '*Close* friends. Inseparable, they were. Maris nursed her father when he became ill and Quint took up a place in the Knights' Academy. They were happy times, exciting times! I often think about old Sanctaphrax, and that long cold winter . . .' The spindle-bug's eyes closed completely, and he seemed to have fallen asleep.

'Tweezel?' said Xanth. 'Tweezel? Maris and Quint . . . What happened to them?'

The spindlebug opened his eyes and shook his huge, glassy head. 'Many, many things,' he said. 'They got married, they set sail on a sky ship captained by a brutal rogue by the name of Multinius Gobtrax . . .' He shuddered.

'And?' said Xanth, struggling to contain himself.

'They were shipwrecked,' said Tweezel simply. He took Xanth's glass and topped it up with tea. 'I never quite got to the bottom of exactly what took place out there in the skies above the Deepwoods. Quint wouldn't talk about it, and poor Maris couldn't talk about it. There was a storm, that much I know. And, in the tumultuous wind and rain, Maris gave birth to a son on board the sky ship. Then . . .' The great creature's eyes misted over. 'Oh, my poor mistress,' he said, his voice quavering with emotion. 'Even now I find it hard to think about what happened.'

'What?' said Xanth.

'They had to make a terrible decision,' said Tweezel. 'They were stranded in the middle of the Deepwoods with a new-born baby, and Gobtrax and the rest of the crew refused to take it with them. Quint and Maris both knew the young'un would never survive the journey on foot back to Undertown.'

Xanth's jaw dropped. 'What did they do?' he murmured.

'They found themselves near a woodtroll village. They knew that woodtrolls feared and distrusted sky pirates – but a foundling might just stand a chance,' said Tweezel. 'So they left the young'un there and set off for Undertown.' He shook his head. 'Maris never spoke again.'

'That's terrible,' said Xanth.

Tweezel nodded. 'The guilt, Xanth; it was the guilt that almost killed them both. I came the moment I heard that they'd made it back to Undertown. And a sorry sight they were, too. They were both half-starved and Maris had come down with a fever. Nothing but a bag of bones, she was. I found them in lodgings above a tavern – the Bloodoak Tavern, run by an avaricious old bird-creature by the name of Mother Horsefeather. Quint, by this time, was calling himself by his sky pirate name – Captain Cloud Wolf . . .'

'What did you do?' asked Xanth.

'The only thing I could do,' said Tweezel. He placed his empty glass down gently on the tray. 'I packed up my belongings and left Sanctaphrax at once. After all, since Linius Pallitax my master had died, there was precious little to keep me up there. Besides, I had known the young mistress since *she* was a baby. I nursed her back to health, though it was touch and go for a few weeks, I can tell you.'

'And Cloud Wolf?' said Xanth.

'Cloud Wolf set sail in a sky pirate ship of his own,' Tweezel explained, 'with money lent to him by Mother Horsefeather. He hated leaving Maris, but he'd promised her that if they made it back, he'd return to the Deepwoods to find their child. I think he realized what a terrible thing they'd done. Of course, Mother Horsefeather was only interested in the lucrative cargoes of timber Cloud Wolf would bring back.'

'Did he find the baby?' said Xanth.

Tweezel shook his head. 'No,' he said sadly. 'Voyage after voyage he made, each time returning with a heavily-laden ship – but without the one thing he'd actually set out for. And all the time, I could see the guilt eating away at him. It got so bad that eventually he couldn't bear to see the look in Maris's eyes when he returned empty-handed. At last, he just stayed away from the tavern.' Tweezel sighed heavily.

'When Maris finally recovered from her fever,' he went on, 'she had changed. She, too, was racked with guilt, that much was plain to see in her face. And, like Cloud Wolf, she set out to do something about it. Each night, she would leave the tavern by the backstairs and roam Undertown, looking for young'un waifs and strays with no parents of their own, and bring them home with her.

'The first one, I remember, was a young gnokgoblin whose parents had disappeared in the Mire. Then a pair of slaughterers. Then a young mobgnome lass who had had to run away from her violent uncle . . .

'And yet, despite the good she was undoubtedly doing, Maris was never truly at peace. Her terrible loss weighed too heavily on her heart, and she yearned to go back to the Deepwoods.'

'To search for her lost child?' Xanth asked.

'I thought that, at first,' said Tweezel, 'but I think there was more to it than that. I think she wanted to face up to her guilt, and ease it by trying to put right the terrible thing she'd done. If she couldn't find her own abandoned baby, then she would find and care for those abandoned by others. I think *that's* what she yearned to do.'

'And did she?' said Xanth, feeling the weight of his own guilt tugging at his heart.

'Let me finish my story,' said Tweezel, 'and you can decide for yourself.' The spindlebug took a long, slow breath that set the papery tissues of his lungs fluttering inside his chest. 'It was a cold and stormy night when we all set off – Maris, myself, and our little family of Undertown orphans, on foot . . .'

'On foot!' said Xanth, amazed.

'Certainly,' said Tweezel. 'We were in no hurry. And as we travelled, across the Mire, through the treacherous Twilight Woods – led blindfolded by a shryke-mate, Dekkel, his name – and into the Deepwoods themselves, we picked up waifs and strays every step of the way. Through woodtroll villages, slaughterer encampments and gabtroll clearings we wandered, attracting more and more young'uns wherever we went – orphans with no future, drawn to our growing band, because no one else would have them. And you should have seen Maris!' Tweezel's antennae trilled at the memory. 'She was radiant. Like a mother to them all!

'Of course, it was dangerous,' Tweezel continued, his eyes narrowing. 'The Deepwoods is a treacherous place at the best of times, even for well-armed sky pirates – though I like to think that my own considerable know-ledge of the place helped us survive. There were flesh-eating trees, bloodthirsty carnivores, slavers with wolf-packs and innumerable shryke patrols. Many was the time we had to take to the trees, or hide out in hollows, until the dangers had passed. And that's the way it would have continued if we hadn't found what we were looking for . . .'

'And what *were* you looking for?' asked Xanth, intrigued.

'A home, Xanth,' said Tweezel, a smile playing on his face. 'A home.'

'Where?'

'Can't you guess, Master Xanth?' The spindlebug trilled with pleasure. 'I remember it as if it was only yesterday. We emerged from the dark depths of the forest into the most beautiful place any of us had ever seen.

'There was a wide expanse of grassy slopes, strewn with flowers and fruit bushes, which led down to a crystal clear lake, one of three stretching out in a line. In the centre of one was a small island, the lullabee trees growing upon it filling the air with a soft, turquoise mist. To our left was a tall cliff, studded with caves and rising out of the forest like a vast, curved edifice; to our right, on the other side of the lakes, an ironwood stand, with trees so tall and straight, it seemed as if they were skewering the clear blue sky, high above our heads. The sun was shining. Birdsong filled the air, joined at once by the sound of laughter and singing as the young'uns gambolled down the grassy slopes to the water's edge.

'And when I turned to my mistress, Maris, I could see by the look in her eyes that our long trek was over. We would wander no more.'

Xanth gasped. 'It's the Free Glades, isn't it?' he exclaimed. 'You'd found the Free Glades!'

'Indeed we had,' said Tweezel. 'Indeed we had. That first night, we camped out beneath the stars. No creatures disturbed us; no tribes attacked. It was as if we were surrounded by an invisible mantle that kept us safe from danger.

'The following morning, we began to explore the area. It was, for the main part, uninhabited, but we discovered first that there were oakelves living on the island of lullabee trees, and later that a colony of spindlebugs dwelt in caverns beneath the Ironwood Glades.'

'Spindlebugs!' said Xanth, and chuckled.

'To our eternal good fortune,' said Tweezel, nodding. 'I was able to persuade them to take us in, and we stayed with them until we had constructed the first buildings which were to become New Undertown.' He paused. There were tears in his great eyes. 'And that's how it all began, Xanth. From such simple and humble beginnings . . .'

Xanth could feel a lump forming in his own throat once more.

'Soon others came, and stayed. Everyone who arrived at the Free Glades immediately felt at home. Slaughterers and woodtrolls established villages to the south, while cloddertrogs, inspired to give up their nomadic existence, started living in the eastern caves. Even passing goblins decided to stay, and settlements sprang up all along the eastern banks of the lakes . . .'

'And Maris?' asked Xanth. 'What happened to her?'

The spindlebug cocked his head to one side. 'Ah, Maris,' he said, and smiled. 'She was the mother of the Free Glades and, I think, as she saw the young'uns grow and settle down and have families of their own, she found the peace she had searched so long for. And when, some years later, she died, she was as happy as I had ever seen her – even though she had never again set eyes upon her son . . .'

'So the Free Glades made her well,' said Xanth thoughtfully, speaking as much to himself as to the great spindlebug. He stared down bleakly at the half drunk glass of tea, cold now, before him. 'She found peace,' he murmured.

'For many, the Free Glades have been a place of healing,' Tweezel broke in. 'To those who are lost or abandoned or mired in their own unfortunate pasts, it can be a place of sanctuary and rebirth.' He paused. 'Of course, the first step is to confront the guilt you carry, not hide from it . . .'

Xanth flinched. 'Is that what I've been doing?' he said. 'Hiding from my guilt?' His face paled. 'But if I face it, will I really be able to live with it? Or will it destroy me and . . ?' He fell silent, unable to put the terrible thoughts into words.

Tweezel leaned forwards. 'That,' he said, 'is what we'll find out at your Reckoning.'

·CHAPTER FOURTEEN·

THE NEW GREAT
LIBRARY

As they walked through the lush farmland that stretched before them, Rook glanced back over his shoulder. New Undertown, with its narrow cobbled streets, bustling squares and thronging lakeside, had almost disappeared from view. The mighty Lufwood Tower poked up above the gently undulating hills and the tall, irregular pinnacles of the gyle goblin colonies to the west glimmered in the morning sun – but the roofs of the Hive Huts were lost from view, and Lullabee Island to the east was no more than a distant memory.

At the top of a low hill, criss-crossed by small fields and edged with copperleaf hedges, Rook stopped, threw back his head and let out a great, joyous shout.

'Oh, Felix,' he laughed. 'I can't tell you how good it is to feel the sun on my back and the wind in my face, and to be surrounded by all this.' He spread his arms wide.

Felix laughed in turn. 'You mean sour cabbage and glimmer-onion fields?' he said.

Several low-belly goblins looked up from the field next to them, where they were pulling large red turnips, and doffed their harvest-bonnets in greeting.

'No,' said Rook. 'I mean . . . well, yes, *all* of it. The Free Glades, all around us. Isn't it wonderful!'

'Well, it certainly beats Screetown, I'll give you that,' said Felix. 'Now, if you've quite finished disturbing the peace, let's get a move on, or we'll never get to Lake Landing!'

They set off again down the hill. Ahead of them, the three banderbears – who had out-paced them – were waiting patiently for their two friends to catch up. They seemed distracted, Rook noticed, their small ears quivering and their noses twitching as they cast longing glances at the Deepwoods' treeline far in the distance.

'Wuh-woolah, weeg wullaah!' Rook called as he approached. *Forgive me, friends, my feet are slow, but my heart is light!*

'Wella-goleema. Weg-wuh,' Wumeru replied, turning from looking into the distance and falling into step. *It's good you are recovered.* 'Wug-wurra-wuh. Wuh-leera,' she yodelled softly in his ear. *We will wait for you as long as you need us, friend.*

Ahead of them, to the east, the impenetrable wall of thorn-oaks that surrounded the mysterious Waif Glen stood out, dark blue and black against the bright cloud-flecked sky. They continued past fields of gladewheat and blue barley swaying in the breeze before, once more, coming to a halt. Before them, the lake shimmered in the morning sun, the huge silhouette of the Ironwood Glade on its far shore mirrored in its glassy surface.

'It takes my breath away,' said Rook. 'It always did.'

'It's spectacular,' replied Felix, 'I'll give you that.'

To the east, the woodtroll villages in their clumps of lufwood trees were stirring. A long line of hammelhorn carts, laden with logs, was already snaking out from the timber yards in their midst and making for the near shore of the Great Lake and the tall tower on the large wooden jetty which jutted out into its waters.

'Lake Landing,' breathed Rook as he gazed down at the Librarian Knights' Academy, where he had learned about the secrets of sky-flight so long ago – or so it seemed to him. 'It's hardly changed . . .' he began. 'But what's that?'

Felix followed his friend's gaze and smiled. 'I was wondering when you'd notice,' he said. '*That* is my father's pride and joy. The new Great Library of the Free Glades – or rather, it will be when it's finished.'

Rook stared at the massive construction, wondering how on earth he had failed to see it immediately. It was tall and round and had been built on the end of a wooden pier directly opposite Lake Landing. Although clearly, as Felix had pointed out, there was still work to be done, with scaffolding enclosing its upper reaches, the library was already an impressive building. What was more, it looked familiar.

'But I've seen this somewhere before,' said Rook.

'Not another of your cocoon dreams, Rook,' said Felix, with a smile.

Rook shook his head. He'd told Felix about the strange dreams he'd had on Lullabee Island as they'd walked, but this wasn't one of them.

'No,' he said. 'This building is an exact copy of the Great Library of old Sanctaphrax! I remember seeing drawings of it on barkscrolls . . .'

'Barkscrolls, eh?' said Felix. 'Once a librarian, always a librarian, eh?' He nudged his friend. 'Well, come on if you're coming. My father's waiting to see you.'

As Rook and the banderbears followed Felix down the track leading to the Great Lake, the already massive building grew larger. The main circular wall stood some eighty strides or so tall. Above it, the roof soared up into the air like a vast pleated cone, with flying buttresses and jutting gantries sticking out from it on all sides, their horizontal platforms constructed as landing-decks for the skycraft which buzzed all round.

At first sight, with the noise and the bustle, the whole area looked like one of utter chaos. But as Rook stared, he could see that there was an order to everything taking place, with everyone working together, all under the bellowed commands of the goblin foremen and librarian overseers.

From the south-east, the long line of hammelhorn carts, driven by woodtrolls and laden with felled trees, came trundling down the dirt track from the timber yards to the lakeside, where they deposited their loads in huge piles. Cloddertrogs and flat-head goblins were stripping the branches and bark from them and sawing the logs into broad planks. Gnokgoblin tilers crawled over the great wooden roof, hammering lufwood and leadwood shingles into place in neat lines and intricate patterns. Slaughterers and mobgnomes with cranes were tying ropes round the bundles of prepared timber and winching them up to the top, where joiners and carpenters were constructing the gantries.

'It's amazing,' Rook gasped, as he strode closer. 'There's so many of them, and they're working so quickly.'

'Yes, when these Freegladers set about building something, they don't waste any time,' said Felix, obviously impressed. 'You should see my father, Rook. I've never seen the old barkworm happier! Talking of whom . . .'

They were approaching the huge ironwood doors of the new library, and the din of hammering, sawing and shouted commands up above was almost deafening. The entrance was full of Undertowners, laughing and joking and congratulating one another.

'You made it, Hodluff!' exclaimed a gnokgoblin, clapping a cloddertrog on the back. 'I lost sight of you at the lufwood mount. Are your young'uns safe?'

'Yes, Sky be praised,' said the cloddertrog. 'We've all settled in a beautiful cave, and we've come to hand over our barkscrolls.'

'Me, too!' laughed the gnokgoblin joyfully.

In the midst of the throng stood the portly figure of Fenbrus Lodd himself, the High Librarian, a huge smile on his heavily bearded face.

'Friends, friends!' he was booming. 'Welcome to the new Great Library. Find a librarian and hand over your barkscrolls for cataloguing, and may Earth and Sky bless you all!'

Rook approached him and gave a short, respectful bow. 'Rook Barkwater, librarian knight,' he said. 'Reporting for duty.'

'Ah, Rook, my boy,' said Fenbrus, his eyes lighting up. 'So it is, so it is – and looking so much better, I'm pleased to see.'

'Oh, I am better, sir,' said Rook. 'Fully recovered.'

'Excellent,' said Fenbrus. 'Then you can begin straight away. As you can see, we have a steady stream of barkscrolls returning to us, all needing to be catalogued . . .'

'But,' began Rook, 'I was hoping to return to sky-flight, with the librarian knights . . .'

Fenbrus frowned. 'But I understood that you lost your skycraft in old Undertown,' he said.

Rook nodded, a lump coming to his throat as he remembered the *Stormhornet* lying smashed in the rubble of Screetown.

'Then you'll have to speak to Oakley Gruffbark the woodmaster about carving a new one. He's busy carving a likeness of yours truly up above the main entrance as we speak . . . In the meantime, you can be of use here in the library.' He beamed happily. 'Isn't it magnificent?'

Rook nodded.

'Speaking of which, Rook,' said Fenbrus Lodd. 'I hope the barkscroll *you* were entrusted with is safe.'

Rook reached inside his shirt, and pulled out the leather pouch into which he'd pushed the roll of parchment. He held it out.

'Excellent,' said Fenbrus, giving it a loving examination. '*Customs and Practices Encountered in Deepwoods Villages*. Perhaps you'd like to start by cataloguing it yourself,' he said. 'It'll give you a chance to appreciate what we've built here.'

Rook nodded a little reluctantly. Library cataloguing was not what he'd had in mind when he left Undertown for the Free Glades – though he was, it was true, intrigued to see the building beyond the entrance he was standing in.

As he entered the cavernous, vaulted chamber of the new Great Library, Rook's heart missed a beat. It was even more impressive from within than without. Tall tree-pillars stood in lines, hundreds in total and each one with a little plaque at its base. Rook looked up into the shadowy roof space, where the tree-pillars divided and sub-divided into branchlike sections, each one housing a different category. This was where the scrolls were stored, high up in the well-ventilated, pest-free upper reaches.

The whole place was a hive of activity. At ground level, and up on raised platforms around the walls, research was already in progress, with bent-backed academics poring over treatises and scrolls and labour-ing over work of their own. In the central areas, the activity was more frenetic, with innumerable librarians scaling the tree-pillars, winching themselves along the branches in their hanging-baskets and loading up the clusters of leather tubes where the individual barkscrolls were stored.

Taking his cue from the signposts dotted about at the junctions, Rook hurried to the far side of the library where, in the Deepwoods' section, he found a tree-pillar with a plaque marked *Social Behaviour*. He started climbing, taking the rungs two at a time, right up to where the first fork occurred. Already, he was high above the library floor. He forced himself not to look down.

Historical/Legendary were the words on each of the forks. He took the former. *Past* and *Present* were the next choices. He dithered for a moment, before taking *Present*. Then *Societal* and *Individual*. Then *Nocturnal* and *Diurnal* ... And so it went on, defining and redefining the treatise in his hand increasingly specifically. When the forking branches became too thin and weak to support his weight, he climbed into one of the hanging-baskets and, grabbing a rope, winched himself across.

He was now high in the upper rafters of the huge domed roof and could feel a gentle, modulated breeze on his face. All around him, the barkscrolls in their holders rustled like leaves in a forest. Finally, he arrived at the woodgrape-like bunch of leather tubes.

Most were still empty, though a couple had already been stuffed full with scrolls. Just to make certain he had found the right place, Rook pulled one out and inspected it. *'Practices and Customs in Deepwood Village Life,'* he read. The subject matter was almost identical.

He had done it!

Pushing his own scroll into the adjacent tube, he began the long descent to the ground. To his surprise, he had found the whole process exhilarating, and when he reached the floor, his heart was racing.

'My word, lad, that was quick,' said Fenbrus Lodd as he arrived back. 'I can see you're going to make a first-rate scroll-seeker!'

Rook smiled. 'I suppose so,' he said quietly. 'Until I can fly again.'

'Yes, well, go and find Garulus Lexis,' Fenbrus went on. 'He'll assign you a sleeping-cabin in the upper gantries. They've just been completed. Quite spectacular views and you'll be able to watch your knight friends on sky patrol.' He paused and gazed over Rook's shoulder. 'Are those banderbears with *you*?'

'Yes,' said Rook, looking across at his three shaggy friends standing waiting for him, their ears fluttering as they listened to what was being said. 'They've been with me ever since I became a librarian knight . . .'

'That's as may be,' said Fenbrus sternly. 'But bander-bears are creatures of the forest. They certainly don't belong in a library. Surely you can see that?'

Rook noticed the banderbears' eyes light up. Wumeru stepped towards them, her great clawed arm raised.

'Wulla-weera. Wuh,' she yodelled. *We hear the Deepwoods calling us, yet for you we would stay, friend.*

Rook trembled. 'You brought me here,' he said to Wumeru. 'I am indebted to you – to *all* of you. You've done so much for me. Now, it is plain that I must do something for you . . . Let you leave . . . Oh, Wumeru!' he cried, and fell into the great creature's warm, mossy embrace.

'Loomah-weera, wuh,' the banderbear replied, scratching his back gently with her claws. 'Wurra-moolah-wuh.' *Farewell, my friend. The moon will shine on our friendship for ever.*

'Wuh. Uralowa, wuh-wuh!' the others chorused. *You shall sleep in the nest of our hearts, he who took the poison-stick. Farewell!*

Tears in his eyes, Rook watched as the three great shambling banderbears left the library behind them. Weeg, with the great scar across his shoulder; Wuralo, with her curious facial markings, whom he had once rescued from the Foundry Glades, and Wumeru – dear Wumeru; the banderbear he had first befriended all that time ago in the Deepwoods. How he loved all of them. Now they were going. Rook swallowed away the painful lump in his throat and waved.

'Farewell,' he called. 'Farewell!'

'I think it's time *I* was heading off as well,' came a voice from his left. 'Back to New Undertown.'

Rook spun round to see Felix lurking in the shadows behind the great ironwood doors. Fenbrus had his back to them and was surrounded by a fresh crowd of happy Undertowners.

'What are you doing there?' Rook hissed.

'Didn't want my father to see me,' said Felix. 'He keeps trying to rope me into working in this boring old library of his. Says I need to settle down. Me! Settle down!' He laughed and edged towards the door. 'Say hello to the old barkworm from me, and tell him that his ever-loving son is busy with his ghosts and sky pirate friends in New Undertown.'

'But Felix!' protested Rook. 'Do you have to leave right now?'

'Sorry, Rook.' Felix shrugged his shoulders and grinned. 'Said I'd meet Deadbolt at the Bloodoak. Must dash! Have fun up there in the rafters!' he laughed, and with that he was gone.

Rook turned and wandered back into the library, all of a sudden feeling very alone. His banderbear friends had left, returning to a life in the Deepwoods. Now Felix, too, had gone – back to the bustle of New Undertown. And here he was, Rook Barkwater, on his own.

He looked up. The reading gantries were crowded with librarians; the rafters above, full of baskets swinging backwards and forwards. And as he looked, Rook knew in his heart of hearts that this wasn't the life for him, and never could be. No, he needed to get out there, into the clear, sunlit air of the Free Glades.

Mind made up, he turned and strode through the library doorway. Pausing in front of the lufwood scaffolding outside, Rook peered up and squinted. And sure enough, high above his head was the familiar short, stocky figure of Oakley Gruffbark, the master carver who had taught him everything he knew about carving a skycraft.

Crouched down on a narrow platform laid out across the scaffolding, a chisel and mallet in his hands, the old woodtroll was busy carving a massive likeness of Fenbrus Lodd from a single block of wood. Although only half complete, the head – with its corkscrew hair, thick beard and intense stare – was already unmistakable.

Pausing just for a moment to catch his breath, Rook began scaling the scaffolding that criss-crossed its way up the front of the building. Compared with the roof-beams and swinging baskets, climbing the lufwood scaffolding was easy.

As he emerged on the platform beside Oakley, the woodtroll turned. His bright orange hair, twisted into the traditional tufts Rook remembered so well, was flecked with grey and white now. Otherwise, he looked no different. Neither, it seemed, did Rook, for Oakley recognized him at once.

'Rook Barkwater of the *Stormhornet*!' he cried. 'I never forget an apprentice, or their skycraft. Well, I declare! And how is life treating you, lad?'

'All right,' said Rook, 'although I'm afraid I lost the *Stormhornet* on patrol over old Undertown.'

The woodtroll tutted sympathetically. 'I'm sorry to hear that. It's a terrible loss,' he said softly. 'Like losing a part of your self.'

'Yes,' said Rook, tears welling up in his eyes at the memory.

Oakley laid his tools down, turned his back on Fenbrus Lodd's half-finished beard and clamped his large, leathery hands around Rook's shoulders.

'Now, tell me truthfully,' he said, looking deep into Rook's eyes. 'A loss like that takes time to get over. Do you think you're ready to start carving a new skycraft?'

'Yes, yes,' said Rook. 'I've made up my mind. I want to return to the skies as soon as possible.'

Oakley nodded. 'Well, Rook, you know what you have to do. There are no short cuts. You must go to the timber yards and select for yourself a large piece of sumpwood. Choose carefully and think long and hard before you first put your chisel to the wood, because that's the thing with carving – it can't be rushed. It has to . . .'

'Come from the heart,' Rook finished for him.

'Precisely,' said Oakley. 'You know the score, Rook Barkwater.' He gestured back at the carving of Fenbrus. 'With a bit of luck I should be finished with the High Librarian here in the next week or so. I'll come and look in on you then, and see how you're doing.'

'Thank you,' said Rook. 'I'll start straight away!'

*

Two weeks later, Rook's carving was not going well. Although he had selected the best, finest-grained piece of sumpwood he could find in the woodtroll timber yards, he could still not decide what to carve. Each time he put his chisel to the wood and raised the mallet, his mind was filled with images of the stormhornet. And yet try as he might, he couldn't see the curves and arches of a stormhornet – or any other creature – in this piece of sumpwood. And if he couldn't carve the prow, then he couldn't make a skycraft. And if he couldn't make his own personal skycraft, then he couldn't fly. And if he couldn't fly, then he couldn't rejoin the librarian knights. He was stuck staring at this lump of wood – and there was no sign of Oakley Gruffbark.

Finally, Rook left the workshop in the timber yards and returned to the library to look for him. He found the old woodtroll still hard at work on his carving, high above the ironwood doors of the new Great Library. Not only was the High Librarian's beard finely chiselled and minutely rendered, but now the head and shoulders had outstretched arms and lovingly carved fingers.

'Can't help it, lad,' said Oakley, catching the disappointment in Rook's eyes when he told him he was too busy to help him. 'The wood is our master. It tells us what lies within. And this here wood demanded arms held out in greeting.' He stroking the carving gently. 'And two solid legs as well before I'm finished.'

Rook sighed. He knew that in the meantime, he had no choice. He reported back to the High Librarian, who was most understanding.

'The main thing is to keep busy,' Fenbrus said, patting him on the back. 'You're a fine scroll-seeker, Rook – just made for the roof timbers!'

So Rook had returned to cataloguing and fetching barkscrolls high up in the new library, frustrated and longing more than ever to take to the sky outside.

It was late one cool, sunny evening when, following yet another long day's filing, Rook was walking down the wooden jetty at Lake Landing. Halfway along, he paused, crossed to the side and leaned over the balustrade, looking at the rippled water below him.

It wasn't that he was unhappy at the library. He enjoyed working with the scrolls, reading for long hours on the platforms and mastering the baskets until he could reach even the farthest corners of the high dome. It was just that he missed sky-flight so much. Each evening, as the librarian knights returned from patrol, he'd see them from his sleeping-cabin – Varis and the Professors of Light and Darkness at the heads of their squadrons. And he'd feel his heart breaking as they swooped down through the air. He longed to join them – but the carving simply wouldn't come.

'Hey, Rook!' called a voice from up ahead, breaking into his thoughts. 'Is that you?'

Rook looked over to see the familiar, stout figure of his old friend Stob Lummus silhouetted against the sinking sun. He acknowledged him with a wave, but stayed where he was. It was Stob who came to him, stopping beside him and looking out across the water.

'Haven't seen you for a while, Rook,' he said at length.

'Keeping you pretty busy at the new Great Library, I hear. Nearly all the barkscrolls have been handed back. A wonderful achievement, I must say! You must be very proud.'

Rook nodded. 'I am, Stob. But what I really want is to fly again.'

Stob chuckled. 'Do you remember *my* first attempt at flight?' he said. 'Ended up steering the old *Hammelhorn* straight into an ironwood pine. Just over there, if I remember correctly. I was never really cut out for sky-flight.' He paused. 'I enjoy what I do now . . .'

'You're Parsimmon's assistant, aren't you?' said Rook. 'Keeping all those young apprentice knights in order, I hope.'

Stob laughed again. 'Doing my best, Rook,' he replied.

There was another long pause. Rook liked Stob, but he was tired and fed up and didn't feel much like talking.

'Talking of apprentice knights, looks like our old classmate, Xanth, is getting his come-uppance,' said Stob finally. 'I never trusted him. Something deceitful in his eyes . . .'

Rook shrugged. 'I feel sorry for him. All the librarians tell such terrible stories about him, but I only remember him as an apprentice here at Lake Landing . . .'

'It'll all be sorted out at the Reckoning,' said Stob. 'The Free Glades will be better off without his sort.'

They stared out across the lake in silence.

'I was really sorry to hear about Magda,' said Stob, breaking into the stillness again. 'Now she *was* a true friend. I'll miss her.'

'Me, too,' said Rook glumly. 'Looks like it's just you

and me now, Stob – and neither of us flying. Fine librarian knights *we* turned out to be!'

The sun dropped down beneath the horizon, and the pink and orange light spread out across the surface of the lake like shimmering oil. The wind dropped. The water fell still. Out of the silence, Rook heard a low humming sound, and turned to see the red and black striped body of a stormhornet flying low over the lake.

'A stormhornet!' said Stob, breaking the silence. 'Wasn't that . . ?'

'Yes, thanks for reminding me,' said Rook. He turned to his erstwhile friend, seeing him properly for the first time. He had grown paunchy, and deep lines were etched into his face down the sides of his mouth. Yet he looked happy for all that – a contented schoolmaster. 'Oh, Stob,' he groaned. 'How I envy you!'

'*You* envy *me*?' said Stob, surprised.

'Yes,' said Rook. 'You're obviously happy teaching here at Lake Landing – whereas I . . .' He paused.

'You want to fly again,' said Stob. 'Yes, I know, you told me. So what's stopping you?'

Rook brought his fist down on the balustrade in frustration. 'Everything, Stob! Everything! I can't carve another skycraft, it just won't come. And Oakley Gruffbark can't help me. And Fenbrus Lodd – he wants me to stay at the library. I'm stuck there from dawn till dusk . . .'

Just then, echoing across the water, came the insistent sound of trumpeting tilder horns, followed by the clatter and clomp of heavy footfalls. Rook looked up. There, bathed in lantern light and golden twilight glow, he saw

a great troop of prowlgrins galloping along the edge of
the lake. Surcoats flapped and pennants fluttered and
the polished armour of the riders glinted brightly.

'Earth and Sky,' Rook breathed. 'Who are *they*?'

Stob looked at him surprised. 'You really don't get out
much, do you?' he said. 'They're the Freeglade Lancers,
of course. That's the dusk patrol. Make a pretty fine
spectacle in this light, don't you think?'

'The Freeglade Lancers,' Rook repeated, awestruck.
'Heroes of the Battle of Lufwood Mount . . .'

Stob looked at his friend. 'Rook, are you feeling all
right?' he asked, concern plain on his plump features.

'They're magnificent!' said Rook. 'Magnificent!'

CHAPTER FIFTEEN

CHINQUIX

Late the following morning, Rook set off. He had swapped his librarian robes for the green leather flight-suit of a librarian knight, a kit-bag strapped to his shoulders and his sword at his side. All round him, as the sun rose higher in the sky, it was business as usual on the banks of the Great Lake. Cloddertrogs and mobgnomes, flat-heads and slaughterers; they were all hard at work, endeavouring to put the finishing touches to the magnificent new library before the current spell of good weather broke.

Rook, however, was leaving it all behind. He'd spoken to Felix the night before, and Fenbrus Lodd earlier that morning. Felix had been his usual self, full of enthusiasm and encouragement.

'Freeglade Lancers, eh, Rook?' he'd laughed. 'Not bad for a bunch of tree hoppers, and they *did* get us out of a tight spot at Lufwood Mount. Good luck to you!' He'd raised his tankard to the rest of the regulars in the New Bloodoak. 'To Rook's new career!'

Fenbrus Lodd's response, of course, had been quite different. The High Librarian had tried to persuade him to stay – though there was nothing he could say to change Rook's mind. There was a jaunty spring now in the young librarian knight's step, a joyful whistled tune on his lips and, as he strode off along the lakeside, his spirits soared.

He passed the lines of woodtrolls on hammelhorn carts, still arriving from the east with their cargoes of felled trees, and departing the same way with rubble and rocks and off-cuts of timber.

Gradually, the sounds of hammering and drilling, carving and sawing, the shouts and the cries, all faded away. Water splashed softly against the muddy banks where reed-ducks and rockswans nested, and sleek young fromp-pups playfully scampered and tumbled.

Reaching a narrow track, Rook left the water's edge and headed up through windgorse and woodfurze towards the Ironwood Glade. Far ahead, he could see its dark, imposing trees swaying gently in the breeze and heard the distant sound of their needle-like leaves hissing like running water.

Soon after, the undulating land went down into a deep dip and, with the thorny shrubs rising up all round him, the glade disappeared from view, the hissing stopped and another sound filled the air – the sound of happily singing voices. Rook continued and, as he rounded a corner in the twisting track, he saw a large band of gyle goblins before him, heavy pails of pink honey swinging from their clenched fists, coming from the opposite direction.

'Morning, Freeglader,' the gyle goblins greeted him warmly as they drew nearer.

'Good morning, Freegladers,' said Rook, returning their greeting with a smile.

The gyle goblins clustered round him and a couple of them politely offered him some of their raw honey to drink.

'We prefer it boiled up in our mother's cooking-pots,' said one. 'Nice 'n' warm.'

'But you might like it as it is,' said another, offering him a beakerful. 'Sweet and refreshing.'

Rook took the beaker and sipped at the pink liquid. It was indeed delicious – and far more refreshing than he would have thought possible. 'Thank you, thank you,' he said, grinning at the gyle goblins each in turn. 'It's marvellous.'

'You're most welcome, friend,' came the reply.

The gyle goblins continued on their way and Rook waved after them. Alone once more, he turned and resumed his journey with renewed energy and, as he climbed the slope on the far side of the dip, his thoughts returned to Fenbrus Lodd and the meeting they'd had early that morning.

'You're absolutely sure this is what you want to do,' the High Librarian had pressed him. The pair of them had been standing in Fenbrus Lodd's study inside the library, the hushed purr of academic activity softly echoing all about them. 'The Freeglade Lancers do an excellent job patrolling our borders, but they're a rough and ready lot, you know.'

Rook had laughed. 'Unlike the librarian knights, you mean?' he said.

'Yes, well, we've got some pretty interesting characters in our ranks as well, I grant you,' Fenbrus had said. 'But that aside, Rook, there's a great future waiting for you here in the Great Library if you would only accept it. You've got the skills to make a superb librarian; the perseverance, the agility and accuracy – why only yesterday, my assistant Garulus Lexis was saying what a terrific start you've already made as a scroll-seeker.' His brow had furrowed as he surveyed the youth warmly. 'The Great Library *needs* bright young academics like you, Rook.'

'I . . . I'm very flattered, sir,' Rook had said, his cheeks reddening, 'really I am. And I love the library, of course,' he'd added, looking out through the study door at the magnificent roof timbers, bedecked with hanging barkscrolls. 'And yet, I . . . I need something else . . . I'm a librarian knight who has lost his skycraft. Perhaps by joining the lancers I can serve not only the librarians but all Freegladers.'

'By Earth and Sky, you sound just like Felix,' Fenbrus had said, his eyes twinkling. 'Can't seem to get him to leave the ghosts and join us in the Great Library. But I had such high hopes of *you*, my lad. Still,' he'd said, shaking his head resignedly, 'I can see I'm not going to change your mind.' And he'd reached out, seized Rook by the hand and pumped it heartily up and down. 'I shall miss you, lad, but I wish you all the very best. The library's loss is the Freeglade Lancers' gain. And remember, there'll always be a welcome for you back here at the library, any time you choose to return. Any time at all!'

'Thank you, sir,' Rook had said and was about to leave, when Fenbrus had told him to wait just a moment longer.

He'd hurried over to his desk, pulled a drawer open and rummaged about noisily inside it, returning a moment later with a roll of parchment, which he'd handed over. Rook had looked at it, curious.

'Open it up, lad,' Fenbrus had said, his eyes gleaming excitedly. 'Given your chosen career, I think you might find it quite helpful.'

'*On the Husbandry of Prowlgrins*,' Rook had read out loud. '*A treatise by . . .*' He'd stopped, then smiled. '*Fenbrus Lodd* . . . So this is . . .'

'My very first treatise, that's right, Rook,' Fenbrus had said. 'Keep it safe and return it to me one day – possibly with additions of your own. After all, you did say you enjoyed treatise work. And if you're not going to be a scroll-seeker, then we'll get you working as a scroll-*writer*, eh?

Go on, then. Get out, before I change my mind and have you assigned to quill-sharpening duty.'

The High Librarian had sounded gruff, but Rook had noticed the moistness in his eyes. Despite his bluster and stern manner, Fenbrus Lodd has a kind heart, Rook thought, as he struggled up the overgrown slope – I wonder why he never lets his own son see it?

Reaching the top of a ridge at last – red-faced and out of breath – he looked up and saw the towering trees of the Ironwood Glade just before him. He stepped forwards and entered the huge stand of trees. It was like entering a gigantic, windowless hall. The temperature dropped and the sounds of the Free Glades outside became muffled.

Stepping gingerly over the glade floor, his feet sinking into the thick mattress of pine needles, Rook looked down. Somewhere far below him lay the Gardens of Light, where Xanth Filatine was being held.

Poor Xanth, he thought. Nobody seemed to have a good word to say about him, and yet ... No, it was no good. Try as he might, Rook couldn't remember anything about his friend's betrayal so long ago.

From high above his head, as he plunged deeper into the shadow-filled coolness of the glade, he heard sounds – the soft whinnying of countless prowlgrins; the low buzz of voices. And looking up into the tall trees, their huge branches criss-crossing, not unlike the roofbeams of the library, he saw that he was below the Prowlgrin Roosts. Hundreds of the creatures perched overhead – snuffling, nuzzling, resting and preening; some gnawing on bones, some wandering from branch to branch. And amongst them in the half-light, Rook could just make out individuals, with chequered green and white at their necks and red figures emblazoned on their chests.

'The Freeglade Lancers,' Rook murmured.

He started up the nearest ironwood pine, finding handholds and footholds in the rough bark and climbing at an angle, crossing from branch to branch, as he made his way up the close-growing trees. It was just like climbing the roof timbers at the new Great Library, only on an altogether bigger scale. Soon, he was far above the ground and all around him, in place of barkscrolls, were prowlgrins of all ages and sizes.

They ambled this way and that freely, purring contentedly as they grazed on the tilder-carcasses which hung from heavy hooks, and sometimes snorting loudly as, in a sudden display of activity, they launched off from one branch with their powerful back legs and grasped hold of the next with the long claws of their stubby forelegs. Clearly used to the lancers in their midst, none of them paid Rook any attention.

Nor, at first, did the lancers themselves. Those who were not asleep in hammocks, slung from the overhead branches, were busy with their duties. Some sat cross-legged, sharpening their ironwood lances with notched jag-knives. Some polished their breast-plates and limb-guards with tilder grease. Others – in twos and threes – were grooming their prowlgrins, brushing their fur and oiling their great paws.

Most of them, Rook noticed, were gnokgoblins, small,

wiry creatures whose close relationship with the great
roosting beasts was similar to that of the gyle goblins
and spindlebugs in the Gardens of Light below. But there
were a smattering of others – mobgnomes, lop-eared
goblins, slaughterers . . . It was, in fact, a slaughterer
who first noticed Rook. Looking up from the broken
harness he was busy repairing, he caught sight of the
young librarian.

'Well, well, if it isn't a librarian knight,' he said. 'And
what can we humble lancers do for you?'

Others looked round to see who their comrade was
talking to.

'Greetings, Freeglader,' Rook said. 'If you could take
me to see your captain . . .'

'Captain, eh?' said one of the gnokgoblins. 'And what
would you be wanting with him?'

'Certainly don't get many librarian knights around
here,' said his companion. 'I thought you lot preferred
being up in the sky.'

''S safer up there, innit?' said the first gnokgoblin,
raising his eyebrows and provoking laughter from the
others.

Rook's face reddened. 'I . . . I want . . . I wanted . . .' he
stammered.

'Spit it out, lad,' said the slaughterer. 'Stone me, I
thought you librarian knights were meant to be good
with words – what with all them barkscrolls and that . . .'

'Come on, now, you lot, cut it out,' came a gruff voice.

'Captain Welt,' said two of the gnokgoblins as one.

Rook looked round to see a short yet heavily-built

gnokgoblin swinging down on a rope from a higher branch and landing squarely beside him. He had dark eyes, a low brow and a deep scar that crossed his cheek, clearly made by the knife that had left one of his ears half the size of the other.

'In't there something useful you could be getting on with, eh, Grist, Worp, Trabbis?' he asked, turning from one gnokgoblin to the other, 'rather than joshing the lad here? And as for you, Ligger,' he added, turning to the slaughterer, 'I distinctly remember telling you to skin those tilders before the prowlgrins got their teeth into them. We need the pelts!'

'Yes, Captain. Sorry, Captain, sir,' said Ligger, and hurried off.

The gnokgoblin captain turned to Rook. 'Well, son?' he said. 'Why *are* you here?'

The gnokgoblins busied themselves, while listening closely.

'I want to join the Freeglade Lancers,' Rook replied, trying to ignore the smirks of the gnokgoblins watching and listening from the surrounding branches.

'Do you now?' said the captain. 'Can you ride?'

'I . . . I have ridden a prowlgrin before, sir,' said Rook. 'I'm sure, with a little practice . . .'

'Practice!' the captain snorted. 'I'm sure with a little practice, *I* could fly a skycraft, but that wouldn't make me a librarian knight. What makes you think you could make it as a Freeglade Lancer?'

'It's just that . . . well . . .' Rook began, his face falling. 'I lost my skycraft – crashed over Screetown – and I can't seem to carve a new one, and I've been stuck in the library in the meantime. And . . . and then I saw you out on patrol the other evening. And I talked to Felix about it, and *he* said . . .'

'Felix?' said Captain Welt, his good ear twitching. 'Felix *Lodd*?'

'Yes, sir,' said Rook.

'Felix Lodd of the Ghosts of Undertown?'

Rook nodded. 'Felix said I could do a lot worse than join the Freeglade Lancers, especially after what you did at the Battle of Lufwood Mount.'

'Did he now?' said the captain, nodding sagely. Behind him, Rook could hear the eavesdropping gnokgoblins murmuring to one another. They were all clearly impressed.

'Well, why didn't you say so before?' said Captain Welt. 'Any friend of Felix Lodd is welcome to join us, and Sky knows we could do with new riders. We lost a lot of good lancers at the lufwood mount.' He shook his head for a moment, then reached forward and slapped Rook on the back. 'String your hammock up over there,' he said. 'Grist and Worp'll sort you out – and report to me tomorrow morning at eight hours. Understood, Lancer?'

'Understood, sir,' said Rook happily.

Rook slept well. The cool night air suited him so much better than the stuffy atmosphere inside a sleeping cabin; it always had. He was woken at sunrise by Ligger the slaughterer, who had prepared a breakfast of smoked rashers of tilder and pine-hen eggs for himself, Rook, and the three gnokgoblins, Grist, Worp and Trabbis. The five of them were soon hunkered down on the broad branch, tucking in.

'So, Worp tells me you're an Undertowner,' Grist was saying, as he chewed the salty fried meat.

'I was brought up in the Great Library in the sewers of old Undertown,' Rook nodded. 'But I was born out here in the Deepwoods, so I'm told.'

'Told?' said Worp. 'Don't you know?'

'Let the lad enjoy his breakfast in peace,' Ligger interrupted, and gave Rook a nudge. 'Don't mind them. Gnokgoblins are nosy – you can tell that just by looking at them!'

The three gnokgoblins laughed so hard, Rook thought they might fall off the branch if they weren't careful.

'It's all right,' he reassured Ligger. 'I don't mind. I'm an orphan. My parents were killed by slavers when I was little, and the librarians took me in and raised me.'

'Undertowner, librarian, gnokgoblin or slaughterer – it's all the same,' said Worp, wiping his mouth on his sleeve. 'We're all Freegladers now.' The others all nodded. 'Though for a moment back there, I didn't think we'd make it,' he said quietly.

'You were at the Battle of Lufwood Mount?' asked Rook, putting down his plate.

'We all were,' said Ligger.

'We lost some good lancers that day,' said Grist, shaking his head grimly.

'Them shrykes had the frenzy upon them,' said Worp and shuddered. 'The hunger . . .'

'If the roost-mother hadn't been killed, we'd have lost a whole load more,' said Trabbis.

'You're not wrong there,' said Worp and the others nodded earnestly.

'I saw it happen,' Ligger said, 'just as Vanquix and me made it through to the Undertowners' lines. Never saw the like of it in all my days. This young lad stepped up – shaved head, big flash-looking sword. Sliced her head off in one blow, he did! Right in front of us. The whole shryke flock just went crazy – turned and started attacking each other.' He shuddered at the memory of it. 'So where were you?' Worp asked Rook. 'Head in the clouds?'

'Well, sort of,' said Rook, smiling. 'But not in the way you mean . . . I'd been struck by a sepia storm, way out in the Edgelands. I was half dead. My banderbear friends took me away from the mount before the actual battle began. They made their own way to the Free Glades, taking it in turns to carry me. I remember very little about it . . .'

'A friend of banderbears, eh?' said Ligger, obviously impressed.

'Fine, noble creatures,' the gnokgoblins were all agreeing, when all at once a tilder horn sounded, the rasping cry echoing round the glade.

'Eight hours already,' said Ligger. 'Time to muster.'

The gnokgoblins hurriedly finished the rest of their breakfast and drained their mugs. Ligger grabbed Rook by the arm.

'Come on,' he said. 'You've got an appointment with Captain Welt.'

The next two weeks were among the most challenging of Rook's life. Despite his training as a librarian knight, nothing could have prepared him for what followed. Instead of the elegant arts of ropecraft, sail-setting and flight practice, Rook learned the bone-crunching techniques of branch-riding and iron-wood jousting.

Gripping on to a slender lower branch with his legs, and dodging the incoming iron-wood pine-cones, he had to remain in position as the branch was bounced up and down by ropes, tugged and jerked by bellowing lancers. Time and again he was unseated, and fell down onto the soft pine needles below, only to climb back onto the branch

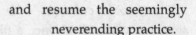

and resume the seemingly neverending practice.

And as if that wasn't bad enough, every day there were the endless tilts at the quintain, with the heavy ironwood lance clasped under one arm while the other was strapped to his side. Suspended from a branch in a narrow rope-swing and pushed, Rook swung to and fro, hitting the target and being hit in equal measure by the quintain's pivoting padded arm. At night – despite the others sniggering at the bookish former librarian in their midst – he read from Fenbrus Lodd's treatise, soaking up every word and learning all about the prowlgrins he had yet to ride.

In the third week, he was introduced to the creatures

at last and instructed how to clean and groom them, how to file their claws and oil their leathery feet. He patted them on the sides of their great heads and tickled them with his fingertips, just the way the treatise had taught him to. He learned about tack; the harnesses, saddles and reins, and the heavy bits that were held between their great, gaping mouths which enabled them to be controlled.

Ligger and the gnokgoblins all had prowlgrins of their own, on whom they lavished great care and attention. They were tame – sleek grey, brown, orange and black creatures who had formed strong bonds with their riders. But there were also others – some young and unbroken; others ownerless since the loss of their Freeglader riders. These, Rook and the other new recruits looked after. It was at the end of that third week that Captain Welt himself came up to Rook at the close of yet another gruelling day.

'I've had my eye on you, Rook Barkwater,' he said. 'You're a quick learner and no mistake. I think the time's come for you to choose a prowlgrin of your own. Ligger,' he said, turning to the slaughterer. 'Take him with you to the central-corral. Tomorrow, he'll ride beside you on patrol.'

'Thank you, sir,' said Rook, breaking into a broad smile. It was the moment he'd been waiting for.

He and Ligger set off at once, cutting through the Ironwood Glade, towards the great central roost, chatting excitedly as they went. As they got closer, the air grew musty and Rook could hear the sounds of whinnying and snorting as the roosting creatures sensed their approach. They were greeted by the roost-marshal, Rembit Tag, a small, muscular gnokgoblin with thick, black hair.

'We've been sent by Captain Welt,' Ligger announced. 'Rook here needs a prowlgrin mount.'

'Does he now,' Rembit said, eyeing Rook up and down, gauging his size and weight. He selected a saddle for him and handed it over. Then, turning, he nodded towards the herd. 'I'd go for one of the large greys,' he said. 'Not too much spirit, but dependable.'

Rook looked. They were a mixed flock. There were the large brown, grey and black prowlgrins, with thick, muscular hind-legs and tiny front paws. Then the slightly smaller, but more skittish, orange prowlgrins – sleek and fast, but harder to handle. Rook stepped forwards, and walked amongst them, patting them, stroking and tickling them. The prowlgrins purred and nuzzled against him. Rembit was impressed.

'They like you,' he said. 'You seem to have a natural way with them.'

Rook nodded. *The prowlgrin has forty-three places receptive to stroking, patting and tickling: the eyebrow, the middle digit of the toe . . .* Fenbrus's treatise intoned in his head.

There was one prowlgrin he'd noticed, perched on a branch some way off from the others. Unlike them, with their yellow eyes and plain coats, this one had eyes of bright, piercing blue and a skewbald pattern of dark brown patches on snow-white fur.

The white, spotted prowlgrin – exceptionally intelligent,

but temperamental. Rewards careful handling, but easily ruined by a heavy hand . . .

'What about that one?' he said.

'Ooh, no,' said the marshal. 'You don't want that one. It was ridden by Graze Flintwick, a flat-head. Cut down in the Battle of Lufwood Mount, he was. Won't let anyone else near it. I only keep it out of respect for old Flintwick . . .'

But Rook was intrigued. There was something about the way the prowlgrin with the beautiful markings skittered about, its gaze flickering anxiously, that caught his eye. Passing through the more docile prowlgrins which nuzzled against him as he went, he approached the skewbald creature slowly. Ligger and the marshal went with him.

'What's his name?' said Rook.

'Chinquix,' Rembit replied. 'But believe me, he can't be ridden. In fact, I'm amazed he's allowed you to get this close.'

Rook nodded and, with his head lowered, but eyes holding the gaze of the nervous beast, moved towards it. 'Chinquix,' he said softly. 'It's all right, lad.'

Approach a nervous prowlgrin from the side, maintaining eye contact at all times, and blowing softly . . .

The prowlgrin reared up and let out a yelp of distress.

'Yes, yes, I know,' Rook whispered. 'Steady now. Steady . . .'

Keep hands at one's side, and head lowered . . .

'I really can't advise this,' Rembit began, but Ligger took his arm and stilled him.

. . . Introduce oneself to the prowlgrin by means of smell . . .

Rook stepped closer to the creature. He licked his fingers and traced them gently round the prowl-grin's flaring nostrils, whispering as he did so.

'Chinquix, Chinquix . . .'

As he did so, the prowl-grin breathed in. It stopped pawing the ground and seemed to listen. Rook smiled softly and, still holding the great creature's nervous gaze, he leaned forwards and blew softly.

The prowlgrin blew back and its bright blue eyes softened. The yelping sound subsided, and in its place, rumbling from deep down inside its throat, came a low, contented purr.

'Good lad, Chinquix,' said Rook, throwing the saddle over its back and tightening the straps under its belly, tickling and stroking it all the while. 'Good, good lad!'

'Well, I never,' said Rembit. 'Most incredible thing I've ever seen. Where on earth did you learn to do that?' he asked.

Rook turned towards the marshal, only to find Chinquix nuzzling against him, greedy for more attention. He patted the barkscroll in his top pocket. 'Just something I read,' he said.

Rembit shook his head. 'If I hadn't seen it with my own eyes . . .'

Behind him, Ligger had mounted his own prowlgrin, an orangey-brown beast by the name of Belvix. He trotted over to Rook.

'Very impressive,' he said. 'Now, let's see how you get on in the upper branches.'

Rook didn't need telling twice. Steadying his prowlgrin, he swung himself into the saddle and gave the reins a small flick. Almost immediately, Chinquix bounded into the air, and Rook found himself racing through the branches, the blood coursing along his veins. Not since *Stormhornet* had he felt such exhilaration.

'I'm alive, Chinquix!' he cried, his voice echoing round the Ironwood Glade. '*I'm alive!*'

·CHAPTER SIXTEEN·

CANCARESSE

Inside the tall, dense ring of spike-briars and milkthorn trees, their curved thorns sharp and forbidding, Waif Glen was bathed in the pale yellow light of early morning. Everything had been made ready.

The winding gravel paths were newly raked, the pools and waterfalls clear, the rockeries tidy, while the ornamental evergreen trees with their small, dark, waxen leaves, had been freshly clipped into intricate, angular shapes. Arbours and alcoves had been prepared for those who would soon sit in and walk around them. At the centre of the garden was a circular lawn of fragrant herbs, recently mown, out of which towered an ancient gladewillow, its mighty branches falling like a golden curtain to the ground.

Cancaresse the Silent, Keeper of the Garden of Thoughts, stood in the shadows beneath the glade-willow, her shimmering robes hanging loosely from her bony shoulders and the tips of her long, spidery fingers pressed together in concentration . . .

They were coming, that much was certain. As her large, papery ears fluttered, she could hear them – all the ones who had been summoned to the Reckoning, plus those others who, for their own reasons, desired to be present.

Even now, her waif attendants were helping the visitors to navigate the seemingly impenetrable wall of thorns that kept the sounds of the outside world at bay. She sensed their amazement as the path through the treacherous thorn trees and briars opened up before them and felt their jolt of unease as they noticed the various waifs – ghostwaifs, greywaifs, flitterwaifs, nightwaifs – staring back at them from out of the shadows. One by one, they began to appear, emerging from the thorny wall of undergrowth and blinking into the light.

Welcome, she said, her soft

voice cutting through the cluttered thoughts in their heads.

Keeping largely to themselves, the visitors moved round the garden, unknowingly seeking out the places where they felt most comfortable. Some contemplated their reflections in the deep, limpid pools, some sat beneath the swaying sallowdrop trees, while others continued walking, lost in contemplation, their footsteps crunching softly in the gravel. And, as more and more individuals joined the slowly growing number, the sounds of their thoughts filled Cancaresse's head.

She trembled, her frail body quivering at the jumble of voices as they hummed and buzzed like woodbees. Already though, as the calming atmosphere of the garden took hold, they were beginning to quieten down; to be stilled and soothed and steered to clear, uncluttered thought.

A faint, inscrutable smile plucked at the corners of her mouth as she slowly parted the gladewillow curtain and cast her gaze round the garden. Normally, there would be a troubled cloddertrog or two soothing their anger by the pools, or a solitary gyle goblin easing his melancholy on the gravel paths. But on days like this – Reckoning Days – it seemed as if all of the Free Glades had turned up, their heads filled with noisy thoughts.

As they moved around, Cancaresse began to listen in to them, one after the other. Some had dark thoughts, full of anger and blame. Some had sympathetic thoughts, full of sadness, whilst the majority had minds buzzing with the inquisitiveness and gossip-fed interest of the casual onlooker. Cancaresse moved swiftly over these and concentrated on only the strongest emotions she could sense coming from the various corners of the garden.

There was a young sunken-eyed librarian knight brooding by the healing-pools. And there, a fussy under-librarian delicately sniffing a sallowdrop blossom to ease his pain. And over on the straight gravel path, the High Academe himself, head down and hands clasped behind his back, while in the wicker arbour there lounged a tense and fidgety ghost, his muglumpskin jacket bright against the dark evergreen bushes behind him. A little way beyond, two Freeglade lancers edged their way round the waterfalls of memory. Their thoughts intrigued her – she would get to them in due course.

A soft, scent-laden breeze wafted across the manicured lawns and neatly clipped bushes. Cancaresse paused. Her ears trembled and twisted round.

'Aah,' she sighed.

Behind her, standing in the deep shadows by the gnarled and knotted trunk of the gladewillow, was the object of all their thoughts: a youth with short cropped hair. He was pale and looked anxious, like a startled lemkin – but then, she thought, who wouldn't at his own Reckoning?

She closed her eyes for a moment and breathed in, her frail body quivering as she did so. It was time to begin.

She stepped through the curtain of gladewillow leaves and made her way across the lawn and onto the gravel paths, stepping so lightly that her feet made no sound.

She wandered unnoticed, mingling with the visitors, seeking out those whose emotions ran deepest . . .

In front of her, kneeling on the marble surround of a pool, was the sunken-eyed librarian knight, his thoughts as deep and dark as the water he was staring into. There was pain and hurt in his thoughts, and a rage so strong, it made her papery ears flutter with its intensity. She approached him, and laid her spidery fingers against his chest.

Show me, she spoke inside his head.

The youth unbuttoned his flight-jacket and hitched up his undershirt. A jagged scar crossed his ribs. Cancaresse reached out and traced a finger along the angry red line, staring deeply all the while into the youth's eyes.

Yes, she said, her voice full of sadness and regret. *Yes, I see. An ambush – in the terrible city of the bird-creatures . . . Your friends, so young, so brave, hacked to pieces, one after the other by the vicious shryke-sisters. The blood, the screams, one, two, three, four – and now it is your turn . . .*

She shuddered, her tiny body quivering as it felt the librarian knight's pain.

A slash of a razor-sharp claw . . . And then you're running, running! Running!

Cancaresse closed her eyes and probed deeper into his memories.

Cowering in the shadows of a walkway; watching, waiting, praying that the shrykes won't find you. The terror. The pain.

The sound of the bird-creatures' triumphant cries . . .
'Betrayed by their own! Betrayed by their own!'

She opened her eyes and stared into the librarian knight's face, the memory of the shrykes' taunting screech still fresh and raw.

'Thank you, Xanth!' the shryke's voice cackled. *'Xanth Filatine!'*

Cancaresse let her thin arms fall limply to her side. She turned and walked away from the pool and across the gravelled paths, leaving the youth to his brooding. There were others whose thoughts she must hear. She crossed the scented lawn and wandered through the sallowdrop trees, their branches heavy with yellow and white blossom, stopping in front of the fussy under-librarian. She regarded him with large unblinking eyes.

He was slight, but spritely-looking, with half-moon spectacles which had slipped down over the bridge of his long, thin nose. His thinning hair had turned to a shade of grey, yet from the way the bright sun glinted on it, Cancaresse could see that once it had been as red as copperwood leaves. Inside him, the waif sensed a hole, a gap – something missing that could never be replaced.

Tell me, she said. *Open your thoughts to me.*

She leaned forwards, reached up and placed her hands on either side of his head, and gasped as his pain washed over her.

Your son. Cancaresse's heart ached. *Your poor, dear son*

... Artillus, rosy-cheeked, ginger-haired. Your pride and joy. You told him not to wander off in the sewers; you told him it wasn't safe, but he didn't listen ... So young, so impetuous ...

The waif shuddered.

You only found out the true horror later ... A sky patrol high over old Undertown saw it and reported back ... Captured by Guardians, dragged into the Tower of Night and ... and ...

The pain was almost too much to bear. Cancaresse trembled.

Your son, and another young prisoner, lowered in a cage from the tower, into the ravine below ... A ravine full of hideous creatures – rock demons ... They didn't stand a chance. She shook her head. *Sacrificed by the High Guardian of Night and his young deputy – interrogator of all prisoners brought to the Tower of Night ... Xanth. Xanth Filatine ...*

Cancaresse moved away, leaving the stricken under-librarian to the thoughts that time might soften, though never heal.

Ahead of her on the gravel path, she saw an elderly academic dressed in simple, homespun robes, staring into space. His eyes were green and kindly, yet behind them the waif detected years of pain and torment, with every line on his wrinkled face telling its own tragic story. Despite all this, Cancaresse could sense that the Most High Academe, Cowlquape Pentephraxis, was not a bitter man – indeed his thoughts about the youth were kind and warm. And yet, behind them, deeper down ...

The waif took his hands in her own, and squeezed them lightly. Cowlquape's thoughts echoed inside her head.

So, she said, *you consider him a friend?*

A smile passed over the High Academe's thin lips. Cancaresse smiled in turn.

Yes, a friend. So many, many hours talking together of the Deepwoods ... Its mysteries and wonders ... Of your adventures there with the great Captain Twig ... Oh, how Xanth loved to hear you speak of them!

The waif frowned.

But what is this? In what dark, fetid place do you two friends sit talking?

An involuntary shudder ran down the length of her spine.

A prison! A terrible prison, deep in the bowels of the Tower of Night ... How you suffered ... The stench, the filthy rags, the lice and ticks ... Year after year, on a jutting ledge in the darkness ... And ... The key in the lock ... The heavy door opening ... Your jailer entering ...

Xanth. Xanth Filatine!

As the waif pulled away from Cowlquape, he had already immersed himself once more in the colour and grandeur of the Deepwoods – the place which, throughout his long years of incarceration, he had returned to in his thoughts time and time again. There was a smile on his lips and a dreamy look on his face. The Most High Academe was truly happy.

But what of the youth? Cancaresse sighed.

Xanth Filatine had clearly done much to be ashamed

of. He had been a spy, a traitor, a torturer, a jailer . . . He had caused great suffering and pain, strong emotions that flowed through the thoughts in the garden.

The waif paused in her tracks, and looked round. There, to her right, was the youth in the muglumpskin jacket whom she'd noticed earlier. He looked more fidgety than ever now, pacing up and down beside the wicker arbour.

Ah, the bold young Ghost of Screetown, Cancaresse thought. *Let me see now what he has to say.*

She stole up beside him and took him by the hand. The frenetic pacing slowed. The youth turned and looked deep into her eyes, and as he did so, Cancaresse felt a hot rush of anger boiling up in his thoughts.

Your best friend, Rook, betrayed by this Xanth creature! . . . Once a Guardian, always a Guardian . . .

It was so hot and fiery inside the ghost's head that Cancaresse felt almost as though she were passing her fingers over a flame . . .

He lured him off into the Edgeland mists – he was almost killed thanks to him. Then he steals Rook's sword . . . The sword you gave him! Typical of a Guardian, and no more than you'd expect of Xanth Filatine!

Cancaresse dropped the hot-blooded ghost's hand and sighed. It seemed that Xanth Filatine really was no good. All around her she was aware of the thoughts of the Freegladers.

Worthless traitor!

You can see the evil in his eyes.

The Free Glades are better off without his sort!

She brushed them away, as if swatting troublesome woodmidges, and walked on. When she reached the waterfalls of memory, she stopped and gazed at the cascading water. And as she did so, Tweezel's thoughts came back to her.

She had taken tea with the great spindlebug the previous evening, just as she always did before a Reckoning, in order to benefit from his wisdom.

'I have looked into his heart,' the old spindlebug had told her. 'There is a lot of guilt there. Guilt that grows like a great mushroom, but only because it has the soil of goodness to grow upon. Beneath the guilt, I believe Xanth Filatine's heart is good.'

Cancaresse's thoughts were suddenly interrupted by a high-pitched cry of joy, and she turned from the waterfall to see a gnokgoblin young'un come bounding past her, a delighted look on her face. She rushed towards one of the two Freeglade lancers who were standing to one side of the flowing water, and threw herself into his arms.

'Rook! Rook!' she squealed. 'It *is* you!'

'Gilda!' cried the Freeglade lancer. 'Gilda from the misery hole in old Undertown! I can't believe it! You made it to the Free Glades!'

The pair hugged each other delightedly. Cancaresse approached and held out her long-fingered hands.

What joy! What delight! her voice sounded in both their

heads at the same time. *Come, take my hands and share it.*

The Freeglade lancer and the gnokgoblin each took Cancaresse's hand, and the three of them walked together.

Two friends re-united! A joyful reunion . . .

She looked down at the little gnokgoblin, who smiled up at her. *You have suffered, little one . . . First the misery hole . . . And then the long journey to the Free Glades. But you carried something with you . . . A sword . . . A sword that belongs to Rook, the librarian knight who risked his own life to save yours in old Undertown! You kept it safe on your journey, and then . . . Oh, little one! You didn't want to disturb him! You left it outside the banderbear nest in the Deepwoods . . .*

Cancaresse felt Rook's hand tighten around her own. She looked up into his eyes.

Yes, Rook! Her voice was light and joyful in his head. *Xanth didn't steal your sword. He found it! And that's not all . . .* Her eyes narrowed as she gazed at him. *Your thoughts are hidden deep . . . Confused and blasted by the sepia storm . . . But I can bring them back within your grasp . . . Yes . . . There it is . . .*

The Edgelands . . . You, in a sepia storm, being swept across the rocky pavement towards the Edge itself . . . A hand reaching out, grasping yours and pulling you back to safety . . .

Xanth's hand, Rook. Xanth Filatine!

Rook frowned. 'Yes,' he whispered softly. 'I remember.'

And there is more, the waif continued. *At great risk to himself, he picked you up, cradled you in his arms, and carried you back across the Edgelands and through the Deepwoods. He did not rest until he had delivered you safely to the banderbears.*

'Yes, yes,' said Rook. He remembered it all now; every terrible step of the long journey. 'He rescued me,' he murmured. 'Xanth Filatine. He saved my life.'

Cancaresse smiled and let go of his hand. *He has been a faithful friend to you. Now enjoy this happy reunion.*

She smiled as Rook took Gilda's hand, and the two of them strolled across the scented lawn. Behind her, she was aware of another voice – hard, callous, and yet with a tender edge to it. She turned and gazed into the eyes of the second Freeglade lancer, a short, stocky slaughterer with spiky flame-coloured hair.

So you were at Lufwood Mount? she asked.

The slaughterer nodded, and she sensed the pain and loss of brave comrades.

You saw the slaying of the roost-mother . . . A shaven-headed youth with a fancy sword . . . Bravest thing you ever saw . . . Turned the tide of battle . . . A hero . . . Xanth Filatine!

Cancaresse left the Freeglade lancer gazing at the waterfall and wandered off through the garden once more. The sun had climbed to its highest point in the sky and was beating down warmly, shrinking the shadows in the gardens. The time had come, the waif realized, to hear from Xanth Filatine himself. She crossed the lawn, drew back the gladewillow curtain and beckoned to the youth to join her.

Xanth emerged from the shadows and stumbled out into the brilliant sunshine, his shoulders hunched and his eyes screwed up against the light. As he drew close, Cancaresse sensed his unhappiness and uncertainty, and the power of his conflicting emotions. There was guilt, remorse, hurt and unhappiness. He was alone – shunned and despised.

She placed her hand on his shoulder. He turned, and looked at her with his dark, haunted eyes. And as their gaze met, everything changed. It was as though a dam had been breached, and she was suddenly drenched in a torrent of thoughts that poured out over her.

I served a terrible master for years, loyally carrying out his evil plans. It was wrong, it was wrong; I know it was wrong – but I was so young . . .

But no! This is no excuse. This cannot take away the horror of what I did.

Cancaresse nodded.

I betrayed them. I betrayed so many. My hands are stained with blood that I can never, ever wash away.

Cowlquape gave me hope of escape with his stories of the Deepwoods, and yet the only way to get there was as a spy for the Guardians of Night! How many valiant apprentice librarians must have died because of my treachery! And then I was unmasked and fled, like the coward I was, back to the Tower of Night!

Oh, if only I could have stayed in the Free Glades, where, for

*the first time in my life, I had encountered enduring friendship
– Rook, Magda, Tweezel ... But it was impossible ... I let
them all down. Each and every one of them. How can I ever
undo the wrong I have done?*

He paused, a haunted, despairing look in his eyes.
Almost at once, the torrent of thoughts, pent up for so
long, gushed forth once more.

*I tried! Earth and Sky know, I tried, but to what avail? I was
a traitor. A spy. A curse on all who came close to me and
trusted me. Yet, I did try, you have to believe me ...*

Cancaresse nodded again, slowly.

*Back in the tower, I could see more clearly than ever how
wicked the High Guardian of Night truly was. I did everything I could to stop the madness.*

*My heart was full of joy when Cowlquape was rescued from
the Tower of Night – and how I wished I could go with him ...
Yet, I knew I could not. I had to stay and do everything I could
to lessen the evil my master was doing.*

That was my punishment.

*I did what I could for those who fell into the Guardians'
clutches. I tried so hard to rob the cages of their sacrifices – to
find excuses in my interrogations to set them free. Yet Leddix,
the executioner, would often whisk them away ...*

*Oh, but how the loss of those I couldn't save sickens me to
the very bottom of my heart ...*

Cancaresse nodded. She could feel his pain clearly.
The youth fell to his knees in the middle of the sunlit
lawn and buried his face in his hands. Sobs racked his
body and, from all corners of the garden, Freegladers
gathered round. The moment of Reckoning had come at

last. All eyes fell on the tiny figure of Cancaresse the Silent, Keeper of the Garden of Thoughts.

Friends, her soft voice sounded in a thousand minds. *I have looked deep within many minds, shared deep sorrows and terrible pain . . .*

She looked round at the faces in front of her; at the librarian knight with the terrible scar, the grieving under-librarian and the care-worn High Academe.

I have also felt loyalty, bravery and friendship, the waif continued.

She noticed Rook and the slaughterer nodding, and Felix, the ghost, looking ashamed.

I have weighed the good and the evil Xanth Filatine has done, and though the scales are more finely balanced than at first I thought . . . She looked down at Xanth, sorrow plain in her eyes. *I'm afraid, Xanth, that . . .*

The youth stared back at her, his face a stark white in the brilliant sunshine.

'Stop! Wait!' A voice broke the silence.

A gasp went round the Garden of Thoughts as a newcomer suddenly burst through the crowd of Freegladers.

'But you were shot down!' cried one.

'We thought you were dead!' called another.

Magda Burlix, her flight-suit torn and grimy, limped towards Xanth and the waif. 'Forgive me, but I must speak with you,' she said urgently.

Cancaresse stepped towards the young librarian knight, her great veined ears fluttering. *Tell me what you know*, she said.

The librarian knight knelt before her, and the waif placed her long thin hands on Magda's head.

He rescued you from the Tower of Night, she said, her soft voice resonating in the heads of everyone present. *He risked his life guiding you through the sewers and back to the safety of the librarians even though he knew they hated him and would shun and despise him ... He did this with no thought of reward – only that you might live ...*

Cancaresse looked up. *The moment of Reckoning has come*, she said silently, and around the garden, every head nodded.

She turned to Xanth and raised her arms, the palms of her hands turned upwards. Her robes shimmered in the midday sunlight.

'Welcome, Xanth Filatine,' she said. 'Welcome, Freeglader.'

PART 3

WAR

CHAPTER SEVENTEEN

GLADE-EATER

'Aaagh!' the low-bellied goblin cried out in agony as he fell heavily to the filthy foundry floor. He curled up into a ball, but the blows kept coming.

'Ignorant, clumsy, half-witted oaf!' the flat-head guard bellowed, punctuating each word with lashes from his heavy whip.

'Forgive me! Forgive me!' the low-belly whimpered. The whip cracked louder than ever, tearing into the skin at his back and shoulders, drawing blood. 'Aaaagh!' he howled. 'Have mercy on this miserable wretch . . .'

The guard, a brawny flat-head with zigzag tattoos across half of his face and over both shoulders, sneered unpleasantly – though he did at last stay his arm.

'Mercy?' he snarled. 'Another accident like that and I'll finish you off for good. I've got quotas to meet, and I'm not gonna meet them with no-good slackers like you. Y'understand me, huh?'

The low-belly remained curled up and motionless, too frightened to speak in case he incurred the goblin's violent wrath once more. It wasn't his fault he'd stumbled. It was blisteringly hot in the metal foundry, and he was parched, and weary, and so weak with lack of food he could barely see. His head was swimming, his legs had turned to rubber. And when the moulds were full of the glowing molten metal, they were *so* unsteady . . .

'*Understand?*' the flat-head guard roared.

'Yes, yes, sir, he understands,' said a second low-belly goblin, scurrying to his brother's side. Taking him by the arm, trying not to touch the raw, open wounds on his back, he helped him to his feet. 'Sir, it won't happen again, sir. I give you my word.'

The flat-head spat with contempt. 'The day I take the word of low-belly scum like you is the day I hang up my hood and whip,' he sneered. 'Get that mess cleared up!' he roared, nodding down at the floor where the spilled molten metal had solidified into a huge, irregular lump. 'And you lot,' he added, cracking his whip at a small group of gnokgoblins over by the ore-belts. 'Give 'em a hand.'

Warily eyeing the guard's whip, with its three tails, each one tipped with a hooked spike, the gnokgoblins approached. Then, together with the low-bellies, they tugged and heaved the huge lump of metal, grunting loudly as they did so, gradually shifting it over the floor through the smoke-filled foundry.

All round them, the place throbbed with ceaseless noise as the enslaved workforce toiled in their individual groups, stripped to their waists, their grimy, sweaty bodies gleaming in the furnace-glow. There were hefters and stokers, smelt-lackeys and mould-navvies – each one of them cowed, half-starved and racked with foundry-croup – working at the feverish pace dictated by the slave-driving guards.

With military precision, logs were turned to heat in the main furnace, ore was turned to iron in the smelting-vats, and the long, heavy moulds – suspended on chains from ceiling-tracks high above – were filled with brightly glowing molten metal and steered towards the cooling-bays. It was raw materials to finished product in less than an hour.

And what a finished product! Huge, curved scythes which, once expertly hammered, honed and polished, were set aside in long racks, waiting to be taken off in hammel-horn-drawn carts to the assembly-yards.

Fighting against the intense, choking heat that was driving them back, the group of hapless goblins struggled on towards the smelting vat.

'One – two – three ... *Heave!*' cried one of the gnokgoblins.

Groaning with effort, they all clasped the huge lump of metal and pushed it up, up, over the lip of the pot-bellied vat, and down into the molten metal within. It landed with a splash, a hiss and a puff of acrid smoke, before rolling over and melting like butter in a fire. The poor low-belly who had spilt the molten metal in the first place slumped to the ground.

'Get up,' the other urged him, glancing anxiously round to see whether the flat-head goblin guard was paying them any attention.

'Can't, Heeb,' came the reply, little more than a grunt.

'But you must,' his brother insisted. 'Before he accuses you of slacking again.' He shook his head grimly. 'I can't lose you, too, Rumpel. Not after the others . . . Rudder, and Reel. You're all I've got left. You *must* get up . . .'

'*Pfweeeep!*'

A shrill steam-whistle blasted loudly, cutting through the thick, noisy air of the foundry and signalling the end of the shift. The rhythmic hammering and teeth-jarring screech of the sharpening-rasps abruptly ceased, as the goblins downed tools and shuffled away, leaving their posts empty for the next shift. Soon, only the roar of the furnace remained.

'Thank Earth and Sky,' Heeb murmured. 'Come, Rumpel,' he said, taking his brother by the arm a second time. 'Let's get out of here.'

Rumpel struggled to his feet and, without a word, let himself be led from the foundry, stumbling clumsily like a hobbled hammelhorn. His head was down, his ears were ringing, his back felt as though it was on fire.

Outside – as the line of exhausted goblins brushed past those arriving for work – the sky was the colour of congealed gruel and a soft, cold drizzle was falling. At first, it soothed the vicious, blood-encrusted weals in the low-belly's flesh. It wasn't long though before what had started as cooling, after the blistering heat of the foundry, became bitterly cold as Rumpel's feverish body was chilled to the marrow.

'C . . . c . . . c . . . can't t . . . t . . . take it no m . . . m . . . more,' he stammered, his teeth chattering and body shaking. And as the caked smoke in his lungs began to loosen, so his frail, bony body was racked once more with the hacking cough that tormented every one of the Foundry Glades slave-workers.

Heeb looked round at his brother. The pair of them were making their way across the glade to the hovel that had become home to them and seventy others. He noted the deathly pallor to his skin, the dark charcoal-grey rings beneath his eyes, and the rheumy, unblinking stare – as if his gaze were already fixed on the world beyond the unceasing cruelty of this one. It was an expression he had seen before – in the faces of his other brothers, Reel and Rudder, shortly before they had died.

'Hang on in there, little brother,' Heeb said softly. 'I'll get those wounds dressed, we'll have something to eat, and you can rest up.' He smiled weakly. 'It's going to be fine, you'll see,' he added, only wishing that his words were as easy to believe as they were to say.

Ahead of them now, bathed in the fine, grey rain, were the slave-huts. Their own – a rundown, ramshackle hovel – was situated slap-bang in the middle of the row. The ground had been churned up, and they had to drag themselves on those last few strides through thick, claggy mud that clung to their tattered boots. There at last, Heeb helped Rumpel up the three wooden steps, lifted the latch and pushed the door open.

A blast of stale, fetid air struck them in the face, a mixture of rotting straw, running sores and unwashed bodies. The two of them stumbled inside.

'Shut that door!' someone bellowed, before his voice gave way to a thick, chesty cough, which was soon joined by several others, until the whole hut was echoing with loud, febrile coughing.

'Shut up! Shut up!' a voice kept shouting from the far end. 'Shut that infernal row!'

Heeb steered his brother down the central aisle of the hut towards the place where they slept – two wooden pallets covered with rank, mildewed straw. Forgetting for a moment the cuts and weals on his back, Rumpel fell down onto the makeshift bed – only to cry out and roll over the next moment.

'Shut up!' the voice came back with renewed vigour. 'I'm trying to sleep here!'

'Shut up yourself,' someone else shouted back and a

heavy clod of earth was lobbed at the complainer. 'If you can't sleep, then you haven't been working hard enough!'

With everyone on different shifts, there were always some trying to sleep while others were coming and going; eating, drinking, muttering to themselves ... dying.

Heeb knelt down beside his brother, pulled a small pot from his trouser pocket and unscrewed the lid. The sweet, juicy smell of hyleberry salve wafted up – though the pot was almost empty. Licking the grime from his finger as best he could, Heeb scraped out the dregs of the salve from the corners of the pot, top and bottom.

'Lie still,' he said, and proceeded to smear the pale green ointment around the worst of his brother's wounds. Rumpel flinched, and moaned softly when the pain got too much. 'You've got to hold on a little bit longer,' Heeb told him, as he massaged the salve into the skin. 'We're almost done now. It's almost over . . .'

'Al . . . almost o . . . o . . . over,' Rumpel repeated, every syllable a terrible struggle.

'That's right,' said Heeb encouragingly. 'The catapult cages have been completed. *And* the step-wheels and lance-launchers. And the boiler-chimneys. And the long-scythes will soon be ready as well.' He tried to sound cheerful. 'Won't be long now before we're finished . . .'

'F . . . fi . . . finished . . .' grunted Rumpel.

'Glade-eater? Pah!' said Heeb. 'Goblin-crippler, more like!' He shuddered as he replaced the lid on the small pot. 'You stay there, bro',' he said gently. 'I'll get us something to eat.'

He climbed wearily to his feet, grabbed his and Rumpel's mug and bowl, and shuffled off towards the gruel-pot at the end of the slave-hut, which bubbled slowly under the watchful eye of a web-foot trustee. Heeb groaned. The fact that his brother was in a worse state than himself did nothing to lessen his own exhaustion. His cheeks were hollow, his eyes were sunken and his ribs stuck out like bits of kindling. Like his brother and the other low-belly goblins, he had little need for the belly-sling that hung loosely at his front – for just like them and all the others in the slave-hut, he was slowly being worked to death.

The gruel was grey and slimy and smelled of drains, and as it was ladled into his and his brother's bowls, Heeb couldn't help heaving. He filled the mugs with dirty water from the barrel and returned to the sleeping pallet.

'Here we are,' he said, placing everything down and pulling out a spoon from his back pocket. 'Do you want me to feed you?'

Rumpel made no reply. Heeb wasn't even sure he'd heard him. Lying on his side, he was simply staring ahead, his breathing rasping and irregular.

Heeb swallowed anxiously. 'Don't die on me,' he whispered softly. 'Not now. I couldn't bear it.' Tears welled up in his eyes. 'I told you, Rumpel, it's almost over. They've almost finished. Trust me, it's not long to go now. Not long . . .'

*

Lummel Grope dropped his scythe, stood up straight and stretched. 'Earth and Sky, but this is backbreaking work, Lob,' he said, and he reached inside his belly-sling to scratch the great, round, hairy stomach it supported.

'You can say that again,' said Lob. He pulled his straw bonnet from his head and mopped his brow on his sleeve. 'And thirsty work, to boot,' he added.

Lummel picked up the half-empty flagon by his side, pulled the stopper out with his teeth, and took a long swig of woodapple cider. 'Here,' he said, handing it over to his brother.

Lob wiped the top with the palm of his hand and did the same. '*Aaah!*' he sighed. 'That sure hits the spot.'

The two brothers were in the middle of a blue-barley

field. Half of the crop had already been scythed down and gathered up into neat, pointed stooks. The other half was still waiting to be cut and bundled. It was over-ripe, with the heavy ears of barley showing the first signs of spoil-bloom, and no matter how hard the two low-bellied brothers worked, both of them knew it could never be fast enough.

'If only it weren't just the two of us,' Lummel grumbled.

'I know,' said Lob, nodding sadly. 'When I think back to last year . . .' He shook his head miserably. 'I just hope and pray the others are all right.'

Lummel took the flagon back, and tipped another mouthful of cider down his throat.

'Rumpel, Rudder, Heeb, Reel . . .' Lob's eyes welled with tears at the thought of their absent brothers. 'Dragged off to those accursed Foundry Glades like that . . .' He swung his arm round in a broad circle that included the farm-holdings owned by their neighbours, their fields as full of uncut blue-barley as their own. 'The Topes, the Lopes, the Hempels . . . Half of them already gone, and the other half waiting to be rounded up and carted off with the rest . . .'

'And we'll be next, you mark my word,' said Lummel. 'Any time now those flat-heads'll be back. And this time, it'll be to send us off to war.'

'And it won't just be us low-bellies, neither,' said Lob. 'No one's going to be spared this time round. Gonna send us all off to fight, so they are. And then what's to become of the harvest? You tell me that.'

Lummel nodded sagely, and the two brothers stood in

the field, side by side, passing the flagon back and forth as they surveyed the sprawling patchwork landscape of fields, villages and settlements spread out before them.

The Goblin Nations had come such a long way since its beginnings as a single gyle goblin colony, with tribe after tribe from all the major clans settling down as neighbours. Peaceable symbites had arrived first; as well as the gyle goblins, there were tree goblins, web-foots and gnokgoblins, settling round the dew ponds and in the Ironwood Stands. But later, others had joined them – warrior-like goblins who, despite their traditional root-lessness, had become increasingly attracted to this more stable and reliable way of life.

Tusked and tufted goblins, black-ears and long-hairs, pink-eyed and greys – they had constructed nondescript huts at first, often clustered round a totem-pole carved from the last tree left standing when a patch of forest was cleared. Later, some individual tribes had branched out – both geographically and architecturally – building towers and forts, round-houses and long-houses. Even some groups of flat-heads had seen the advantages of settling down and had taken land for themselves where they'd erected their own distinctive wicker hive-huts.

The two brothers stared ahead in silence at the scene. In the middle distance, the jagged Ironwood Stands where tree-goblins dwelt and long-hairs trained were silhouetted against the evening sky. Due south and east, the flat-heads' and hammerheads' wicker hive towers broke the distant horizon where, even now, dark forbidding clouds were gathering.

Further to the north, beside the mist-covered web-foots' dew ponds, the pinnacles of the gyle goblin colonies glinted in the rays of the sinking sun, while far to their right, in the partially cleared forest areas, they could see smoke spiralling up out of the chimneys of the huts in the new villages – some not yet even blooded – where the latest tribes and family groups to arrive had begun to settle.

Lob's face tightened with anger. 'Why can't the clan chiefs just leave us in peace? Why must we go to war? Why, Lummel, why?'

Lummel sighed. 'We're just simple low-bellies,' he said, slowly shaking his head. 'The mighty clan chiefs don't concern themselves with the likes of us, Lob.'

'It's not right,' said Lob hotly once more. He nodded round at the blue fields, the barley swaying in the rising easterlies. 'Who's gonna harvest that lot, eh? No one, that's who. It'll just get left to spoil in the fields.'

'S'already starting to turn,' said Lummel.

''Xactly,' said Lob. 'And what's there gonna be to eat on those long, cold, winter nights then? You tell me that!' He took the flagon back from his brother, drained it and wiped his mouth on the back of his hand. 'One thing's for certain, those high and mighty clan chiefs won't go hungry.'

'You're right, brother,' said Lummel. 'They'll be feasting in their clan-huts while we do the fighting and dying in this war of theirs.'

'Clan chiefs!' said Lob, his voice heavy with contempt. He spat on the ground. 'We'd be better off without them.' He picked up his scythe, turned his attention to the waiting barley and began cutting with renewed vigour. 'What you and I need, brother, are the friends of the harvest . . .'

'Lob,' said Lummel, his voice suddenly hushed and urgent.

'You heard what was said at that meeting,' Lob continued, scything furiously. 'There's a whole load of goblins like us, from every tribe and all walks of life who think just the way we do . . .'

'Lob!'

Lob paused and looked up. 'What?' he said. 'It's true, isn't it? . .'

And then he caught sight of what his brother had already seen – a long line of scrawny web-footed goblins tramping through the fields towards them from the northeast under heavy armed guard. They were dripping wet from head to toe. Clearly, the flat-head guards had interrupted their sacred clam-feeding and dragged them out of the water without even allowing them to return home for a change of clothes. The thin, scaly creatures looked lost and forlorn away from the dew ponds and the giant molluscs they tended that lived in their depths.

Lob gasped. 'By Earth and Sky,' he whispered, his voice trembling, 'if they're picking on harmless symbites now, then no one in the Goblin Nations is safe any more.'

'Oi, you two!' one of the flat-head guards bellowed across the blue-barley field. 'Get over here and join the ranks at once.'

Lob and Lummel looked at one another, their hearts sinking. The moment they had both been dreading had arrived, and much earlier than their worst fears. Where were the friends of the harvest now?

'Look lively!' shouted the flat-head. 'You're in the army now.'

'But . . . but the harvest,' Lob called back. 'We haven't finished bringing it in . . .'

'Forget the harvest!' the flat-head roared, his face blotchy crimson and contorted with rage. 'Let it rot! A richer harvest by far awaits us in the Free Glades, and all *you* have to do to reap it is to follow in the tracks of a glade-eater!'

Flambusia Flodfox was down on her knees, her large head lowered and her great rear raised. She was feeling more sorry for herself than she had ever done before in her life. She'd lost weight on her meagre, tasteless diet of black bread and barley gruel, her chest was bad, her joints were swollen, her hands had been chafed red raw and her corns were playing up. To crown it all, she hadn't seen Amberfuce for days.

To her right stood a metal pail, filled with cold water

and overflowing with soapy suds. Time and again, as she shuffled forwards on her inflamed knees, she plunged a big, bristly brush into the water and scrubbed vigorously at the muddy marks on the white marble floor, muttering under her breath as she did so.

'Oh, if only they'd let me see him,' she complained, her voice weak and peevish. 'Why, if Amby knew just how they were treating me . . .'

Just then she heard a noise. She paused, and pushed a greasy hank of hair back, revealing the puffy, red-rimmed eyes behind. From behind her, the heavy clomping of boots came closer.

Muddy boots, most like, she thought miserably. And then I'll have to scrub the whole floor all over again.

Not that Flambusia was about to complain out loud. She'd tried that once – and still had the angry welts across the backs of her legs to prove it. That Foundry Master was a tyrant all right. The footsteps approached and passed her by without stopping.

Casting a sideways glance round, she saw that there were two of them. Hemuel Spume was one, his longcoat hissing as it glided over the floor, the purifiers on his angular hat wreathing his head in aromatic smoke. He ignored her completely. Beside him was his esteemed visitor, in whose honour she, Flambusia, had been ordered to scrub the marble floor spotless. Hemtuft Battleaxe, he was called, a savage-looking long-haired goblin with a long feathered cloak that swept back behind him as he and Hemuel hurried up the stairs beyond – leaving, just as she'd feared, a trail of muddy footprints behind them. A moment later, she heard an upper door slam.

Bang!

Flambusia looked up, an expression of utter misery in her rheumy eyes. 'Oh Amberfuce, my love,' she moaned pitifully. 'What are they doing to you up there?'

Upstairs in the treatment room adjoining his bed-chamber, Amberfuce the Waif, once High Chancellor to the Most High Academe of old Sanctaphrax, was still not absolutely convinced he hadn't died and gone to the great Eternal Glen. The last thing on his mind was his former nurse. In fact he wasn't thinking of anything except his own pleasure. Even when Hemuel Spume knocked on the door and entered, with Hemtuft Battleaxe close on his heels, it was as much as he could do to open his eyes and raise a thin, spidery hand in greeting.

The soak-vat – or 'cooking-pot', as his attendant gabtrolls called it behind his back – was, to Amberfuce's mind, the most wonderful contraption ever invented. It was round and squat, fashioned from burnished copper and filled with warm liquid. Amberfuce sat inside it on a small stool, only his head protruding from the top.

There was a series of pipes attached to the outer shell

of the vat, delivering hot water, silken balms and salves and purified air – which bubbled through the fragrant, oily liquid inside – from the bottom, and removing the cooled overflow from the top. And as if that were not enough, the team of gabtrolls – their tongues slurping constantly over their eyeballs in the steamy room – were fussing about Amberfuce's head, stroking his ears and temples, massaging his cranium and rubbing sweet-smelling unguents into his skin.

Hemuel approached him, the stocky goblin following close on his heels. Amberfuce's eyelids fluttered as he struggled to concentrate on the visitors to his room.

Leave us a while, he told the gabtrolls, speaking directly inside their heads.

The gabtrolls did as they were told, putting down their sponges and loofahs and vials of aromatic oils, and withdrew. Hemuel Spume stepped closer.

'You're looking so much better, dear friend,' he said, a smile tugging the corners of his tight mouth as he looked round the steamy room, scented candles with misty haloes burning on every surface. He pulled off his steel-rimmed glasses and wiped the steam from the inside of the glass. 'I trust the gabtrolls are taking extra-special care of you, as I ordered.'

'They're wonderful, wonderful,' Amberfuce gushed. 'I haven't felt so good in years.'

'You've earned it,' said Hemuel. 'Those blueprints were invaluable.' He raised his arm, and gestured to his companion. 'I've just been showing our visitor here how well our work is progressing,' he explained.

'Indeed,' said Hemtuft, nodding gravely. 'Most impressive . . .'

I see, said Amberfuce, his soft voice hissing inside the long-haired goblin's head.

Hemtuft winced. He despised waifs at the best of times, with their soft, weak bodies and insidious thoughts. And this one – pampered and sibilant – was a particularly unpleasant specimen. Then again, as Hemuel Spume had explained, he'd stolen the plans from Vox Verlix which had made everything possible, and the goblin general made a note to himself to keep his contempt and disgust reined in.

'My army is assembled,' he told them both. 'The Goblin Nations are ready to march!'

To march? The waif's voice sounded contemptuous. *Don't you mean* to follow, *General?*

For a second time, Hemtuft winced. He would never get used to the way the frail-looking creatures would invade thoughts, and he resented the waif's tone – but he tried to mask his anger as he turned to Hemuel.

'The axes of the long-hairs are sharpened,' he said, 'the swords and scythes of the hammerheads and flat-heads whetted. The lances of the lop-ears are oiled, the quivers of the pink-eyes are full and the clubs of the tusked and underbiters all freshly studded. We are ready!'

Hemuel Spume smiled, a twinkle in his eye. 'As are my glade-eaters,' he rasped.

CHAPTER EIGHTEEN

SUNSET IN THE FREE GLADES

'Good luck, Blad,' said Felix, raising his tankard to the ruddy-faced slaughterer in the muglumpskin jacket who was seated beside him. 'Here's to your new life in the Silver Pastures!'

'The Silver Pastures!' echoed the other ghosts clustered round the huge, circular table in the Bloodoak Tavern.

'Though why you'd want to spend your days chasing after herds of hammelhorns beats me ... Stupid great creatures!' laughed a mobgnome named Skillet, nudging his wiry gnokgoblin companion. 'Skut and I are off to the southern fringes to trap fromps.'

'That's not all you'll trap if you're not careful,' said Brove, a lugtroll, darkly. 'That's hammerhead country, so they say. The forests up there are crawling with them.' He shook his head and tapped his bone breast-plate. 'Once I take this off, it's the quiet life for me. Got a nice little cave in the northern cliffs picked out, I have, a small plot to grow tripweed, and a hammelhorn cart to take it to market . . .'

'Well, now I've heard everything!' Felix burst out, clapping the lugtroll on the back. 'Brove Gloamcheek, the toughest troll in all of Screetown, scourge of the Guardians of Night, is about to become a gardener!'

The whole table exploded with laughter and the ghosts raised their tankards once more.

'To fromp trapping!'

'To tripweed!'

'To Brove the gardener!'

The locals sitting round the tavern turned and looked at them with a mixture of curiosity and amusement. Meggutt, Beggutt and Deg toasted the rowdy group before plunging their heads back into their drinking trough. Zett Blackeye smiled a gap-toothed smile and his hefty cloddertrog sidekick, Grome, raised his drinking-pail in salute. Only the old sky pirate in the corner ignored the ghosts and sat instead staring into his goblet of sapwine with pale, unblinking eyes.

Draining his tankard in one huge gulp, Brove turned to Felix. 'So what about you?' he said. 'Once we're disbanded, there'll be no one to listen to your muglump-hunting stories . . .'

'Or to lead raids on the Tower of Night . . .' chipped in Blad.

'. . . Or to swim 'cross the Edgewater in the middle of the night,' added Skillet.

'In full bone-armour!' Skut reminded him.

'Happy days,' said Brove, and put his tankard down on the table.

An awkward silence fell over the ghosts as they each remembered their former home; the rubble-strewn, demon-haunted desolation of Screetown, so different from the peaceful tranquillity of the Free Glades. None of them liked to admit it but, despite the dangers and hardships they'd had to endure, they were going to miss their former lives as ghosts – and none more so than their young leader, Felix Lodd.

Felix peered into the depths of his tankard thoughtfully before breaking the silence. And when he did, his voice was raw with emotion. 'My father wants me to join him in the new Great Library.' He shrugged. 'He says it's my duty to the librarians – and to him . . .'

'Felix Lodd, a librarian,' said Skillett, his face cracking into a broad grin. 'Who'd have thought it?'

The others laughed – though a little uncomfortably. They could sense their leader's inner turmoil and unhappiness.

Felix shrugged again. 'Still, if it'll make the old bark-worm happy . . .'

Suddenly, the heavy ironwood door burst open with a loud *crash* that made the roof timbers of the New Bloodoak Tavern shake, and in strode Deadbolt Vulpoon, followed by a stream of sky pirates.

'Well, lads, look what old Deadbolt's found, skulking in the woods of the western fringes,' he said, nodding over his shoulder.

The two sky pirates behind him wrestled with a

hulking figure in an iron collar attached to a chain. The acrid smell of rotting meat and dank vegetation was unmistakable. The figure stopped struggling and straightened up, ear and chin rings glinting in the lamplight. Two bloodshot eyes surveyed the ghosts from beneath heavily tattooed brow-ridges. An upper lip curled in disdain, to reveal two rows of sharp, pointed teeth.

Felix rose to his feet. 'A hammerhead,' he said with awe.

Though the sky pirates on either side of the goblin were big, strapping individuals, beside the hammerhead they looked decidedly small. Luckily for them all, the goblin's wrists were tied securely behind his back and his legs were hobbled by a short length of stout chain.

'A *warrior* hammerhead,'

said Deadbolt proudly, ignoring the murderous look the goblin gave him. 'Fresh from the Goblin Nations. Armed to the teeth and looking for trouble. We were fromp trapping when we surprised his war band.'

'What did I tell you?' said Brove to Skillet. 'Dangerous thing, fromp trapping.'

Skillet swallowed uneasily.

'War band?' said Felix with surprise.

'That's what it looked like to me,' said Deadbolt. 'They weren't carrying their birthing-bundles or their weaving-rods, just weapons – and plenty of them! They were looking for trouble all right.'

The goblin sneered and fell to his haunches, his eyes darting round the tavern.

'His mates turned and disappeared into the woods as soon as they saw us.'

'*They ran away?*' Felix could hardly believe it.

The goblin spat on the floor and leered up at him. 'Run now, fight soon,' he said in a low, guttural voice.

'When?' said Felix, dropping to his knees and staring into the goblin's face. '*When* will the hammerheads fight?'

'Soon,' said the hammerhead, his smile revealing his jagged white teeth once more. 'Hammerheads fight *soon*.'

'That's as much as we could get out of him,' said Deadbolt with a wave of his arm. 'He must have been at the woodgrog, because when his mates fled, they left him curled up under a sapwood tree, snoring his head off. Speaking of which, where's Mother Bluegizzard? I'm parched!'

'Woodgrog!' said the hammerhead, licking his lips. 'Teg-Teg want woodgrog!'

'I think he's had enough!' said Mother Bluegizzard, flapping over with a heavily-laden tray, her mate, Bikkle, hiding behind her skirts. 'Now, if you wouldn't mind, please remove your visitor, Captain Vulpoon. He's upsetting my regulars!'

'Take Teg-Teg here to the Hive Huts,' said Deadbolt. 'And see about getting him a bath,' he added. 'He smells worse than a halitoad!'

As the sky pirates bundled the great hammerhead out of the tavern and the door slammed shut behind them, everyone in the Bloodoak let out a sigh of relief. Meggutt, Beggutt and Deg resumed their drinking, thirsty after all the excitement. Zett and Grome exchanged glances, while in the corner the lone sky pirate looked back down at the table before him.

'Earth and Sky, wouldn't fancy meeting someone like him on a dark night,' said Skillett, draining his tankard and catching Mother Bluegizzard's eye for a top-up.

'Me neither,' added Blad.

'Maybe not,' said Deadbolt Vulpoon, as he and the remaining sky pirates joined the ghosts at the table, 'but I have the horrible feeling we're going to. You heard him. "Fight soon", he said, and I for one believe him.'

Felix's eyebrows drew together darkly. 'You reckon the hammerheads you disturbed were snooping then?' he said.

'No doubt about it,' said Deadbolt darkly. 'And they didn't want to be seen either. Scouting out our defences, if you ask me.'

Felix frowned. 'How many did you say there were?'

'At least two hundred,' said Deadbolt grimly. 'And we found evidence of many more. Camp fires, clearings and old hive-huts, freshly used' – he wrinkled his nose – 'by the smell of them. I reckon we've got half the Goblin Nations out there, just waiting for the chance to attack.'

Felix leaped to his feet, his eyes blazing. 'Well, what are we waiting for?' he said, the excitement plain in his voice. 'We must warn the Freeglade Council at once and prepare for war!'

'Good luck with that!' said Deadbolt with a snort. 'You know what these Freegladers are like. So long as there's crops in the fields and timber in the yards, they're happy. Even the librarians are more concerned with that library of theirs than anything else.'

'Then it's up to us!' said Felix with a triumphant smile.

He looked round the table, his gaze fixing moment-arily on each of his ghosts. 'You're going to have to put those plans of yours on hold, lads,' he said. 'Blad, the Silver Pastures will have to wait. Skut and Skillet, it's goblin fighting not fromp trapping for you. And Brove, forget the gardening and hang onto your bone-armour. You're going to need it!'

'Aye, Felix,' he said.

'And as for me,' he said, his eyes blazing brightly. 'It looks as if the librarians will just have to get along with-out me for the time being.' He raised the tankard which Mother Bluegizzard had just refilled. 'Forget the Ghosts of Screetown,' he said. 'Here's to the Ghosts of New Undertown!'

*

All clear to the west, the young skycraft pilot signalled, before swooping down low and fast, skimming over the long, pale green grass of the Silver Pastures and soaring back, high into the air.

Steady, Xanth! his companion signalled back, adjusting her sail with a deft flick of her tolley-rope and rising up beside him.

'Still trying to impress the tilderherders, I see!' Magda shouted across to Xanth with a smile.

'Just enjoying the *Ratbird* again!' Xanth shouted back, patting the carved prow of his skycraft. 'It handles even better than I remember,' he added, laughing out loud as, with a skilful twitch of the loft and nether-sail ropes, the spidersilk sails billowed and the little craft soared up high above his flight partner.

'We're not here to enjoy ourselves! We're on patrol!' Magda called after him, stroking the carved prow of the *Woodmoth*. It was true, it was exhilarating to be back in the air. After the shryke fireball had torn through her spidersilk sail and sent her spiralling out of control to slam into the forest floor, she had feared *Woodmoth* would never fly again. But she'd picked herself up and, pulling the stricken skycraft behind her, had trudged for days through the Deepwoods. It had taken weeks to recover from that terrible journey, not to mention to repair the *Woodmoth*. And now, here they were once more, soaring through the clear Free Glades air.

High above, Xanth tugged on the hanging-weights and swooped back down through the sky, panicking a herd of tilder grazing below him, and sending them galloping off across the grasslands. In the distance, several slaughterers on skycraft waved in salute and gave their characteristic whooping calls. There was nothing a seasoned tilderherder appreciated more than skilful flying. Xanth waved back and swooped round in a slow arc to rejoin his companion.

Come on, Magda signalled, trying not to smile. *Let's head back. We need to make our report.*

Xanth nodded and followed her as she set a full sail. Below them, the vast grasslands of the Silver Pastures shimmered in the morning light and great herds of bellowing hammelhorns grazed beside skittish runs of leaping tilder.

Beyond the Silver Pastures, the rolling green canopy of the Deepwoods stretched out seemingly for ever. Far, far away were the tiny specks that marked the beginning of the Goblin Nations, and on the distant horizon the inky smudge of the Foundry Glades glowered like a bad dream. Here in the bright sunshine, all was peace and tranquillity. Xanth caught Magda up and signalled across to her.

Race you back to Lake Landing!

Magda made no reply, but from the way the *Woodmoth* abruptly darted off through the air in the direction of the Free Glades, it was clear that she had not only seen his challenge but had also taken him up on it. Like two snowbirds in a windstorm, the skycraft streaked across the sky.

Past the look-out tower they went, leaving the Silver Pastures behind them; over the spiky tree-tops of the forest ridges and down towards the Free Glades. Far below them, the great northern cliffs dotted with cloddertrog caves came into view. A moment later, New Undertown appeared, with the three lakes spread out before them, their still, deep waters reflecting the midday sky like burnished mirrors. And as they flew on, they were joined by other librarian skycraft as patrols flew in from every direction towards Lake Landing.

The Great Lake came closer and Magda eased off, letting the loft-sail go slack. *It's OK!* she signalled. *You win! If Varis sees us racing, we'll be for it!*

Xanth brought the *Ratbird* round and gently steered it

in. The pair of them landed amongst many others on the
thronging platforms of Lake Landing.

'Timid lemkin,' whispered Xanth in Magda's ear as
they secured their skycraft.

'Show off!' she responded and stuck out her tongue.

The dozens of skycraft, tethered to jutting mooring-
bars, bobbed around in the warm breeze that was getting
up, while the gantries and flying-walkways were filled
both with those librarian knights who had just landed
and those who were about to take off. Magda and Xanth
headed off along the jetty to where a cluster of young
librarian knights had assembled and were deep in loud,
animated conversation with each other. As they joined
them, so too did Varis Lodd, striding up from the
direction of the refectory tower, her green flight-suit
gleaming in the bright sunlight.

'Librarian knights!' she said, her voice sharp-edged
and commanding. 'Stop gabbling like a bunch of
woodgeese and make your reports!'

The librarian knights snapped to attention, eyes facing
forwards and divided into twos. All raised their hands
and signalled their reports with crisp precision.

Movements to the south. Suspected flat-head party.

Varis nodded, her eyes narrowing.

Forest fires near the Foundry Glades. Spreading this way.

Varis nodded again, her face stony and expressionless.

*Fired upon over the southern fringes. Grey goblins' barbed
arrowheads. No casualties.*

Varis moved along the line, nodding curtly as each
librarian pair reported in turn. There had been goblin

sightings, recently deserted clearings and glowing camp fires all round the borders of the Free Glades.

'And you two?' Varis's voice, stern and strident, cut through the silence.

Magda and Xanth, who'd been nudging each other and trying to make one another giggle, looked up guiltily. Magda raised her left hand and signalled the wide arc of the Silver Pastures, while Xanth circled his thumb and forefinger and bowed his head.

'All quiet in the Silver Pastures, eh?' Varis gave a thin smile. 'At last, some good news. Though with all that fancy flying and racing, I'm not surprised you two didn't notice anything. Thank goodness for the slaughterer herders. At least *their* reports are reliable!'

Magda and Xanth both reddened as all eyes turned to them.

'Librarian knights, dismissed!' Varis barked, and the ranks broke up and headed for the refectory tower.

'Xanth!' Varis's hand was on the librarian knight's shoulder. As she drew him to one side her voice became low and confidential. 'Talking of herders' reports,' she said, 'a certain slaughterer tells me that your flying this morning was the finest he'd ever seen.'

Xanth's face reddened once again, but this time he was smiling.

'If things are as bad as I suspect, your flying skills will soon come in useful.'

'They will?' said Xanth.

'Yes,' said Varis, smiling in turn. 'As my flight marshal.'

*

'Steady, boy,' Rook whispered as he felt Chinquix quiver beneath him.

The branch the prowlgrin was perched on seemed impossibly slender, but Rook had learned to trust his mount's judgement completely. In all their exhilarating treetop gallops through the Deepwoods, the powerful skewbald prowlgrin had never put a foot wrong. And in contrast to its bigger brown and orange cousins, Chinquix was fast and quick-witted. Rook had only to touch the reins or squeeze his legs with the slightest pressure for the prowlgrin to respond instantly.

But there was more to their bond than simply *mount* and *rider*. Whenever Rook appeared in the roost, Chinquix's blue eyes would light up and his thin, whiplash tail would thrash the air excitedly. Then Rook would tickle Chinquix just above his nostrils and the prowlgrin would close his eyes and let out a low rumbling growl of contentment.

'What is it, boy?' whispered Rook, leaning forward in the saddle. Chinquix's nostrils were quivering as he sniffed the air. 'What can you smell?'

Rook scanned the horizon. To his right, the undulating ocean of leaves continued into the distance; before him, a similar view was interrupted in several places by iron-wood stands, the stately pines reaching up high above the rest – while to his left . . .

He gasped. His jaw dropped and his eyes widened, unable to believe what they could see.

'What in Sky's name?' Rook murmured.

For two long days, the troop of Freeglade Lancers had been out on patrol. They'd started off far to the north-west of the Free Glades, and had gradually made their way eastwards, skirting round the outer fringes and making occasional forays deeper into the forest. Up until now, they'd discovered nothing untoward. In fact, if anything, the forest had seemed quieter than usual, and on that first night spent in his swaying hammock, Rook had slept better than he had done for years.

The following morning, however, the deep sonorous calls of giant fromps from distant ironwood stands had woken them, and the troop had set off to investigate the cause of the disturbance. As they rode, leaping through the upper branches, their lance pennants fluttering, they had passed Deepwood creatures fleeing through the forest below.

Now, Rook could see why. Beneath him, Chinquix gave a low growl of alarm. Other riders joined Rook, high up above the leafy canopy: the gnokgoblins Grist, Worp and Trabbis, Ligger the slaughterer, and Captain Welt himself.

'Earth and Sky!' the captain exclaimed. 'What is *that*?'

Rook shook his head. Countless trees had been felled, leaving a bald swathe of scorched earth through the forest. Beyond it was a second track, even broader than the first, and thick with chips of wood – all that remained of the magnificent lufwoods, leadwoods and lullabees that had until so very recently been standing there.

'The trees have been decimated,' cried Grist, pulling

on the reins and steadying his prowlgrin.

'Razed to the ground,' added Worp.

'Flattened and incinerated,' gasped Ligger.

'And scythed,' added Ligger. 'Look at these saplings. They've been sliced right through.'

Grist turned to Captain Welt. 'Goblins?' he asked.

But the captain shook his head. 'No goblin work party I've ever seen could clear the forest like this,' he said. 'It takes weeks to fell an ironwood stand, yet look . . .'

The lancers looked where Welt was pointing. The stumps of the mighty pines stuck up from the devastated forest floor like the gap-toothed smile of a gabtroll. All round them lay the charred remains of twenty or so huge fromps, still clutching branches in their great curved claws.

'And we heard the fromps calling just this morning,' the captain said grimly.

'So, who or what did this?' asked Ligger, his red face anxious and drawn.

'It beats me,' said Welt.

'Well, whatever it was,' said Rook, pointing down the tracks to smoke on the horizon, 'it's heading straight for the Free Glades!'

As evening fell over New Undertown and the sky turned from gold to deepest copper, the lamps of the Lufwood Tower were lit, one by one, until the whole magnificent building was ablaze with flickering light. High in the tower, on the open platform just below the roof, the Council of Eight had gathered. Garlands of flowers hung from the pillars, the posts and the balustrades, their fragrance as intoxicating as the goblets of sweet winesap on the table before them. Above, the bell in the cupola tolled nine and Cowlquape Pentephraxis raised his goblet.

'Fellow members of the Council of Eight,' said the High Academe, looking round at the gathered assembly. 'Or should I say, friends. I would like to propose a toast.'

Parsimmon, the Master of Lake Landing, and Fenbrus Lodd, the High Librarian, exchanged knowing glances. The Professors of Light and Darkness picked up their goblets with a smile, while stony-faced Varis Lodd took hers in both hands. Hebb Lub-drub, Mayor of New Undertown, looked embarrassed and clicked his fingers for his empty goblet to be refilled, while Cancaresse, Keeper of the Gardens of Thought, fluttered her huge ears as she raised her tiny thimble of winesap.

'Hebb informs me that the harvest has been gathered

in,' Cowlquape proceeded, 'that the grain-stores, the beet-houses, the fruit-lofts and milch-barns are all full to bursting . . .'

Everyone raised their goblets to the low-belly goblin, who smiled delightedly.

'While Parsimmon, here, reports the largest graduation of apprentices from the Lake Landing Academy in living memory!'

'Hear, hear!' said the Professors of Light and Darkness together, bowing to the gnokgoblin master.

'And Cancaresse reassures me that the Undertowners have settled into their new lives here in the Free Glades with great success.' Cowlquape smiled at the tiny waif, who nodded in agreement. 'But perhaps our greatest achievement here,' the High Academe continued, spilling a drop of his winesap as he raised his goblet high above his head, 'is the completion of the magnificent new library under the guiding hand of Fenbrus Lodd. To the Great Library!'

'To the Great Library!' chorused the Council of Eight as one, and drained their goblets.

But wait . . . Cancaresse's soft voice sounded in everyone's head. *One of our number does not share our happiness* . . . The waif turned to Varis Lodd, her ears fluttering like paper. 'You are troubled?' she asked quietly.

Varis nodded. 'There are disturbing reports coming in from the forest fringes all round the Free Glades,' she said, putting her goblet down on the table.

'Reports?' said Cowlquape with concern. 'From whom?'

'From my librarian knights, from the sky pirates *and* from the ghosts ...'

'*Pah!*' interrupted Fenbrus Lodd. 'The ghosts, indeed. That's just that son of mine out looking for trouble ...'

'No, father.' Varis's voice was stern. 'I believe there's more to it than that. I believe that the Free Glades are in great danger ...'

Just then, there came a clattering sound followed by a loud whinny, and a powerful skewbald prowlgrin appeared on a buttress below and launched itself up onto the platform balustrade, scattering the garlands of glade-lily and pasture-violets. A Freeglade lancer slipped from the saddle and thudded to the floor, where he knelt in front of the Most High Academe, his head bowed and his breath short and panting.

'Rook!' said Cowlquape. 'Rook Barkwater, is that you?'

'I ... I bring ... urgent news ...' Rook gasped, gulping in lungfuls of air, 'from Captain Welt ... of the Lancers ... He sent me on ahead ... Chinquix was the fastest ...'

'Yes, yes,' said Varis. 'What news, Rook?'

'The Free Glades ...

are in . . . great . . . danger,' he panted.

'Danger?' said Cowlquape, 'from what?'

'From that!' said Rook, leaping to his feet and gesturing towards the distant horizon.

Cowlquape and the council crossed to the balustrade and peered out at the reddish glow in the distance.

'From the sunset?' said Cowlquape. 'I don't understand . . .'

'Sunset!' Rook interrupted, his voice breaking with emotion. 'Believe me, Most High Academe, sir, that is no sunset!'

·CHAPTER NINETEEN·

INFERNO

'Rook Barkwater reporting back!' the young lancer cried out as he tugged at the reins of his powerful skewbald prowlgrin.

Captain Welt acknowledged him with a nod of the head and a barely perceptible smile. Behind him, the massed ranks of the Freeglade Lancers – five thousand strong in all – stretched out across the meadowlands of the southern fringe. They wore green and white chequerboard collars, white tunics emblazoned with the red banderbear badges and, with their long, glittering ironwood lances raised, resembled nothing so much as a gigantic bristle-hog basking in the evening light.

'Captain,' Rook began, and patted Chinquix, who was panting and snorting, his great pink tongue lolling out of the corner of his mouth as he sucked in huge gulps of air. 'The Council of Eight send their compliments to the Freeglade Lancers and their illustrious leader . . .'

'Yes, yes, Rook, lad,' interrupted Captain Welt. 'You and Chinquix here have made excellent time getting back from the Lufwood Tower. Don't waste it now with empty greetings. What exactly did the council *say*?'

Rook took a deep breath. 'The librarian knights are taking to the air,' he told him, 'and the ghosts and sky pirates are organizing the defences of New Undertown, but . . .'

'But?' said Welt, his low brow creased and his dark eyes boring into Rook's.

'But they need time to evacuate the villages of the woodtrolls and slaughterers to the cloddertrog caves in the northern cliffs . . .'

'Then we shall buy them that time!' said Welt, glancing round, 'if necessary, with the blood of the Freeglade Lancers!'

Behind him, the lancers roared their approval and thrust their ironwood lances high in the air. Rook smiled.

'You've done well, Rook, lad,' said Welt, wheeling Orlnix, his orange prowlgrin, round on the spot. 'Now find your troop and fall in. We've got a long and bloody night ahead of us!'

He spurred his mount and trotted out along the edge of the meadowlands in front of the lancers. All eyes turned to the treeline in the distance. Above the jagged silhouettes of the copper-elms and gladebirch trees, the sky was an angry crimson, as columns of smoke rose up from the depths of the forest all along the southern fringes of the Free Glades.

Rook found Ligger the slaughterer, and Worp, Trabbis and Grist the gnokgoblins, sitting grim-faced astride their prowlgrins in the centre of the line. There was no time for greetings. An ominous rumble, like rolling thunder or the growl in the throat of a monstrous beast, was rising up from the forest in front of them, growing louder and louder as the light faded.

'By Sky,' Ligger murmured, his lance trembling in his hand. 'What *is* that?'

Beside him, Grist shook his head. Worp and Trabbis exchanged troubled glances. The next moment a loud splintering crash rang out across the meadowlands as a dozen or so towering copper-elms on the fringes of the glade abruptly toppled to the ground. An instant later, from a couple of places further to the right, more trees creaked and splintered and crashed to the forest floor.

The line of trees in front of the massed ranks of lancers now looked suddenly ragged. The ominous rumbling became a deafening roar as, out of the gaps in the treeline, in a flash of flame and screech of metal, came first one, then two, then four huge metallic monsters, heaving themselves out into the meadowlands.

The first was like a giant battering-ram, with a long, curved metal spike protruding from its front. The next had long whiplash chains that spun round and round,

encircling everything
before it and tearing
it from the ground,
while the third had
sweeping scythes
that slashed through
the air – now high,
now at ground-level – cutting down everything that stood

in its way. Each infernal machine was propelled by a
mighty lufwood-burning furnace, and as the energy of
the buoyant wood was converted into power by screeching chain-belts and pulleys, so thick, black, spark-filled
smoke billowed from the furnace chimney above.

Rook looked at the terrible machines, one after the
other, his stomach sinking. From beside him, he could
hear Ligger whisper the same three words over and over.

Sky protect us. Sky protect us. Sky protect us . . .

With a deafening crash, two more of the
hulking glade-eaters burst
through the tree-
line, one hurling
massive rocks from
a three-armed cata-
pult; the other firing
blazing logs.

'Stand firm,
Freeglade
Lancers!' Captain
Welt commanded.

The rows of lancers did as they were told, holding their skittish prowlgrins steady while struggling hard to stop their lances from shaking as the blazing logs and massive rocks landed in their midst. As the machines crashed forwards, they scorched a path across the meadowlands every bit as pulverized as the tracks through the Deepwoods. And trailing behind – shields up, weapons at the ready and keeping to the smoking tracks – marched phalanx after phalanx of the goblin army; hammerheads, flat-heads, huge tusked goblins and small greys, lop-eared, long-haired and tufted, all tramping in the twake of the glade-eaters.

Rook wrapped the reins around one hand and gripped his lance tightly. He bent down and whispered to Chinquix. 'Easy now, lad.' His voice quavered. 'Wait for the command.'

Just then, Captain Welt's bellowed cry pierced the air.

'CHARGE!!'

The full moon's reflection in the glassy surface of the Great Lake barely rippled as, with the faint sigh of wind on spidersilk, nine hundred skycraft rose into the air from the great wooden platform of Lake Landing. Silent as moonmoths, their sails billowing, the craft climbed high above the black silhouette of the Academy Tower and hovered for a moment. Then, as silently as they had risen, the swarm of skycraft separated into three and streaked off across the sky – one to the east, one to the west and one to the south.

Xanth Filatine set his nether-sail and swooped down

in a wide arc round the three hundred skycraft of Varis Lodd's squadron. He signalled as he went.

Keep in formation, Grey Flight . . . Close up on the right, Green Flight . . . Steady, Centre Flight, follow the flight-leader's course!

The flights – each a hundred skycraft strong – fell into graceful arrowhead formations and followed Varis Lodd as she set a course for the southern fringes. Xanth checked his hanging-weights and swooped down to join the leader of the Grey Flight, who looked up with a smile.

Looking good, Flight Marshal! Magda signalled.

So are you, Grey Leader, Xanth signalled back. *Just keep close when we get to the meadowlands.*

Magda nodded, and Xanth peeled away to circle the squadron again. As he marshalled the stragglers back into formation, the moon appeared from behind the swiftly moving banks of cloud and shone down brightly, glinting on the carved and varnished heads of the individual skycraft. To the north, Xanth could see the Professor of Light's squadron, now just distant specks, flying low over the farmlands towards New Undertown. To the east, the Professor of Darkness's squadron skirted over the tall, tree-covered bluffs beyond the woodtroll villages.

Xanth checked his equipment for the hundredth time as the squadron flew high above the waif glen and the glistening lakes, and over the spiky treetops of the iron-wood pines. His crossbow was in the holster strapped to his leg. It was oiled and loaded. The bolts hung from his flight-harness, sixty in each quiver, thorn-tipped and razor-sharp. His stove glowed from the saddle hook to his right, and the pinesap darts were strapped to his back along with a gladebirch catapult and a sack of rock-hard ironwood pellets for good measure.

That should do for the time being, he thought, but just in case . . . He slipped his hand inside his tunic and felt the handle of a sharp straight dagger. He had no intention of being taken alive.

It was quiet up so high in the air, away from the hubbub of Lake Landing. Only the single thrummed note of the wind whistling through the taut string of his crossbow broke the silence – now loud, now soft – as the wind rose and fell.

Some way beyond the Ironwood Glade, at Varis Lodd's signal, the entire squadron bore round and headed west. Below them now, Xanth spotted the fringes of the Free Glades picked out in the moonlight as farm-land gave way to meadowland. He saw at once that all was not well. The forest had been sliced through in broad swathes, the great glowing scars extending out across the meadowlands like slime-mole trails. Along these tracks, at least twenty in number, the torches of the innumerable goblin hordes pouring into the Free Glades glittered like marsh gems.

But that was not all.

As Varis signalled for the squadron to hover and Xanth dropped down in the air to gather in the strays, he could see, at the head of each glowing trail, a huge furnace, its fiery mouth belching heat and sparks, its chimney spewing forth thick smoke.

Squadron! Varis signalled. *Prepare for attack in flight formation, on my command . . .*

Xanth tensed in his saddle as he steered the *Ratbird* round and joined the hovering Grey Flight, already busy setting their sails with feverish intensity. *Good luck, Magda!* he signalled across to the *Woodmoth*.

Good luck, Xanth! See you on the other side! Magda gestured back with a sweep of her arm.

Just then, far below, came the sound of a tilder horn sounding a charge, and a great spiky formation of Freeglade Lancers hurtled over the meadowlands towards the glowing furnaces. Varis sped across the sky in front of the squadron, her clenched fist held straight ahead in the unmistakable signal.

ATTACK!!

Up ahead of them, Lob could see the tall chimney of the glade-eater spewing out the acrid, black smoke that caught in their throats and made their eyes stream. The furnace glowed purple-blue as the goblin crew fed it with huge lufwood logs under the steady crack of a flat-head overseer's whip. Beside him, Lummel stumbled and almost lost his long-handled scythe as he tried to regain his balance on the churned up, splinter-strewn ground.

'Careful, brother.' Lob held out his hand to help him. 'That's a good scythe, that is. You don't want to go throwing it away!'

From the rear, a flat-head goblin let out a throaty roar. 'Close up in the ranks, you symbite pond-slime!' And the air rang out with the sound of a bullwhip cracking and anguished whimpers of pain.

The web-footed goblins behind them – some three thousand strong – were suffering cruelly at the hands of their flat-head captains. Most were armed only with nets and fishing-spears, and were being horribly tormented by the burning sparks that blew back from the huge glade-eater they were forced to follow. They tried to fall back, to protect themselves, but the flat-heads were having none of it.

'Keep up close to the glade-eater!' they roared, cracking their whips. 'You can bathe your scabby scales at the lakeside in New Undertown by sunrise!'

As Lob and Lummel stumbled forwards, the wind changed and blew the furnace smoke out of their faces, and for almost the first time since their hellish march had begun, they could see clearly. Ahead of them, New Undertown gleamed in the moonlight. There were tall buildings with crystal windows and spiky turrets, broad avenues lined with lights, stretches of water, fountains and statues, gardens and parks, the like of which none of the low-belly or symbite goblins dragooned into marching on the place had ever seen or even dreamed of before.

'Hive-huts, look,' whispered Lob.

'And webfoot wicker-huts,' Lummel whispered back.

'And look at that dome there. I ain't never seen nothing so tall and grand and beautiful . . .'

'. . . And deserted,' Lummel interrupted.

Lob looked round and frowned. It was true. Despite the smells of woodale and perfume still lingering in the air; despite the lamplight, the open windows, the chatter of pet lemkins and distant lowing of hammelhorns, there was no sign of any New Undertowners. The taverns were empty. The streets were deserted. It was as though the whole place had been abandoned.

'Where's everyone gone?' whispered Lob.

Lummel shrugged. 'I don't know,' he whispered back. 'Perhaps they heard we were coming and ran away?'

Ahead of them the glade-eater gave a screeching roar as the Furnace Master thrust full power onto the drive-chains, and the monstrous machine trundled forwards onto the cobbles of New Undertown.

'To the Lufwood Tower!' roared the flat-heads on either side of Lob and Lummel. 'New Undertown is ours!'

They surged forwards, waving their bullwhips in the air, forgetting the low-bellies and web-feet in their eagerness to follow the glade-eater. Suddenly, as Lob and Lummel looked on open-mouthed, the cobblestones beneath the huge machine gave way and the glade-eater disappeared into the ground with an almighty *crash*!

For a moment there was a stunned silence as everyone stood rooted to the spot, a cloud of dust billowing over them and turning them white as it settled. The flat-head goblins in front looked like statues, Lob thought; big, ugly, startled statues. He started to laugh.

Suddenly something whistled past his nose with the sound of an angry woodwasp. It was followed by another, and another. At first Lob thought they had disturbed a nest or a hive, until he saw the statues crumple in front of him, crossbow bolts embedded in their chests like red badges.

He looked up and, with a lurch of his stomach that threatened to burst his belly-sling, he saw that the rooftops of New Undertown had sprouted white-clad figures in muglumpskin armour, swinging ropes and bristling with crossbows. Suddenly he became aware of Lummel bellowing in his ear.

'Lob! Lob! Snap out of it and run!'

Without another thought, he dropped his long-handled scythe, turned on his heels and ran as fast as his legs could carry him back to the comparative safety of the treeline. Behind them came a deafening explosion as the furnace of the glade-eater exploded. Burning lufwood logs shot up from the sunken pit and blazed a trail across the sky.

Catching up with Lummel, Lob slumped to his knees on the forest floor. 'What now?' he wheezed, panting for breath.

His brother shrugged as he looked round. 'Maybe we can go home,' he said.

'Not so fast,' came a low growl and the low-bellies looked up to see a phalanx of hammerhead goblins glaring down at them from the forest shadows. Their captain stepped forward, his brow rings jingling, his lips set in a contemptuous curl. 'The battle,' he snarled, 'is only just beginning.'

At the sound of the tilder horn, Chinquix leaped forwards – his muscular rear-quarters propelling him up half a dozen strides into the air and down again. All round, flashes of orange and brown bounding across the meadowlands told Rook that his friends were following. In front, the huge shape of a glade-eater raced up to meet them, its forward platform bristling with spears.

With another huge bound, Chinquix leaped past the rumbling machine as the air filled with the hum of serrated spears. Rook stood high in the saddle and gripped his ironwood lance tightly as they came down in the midst of the following goblins. A jolt ran down from his elbow to his shoulder as the lance struck

something solid – and then Chinquix was back in the air with another huge leap.

Rook looked down and noticed that the lance was dark with blood. Behind him, there were gaping holes in the ranks of the goblins – but with the scattered corpses of prowlgrins, too. He twitched on Chinquix's reins and the powerful creature bounded forward as another glade-eater reared up in front of them. Rook gripped his lance with all his might and felt Chinquix's powerful legs tense once more as they prepared to spring.

The glade-eater roared, the air black with smoke, as Rook and Chinquix sailed up to meet it. He felt his lance buckle as it struck the metal side of the furnace, then shatter. Chinquix's reins snapped out of his grasp and the stirrups were ripped from his feet as Rook felt his prowl-grin fall away beneath him. With a deafening *clang*, Rook hit the burning hot metal of the furnace and rebounded from it with a soft hiss, before falling back to land in the soft meadowland grass with a bone-jarring thud.

Struggling for breath, he leaped to his feet and drew his sword. The glade-eater trundled past belching flames and sparks, and Rook found himself confronted by a war band of powerful long-haired goblins in ornate tooled armour, wielding huge double-bladed axes.

With a savage roar, a massive black-haired goblin, his beard glinting with rings and his blue eyes flashing, swung a copper-coloured axe at Rook's head. Although his helmet crest deflected the blow, Rook was knocked back down to the ground. The goblin towered above him, hate blazing in his eyes.

'Death to the Freeglader scum!' he screamed, raising his axe. '*Unnnkhh!*'

The blue eyes glazed over suddenly as an ironwood pellet embedded itself in the goblin's forehead with an audible skull-splitting crack.

Rook tore off his shattered helmet as, overhead, skycraft flashed past, their riders raining down a deadly shower of bolts, flaming darts and ironwood pellets.

The long-hairs scattered, swinging their mighty axes above their heads with howls of rage.

Rook climbed to his feet. The Freeglade Lancers' charge had cut a swathe through the goblin army, but at a terrible cost. All around, desperately wounded prowl-grins thrashed about amid heaps of goblin dead. What was more, the charge had failed to halt the glade-eaters, which trundled on ever deeper into the heart of the Free Glades. And, as Rook looked, fresh goblin war bands swarmed out of the Deepwoods and along the scorched tracks.

Suddenly, a flash of white in the corner of his eye, made Rook spin round. And there beside him stood Chinquix, his nostrils quivering and the veins in his temples throbbing with exertion.

'Chinquix! There you are!' Rook cried, leaping into the saddle as the long-hairs regrouped and came on again. Rook raised his sword and urged Chinquix forward, a defiant cry on his lips.

'FREEGLADER!!'

*

Xanth pulled on the flight rope and climbed high above the meadowlands of the southern fringes. The squadron was regrouping flight by flight, the holes in their formation a testament to the desperate fight they'd been in. He looked back over his shoulder and shook his head ruefully. The charge of the Freeglade Lancers had been truly magnificent – more so, even, than the Battle of Lufwood Mount.

But at what cost?

All along the southernmost borders of the Free Glades, orange, black and brown corpses lay amidst heaps of bodies, marking the course of the lancers' charge. It had cut through the advancing columns of the goblin army, but had failed to stop the advance of the monstrous glade-eaters. Even now as he looked, Xanth could see the fiery furnaces glowing as they cut a swathe through the Timber Yards to the east.

The librarian knights had done what they could to help the lancers, flying down low over the goblin army time after time until their quivers were empty and their missiles spent. And they'd paid dearly for their persistence. Green Flight was down to two dozen craft, Centre Flight had lost fifty and Grey Flight . . .

Xanth let out his loft-sail and urged *Ratbird* forward. The remnants of the Freeglade Lancers had fallen back towards New Undertown, their sacrifice buying time for the woodtrolls and slaughterers to find safety in the caves of the northern cliffs. Now the librarian knights had to look after their own.

Xanth gathered speed and caught up with the tattered

scattering of skycraft that, at first, he had taken to be stragglers, but now saw – as he approached – were actually all that was left of Grey Flight.

Your Flight Leader? he signalled to a librarian knight who was struggling with a torn nether-sail. *Where is she?*

The librarian gestured ahead. There, at the head of no more than twelve skycraft, Xanth saw the unmistakable prow of the *Woodmoth*, a figure slumped low in its saddle.

'Magda!' he called out. 'Magda! Are you hurt?'

Magda looked up with dull, glazed eyes, her face black with soot – except for white tear-streaks. *I'm fine, Flight Marshal*, she signalled. *But look what they've done to my Flight.*

She slumped forward again, and they flew on together in silence towards Lake Landing as the thin light of dawn rose behind the dark treeline. Or, at least, what the librarian knights of Varis Lodd's depleted squadron took to be the dawn. It was only as they approached the Ironwood Stands and dropped lower to skim over the Great Lake and down to Lake Landing that they realized their mistake.

There was a glow in the sky all right, but it didn't come from the dawn. Instead, a red tinge lit up the drawn and weary faces of the librarian knights as they approached the lake.

'The Great Library!' gasped Varis Lodd, raising her arm to signal the following skycraft to hover.

In front of them, on the lake shore opposite Lake Landing, the new library blazed like a lufwood torch. All round it, a mighty goblin army danced and howled as a dozen mighty glade-eaters shot burning logs into the inferno. On the library steps, the bodies of librarians were piled high, their robes smoking as the burning embers of the blazing new library showered down on them.

Varis put her head in her hands. 'Father, father, father,' she sobbed.

The librarian knights clustered round, hovering uncertainly, unnerved by their leader's breakdown. But when Varis looked up, her eyes were blazing and her face was a mask of stone.

They haven't got to Lake Landing yet, she signalled. *The sight of the Great Library burning has proved too much of an attraction . . .*

Her eyes glinted with a fierce hatred.

Flight Marshal! She turned to Xanth. *Take Grey Flight and save the apprentices at Lake Landing,* she signalled – and Xanth could tell by the look on her face that it was useless to argue.

And you? he signalled back.

We have the honour of the Great Library to uphold! Varis's hand touched her forehead and then her heart. She turned to the others. *Are you with me, librarian knights?*

In Centre Flight and Green Flight, all seventy heads nodded as one.

Then follow me!

Varis Lodd fed out a length of rope in a graceful arc, and her spidersilk loft-sail billowed out like an unfurling woodapple blossom. Around her seventy librarian knights did the same and, with a soft sigh, they sped away over the still waters of the Great Lake like silent stormhornets.

Xanth felt a hand on his forearm. It was Magda, tears streaming down her face. 'Make them come back!' she sobbed. 'Xanth, please! Hasn't there been enough useless sacrifice?'

Xanth turned back to her, the old haunted look in his face that she hadn't seen since the Reckoning.

'Stob Lummus and three hundred apprentices who have never flown before need our help to get to New Undertown. Varis and the squadron have laid down their lives so that we might succeed.' He gazed into Magda's eyes. 'A sacrifice, yes, Magda,' he said softly as the squadron approached the burning library in the distance. 'But not a useless one!'

·CHAPTER TWENTY·

THE THREE BATTLES

i
The Battle of the Great Library

The following morning, seemingly out of nowhere, an incoming leadwood log smashed into the side of the New Bloodoak Tavern with a great *crash!*, setting its foundations trembling and opening up a crack that ran from the bottom to the top of the eastern wall. Cleeve Hakenbolt shuddered, the paraphernalia at the front of his heavy sky pirate coat jangling, and gripped his pikestaff with white-knuckled ferocity.

'That was close,' said Rickett, the wiry ghost at his side. He peered up anxiously at the wall of the tavern. 'Another direct hit like that and the whole lot's gonna come crashing down on top of us.'

Cleeve nodded, the expression on his face drawn and sombre. 'What are they waiting for?' he snarled, poking his head up over the barricade of hastily constructed drinking troughs and tavern tables.

'They've got us surrounded. Why don't they attack?'

On the outskirts of New Undertown, the glade-eaters crouched like monstrous fire-bugs, gleaming in the dawn light. Their furnaces sparked and rumbled; their chimneys smoked. Behind them stood a vast mass of symbite goblins – gyle goblins, web-foot, tree and gnokgoblins, together with low-bellies and their lop-eared cousins. They shuffled from foot to foot miserably, and the air was filled with the sounds of their coughing and spluttering.

'They're softening us up,' said Rickett, his face appearing next to Cleeve's at the barricade. 'Using those infernal machines to batter Undertown to pieces, and then ... *Get down!*' he bellowed, as a huge boulder whistled overhead and crashed into a section of the barricades to their left.

Dusting himself down, Rickett saw a couple of sky pirates emerge from the rubble and begin repairing the shattered section of barricade with matter-of-fact efficiency. He turned to Cleeve.

'It'll take more than a few leadwood logs and boulders to soften you lot up. Tough as old Mire ravens, so you are!'

'Well said, Rickett, lad,' the sky pirate smiled. 'And as for you ghosts, this must seem like a home away from home, what with all this rubble!'

They laughed heartily as they peered over the barricade once more. Just then, there was a soft, whistling hiss from above, followed by a muffled thud. Rickett and Cleeve spun round to see a young ghost in a muglumpskin jacket and bone-armour standing before them. He coiled up the rope he'd just slid down on and tossed it over his shoulder.

'Care to share the joke, lads?' he said.

Rickett grinned. 'Just keeping our spirits up, Felix,' he said. His face grew more serious. 'Though Cleeve here was wondering why they haven't attacked yet . . .'

'They're firing up their furnaces with fresh lufwood,' came a voice behind them, and the three of them turned to see Deadbolt Vulpoon striding towards them, with the Professors of Light and Darkness in tow. 'When they're good and hot, they'll attack all right. And when they do . . .'

Felix clapped his friend on the back. 'We'll be ready for them, won't we, Deadbolt!' he said cheerfully.

'The sooner the better!' the sky pirate captain roared, waving a fist in the direction of the goblin army. 'If they think they can bash the best tavern in Undertown to bits and get away with it, they've got another think coming!'

Felix laughed – but when he saw the expressions on

the two professors' faces, he stopped. 'Forgive me, Professors,' he said gravely. 'I see from your faces that the librarian knights have had a difficult night . . .'

The Professor of Darkness bowed his head to Felix. 'My squadron covered the retreat from the slaughterer and woodtroll villages. I lost a hundred of my best knights.'

'And we fought in the northern fringe until we could fight no more,' added the Professor of Light simply. His white tunic was ragged and stained with blood. 'I lost more than half my squadron.'

Felix nodded. 'The population of the Free Glades is safe in the cloddertrog caves, thanks to the heroism of you and your knights,' he said quietly. 'Now we must make our stand together – ghosts, sky pirates and librarian knights alike – here in New Undertown!'

At that moment, a flurry of missiles flew overhead and smashed into the surrounding buildings, sending the group ducking for cover.

'We're all in this together, all right!' said Deadbolt darkly, spitting dust from his mouth and clambering to his feet. 'Like oozefish trapped in a barrel . . .'

A loud whistle cut him short. Felix looked up to see one of his ghosts standing on the upper gantry of the Lufwood Tower, pointing into the distance.

'Felix! Felix!' he called down. 'Over there!'

Felix unhitched his rope and hurled it high above his head, and in an instant, swung up onto the rooftops.

'That lad,' said Deadbolt, peering up after him, 'never stays still for an instant!' He put his telescope to his right eye.

The professors climbed to their feet and set off for the Lufwood Tower at a run.

'The third squadron!' said Deadbolt, focusing the telescope. 'I wonder what kept them? Hey, Professors!' He snapped the telescope shut and gave chase. 'Wait for me!'

At the Lufwood Tower, Felix landed on the gantry with a soft thud and scanned the horizon for himself. Far ahead and low in the sky, was a smudge of tiny specks, dark against the lightening backdrop. As they got closer, he could see that they did indeed form a squadron of skycraft, flying like woodgeese in their familiar V-shaped formation.

'There you are, sister,' he murmured. 'I was beginning to get worried . . .' He frowned. Something wasn't quite right. 'They're all over the place,' he said.

'That's just what I was thinking,' said the Professor of Darkness breathlessly as he climbed up the steps to join Felix, the Professor of Light close on his heels.

There was definitely something wrong with the squadron. Although there was a skycraft clearly leading at the front, followed by ten more in full sail and steady formation, and a sky-marshal darting back and forth bringing up the rear, the vast majority of the skycraft – almost three hundred of them – were wavering about uncertainly, their sails loose and flapping and their hanging flight-weights dragging them off course.

'Good old Varis. Looks like a full squadron,' muttered the Professor of Light. 'No casualties!' He shook his head. 'But what *is* wrong with them?'

'They're flying like apprentices,' said the Professor of Darkness. 'No sail discipline. And look at that flight-marshal. He's having to fly in circles just to keep them together!'

'Come on, come on!' Felix urged through clenched teeth.

As the fluttering skycraft came closer, the goblin army gathered round the glade-eaters noticed them. All at once a tremendous volley of flaming arrows and missiles flew up from its ranks towards the skycraft passing overhead. Almost immediately, the sounds of distant screams reached the onlookers in the Lufwood Tower as the goblin missiles found their mark.

Skycraft after skycraft was hit, their sails collapsing and their riders spiralling down to earth.

'Tack and dive!' urged the Professor of Light desperately. 'Pull in the nether-sails for Sky's sake! You're making yourselves easy targets!'

The squadron formation now showed ragged holes as it approached the outskirts of New Undertown and more skycraft were falling with every passing second.

'Come on, come on,' Felix muttered grimly. 'You can make it!'

Below them, the defenders of New Undertown had noticed the incoming flight, and cheers and cries and shouts of encouragement echoed through the air. At the front of the squadron, Felix saw the flight-leader and a tight formation of ten skycraft expertly adjust their sails and prepare to land. They came down silently in the square below the Lufwood Tower to the wild cheering of

ghosts and sky pirates –
which they ignored.
Instead, leaping from
their own skycraft, they
began signalling urgently to
the skycraft straggling behind.

One by one, they came in to
land, unsteadily and so lack-
ing in control that most of
them slammed down and
their riders were
thrown from their
saddles and tossed
ignominiously to the
ground. The square was
soon thronging with
librarian knights, sky
pirates and ghosts, all
helping the dazed riders back to their feet. Felix
swooped down from the gantry and landed in their
midst, while the professors hurried down the steps.

'Varis!' he cried, rushing towards the flight-leader.
'Varis! What kept you?'

The flight-leader turned and removed her helmet and
goggles. Felix started back, a look of bewilderment on
his face.

'M ... Magda?' he stuttered. 'Magda Burlix ... But
where's my sister?'

The Professors of Light and Darkness jostled their way
through the crowd in the square to join Felix.

'But these are apprentices!' exclaimed the Professor of Light.

'From Lake Landing,' interrupted the Professor of Darkness. 'Sky be praised – we thought we'd lost you!'

'But where is Varis Lodd's squadron?'

Exhausted, Magda bowed her head, her face ashen white. A tear fell and splashed on her green flight-suit as she struggled to speak.

Stob Lummus, Assistant Master of Lake Landing, climbed from his skycraft and stumbled over. He gestured behind him.

'Xanth Filatine can tell you best,' he said. 'It is thanks to Magda and him, and their brave knights, that we made it this far.'

Felix turned. The last skycraft – that of the flight-marshal – was fluttering in to land. It had stayed airborne until the others had all landed. The carved ratbird prow was studded with goblin arrows; the sails ragged and scorched. Its rider climbed from the saddle and approached. There was blood on his flight-suit.

Xanth bowed solemnly. All round him, the ghosts and sky pirates were barking orders to clear the square and the librarian knights were helping the dazed apprentices to find shelter. Felix stood, completely oblivious to the missiles falling and the shouts to 'take cover!'. His eyes bore into Xanth's with a savage intensity.

'Tell me,' he said.

'We came down low across the Great Lake, what was left of us after the fight in the southern meadowlands,' Xanth began, his voice low but steady. 'That's when we saw it . . . The Great Library in flames, surrounded by goblin hordes and glade-eaters. It was plain that Lake Landing would be next. So Varis sent Grey Flight – the twelve of us – to save the apprentices, while she . . .' His voice faltered.

Felix's eyes never left his. 'What did she do?'

'I saw it all,' said Xanth, 'from the saddle of the *Ratbird* as I circled Lake Landing. It was a magnificent battle . . .'

'Magnificent?' said Felix fiercely.

'Yes,' said Xanth, his voice now grimly determined. 'Magnificent. In close formation, skimming the Great Lake, with Varis in front, the squadron charged the Great Library. They hit the shoreline with a murderous volley, the last they had, and then swarmed round the flaming building, ripping burning timbers from it with their flight-ropes, and raining them down on the goblins below. They fought till their sails were aflame and their skycraft were on fire . . . And then I saw them sail over the dark treetops followed by the enraged goblin hordes.'

Xanth's eyes were blazing now and his voice had risen.

'They followed them, like woodmoths to a flame, into the Deepwoods and away from Lake Landing until, one by one, I saw the flames go out. Then the goblin army streamed back, past the Great Library and towards Lake Landing. But by that time we'd got the apprentices airborne and were making for New Undertown.'

'So, my sister is . . .' Felix's voice choked.

'She sacrificed herself and her squadron for the

apprentices. Without the Battle of the Great Library, we would never have made it.'

Felix placed a hand on Xanth's shoulder. 'Varis would have been proud of you, Xanth Filatine,' he said simply.

The square was almost empty now, the skycraft tethered to mooring-poles beside the Lufwood Tower, and the defenders of New Undertown huddled behind the barricades. Overhead, the missiles continued to fall.

Felix was turning to go when Deadbolt arrived, Fenbrus Lodd at his side. The High Librarian was gesticulating wildly and booming in the sky pirate's ear. Behind them came a motley crowd of under-librarians armed with a mishmash of assorted weapons. Fenbrus stopped in front of Felix and glared round, red-faced with indignation.

'This sky pirate friend of yours thinks we librarian academics can't fight, Felix! The goblins burnt down our magnificent library, didn't they? Of course we're going to fight! You try and stop us. Tell him, Felix. Go on, tell him!'

Deadbolt rolled his eyes and shrugged.

'I'm ... I'm so sorry, my dear Fenbrus,' said the Professor of Light, turning away.

'Such a terrible loss,' murmured the Professor of Darkness.

'The Great Library?' said Fenbrus Lodd. 'Yes, yes. Time to think about that later. Now we must fight!'

Felix stepped forward. 'It's Varis, father,' he said softly.

'Is she back?' Fenbrus began.

Felix swallowed. He shook his head. 'She's not coming back.'

'You mean . . .' said Fenbrus again, his voice little more than a croaking whisper.

'Yes, father,' said Felix. 'Varis is dead.'

Fenbrus let out a small wheezing groan, the sound of a punctured trockbladder-ball losing its air. His beard drooped, the colour drained from his cheeks and it was as if his entire body – the bluster and bombast spent – shrank a little. Felix stepped forward, wrapped his arms round his father and hugged him protectively.

'She died bravely,' he said, 'sacrificing herself for the sake of others . . .'

Felix could feel his father's body trembling. 'Gone,' he heard him sobbing. 'Everything has gone.' The next moment, Fenbrus pulled away.

But Felix wouldn't let him go. He took him by the shoulders and stared deep into his eyes.

'Oh, Felix,' Fenbrus murmured, 'the books, the treatises, the barkscrolls. I can take their loss . . . Fresh young librarian scholars can be sent out to the four corners of the Edgelands. They can gather knowledge and write new books, new treatises, new barkscrolls. And the Great Library . . .' He shook his head. 'So magnificent . . . I can even stand *its* loss . . .'

He sighed. Felix held him tightly.

'But Varis. My beautiful, brave daughter . . .' Tears streamed down his pallid, puffy cheeks. 'Gone for ever . . . I don't think I can stand it.' He tried again to break away, but Felix maintained his grip. 'How can I go on without her?' Fenbrus wailed.

Felix looked down, his voice cracked and quavering. 'You . . . You've got me, father.'

Fenbrus looked into his son's eyes. 'You mean . . ?'

'Yes,' said Felix. 'I shall become a librarian. Together we shall rebuild the Great Library and replace the barkscrolls . . .'

For a moment, Fenbrus fell still. The next, Felix felt himself being pulled towards his father and wrapped up in his warm, strong embrace.

'Oh, son,' he whispered into Felix's ear. 'My dear, dear boy.' He pulled his head away and looked deep into Felix's eyes. 'Do you really think we could do all that?'

Felix nodded. 'Together,' he said simply. 'Together, father, we can do anything.'

At that moment, there came a series of whistles and cries from the top of the Lufwood Tower, and a booming voice filled the air.

'Freeglade Lancers, due south!'

Fenbrus and Felix pulled away from one another. The Professors of Light and Darkness both put their telescopes to their eyes and looked.

'Rook!' gasped Magda, grinning at Xanth through her tears. 'It's Rook!'

Xanth raised his hand and shielded his eyes from the low sun, just rising up above the horizon. Far ahead of him, coming closer with every giant leap, was a band of Freeglade Lancers on prowlgrinback. Most of the mounts were heavy, stolid creatures in shades of orange and woodnut brown. But one – close to the centre at the front – was of a slighter, more sinewy build, and white with dark brown patches.

'You're right,' said Xanth. 'It *is* Rook.'

Bounding in from the north-west, emerging from the treeline and leaping through the colonies of hive-huts, the lancers were skirting round the fringes of the goblin army. Before the goblins had even registered that they were in their midst, the lancers had moved on.

As Magda and Xanth watched, the prowlgrins bounded through the air, leaping higher than the rooftops and dodging the arrows and spears of the goblins. A moment later, the lancers were flying over the barricades and tugging on the reins of their snorting mounts. Rook jumped from Chinquix's saddle and hugged his friends.

'You took your time getting here!' he panted.

His face was bruised, his arms grazed; his surcoat was torn and stained. Yet he was alive and, judging by the grin on his face, well.

'Rook, I'm so glad to see you,' said Magda, her eyes glistening with tears. 'Oh, Rook, where is it all going to end? This fighting. All this killing . . .'

Xanth patted her arm and drew Rook aside. 'She's been through a lot,' he said. 'We all have.'

Rook nodded. 'I know, Xanth, I know,' he said. 'And it isn't over yet. Look after her, Xanth, I must make my report.'

He turned and headed over to where Felix and his father stood, together with the two professors and Deadbolt Vulpoon.

'The glade-eaters,' said Rook. 'They're coming!'

Deadbolt Vulpoon nodded. 'The lad's right,' he said, and pointed to the wreaths of spark-filled black smoke coiling up from the distant machines as a thumping, roaring, screeching sound filled the air. The Professors of Light and Darkness exchanged glances.

'So, this is it, then, Ulbus,' said one. 'First the villages, then the library, now New Undertown itself . . .'

'Indeed, Tallus,' said the other. 'This is where we must make our stand.'

Rook frowned. 'The Great Library, destroyed?'

'Ay, Rook,' said Felix. 'And Varis, dead. My father has taken it very hard. He has lost everything.'

Rook reached inside his jacket, pulled something out and handed it to Fenbrus. 'Not quite everything,' he said. 'You still have Felix, and . . . this.'

Fenbrus found himself holding a familiar barkscroll, the words *On the Husbandry of Prowlgrins* emblazoned across the top.

'The beginning of the *new* new Great Library,' said Rook.

Fenbrus looked up, tears welling in his eyes. All round them now, the sound of the roaring, screeching glade-eaters echoed malevolently. Gripping the barkscroll, Fenbrus Lodd strode towards the barricades, his eyes blazing.

'This is not how it ends!' he bellowed. 'The accursed goblins may well have won the Battle of the Great Library, but they have not won the war!'

ii
The Battle of New Undertown

With an ear-splitting screech and a gut-wrenching roar, the mighty glade-eaters lurched forwards. They sliced through the barricades like an axe through matchwood, and onto the streets of New Undertown in a tumultuous frenzy of destruction. Towers were razed to the ground, street-lamps crushed and crumpled, cobblestones churned up and sent flying off in all directions.

With their battering-rams, their wrecking-balls, their spikes, scythes, chains and flails, the glade-eaters decimated everything which stood in their path. Building after building came crashing to the ground in a

rush of rubble, splintered wood and billowing clouds of dust.

Behind the monstrous machines came the symbites – gyle goblins, gnokgoblins, web-foot and tree-goblins – in a great stampede, viciously driven along by the whips of the flat-heads following close on their heels. In the distance, spread out across the eastern farmlands, stood the massed ranks of the hammerheads and long-haired goblins, looking on. At their centre, the clan chiefs clustered beneath an ornate canopy.

Grossmother Nectarsweet's huge cheeks were wet with tears. 'My poor darlings!' she blubbered.

'Calm yourself,' said Hemtuft Battleaxe. 'Hemuel Spume's glade-eaters will do the hard work. Your symbites will simply "mop up" any remaining resistance.'

'It's not the goblin way!' spat Lytugg the hammerhead disgustedly. 'My warriors need to bathe their blades in Freeglade blood!'

'Don't worry,' said Hemtuft. 'There'll be plenty of Freeglade blood for your warriors when we get to the cloddertrog caves!'

Beside him, Meegmewl the Grey and Rootrott Underbiter exploded into cackles of evil laughter.

In the distance, a cloud of dust and furnace-fumes rose up from New Undertown as the glade-eaters ploughed on. From his position on the steering-platform of the leading machine, Hemuel Spume wiped the dust from his spectacles and cleared his throat. Beside him, the Furnace Master pushed the gear lever forward, and the glade-eater roared as the power was unleashed through the drive chains. The machine smashed through the wall of a half-wrecked tavern and rumbled on towards the Lufwood Tower ahead.

As each building collapsed, the defenders of New Undertown seemed to melt away, while high above, the tiny specks of skycraft hovered like woodgnats, out of reach of the goblin missiles. Hemuel Spume permitted himself a thin smile of triumph. It seemed that his glade-eaters had knocked the fight out of this Freeglader scum. New Undertown would be his! He tapped the Furnace Master on the shoulder and pointed to the tower.

'TO ... THE ... TOWER!' he screamed in his ear above the roar of the furnace. Out of the corner of his eye, he noticed a sudden blur of green as something flashed past ...

With a gurgle and a splutter, the Furnace Master beside him slumped forward. The glade-eater swerved to one side, ramming into a tall statue and lurching on.

'I ... SAID, TO ... THE ... TOWER!!' screamed Hemuel, pulling the Furnace Master back – then stopping when he saw that his own long thin fingers were covered in blood.

There, sticking out from the base of the Furnace Master's neck, was a heavy leadwood bolt.

Now, all around, green skycraft flashed past, spitting deadly leadwood bolts down at the glade-eaters. Hemuel threw himself to the floor with a terrified squeal and curled up into a ball as the great machine trundled on, out of control. Around him, the other glade-eaters were also in trouble as their Furnace Masters fell, in turn, to the crossbow bolts of the librarian knights.

Soon the monstrous machines were beginning to collide with one another. Behind them, the goblins stumbled and slipped, jostling each other in their attempts to stay on their feet.

'Stay steady up there!' the flat-heads roared, whipping the symbites all the harder in their frustration and rage.

Above them, peering down from the rooftops, the pale figures of ghosts appeared. Securing their grappling-hooks, they swooped down on their ropes and landed on the steering-platforms of the glade-eaters. Hastily, they rammed the gears into full throttle, wedging the levers forward with chunks of broken wood, before leaping back to the rooftops on their ropes.

With a deafening roar, the glade-eaters accelerated, the hapless symbites struggling to keep up as their flat-head tormentors flailed at them with their whips. Through bartering-halls and merchant-towers, galleries, taverns, hostels and shops; market-stands, stables and stalls, the mighty glade-eaters smashed an unstoppable path. Ahead, North Lake spread out like a great, glittering circle of burnished silver.

Behind them, from alleyways and rubble-strewn passages, sky pirates appeared with cutlasses and pikestaffs, a sky pirate captain at their head. 'Take out the flat-head overseers!' he roared.

The symbite goblins turned and stampeded back the way they'd come as the sky pirates fell upon the snarling flat-heads. In front of them, at Lakeside, the glade-eaters roared on towards the water's edge, with the goblins on the furnace- and weapons-platforms throwing themselves from them with yelps of terror.

Twenty flat-heads lay at Deadbolt Vulpoon's feet as, around him, the sky pirates bellowed at the backs of their fleeing flat-head comrades. 'Come back and fight!'

'Not so brave now, without your machines, are you?'

'Freeglader!'

'Freeglader! Freeglader! Freeglader!'

All at once, an enormous explosion sounded from Lakeside as the first mighty glade-eater plunged into the lake, its furnace rupturing as it hit the cold water and spewing burning and hissing lufwood logs high in the air. A moment later there was another explosion, then another, and another, as glade-eater after glade-eater dropped down into North Lake and blew up.

Soon a thick steamy fog mingled with the dust in the rubble-strewn streets of New Undertown, and as each explosion sounded, it was greeted by a roar of approval from the ghosts, librarian knights and sky pirates clustered at the lake's shore.

In the eastern farmlands, the goblin army had been waiting. Beneath the ornate canopy, Hemtuft struggled to focus the captured sky pirate telescope on the hazy outlines of ruined buildings.

Then the explosions started.

Meegmewl the Grey spat noisily. 'I don't like the sound of that,' he said grimly.

Rootrott Underbiter nodded. 'Not good, not good,' he growled.

Just then, out of the thickening cloud of dust, burst the symbite goblins in a disorganized stampede, with the Freeglade Lancers snapping at their heels. As the terrified symbites ran towards them, the lancers fell back in a defensive line. Mother Nectarsweet gave a high-pitched scream.

'Look!' she screeched. 'Look what they've done to my darlings!'

As the last glade-eater plunged into the waters of the North Lake and exploded, a huge column of water burst forth into the air like a mighty geyser. Higher and higher it climbed before falling abruptly away. And there, where it had been just moments before, floating head-down on the surface of the water, was the body of the former Foundry Master, Hemuel Spume, his boiled skin looking pinker in death than ever it had in life.

The waters stilled, and the haunting sound of chanting voices echoed out across the surface of the lake from Lullabee Island at its centre.

'Ooh-maah, oomalaah. Ooh-maah, oomalaah. Ooh-maah, oomalaah . . .'

iii

The Battle of the Barley Fields

Lob hitched up his belly-sling and pushed back his straw bonnet. 'It's a sad business all round, and no mistake, brother,' he said.

'It is that, brother,' said Lummel, shaking his head. 'It is that.'

They were standing at the back of a great phalanx of low-belly spear carriers. Around them, the grey goblin archers, pink-eyed sling throwers and barb-spitters of the lop-eared clan clustered in an untidy rabble. Amongst them, standing out like ironwood pines, were huge tusked goblins, their massive clubs resting on their shoulders. Unlike the elite long-haired and hammerhead goblins, this was the untrained bulk of the goblin armies.

'Them poor symbites didn't stand a chance,' said Lob.

'And it'll be our turn next, brother,' said Lummel. 'To pay for the clan chiefs' glory with *our* blood.'

Next to them, a pink-eyed barb-spitter nodded, and a massive tusked goblin gave a low growl of approval. Lummel glanced at them sideways.

'Friends of the harvest?' he asked in a low whisper.

Ahead of them, spread out along the top of the ridge, their weapons, helmets and breast-plates glinting in the bright yellow sunlight, stood phalanx after bristling phalanx of the elite of the goblin army, many rows deep. There were flat-heads to the left, with curved scimitars and studded cudgels, and long-hairs to the right, vicious double-edged battleaxes resting over their shoulders.

At the centre – a head
taller than all the
rest and dominat-
ing the skyline
with their heavy
armour, their
crescent-moon
shields and fear-
some serrated
swords – were
the hammer-
heads.

In front of
them stood the
clan chiefs
beneath the
ornate
canopy, held
aloft by five
huge, tusked goblins.

Mother Nectarsweet of the symbites was sobbing un-
controllably – causing Meegmewl the Grey of the
lop-eared clan and Rootrott Underbiter of the tusked
clan to scowl at her with contempt. Hemtuft Battleaxe
picked at his shryke feathercloak distractedly, while
Lytugg of the hammerhead clan stepped forward and
addressed her warriors.

'The so-called invincible glade-eaters are no more,' she
bellowed, and a wicked smile spread out across her thin
lips. 'Now we shall fight the goblin way!'

*

Out of the ruins of New Undertown came the Freegladers.

On the right were the Freeglade Lancers, still proud and upright on their prowlgrins despite their tattered tunics and blood-stained armour. Rook and Chinquix were at their head, with Grist – the only one of his original comrades to survive – beside him. The lancers were down to eighty now and their prowlgrins looked thin and exhausted.

On the left, the sky pirates marched behind the braziers of their captains, with Deadbolt Vulpoon at their head. They'd polished their breast-plates, compass brass and telescopes, which now gleamed and glittered in the sunlight, and looked impressive despite their ragged greatcoats.

At the centre, led by Felix and his father, Fenbrus Lodd, came the Ghosts of New Undertown and a motley selection of ageing librarians from the Great Library, armed with clubs, scythes, sling-shots and catapults. The ghosts had fought hard but they knew that, numbering less than two hundred, their task against the thousands of goblins facing them was hopeless.

Behind them, leading their skycraft on the ends of tether-ropes and ready to take to the air at a moment's notice, came the librarian knights. Between the Professors of Light and Darkness walked Xanth, his dark eyes betraying both fear and pride. Of the nine hundred librarian knights, fewer than three hundred remained. Their ranks now included the callow apprentices from Lake Landing, led by Stob Lummus – a worried, haunted-looking Magda Burlix at his side.

Behind them all, the ruins of New Undertown smouldered, and beyond that, the white cliffs of the cloddertrog caves glimmered in the afternoon haze. There, holed up and waiting for news, was the defence-less population of the Free Glades, huddled together. All that was standing between them and the bloodthirsty goblin hordes was this rag-tag army.

Tramping through the fields of blue barley – the Waif Glen on one side and the dark fringe of the Deepwoods on the other – the Freegladers approached the huge goblin army, which rippled with anticipation. Felix stepped out and raised his hand.

'We shall stand and fight, here in the barley fields!' his voice rang out.

'And die if we must as Freegladers!'

'Freegladers! Freegladers! Freegladers!' came the response.

Ahead of them, the ranks of the flat-heads, long-hairs and hammerheads lurched for-wards as if in answer to their challenge.

'Earth and Sky be with us all,' Fenbrus murmured by his son's side.

As the goblins bore down upon them, every Freeglader felt his heart race and his stomach churn. The ground itself trembled beneath the marching feet of the massed ranks of the goblins, and as they drew closer, the sun dazzlingly bright behind them, they started chanting – a single word, over and over . . .

'Blood! Blood! Blood! Blood! Blood . . .'

A hundred strides apart . . . Ninety . . . Eighty . . . The Freegladers could smell the foul odour of their enemies' unwashed bodies.

Seventy . . . sixty . . . fifty strides. They could see the tattoos emblazoned on their skins, and hear the sinister jangle of their barbaric battle-rings above the continuing *thud-thud-thud* . . .

Closer and closer. The goblins' chants had turned now into a frenzied, guttural howl mixed with a different noise . . .

Felix gasped. The noise wasn't coming from the ranks of the goblins. It was coming from the fringes of the forest to the east – a loud, yodelling cry that sliced through the still afternoon air.

The goblins seemed oblivious to it. Lost in their blood-lust, they thundered on, closing the gap . . .

Thirty strides . . . Twenty . . .

Now, he could see the reds of their bloodshot eyes. This was it. The Freegladers' last stand . . .

Fifteen . . . Ten . . .

All at once, the yodelling reached fever-pitch and out of the dark-green edges of the Deepwood forest came a great, seething brown mass which tore into the flat-heads on the goblin army's left-hand flank. Mighty goblin warriors were picked up and flung screaming through the air, as the ferocious beasts – all whirring claws and flashing tusks – tore through the goblin ranks like a blade through butterwood.

Rook leaned forward in his saddle as Chinquix snorted and skittered about uneasily. 'Banderbears,' he breathed. 'A convocation of banderbears!'

In front of the Freegladers, the elite of the goblin army was disintegrating. A flat-head swung his studded cudgel, only to have it knocked from his hands like a young'un's rattle – and his head crushed a moment later by a banderbear's tusked bite. A pair of long-hairs, their battleaxes swinging above their heads, were felled as one, as a huge, dark-brown banderbear struck out with one mighty claw.

First one, then two, then three hammerhead goblins were skewered on their own serrated swords, then tossed to the ground and trampled by roaring bander-bears, their fur red with blood.

Those not slaughtered threw down their weapons and fled back towards the mass of lop-ear and tusked gob-lins to the rear, who were looking on in dumbstruck amazement. The banderbears – now as red with goblin blood as the emblem on Rook's tunic – threw back their great heads and bellowed in triumph.

'WUH-WUH!!'

Chinquix gave out a shrill snort of alarm as, out of the mass of celebrating banderbears, three huge, blood-spattered figures approached. Despite their gory disguises, Rook recognized them instantly.

'Weeg! Wuralo! Wumeru!'

'Wuh-weela-wuh, Uralowa,' they yodelled in unison. *We have returned, he who took the poison-stick.*

Rook was about to leap from his saddle and embrace them when Grist clasped his arm.

'Rook!' he hissed urgently. 'Look!'

Rook followed his comrade's gaze. There, on the crest of the hill, coming through the blue barley towards them was the rest of the goblin army, their burnished metal weapons and armour glinting ominously in the evening sunlight.

Rook's heart sank. There were quite simply too many of the goblins to deal with. Countless thousands of them, appearing row after row after row at the crest of the hill and sweeping forward towards them. Not even the banderbears would be sufficient to repel this massive army.

There were tusked goblins, including snag-toothed and saw-toothed individuals, and ferocious underbiters. Tramping down the hills, they looked an impregnable force with their tooled leather armour rattling with battle-rings, their heavy visors and war-fists, and heavier war-clubs, reputedly embedded with the teeth of their opponents.

Marching between them were battalions of other goblins – lighter, more agile, yet no less deadly. Pink-eyed lop-ears, with their back-quivers bristling with poison-tipped arrows; tufted goblins of the long-haired clan, ruthlessly disciplined and skilled both in flailwork and swordplay; black-eared goblins with their characteristic long-pikes, clustered together in their tightly-packed 'stickleback' formations.

There were furrow-browed and thick-necked goblins; tufted, crested and mossy-backed goblins; pink-eyed, scaly and septic goblins. And grey-goblins – thousands of them – fierce and fearless, and armed with their long swords and short spears, all keeping close together in their 'swarms' and waiting for the order to launch a mass attack on their enemy.

As Rook stared at them in horror, he knew that that order would not be long in coming. He braced himself. There in the midst of the goblin army he could just see the heads of the clan chiefs. Rootrott Underbiter, Meegmewl the Grey, Mother Nectarsweet, Lytugg the hammerhead, and there at their centre, Hemtuft Battleaxe, a hideous grimace of triumph on his long-haired face. They bobbed up and down in the midst of their goblins, as if trying to get a better view of their impending victory.

To his right, Rook saw Felix step forwards and stride towards the approaching goblins, sword in hand, his eyes flashing with defiance.

'Very well, then!' he shouted at the taunting faces of the clan chiefs. 'Let us end it now!'

Suddenly, Rook saw his friend drop his sword and sink to his knees, a look of horrified amazement on his face. The goblin army came to a shuddering halt, and five huge tusked goblins shouldered their way through to the front, poles clasped in their massive fists.

Rook looked up. On the end of each pole, instead of an ornate canopy, was a bloodied, severed head. Hemtuft's

hideous grimace greeted the astonished Felix and the
Freegladers. Beside him were the heads of the other clan
chiefs. Then a chant – soft at first, but growing stronger
by the minute – rose up above the clatter of weapons
being dropped to the ground.

'*Friends of the harvest! Friends of the harvest! Friends of
the harvest!*'

EPILOGUE

The Most High Academe and head of the Freeglades Council, Cowlquape Pentephraxis, stood on the upper gantry of the Lufwood Tower and let the warm sun soak into his tired old bones.

What a very long way he'd come, he thought with a smile. And not only him, but all of them in the Free Glades.

He gazed down at New Undertown. Already, the streets were clear of rubble, and the buildings were being repaired. Why, the New Bloodoak Tavern was almost its old self again. You could go down there any evening and hear Deadbolt Vulpoon telling stories of the Battle of New Undertown and the War of the Free Glades . . . War! It already seemed like a distant memory.

Waif Glen was full of goblins now, seeking the peace and tranquillity that Cancaresse offered, and the Goblin Nations were flourishing alongside the Free Glades. There would be no more war, Cowlquape thought, and smiled contentedly.

Over in the distance, the timber wagons of the woodtrolls trundled towards the Great Lake. The work both on the Academy at Lake Landing and on the new Great Library was already underway. He'd never seen Felix Lodd, or Fenbrus, so happy.

Looking towards the Ironwood Stands, Cowlquape saw two skycraft circling. Probably his old friend Xanth, he thought, and Magda – off to take a spot of tea with Tweezel the spindlebug. Yes, things really were getting back to normal . . .

A polite cough brought the Most High Academe out of his reverie, and he turned to see two low-belly goblins in splendid new straw bonnets standing before him.

'Lob! Lummel!' Cowlquape greeted the two newest members of the Freeglade Council. 'Welcome, Freegladers!'

*

The Foundry Glades were silent. The furnaces were all extinguished, and the dense pall of smoke that had hovered in the air above them for so long had thinned and disappeared. The goblin guards were gone and the workshops and forges empty. The slave workers had packed everything they could carry and left for the Free Glades and Goblin Nations.

In a small, upper chamber at the top of the Palace of Furnace Masters, a single occupant remained. He was seated inside the soak-vat, but the water was cold, the bubbles had stopped and the attendant gabtrolls who had oiled him, anointed him and rubbed him vigorously down were nowhere to be found.

'Hello?' he called out weakly. 'Hello? Is there anybody there? Where are my gabtrolls? I'm cold and I'm shivery and I can't get out on my own . . . Please, somebody . . . *any*body! Help me!'

Just then, to his right, he heard a *click* and the door opened. He turned.

'Flambusia!' he squeaked. 'It's you! Thank goodness!'

'So you remember your old nursie,' said the huge, lumbering creature, her bright eyes darting round the room jerkily as she hurried towards him. 'I thought you'd forgotten all about me.' She smiled, her teeth glinting.

'Forgotten?' Amberfuce laughed uneasily. 'Of course I hadn't forgotten . . .'

'All those times I tried to see you,' said Flambusia. 'Standing at that door, calling your name – only to be turned away . . . Beaten . . . Made to wash floors . . . And me, a nurse!'

'How awful,' wheedled Amberfuce. 'I had no idea.'

'Really?' she said, her eyes narrowing. 'You didn't hear my cries? My pleading?'

'No, no, nothing, Flambusia,' he said. 'I really had no idea.'

Flambusia's teeth flashed again. 'Tut-tut, Amby, dear,' she said, crouching down. 'And you a waif. Shame on you. But perhaps Flambusia can take care of you now, then?'

'Yes,' said Amberfuce weakly. 'Yes, that would be nice . . .'

The cloddertrog began pressing buttons, turning dials, switching levers, while Amberfuce looked on helplessly. The water inside the burnished metal vat began churning violently and suddenly began to steam.

'Ouch,' Amberfuce yelped. 'That's a bit *too* warm, Flambusia, my dear,' he said.

'Sorry, Amby, dear, I didn't quite hear you,' said Flambusia. 'What did you say?'

'Too hot!' squealed Amberfuce. 'Scorching, Flambusia!'

'I still can't hear you, Amby,' she said sweetly, giving the dial another violent turn. 'You'll have to speak up.'

'No . . . no . . . no . . . No, please, Flambusia! *Noooo!'*

*

The skewbald prowlgrin tethered to the sallowdrop tree snorted contentedly in the warm evening air. Its rider, a dark-haired youth in the uniform of a Freeglade Lancer, a sword at his side, stood on the small jetty gazing out over the still waters of North Lake to Lullabee Island. From the distant treeline came the far-off sound of a banderbear yodel.

The youth smiled, lost in thought. Then, as if sensing he was being watched, he turned – to find himself staring into the pale eyes of an old sky pirate.

'Lullabee Island,' said the pirate, his voice gravelly with lack of use. 'A place of dreams, they say.'

The youth nodded. 'I've been there,' he said, 'and dreamed the strangest of dreams ... I was thinking about them just now.'

'I guessed as much by the way you were gazing at the place,' said the Mire Pirate, his sad eyes searching the youth's face. He cleared his throat and came to stand beside the youth on the jetty, his own gaze turning to the distant island. 'There was once a great sky pirate captain,' he said. 'I served under him a long, long time ago. He came from a large family. Lived in old Undertown in a grand house, with a beautiful room, a fabulous mural on its wall ...'

The youth turned to look at the old pirate.

'It burned down,' he said. 'Tragically. He lost his mother, and his brothers.'

The youth's eyes opened wide. 'I dreamed that!' he said.

The sky pirate went on. 'He grew up to be a sky pirate

like his father. Took his wife with him ... They had a baby ...'

'But something happened,' the youth interrupted. 'I dreamed that, too. They had to leave their child ... in the Deepwoods.'

The Mire Pirate nodded. 'But the captain found his child again, years later. I was there when he did. And that child grew to be as fine a sky pirate as his father, and his father before him. And I know, because I served under him, too – until ...'

'Until?' asked the youth, hardly daring to breathe.

'Until we were wrecked in the Twilight Woods and I was lost ... lost for such a long time ... I don't know for how long ... Shrykes found me. Sold me in their slave market. I escaped and came to the Free Glades, where I found my brother's son, Shem.' He paused. 'Shem Barkwater!'

The youth gasped. 'Barkwater? You said, Barkwater?'

The Mire Pirate nodded. 'Shem took me in, and gave me a home after all my wanderings. I was so happy. *So* happy ... And then he met Keris, and imagine my surprise and joy when I discovered ...'

'Discovered what?' urged the youth, half remembering his dreams.

'That Keris was the daughter of my sky pirate captain, Twig.'

'Twig!' exclaimed the youth. 'Captain Twig!'

'The very same. He'd married a slaughterer by the name of Sinew. It broke his heart when she died shortly after giving birth, but he did his best to bring his daughter, Keris, up, and he did a good job of it, too. When she grew up and left home, Captain Twig returned to his wanderings in the Deepwoods . . .'

'And that's where I met him!' said the youth. 'Living with banderbears!'

The Mire Pirate smiled. 'Yes, I heard tell of that . . . Well, his daughter married my nephew Shem, and the three of us lived so happily here in the Free Glades until . . .'

'Go on,' said the youth.

'They had a child. A beautiful little boy. Dark, curly hair. He was about four years old when they decided to take him to see his slaughterer relatives in their village. I pleaded with them not to. I *begged* them! But they laughed and set off just the same . . .'

'They wouldn't listen,' said the youth, staring out at Lullabee Island, his dreams coming back to him. 'They rode away into the sunset, and you stared after them, tears streaming down your face . . .'

The Mire Pirate nodded, his eyes glistening. 'When they didn't return,' he said, 'I went after them. I discovered their upturned cart, their scattered belongings and . . .'

Tears flooded down the old pirate's cheeks. 'Their poor, dead bodies. Killed by slavers, they were. But I found no trace of my grand-nephew, Captain Twig's grandson . . .'

'He was found by banderbears, looked after – and then discovered by Varis Lodd, who brought him to old Undertown, where he grew up in the sewers . . . He was . . . is . . .' the youth said hesitantly.

'You,' said the old Mire Pirate. 'Rook Barkwater!'

'And you, you are my great-uncle Tem!' said Rook, amazed. 'I dreamed it. I dreamed it all in the caterbird cocoon!'

The Mire Pirate nodded, his eyes full of sorrow and love, joy and loss. 'But there's one thing you won't have dreamed, I'll be bound,' he said.

'And what's that?' asked Rook.

'This,' said Tem Barkwater, fishing in his pocket and handing Rook a small, round object. 'I took it from your mother's dead hand,' he said, his eyes misting over, 'and I've kept it all these years. It was given to her by her father, who was given it by *his* father. It's yours now.'

Rook looked at the object in his hand. It was a small disc of ancient lufwood, decorated with a miniature painting of a youth staring back at him with a gaze that seemed eerily familiar. He frowned. It was the face he'd seen in the mural on the wall of the Sunken Palace of old Undertown; the face he'd seen in the caterbird cocoon dream.

A young knight academic in old-fashioned armour, with deep indigo eyes and a smile on his face. Behind him was the painted skyline of old Sanctaphrax, the lost floating city, worn, but still recognizable, with the Loftus Observatory at one of his shoulders and the twin towers of the School of Mist at the other.

Tem Barkwater smiled. 'It's your great-grandfather, Rook, lad,' he said, and placed a hand on his grand-nephew's shoulder.

Rook gazed at the portrait of the youth staring back at him.

'Your great-grandfather,' he repeated quietly. 'Cloud Wolf.'

THE FAMILY PALLITAX

 LINIUS PALLITAX
(MOST HIGH ACADEME
OF SANCTAPHRAX)

YENA PALLITAX
(née VESPIUS)

 MARIS VERGINIX
(née PALLITAX)

 TWIG
(ARBORINUS VERGINIX)

 SINE'W VERGINIX
(née TATUM)

 KERIS BARKWATER
(née VERGINIX)

ROOK BARKWATER

THE BLOODING OF RUFUS FILATINE

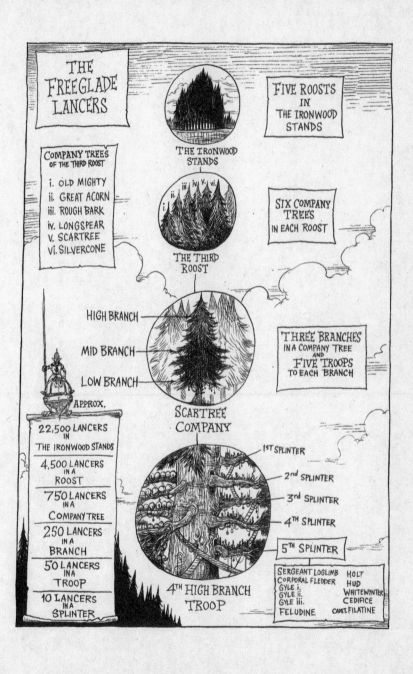

THE FREEGLADE LANCERS

FIVE ROOSTS IN THE IRONWOOD STANDS

THE IRONWOOD STANDS

COMPANY TREES OF THE THIRD ROOST

i. OLD MIGHTY
ii. GREAT ACORN
iii. ROUGH BARK
iv. LONGSPEAR
v. SCARTREE
vi. SILVERCONE

THE THIRD ROOST

SIX COMPANY TREES IN EACH ROOST

HIGH BRANCH

MID BRANCH

LOW BRANCH

SCARTREE COMPANY

THREE BRANCHES IN A COMPANY TREE
AND
FIVE TROOPS TO EACH BRANCH

APPROX.

22,500 LANCERS IN THE IRONWOOD STANDS

4,500 LANCERS IN A ROOST

750 LANCERS IN A COMPANY TREE

250 LANCERS IN A BRANCH

50 LANCERS IN A TROOP

10 LANCERS IN A SPLINTER

1ST SPLINTER

2ND SPLINTER

3RD SPLINTER

4TH SPLINTER

5TH SPLINTER

4TH HIGH BRANCH TROOP

SERGEANT LOGLIMB   HOLT
CORPORAL FLEDDER   HUD
GYLE i.   WHITEWYNTER
GYLE ii.   CEDIFICE
GYLE iii.   CADET FILATINE
FELUDINE

CHAPTER ONE

THE NAMELESS ONE

The creature threw back its massive head and let out a thunderous roar. The sound – a mixture of guttural rage and savage pain – boomed through the Deepwoods. It made the earth tremble and the treetops quiver, while those for whom the great forest was home cowered and cringed with fear.

Colonies of long-armed weezits, feasting high up in the sallowdrop trees, abruptly abandoned the succulent fruit and scattered in howling gangs of fright-spiked fur. Bright flashes of iridescent blue, leaping from branch to branch, revealed themselves to be groups of fleeing lemkins, the smaller ones clinging to the backs of their elders in clusters of three and sometimes four. On the forest floor, a huge herd of tilder – their long snouts flared, and emitting the characteristic whooping call of alarm – stampeded through the forest glades like Edge-salmon leaping a cliff fall. In their wake, the sunlit air was filled with thousands of translucent wind-

spinners, torn from their tendril-grip in the long glade grass and now spinning upwards to the safety of the forest canopy far above.

Sucking in the air in huge, wheezing breaths, the creature continued its frenzied zigzag charge through the forest. It barged into trees, shrubs and bush-clumps, knocking them effortlessly out of its way. And as it battered a churned-up, stump-splintered path through the Deepwoods, shafts of sunlight broke through the shattered canopy, piercing the shadows and illuminating the creature's massive form.

Huge, muscled shoulders bunched at a thick-set and misshapen head, with no discernible neck between. A gigantic belly, pitted and encrusted with boils and pustules, ballooned over relatively short but immensely solid-looking legs, the size and thickness of copperwood tree-trunks. But more remarkable than these – or the yellow tusk-fringed mouth, or the tiny bloodshot eyes, black ringed and glistening – were the creature's arms.

They were gigantic, the knuckles of the great clawed hands at their ends grazing the forest floor as it ran. It was with these arms that the creature smashed its way through the forest, with great scything blows that brought sallowdrop and stinkwood trees crashing to the ground and splintered clumps of shadowbushes and moonshrubs.

The creature paused. As it did so, the unwelcome sunlight glinted in its bloodshot eyes and on the raw fleshy wounds which ran in green-fringed stripes across its shoulders. It glistened on the dripping yellow tusks as the furious creature threw back that huge ugly head and howled once more, a curdled mixture of pain and rage.

A moment later, in a flurry of dust and fallen branches, it was off again, pounding blindly through the forest. It stumbled over a knot of roots and crashed hard against a tall, slender lufwood sapling. Roaring with rage, it wrapped its great arms around the pitted trunk and uprooted the entire tree, then threw it over its immense shoulders. It landed with a heavy crash in a shower of twigs and leaves.

High up in the very topmost branches of a mighty ironwood pine, far above the forest canopy, a prowlgrin and rider emerged from the shadows cast by the great black fir-cones clustered at the tree's summit. The prowlgrin delicately padded along the branch, its large sensitive toes telling it instinctively that the tree-limb would take its weight. It paused at the very tip of the branch and waited, expertly balanced, for instructions.

The prowlgrin's rider was dressed in the distinctive uniform of the Freeglade Lancers; a crested copper helmet with neck and cheek-guards, a white tunic emblazoned with a red banderbear head, finely tooled wood-armour of rich sumpwood and forest elm which protected arms and legs and, most distinctive of all, a thick lance of seasoned iron-wood clasped in a gauntleted hand. Only the collar gave away the fact that, despite appearances, this rider was not quite a Freeglade Lancer. It was solid green, and marked its wearer out as a cadet who had not yet been blooded in battle.

The rider reached down and patted his prowlgrin mount.

'Steady, Lyrinx, lass,' he whispered. 'I hear it, too. Seems to be coming this way.'

Far below, the great bellowing roar of the creature sounded again.

'*Gather, brothers,*' a soft, whispery voice sounded in the cadet's head. '*The glades are threatened . . .*'

The cadet gave a twitch of the reins he held in one hand. In response, the prowlgrin launched herself from the ironwood branch and out over the green forest canopy below. They fell for what seemed like minutes, but was in fact, as the cadet well knew, mere seconds, as the treetops raced up to meet them. Suddenly – like breaking the surface of a green forest pool – they plunged through the leafy canopy and into the depths of the forest below. The prowlgrin's great toes fastened onto a branch as her huge rear-legs braced to cushion the landing.

From branches all round came the gentle creak and leaf-rustle of other landing prowlgrins. Two, three there were. Eight, nine, ten – prowlgrins and riders, clustered in the branches of the surrounding trees.

'*All here, sergeant,*' the whispery voice sounded in every head. The speaker – a tiny waif called Cedifice – gazed at the others with his enormous pale grey eyes, his veined wafer-thin ears quivering. 'Whatever it is, I can tell from the sound of its footfalls, it is enormous,' the waif whispered. 'And it appears to be in pain.'

As if in answer, another howl sounded in the distance, and the waif's prowlgrin – a sleek white beast with a long, knotted beard – shifted uneasily on his branch.

'I can discern no coherent thoughts, Sergeant.' Cedifice's huge ears trembled and the waif winced uncomfortably. 'Only rage . . . And pain. But one thing I can tell you,' the waif concluded, 'is that the creature is heading for the southern fringes of the Free Glades.'

Sergeant Hulm Logglimb tugged at the stump of the ear he'd lost at the Battle of Lufwood Mount many years earlier, and looked around at the expectant faces of his lancers. He was a short, stocky gnokgoblin, battle-scarred and wily, who never asked his lancers to do anything that he wouldn't do himself. For that, they loved and respected him.

'Well, brothers,' he began, tapping his lance on the tree branch as he weighed up his words. 'Seems like there won't be time to call out the rest of the troop, so it's going to be all down to us in the Fifth Splinter to head this creature off before it reaches the Glades. What do you say?'

'I say, yes, sergeant!' the cadet responded enthusiastically. 'Lyrinx and I can scout ahead of the splinter and . . .'

'It's not for you to say anything. You're still just a cadet,' said the first of three short, large-nosed gyle-goblins, each of them mounted on a frisky white and grey prowlgrin.

427

The gyle-goblins admitted to no names individually and were known by the rest of the lancers simply as 'the Gyles'. Draped over their saddles, they each had an elaborate cloak of expertly woven leaves and berry branches which, when worn, rendered them virtually invisible in the forest canopy. Their job was to scout for the splinter.

'The Gyles are right, Rufus, old son,' said Lancer Felludine. He turned to Sergeant Logglimb. 'As for me, sir, I say let's do it.'

Gaddius Felludine was a large, heavy-browed fourthling. He was ungainly but powerful, and when roused to anger a fearsome fighter. A lancer of few words, Felludine never spoke of his past, yet it was common knowledge that he had left a troubled and difficult life behind him. After many long years

of searching he had found
acceptance in the Free
Glades. He was a frequent
visitor to Waif Glen, where
the wounds of his past
were gradually being
healed. Grateful to the Free
Glades, he had no hesita-
tion in laying down his life
for the place he loved, and
his fellow lancers knew it.

'Thank you, Gaddius,'
said the sergeant. He looked up at the three lancers
perched on the branches above him. 'And how
about you?'

All three were, like himself, gnokgoblins. There
was Lance-Corporal Degg
Fledder, heavy-lidded and
cautious, always looking
before leaping, but a skilful
lancer. And then there were
the twins, Hudflux and
Holt. The pair of them were
cheerful and happy-go-
lucky, always ready with a
joke or an encouraging word
– and both were deadly
accurate with a crossbow.

'We're with you, sergeant,' all three replied, suddenly serious as yet another chilling howl echoed up from the forest below them.

'It's getting closer, whatever it is,' said the final lancer in the splinter, a young mobgnome by the name of Tam Whytewinter.

Like his comrades, he wore a collar of white and green chequerboards that denoted that he'd been blooded in battle, fighting alongside the others in his splinter. In Whytewinter's case, his boards had been earned just a few months ago in a nasty skirmish to the south of the Goblin Nations with a roving band of skulltrogs. He'd been wounded in the leg – an injury that still bothered him, though he was always careful not to show it.

'Rufus can ride with me, sergeant,' Tam said. He smiled at the cadet. 'I'll keep him out of trouble! He's far too young to earn his boards just yet.'

The others laughed. Everyone knew that Tam and Cadet Rufus Filatine were practically the same age – and were also the best of friends. In fact, it was only a nasty case of bark-croup that had kept Rufus back at the roost when the company had been called out to deal with the skulltrogs. Otherwise, he would not still be wearing the plain green collar.

'*Patience, Rufus,*' the waif's whispery voice sounded in the cadet's head. '*Your time will come soon enough.*'

Rufus Filatine, his face flushed and unhappy-looking, gazed across into the kindly eyes of Cedifice the waif. Small and physically weak the waif signaller might be, Rufus acknowledged, but Cedifice was a vital member of the splinter. He sent messages, listened out for sounds of danger and, most importantly of all perhaps, spread words of comfort and understanding amongst the group with his telepathy.

'Well, what are we waiting for?' said Sergeant Logglimb, raising his lance and giving the time-honoured battle-cry. 'FREEGLADER!'

'FREEGLADER!' the ten lancers of his splinter replied, their prowlgrins taking off at a gallop and leaping through the treetops after their leader in the direction of the terrible sound.

The Gyles sped on ahead, their white and grey prowlgrins faster and even more nimble than the others.

'Tell them to distract the creature,' Sergeant Logglimb called to the waif. 'We'll ride round and come in from the south.'

'Sir,' the waif whispered back.

'Load those crossbows,' the sergeant called over to Lance-Corporal Fledder and the gnokgoblin twins, who nodded grimly.

'And Gaddius, keep that lance handy,' he said. 'You two . . .' He glanced over his shoulder to make sure Tam and Rufus were following on their prowl-grins. 'Make sure you cover our backs.'

With that, the sergeant urged his own great orange prowlgrin on faster through the trees, the gnokgoblins and large fourthling following close behind. Up ahead, the sound of trees crashing to the forest floor grew suddenly louder.

'You heard what he said,' said Tam, pulling up his prowlgrin, Nixus, and watching the five lancers advance through the trees ahead.

'I know, I know,' said Rufus bitterly, following his friend's example.

Lyrinx halted next to Nixus on the broad branch of a pewterbark tree. Together, the two lancers surveyed the forest floor below.

'*Here it comes*,' Cedifice's voice sounded in their heads. '*It's ignoring the Gyles' slings.*'

Sure enough, up ahead, Rufus could just make out the buzzing sound of the small pebbles being catapulted at the creature by the gyle-goblins in their efforts to distract it.

'*The sergeant says to strike your fire-crystals . . .*' The waif communicated their leader's instructions.

In the treetops in the distance, Rufus saw five pin-points of light suddenly flare up as the lancers lit brushwood torches.

Of course, fire! he realized. The deepest fear of any primitive creature. His hand reached for the two crystals in the small pouch at his belt and he turned to pull a brushwood bundle from his saddle pack.

'*Tam, Rufus,*' came the voice. '*Don't light your torches yet . . .*' The waif passed on Sergeant Logglimb's command. '*We're going to try and turn it before it reaches you . . .*'

Tam and Rufus exchanged glances. As the junior members of the splinter, they knew their role was to stay in reserve – but it was frustrating nonetheless.

Rufus leaned forward in the saddle and scanned the horizon. He could see the torches flaring in the treetops – yet the sound of crashing and splintering trees seemed to be getting closer still.

'*Hudflux! Holt! To the left! Fledder, higher! Double back behind! . . .*' The waif's voice, still a whisper, was tense and urgent. '*That's it . . . That's it . . . Sergeant, look out!*'

Up ahead, there was a deafening howl and Rufus saw a great copperwood tree rise up, then topple back with a crash. Beside him, Tam gasped. But looking up, Rufus saw that his friend's gaze was not on the forest in front of him. No, rather, he was staring down at the forest floor below them. He looked down too, and gasped with horror.

Back from a day's foraging, a party of half a dozen woodtrolls – an old male, three females and a couple of young'uns – were making their way towards the Free Glades. They were carrying baskets and barrels of oak-mushrooms, wood-toadstools, pine-nuts and bark-gourds carefully on their heads and, although from the looks on their faces it was clear that they could hear the commotion ahead of them, they didn't seem to realize the danger they were heading towards.

Rufus twitched the reins and Lyrinx bounded down through the branches to the forest floor.

'Rufus, wait . . .' Tam called after him, but the cadet ignored him.

The woodtrolls were in danger and he had to warn them.

Lyrinx landed on the ground ten strides in front of the small party, and Rufus was about to call out to them when all at once the woodtrolls came to a sudden halt. Their eyes as large as lufwood saucers, the woodtrolls tossed their barrels and baskets of carefully gathered produce to the forest floor, spun on their heels and fled for their lives.

'Rufus! Watch out!' Tam's voice called out from above.

Too late, the cadet swivelled round in his saddle and caught sight of what the woodtrolls had glimpsed over his shoulder. He swallowed hard.

Coming towards him through the forest, its red eyes boring into his own, drool hanging in heavy gobbets from a snaggle-tusked mouth, was the most enormous creature Rufus had ever seen. With a roar of rage, it shot out a great curved claw, forcing Lyrinx to leap out of the way with a yelp of terror.

The movement caught Rufus off-balance and sent him crashing to the earth. He looked up to see the terrifying creature towering over him. It howled with rage. He screwed his eyes shut and clawed at the Deepwoods dirt, his body tensing for the blow he was sure was about to fall.

Above him, the creature's furious howling seemed suddenly to catch in its throat and turn to a spluttering gurgle. Hardly daring to look, Rufus raised his face from the rich, peaty loam of the soil and looked up. The mighty creature stood before him, motionless. Its great arms were spread wide, the chipped claws glistening strangely in the sunlight. There was a look of dazed shock and confusion plastered across its misshapen features.

Then Rufus saw it. Protruding from the creature's barrel-chest, just above its great bloated belly, was the tip of an ironwood lance glistening with blood. With a soft sigh, the creature pitched forwards and crashed to the forest floor with a great thud.

Frozen with shock, Rufus found himself inches from the creature's contorted face, staring at his own horrified reflection in a single glazed red eye.

Sergeant Logglimb appeared a moment later, his

prowlgrin Pheddix panting with exertion. He dismounted and climbed onto the massive creature's back. Then, with a grunt of effort, he slowly pulled his ironwood lance from the body and stood looking at its dripping point ruefully. Rufus climbed shakily to his feet, his heart still hammering away beneath his rib cage.

'I didn't want to do that,' said Sergeant Logglimb quietly. He fixed Rufus with his unblinking gaze. 'But you gave me no choice, cadet.'

Rufus stared back at the sergeant, his face flushing with colour.

'I . . . I wanted to warn the woodtrolls . . .' he began, but the expression on the sergeant's face stopped him.

'Lancer Whytewinter did that from the treetops,' he said. 'You, on the other hand, put yourself in harm's way – and forced me to kill this unfortunate, demented creature.' The sergeant shook his head slowly and climbed down, lance in hand. 'This is no way to earn your boards, Rufus.'

The cadet hung his head in shame and bit his lip. 'I'm sorry, sergeant . . .' he mumbled.

He felt Logglimb's hand on his shoulder.

'That's all right, cadet,' he said, his voice suddenly gentle and compassionate. 'We shall not speak of this again.'

Rufus nodded and, looking up, saw that the rest of the splinter were arriving. They gathered round the body of the strange creature, their eyes wide. Beside him, Tam handed his friend back the reins of his prowlgrin.

'Are you all right?' he asked.

Rufus nodded, and patted Lyrinx's soft orange fur. 'Sorry, lass,' he whispered in her ear.

All eyes were on the dead creature. Cedifice was walking round it, his huge ears quivering.

'Sergeant,' he said at last. 'Look at these marks.'

Sergeant Logglimb turned to the waif, who was pointing to deep wounds on the creature's shoulders.

'These aren't the wounds of an accident . . .' The waif shook his head and inspected the green-fringed stripes, before turning back. 'No, these are rope burns, sergeant.'

'Rope burns?'

'Made by some sort of tight-fitting harness.' Cedifice frowned thoughtfully. 'This creature, whatever it was, has been ill-treated. These wounds alone must have been torment, not to mention these . . .' His ears trembled as he pointed to small criss-crossing scars on the creature's arms and legs. 'Whip marks. No wonder the poor thing was driven half out of its mind.'

'I've never seen a creature like it,' said Corporal Fledder, shaking his head.

'Nor have we,' agreed the gyle-goblins, their leafy cloaks rustling.

Lancer Gaddius Felludine stroked his beard thoughtfully. 'What do you suppose it is?' he asked.

'I know,' said Rufus, stepping forward. 'At least I know what my father and the other librarian academics call creatures like this . . .'

'You do?' said Tam, turning to his friend.

'Yes,' said Rufus quietly. 'They call them the nameless ones.'

. CHAPTER TWO .

THE SKIRMISH AT WOODED CRAG

Rufus pushed the hair from his eyes and, half standing, inched the rough-hewn grooming-stool forward. Lyrinx purred appreciatively and nuzzled the side of her broad head against Rufus's shoulder, glancing up at him through one large blue eye as she did so.

He unsnagged the thick hair of her beard, picking out the twigs and burrs that had got tangled there, he massaged her twisting tail, and he used the curry-comb to brush her orange coat till it gleamed. Rufus patted her, ruffled her fur and gave her a tit-bit of dried offal, which she swallowed gratefully.

'Come on, Lyrinx, girl,' he said softly. 'Let's see to those toes of yours.'

With a low growl, the thrumming sound rising from deep down inside her throat, the prowlgrin shifted her balance to one side and extended her left foot. Rufus, who was perched on the grooming-stool, gently placed the foot on the length of thick

cloth which lay across his lap and inspected each toe closely.

'Oh, what's this?' he said, tutting sympathetically. 'That doesn't look too good, does it?' He took his knife from his belt and, squinting with concentration, removed a sharp piece of ironwood bark which had become wedged beneath one of the broad, ivory-coloured nails. 'That's better,' he said soothingly, 'isn't it, lass?'

Then, resheathing the blade, he picked up his whetstone – a small, porous pebble shaped rather like the hull of a miniature old-fashioned sky ship – and, taking care not to go against the natural grain, began rubbing it along the prowlgrin's nails. Slowly he filed away the ridges and notches on the surface of each nail until they gleamed ivory white.

As he worked, the prowlgrin gently leaned her great round body against him and waited patiently. The feet of a prowlgrin are incredibly sensitive, and it was testament to the trust between rider and beast that Lyrinx allowed Rufus to handle her toes without flinching.

'Good girl,' Rufus whispered encouragingly. 'The hard part is over. Now for the bit I know you enjoy . . .'

Rufus unhooked a spatula from the side of his grooming-stool, picked up the bucket at his feet and began stirring the thick, pale yellow liquid it contained. As he did so, the rich, woody aroma of the oil was released, making Lyrinx emit a deep, rumbling purr of appreciation.

All prowlgrins loved darkelm oil, even those that hadn't been tamed. Herds of wild prowlgrins would gather in the spreading boughs of the massive darkelm trees, shuffling and stamping in a strange undulating dance until their feet were drenched in the oil that seeped through the spongy bark of the tree. Not only did the prowlgrins find it irresistible, but the darkelm oil coated and protected their delicate feet, keeping them in excellent condition.

The head groom organized regular forays into the surrounding forests to keep the prowlgrins of Scartree Company – all seven hundred and fifty of them – well supplied with the precious oil. Each prowlgrin had two grooms assigned to feed and groom him or her, but Rufus preferred to oil Lyrinx's feet himself.

'Here we go then,' he said, plunging his hands into the bucket and then proceeding to rub it into the creases, the knuckles and the soft leathery pads of Lyrinx's left foot. 'That's better, isn't it?' he whispered as Lyrinx closed her eyes dreamily and gave a deep, growling purr.

Nothing, Rufus knew, was more important than caring for your prowlgrin's feet. They were so sensitive they could detect the slightest of movements. At night, while perching, a trained prowlgrin would alert their rider to any tremor or vibration they detected which might indicate approaching danger. And by day, while out riding, the same toes could tell in an instant which branches could support them and which would break under their weight. In prime condition, those toes would carry both rider and mount safely through the very topmost branches of the forest in exhilarating gallops. An untended blister or a neglected splinter could spell disaster out on patrol.

'Good girl,' Rufus whispered. 'Good, good girl.'

All around them, the vast ironwood pine buzzed with activity. On the great broad branch where he sat oiling Lyrinx's paws, the other lancers of the Fifth Splinter were also hard at work.

Lance-Corporal Degg Fledder – a white oakapple flower pinned to his forage cap at a jaunty angle – was sharpening the long straight sabre that was standard issue to all lancers. As he worked the blade to a razor-sharp edge, he smiled to himself and hummed the latest catchy tune that was doing the rounds of the New Undertown taverns. Further along the mighty ironwood branch, the looming figure of Lancer Gaddius Felludine sat surrounded by grappling-hooks, water-bottles, saddlebags and other bits of kit. The big fourthling tutted and muttered darkly as he attempted to sew a patch onto an old pair of breeches with clumsy fingers.

'Sky blast it!' he exploded with exasperation. 'Groom! Groom! Has anyone seen a groom?'

Strictly speaking, all the grooms reported to the head groom – a punctilious mobgnome with a sharp tongue and an obsessive eye for detail – and had responsibility only for the prowlgrins who roosted on the other side of Scartree, in the western branches of the mighty ironwood pine. But here where the lancers lived, on the eastern side of the tree, its branches filled with hammocks and equipment, weapon-stores and armoury-benches, the grooms often found that their services were in high demand.

'What is it, Gad?' said an exasperated-sounding gnokgoblin in the flat felt cap of a groom, hurrying along the branch, an offal bucket clutched in each hand.

'You couldn't patch these, could you, Higg?' said Gaddius, looking up and showing the groom his hopeless efforts to repair the breeches. 'Only, they're my favourite pair.'

'You choose your moments,' said Higg the groom. 'Can't you see it's feeding time in the roost?'

He swung a strong-smelling bucket beneath the lancer's nose. Further along the branch, the three gyle-goblins – who were expertly repairing their camouflage capes with carefully-woven twigs and leaves – all laughed out loud.

'That bucket smells sweet as oakapple-blossom, Higg – compared to Gadd's breeches!' one of them called.

Hudflux and Holt, the gnokgoblin brothers, looked up from the crossbows they were dismantling and greasing, and chuckled.

'Yes, yes, very funny,' growled Gaddius, draping the breeches over the groom's outstretched arm and tucking a thornwood needle and waxed thread into his apron. 'I'll buy you a tankard in the New Bloodoak, Higg.'

'Make it two,' said the groom, as he hurried back along the branch and descended a wooden walkway that spiralled round the trunk towards the western side of the tree. In the distance the barks and growls of hungry prowlgrins could just be heard.

'All right, lass,' said Rufus, patting Lyrinx's great round side. 'Off you go and enjoy your supper.'

With an excited yelping growl, the prowlgrin leaped off the branch and disappeared into the dappled branches below. Rufus stood up, swung his grooming-stool onto his shoulder – then paused. Spread out all around him in the gigantic tree, the seven hundred and fifty lancers of Scartree Company were going about their evening's work.

Rufus smiled happily as he listened to the sounds that in the year that he'd served as a lance-cadet he'd grown to know and love.

There were anvil-clangs and hammerblows as swords were forged, axes honed and lances sharpened. There was the squeak of turning cogs and the rasping hiss of mighty bellows. There was the clash of swords and crunch of maces as the lancers practised their skills, fencing and fighting – as well as the sudden cries of delight or derision as a crossbow bolt either struck a bullseye or missed the target completely. There was the gruff babble of numerous voices; song, laughter, barked commands – as well as the rhythmic rumble of all those weary lancers, curled up in the hammocks suspended from the eastern branches, fast asleep after a long day's patrol.

Coupled with the sounds, the air was filled with smells. High up on a branch of the mighty pine, Rufus breathed in. Aromatic smoke from the hanging braziers mingled with the scent of frying tilder and toasting oakbread as it rose up. From the middle of the tree where the five mid-branch troops were cooking supper before going out on night patrol, there was the odour of scorched metal – and the fumes from the leather-tanning vats from the low-branch troops, who were busy repairing and refitting equipment damaged or lost on recent patrols.

To the west, faint traces of acrid offal and the woody tang of dung drifted up from the roost branches of the prowl-grins, while all around the distinct musty smell of exhausted unwashed bodies floated across the hammocks full of the high-branch lancers getting what sleep they could before dawn patrol.

The company of lancers who lived in Scartree were divided into low-branch, mid-branch and high-branch troops, every troop divided again into splinters – each one occupying their particular place in the mighty iron-wood tree. The Fifth Splinter was situated at the top of Scartree, where the weather was keenest and the views were best – and Rufus loved it.

447

He looked out from the broad branch where the Fifth Splinter – the fourth outfit of five that comprised the high-branch of Scartree Company – were settling down for the night. All around, the other ironwood trees of the roost bustled with activity. Old Mighty, Great Acorn, Roughbark, Longspear and Silvercone each also held a company of lancers some seven hundred and fifty strong. Together they made up the third roost.

There were five roosts in all, their dark silhouettes just visible in the gathering dusk, offering refuge, in total, to over twenty-two thousand lancers in the vast Ironwood Stands that towered over the dark waters of the Great Lake. Twenty-two thousand lancers to patrol the forests around the Free Glades and warn of danger. Twenty-two thousand to ride their prowlgrins into battle and die, if they had to, defending this wonderful place.

And he, Rufus Filatine, was a part of it all. He touched the red banderbear badge stitched to the front of the white tunic he wore, and felt a surge of pride and excitement.

'Lost in thought, green collar?'

Rufus turned to see his friend, Tam Whytewinter. His smiling face, lit by lamplight now that the sun had set, was framed by the great circular darkness of the troop store – a knot hole in the huge trunk of the tree, so big it looked like nothing so much as a deep cave. It was full of supplies of all kinds. Everything from pickled pine-nuts, sumpwood armour polish, dried tilder hams and blood sausage in huge spirals, to wood grog (for medicinal purposes only), whetstones, flagons of darkelm oil, caskets of dried charlock, smoked hyleberry and desiccated thousandfoot. Tam held up a caddy full of aromatic oaktea.

'Fancy a brew?' he said. 'The pot's just coming to the boil.'

Rufus nodded. 'Nothing I'd like better, old veteran,' he said.

Tam laughed and disappeared inside the knot hole. A moment later there was the clink of an iron-wood spoon in pewter mugs and the aroma of freshly brewed oaktea, the splash of creamy hammel-horn milk and the sweet smell of woodhoney. Tam reappeared with two steaming mugs grasped in his hands.

'Here we go, green collar,' he said, striding along the branch and placing the mug down beside him.

Tam's slight limp, Rufus noticed, seemed no better.

'Thanks, old veteran,' he said. 'How's the leg, by the way?'

'Fine, green collar,' Tam replied. 'And thanks for asking.'

Tam lowered himself down onto the branch,

wincing as he did so. Then, legs outstretched, he wrapped his hands round the warm mug and took a sip of oaktea. He glanced over at Rufus, who was sipping his own tea.

'Actually, Rufus,' he said quietly, suddenly serious and unsmiling, 'it's not fine . . . It's not fine at all.'

'Is your leg hurting?' said Rufus.

'It's not my leg so much as . . .' Tam paused and, with a jolt of shock, Rufus realized that his friend was trying very hard not to cry. 'As . . . as . . . this.'

Tam's hand went to the green and white chequerboard collar he wore. For a moment the pair of them were silent, and Rufus was painfully aware of the other lancers exchanging glances, making their excuses and climbing into their hammocks suspended in the shadows below the branch. When the last of them – the waif Cedifice, who preferred to sleep in a corner of the knot hole rather than a hammock – had said goodnight and left them alone on the branch, Rufus put down his mug and turned to his friend.

'Do you want to talk about it, Tam?' he asked.

Tam didn't look at him, but continued to stare into the depths of his own mug, his eyes blank and expressionless. At length, he breathed in and shook his head.

'You were laid up with the croup,' he said quietly.

'I wish to Sky that *I* had been . . .'

'But you earned your boards, Tam,' Rufus interrupted. 'You were blooded . . . !'

A single tear trickled down Tam's cheek and fell into his oaktea.

'Yes,' he whispered. Two more tears plinked into the mug clasped in his hands. 'I was blooded . . .'

For a moment he was silent again. Then, when he started speaking, the words came thick and fast – though his voice betrayed no emotion.

'We left you coughing in your hammock, Rufus, and set off for the southern fringes just as the moon was rising. It was a bright clear night, but the forest shadows were crisp and deep and we made good progress. Nixus was as excited as I was, growling beneath his breath and bounding expertly through the high branches like a prowlgrin twice his age. Reports had come in . . . Perhaps you don't remember them, Rufus – you were running quite a fever at the time. Reports of skulltrogs moving into the forests beyond the slaughterers' camp. A slaughterer herder had spotted a large group of them from his skycraft at a place called Wooded Crag.'

Rufus listened closely. Tam was right. He'd known nothing of those reports.

'Apparently, it looked like they were preparing for one of their feasts.' Tam shuddered. 'Sergeant Logglimb said we had to get there and drive them off before they started. Once these creatures from the depths of the Deepwoods get a taste for blood, he said, they get settled in and make everyone's life a misery. A few well-placed copperwood fire-darts, a whole load of shouting and they'd turn heel and flee, he said, primitive creatures that they are . . .'

Tam swallowed hard.

'And that's what you did, didn't you, Tam?' said Rufus, searching his friend's face for signs of emotion. 'The sergeant reported back to old Marshal Wooden-Leg himself. Fifth Splinter sent those skulltrogs packing – and you earned your boards for being in action. A skirmish, he called it . . .'

'Yes, a skirmish,' said Tam. He put down his mug and turned to Rufus, his face drawn and blotchy. 'Do you have any idea what that simple word actually means, Rufus? A skirmish? Not the mighty war for the Free Glades, or the epic Battle of Lufwood Mount, but just a skirmish – a small forgotten little skirmish? Well, do you?'

'Tell me,' said Rufus, his mouth suddenly dry.

'We arrived at Wooded Crag too late,' Tam continued, staring at Rufus with red-rimmed eyes. 'The skulltrogs had captured a party of low-bellied goblins and . . . and the feasting had begun. Twenty skulltrogs there were, the size of banderbears, clothed in ragged skins, the skulls of previous victims jangling at their necks . . .' He swallowed hard. 'Covered in blood as they competed with each other in tearing their captives limb from limb. The rocks, the trees, the dusty earth; everything was splattered in blood and entrails. Up above, we paused in the top of a copse of copperwoods and looked down.'

'"It's begun," said Sergeant Logglimb, "and they won't give up now until we make them stop – at the end of an ironwood lance." Simple as that. Cedifice then called out the order to form up, lances at the ready, and we charged. The hideous creatures didn't know what hit them. The Gyles took one each at the first leap; Gaddius and Fledder, three, while the twins ran through eight between them. As for Sergeant Logglimb . . .'

'And you?' asked Rufus, softly.

Tam looked down. 'One,' he said. 'Nixus leaped high off the branch, and then down we came, my lance braced and steady, my stirrups forward, heels back. Just like in practice, Rufus. Except this wasn't practice . . .

'He looked up at me, the skulltrog. Deepset eyes, blood-smeared face, all pitted and scarred. And huge great yellow fangs. Bared. Snarling. I felt my lance jump in my hands . . . Jar at my shoulder. Then just sort of slide in.

'The sound, like a bursting woodsap. All fleshy and wet . . . I'll never forget it . . .

453

'The skulltrog groaned, its stinking breath blasting in my face as my lance slid through its body and it lurched towards me. The last thing I remember before Nixus hit the ground and leaped again, was the glistening yellow eye of the skulltrog staring into mine, inches away from my face for a split second. I'll never forget it, Rufus. Never. It was a dead stare. The spark of life had been extinguished – and I . . . I had extinguished it.

'The lance slipped from my hands, greasy with blood, and Nixus and I were up in the treetops, back with the rest of the splinter. Below us – in amongst the barely distinguishable remains of the low-belly goblins – lay twenty skulltrogs, each one run through with ironwood lances. I knew that we . . . that *I*, had to do it. That now the forests round the Free Glades would be safer. But I felt no joy or elation. Just a sick feeling in the pit of my stomach, and a sadness that won't seem to go away.

'Cedifice spoke to me, told me it would pass, and as we rode back in the early light of dawn I thought he was probably right. Then, just as we reached Scartree, I felt a pain in my leg and, looking down, realized I'd been wounded. I'd been so wrapped up in my thoughts that I hadn't even noticed. It was only a scratch. One of the skulltrog's fangs must have caught me as Nixus leaped clear. It's nothing really – only it won't seem to heal. Just aches and aches, and keeps reminding me of that dead eye staring into mine . . .'

'Here, let me take a look,' said Rufus.

Tam pulled off his tilder leather boot and revealed a livid wound cut deep into his calf, oozing with yellow pus. He winced.

'Oh, it doesn't look too bad, old veteran,' Rufus lied to his friend, forcing his voice to sound cheerful and unconcerned.

'Thought earning my boards would be the happiest day of my life . . .'

Rufus reached into the leather bag at his side and dug around, before pulling out a pot of hyleberry salve that worked wonders on Lyrinx's feet.

'Instead, green collar, old friend,' said Tam, fingering his chequerboard collar, hardly noticing as Rufus applied the sweet-smelling ointment to the wound, 'it's only brought me nightmares . . .'

The sound of the wooden leg on the timber boards of Lake Landing Academy was unmistakable. *Tap-tap-tap*, it went, the sound growing louder and louder until, at last, the doors to the Great Lecture Theatre slowly opened.

'Come in, Marshal Heg-tugg,' said the High Master of the Academy, Xanth Filatine.

He was standing by the great window of the academy's magnificent lecture theatre, hands clasped behind his back, looking out across the lake. The sun had just set and the surface of the water was mirroring the red and orange sunset. Silhouetted against the sky were half a dozen librarian-knight apprentices riding their flimsy skycraft. They were coming in to land on the jetty after an arduous afternoon of flying practice.

'Greetings, High Master,' said the elderly flathead goblin. He was dressed in the white tunic and chequerboard collar of the Freeglade Lancers. His wood armour was pitted and scratched, his boots scuffed and worn, but the ornately stitched banderbear badge of gold on his threadbare tunic announced his high rank. Marshal Heg-tugg, or old Wooden-Leg, was High Commander of the Freeglade Lancers of the Ironwood Stands, all twenty-two thousand, five hundred of them. Together with the librarian knights, it was his job to organize the protection and defence of the Free Glades. Which was why – wooden leg or no wooden leg – he had come running when summoned to Lake Landing by the head of the librarian knights, Xanth Filatine.

'So, what have we here? . . .' The marshal stopped and gazed up in astonishment.

There, suspended on a floating cradle of buoyant sumpwood, the light from the great window casting it in vivid light and shadow, was an imposing gigantic creature. In death, the librarians had gently and reverently restored what dignity they could to the Deepwoods monster, for they cherished and studied all aspects of the mysterious forests. The filth and debris had been carefully removed, wounds examined and cleaned, mouth, ears and nostrils gently probed, and the tortured features arranged into a mask of peaceful slumber. And as they'd worked, they had noted and catalogued everything, building up a treatise on this never-before-seen creature that had blundered out of the forest depths.

'My lancers told me it was big, but I had no idea . . .' said the old marshal in awe.

Xanth Filatine turned from the window, a barkscroll treatise in his hand, and joined the marshal in the middle of the Great Lecture Theatre. As the sunset faded, its rose and golden glow was replaced by the warm light of half a dozen globes which hung from the arching timbered ceiling. Xanth stroked his thin straggly beard, once bright russet but now flecked with grey.

'It is what can only be described by us librarians as a nameless one,' he told Marshal Heg-tugg. 'So far as we can tell, creatures as huge and primitive as this one originate in the very darkest depths of the Deepwoods beyond the forest of thorns, beyond the Nightwoods and perhaps even further than Riverrise itself. Life in those regions is often in its earliest state. According to some theories, it is as if it has only recently evolved from the life-bringing "seeds" of the Mother Storm . . .'

'Yes, well, I'll leave such matters to you, High Master,' said the marshal, tapping his wooden leg on the timber floor impatiently. 'What concerns me is, how did it get here? And should we, in the Free Glades, be concerned about it?'

Xanth looked down at the barkscroll treatise in his hand.

'Our librarian knights on their treatise voyages have reported sightings of such creatures skewered on the razor-like barbs of the thornforest,' he said, 'but none has ever found a path through. Until now. But it is such a rare occurrence that I don't think we need to be concerned.' He unfurled the barkscroll. 'What *should* concern us, however, is the treatment this poor, primitive creature evidently received once it had found its way here.'

'Treatment?' The marshal stared up at the creature hovering above, seemingly sleeping peacefully, its massive arms folded over its great distended belly.

'Indeed,' Xanth said sadly. 'According to my librarians' findings, there is evidence of this creature being harnessed and whipped. Scars across its back and legs, and rope burns across the chest and under its arms. It was, we think, harnessed and forced to pull some sort of heavy burden.'

'Have you any idea what?' asked the marshal.

'It's puzzling,' said Xanth, scratching his close-cropped head.

He crossed the floor of the lecture theatre to a floating lectern bobbing on the end of a chain and pulled it down towards him. A moment later, he returned with a small ironwood tray.

'These tiny specks were found beneath the creature's toenails.'

He held the tray up to the light from the globes above. As he did so, the golden glow that fell on the glittering scrapings abruptly diffused, sending shafts of dazzling light shooting off through the air in every direction.

'There's only one substance in all the Edge that does that,' said Marshal Heg-tugg. 'Phraxdust.'

'From the Twilight Woods,' said Xanth thoughtfully. 'Perhaps the creature strayed there . . . But that is not where it was harnessed and enslaved.'

'No?' said Heg-tugg.

'No,' said Xanth. 'We found the nameless one's body spattered and smeared with this.'

He picked up a clod of dried mud from the tray and rubbed it between his finger and thumb, then inspected them. There was a dark, oily stain across his fingertips. He held it up to his nose and sniffed. His brow creased with concentration.

'Rocksulphur,' he said slowly. 'Swarf. Pitch.' He sniffed again. 'Charcoal-grits . . . You can still smell it in the soil.'

'So far as I am aware, one place alone has earth as foul and contaminated as that,' said the marshal, shaking his head. 'And that accursed place has been deserted ever since the war for the Free Glades . . .'

'My thoughts exactly,' said Xanth. He remembered that terrible war only too well. The furnace masters with their war-machines, the glade-eaters, had invaded the Free Glades aided by the massed armies of the Goblin Nations in an effort to enslave the Freegladers. 'Yet these findings suggest it might be deserted no longer.'

Just then, there was a creak from the other side of the hall as the handle turned, and the door to the Great Lecture Theatre opened a fraction. A face appeared in the crack.

'I'm sorry, Father,' came a voice. 'Am I too early?'

'Oh, Rufus, it's you,' Xanth replied. 'No . . .' He turned to the marshal. 'My son, Rufus. He's dining with me tonight. I see all too little of him since he joined those lancers of yours.'

Rufus entered the imposing lecture theatre and shut the door quietly behind him. His eyes fell on the eerie sight of the huge body suspended from the ceiling, the pools of golden lamplight making its curves and crevices look like a statue carved from a great slab of dark wood. How peaceful it looked, he thought. Not at all like the horrific monster he'd encountered in the forest.

Rufus turned and realized he was in the presence of old Wooden Leg himself, Marshal Heg-tugg of the Freeglade Lancers.

'Marshal,' he said, touching his banderbear badge with his right hand. 'Lance-Cadet Filatine, of the Fifth Splinter, Fourth High-Branch Troop, Scartree Company, Third Roost. Servant of the Free Glades.'

'Marshal Heg-tugg of the Ironwood Stands,' said the marshal formally, touching his gold badge with his right hand. 'Also servant of the Free Glades.' He smiled. 'Fifth Splinter, you say?'

Rufus nodded.

'You're making quite a name for yourselves. Weren't you the splinter involved in that skirmish at Wooded Crag?'

Rufus blushed and fingered his green collar. 'I missed that one myself, but yes, the Fifth Splinter was there.'

The marshal exchanged looks with the High Master of Lake Landing before patting the young lancer on his green-collared shoulder.

'Well, it just so happens that your father and I might have a mission for the Fifth Splinter, Fourth High-Branch Troop of Scartree Company . . .'

'You might?' said Rufus, intrigued.

'Yes,' said the old marshal. 'A mission to the Foundry Glades.'

. CHAPTER THREE .

THE DEATH-CHEATERS

'*Open formation,*' Cedifice the waif's voice sounded inside every head. '*Advance at the gallop!*'

Lined up in an orderly row at the southern fringe of the Free Glades, it was the order they'd all been waiting for. The lancers of the Fifth Splinter, Fourth High-Branch Troop, Scartree Company, twitched the reins of their prowlgrin mounts. As one, the great beasts launched themselves high into the air with their powerful back legs.

Rufus clung on tight to the curved saddle roll, braced his legs in the stirrups and waited for his stomach to catch up with him. Lyrinx landed on a branch high in the forest canopy and leaped instantly for another, then another. Leaning forward in the saddle, Rufus pressed himself down as low as he could as his prowlgrin broke through the smaller branches and leafy twigs of the canopy. He felt his ironwood lance judder and buck under his arm as it sliced through the foliage.

They broke through into the bright sunlight. Above the forest canopy now, Lyrinx's feet were a blur of motion as the prowlgrin sped over the leafy tops of the trees at full gallop. Rufus could see the rest of his splinter spread out on either side of him – orange and grey blurs in a sea of green.

Tree-cresting it was called, and it was exhilarating. Up there in the crystal air, leaping from branch to branch, the rider had to entrust his life to the skill of his mount. It was a heart-thrilling, soul-stirring experience. In fact, according to those few lancers who had also piloted a skycraft, galloping across the forest canopy on the back of a prowlgrin – with the lurch and thud of every soaring leap – was more intoxicating than any flight.

Rufus straightened in the saddle and quickly checked his equipment. Broadsword buckled firmly at his side, kitbags secured behind the saddle, knife strapped to his calf – thankfully everything was in its place. When breaking through the upper canopy, it was easy for a whipping branch or thrashing twig to snag any piece of equipment that was not firmly fastened down.

'*Keep formation,*' Cedifice reminded them all.

Rufus looked around. Lyrinx had pulled ahead of the others and he tugged lightly on the reins to check her. The prowlgrin slowed slightly and the gyle-goblins – their camouflage cloaks streaming out behind them – drew level on one side. Beyond them, was the large figure of Gaddius Felludine and his prowlgrin, Dendrix, bounding over the treetops, together with Lance-Corporal Fledder and the gnokgoblin twins, Hudflux and Holt, on their own smaller but no less powerful prowlgrins.

Glancing to the other side, the reassuring figure of Sergeant Logglimb drew level, his ironwood lance – recently sharpened and oiled – glinting in the sunlight. And directly level with him came Cedifice on his own mount, Sulix; snow-white and blue-eyed, the swiftest of all the prowlgrins in Scartree Company.

Beyond them, Rufus noticed Tam and Nixus out on the left flank, speeding ahead.

'*Keep formation, Tam,*' Cedifice reminded him.

Glancing over his shoulder, Tam raised a hand in acknowledgement and reined Nixus in until they were in line with the others.

Up here, tree-cresting over the top of the Deepwoods, high above the thickets, briars and dense undergrowth of the forest floor, the lancers could travel further in one hour than those on foot could manage in a week. And the denser and more impenetrable the forest below, the easier the prowlgrins found it, galloping over the closely packed treetops.

Lyrinx's nostrils flared as she exhaled bursts of air that felt as hot as steaming oaktea against the knuckles of Rufus's hand. Beneath him, Rufus could feel the prowlgrin's great round body expanding and contracting as she filled her lungs with rasping gulps of air. The creature's huge legs flexed and thrummed as the sensitive toes of her feet, splayed wide, sped over the uppermost branches of the trees, causing them to buck and sway in their wake.

Flocks of screeching berry-finches and brightly coloured skullpeckers rose from their perches and scattered before the line of lancers like river spume on an Edgewater current. And from the treetops all around, the forest echoed with the hoarse cries of weezits, the barking alarm-calls of fromps and the squealing of agitated quarms. Tree-cresting might be a speedy way of crossing the vast tracts of the Deepwoods, Rufus realized, but it was also one of the noisiest, alerting everything and everyone in the forest below to their presence.

After an hour or so, and with Lyrinx beginning to tire beneath Rufus, the order came through.

'*Form line.*' Cedifice's voice, as calm and resonant as ever, sounded in Rufus's head. '*Mid-branch canter.*'

Rufus pulled the reins gently to the left and Lyrinx leaned over, one eye peering down through the canopy of leaves as she slowed. Then, following Sergeant Logglimb who was up in front, and with the gyle-goblins falling in behind, Rufus and Lyrinx dropped down into the dappled depths. Rufus stood in the stirrups as they fell, then took the jolt as Lyrinx landed on a broad branch far below.

Ahead of him, Sergeant Logglimb, Cedifice and Tam urged their prowlgrins along the branch in a line. Behind Rufus, the tree juddered as the Gyles, the twins Holt and Hudflux and Lance-Corporal Fledder all landed, their sweating prowlgrins blowing noisily. Rufus twitched the reins and Lyrinx set off in large bounds after the prowlgrins in front.

They snaked through the middle branches of the trees in a sinuous line, like a hunting hover worm, a ripple running along the column now and again as one prowlgrin jumped after the other from tree to tree. Slower, but far quieter down here in the shadow-filled branches – apart from the odd silver-backed quarm whooping at them as they passed – the lancers made steady progress. In the saddle, although Rufus trusted to his prowlgrin to make the leaps from branch to branch as sure-footed as ever, he still had plenty to do.

Peering ahead, he ducked and swivelled as over-hanging branches and foliage sped past in a blur. The air filled with the sweet smell of bruised pine needles and crushed leaves. Occasionally, an acorn-laden sprig or leafy bough would catch Rufus a glancing blow to the helmet or arm, but the long hours of 'branch practice' in the training slings back at the Scartree had served him well.

Deeper into the forest they cantered, Tam at the front of the line, calculating their direction from the sunlight hitting the tree-trunks, heading further and further south. Finally, as the shadows lengthened, the light faded and the forest filled with the echoing calls of night creatures, Sergeant Logglimb gave Cedifice a nod.

'Splinter, halt!' The waif passed on the order. *'Make roost for the night.'*

The Fifth Splinter reined in their prowlgrins and came to a halt in the spreading branches of a dark-elm. The prowlgrins immediately started purring and thrumming their feet on the glistening branches beneath them.

'Perfect spot,' announced Sergeant Logglimb, dismounting and patting his prowlgrin, an orange giant called Pheddix. 'Go ahead, boy, oil those toes of yours. You've earned it.'

'Time to rise, Fifth Splinter!'

Roused to wakefulness by the sound of the waif's voice in his head, Rufus sat up and yawned sleepily. His muscles ached from the exertions of the previous day's ride, but it was a pleasant feeling and he felt well-rested – despite a night filled with dreams of ducking branches and leaping from tree-top to treetop. He rubbed the sleep from his eyes and saw Cedifice and Sergeant Logglimb perched on an upper branch of the darkelm, peering out into the distance, already busy calculating the route of that day's gallop. Above their heads, the bright blue sky twinkled between the dense foliage of the over-head canopy like a mass of jewels.

'Come on, out of those hammocks, you idle lot!' boomed Hulm Logglimb's deep voice. 'Before a rot-sucker has you for breakfast.'

Rufus threw himself enthusiastically into the morning routine of the deep patrol. He groomed Lyrinx and fed her with the rations of dried offal from his forage bag. He rolled up his hammock and strapped it securely to the saddle, and checked over his equipment for any damage caused by twigs and branches. Then he joined the others at the hanging-brazier, where the Gyles and Degg Fledder had prepared a breakfast of cobbley – a lancers' favourite, consisting of fried woodyams, wild mushrooms, kaleaf and chopped rashers of smoked tilder. It was washed down with oaktea. Half an hour later, with their provisions packed and their stomachs full, the Fifth Splinter set off again.

They started at a brief gallop, but soon dropped down to a mid-branch canter for the rest of the morning and into the afternoon. Then, as the sun dropped lower in the sky, the forest began to thin, and they descended first to the lower branches and then to the forest floor itself.

'*Single file,*' Cedifice whispered inside Rufus's head. '*Close order. No talking.*'

The prowlgrins bunched together and padded through the forest. Around them, the mottled-barked, sickly-looking trees with their twisted branches and patchy leaves thinned out further and the soft dark earth began to give off an increasingly stale and dank odour as the prowlgrins' toes sank into it.

As they trotted on, and the gaps between the trees widened, Rufus noticed that the sounds of the forest creatures that had surrounded them ever since they'd set out on patrol the morning before had died away. Now the forest was eerily silent, apart from the snuffling breaths of the prowlgrins, who had grown nervous and skittish.

Finally Sergeant Logglimb raised his lance and pointed to a clump of bleached trees with yellow, diseased-looking foliage just ahead.

'*Roost the prowlgrins and dismount,*' Cedifice relayed the order.

Tam and Rufus exchanged worried looks as they urged their jittery prowlgrins up into the branches after the others. Moments later, they landed on a white-barked branch, dismounted and peered out through the yellow leaves.

The scene before them was one of utter desolation. They were in a tree on the very edge of what, Rufus realized, was the old Foundry Glades – the Foundry Glades that had risen up many years ago, around the time that the Free Glades themselves were beginning. But the two places, Rufus knew from the records of the librarians, could not have been more different.

What had started as a single forest forge in a small glade, set up by Hemuel Spume to provide passing goblin tribes with pots and pans, had developed into a sprawling mass of glades, full of roaring furnaces which voraciously consumed the trees all round them. Before long, the Foundry Glades had destroyed vast swathes of forestland and become one great, polluted blot on the face of the Deepwoods.

Where the Free Glades represented freedom, the Foundry Glades had embraced slavery – at one point forcing even those most noble of creatures, the banderbears, into a brutal life of forced labour. Where the Free Glades existed in harmony with their surroundings, the Foundry Glades destroyed the forest and poisoned the earth. Where the Council of the Free Glades decreed that the land belonged to no one, but that the fruits of the land belonged to everyone, the handful of black-hearted furnace masters who ruled the Foundry Glades were interested only in exploiting their fellow creatures for profit . . .

In short, whereas the Free Glades had always been a beacon of shining light that shone for all the poor, the weak and the downtrodden who wished to start a new life, for any who ended up in the rank mills and dark forges of the Foundry Glades the light of hope was snuffed out for ever. Just reading about the place on those long evenings in his father's study at the academy at Lake Landing, had been enough to cause Rufus childhood nightmares. Now, here he was, on the very edge of those infamous glades. Swallowing hard, Rufus stared down.

At the centre of the great clearing were row upon row of foundries crouched in the dead earth, their blackened chimneys – some cracked, some fractured, some reduced to ugly stumps – pointing to the sky like broken fingers. Some of the forges still had piles of stripped logs outside them, unburned and abandoned. To the right were the slave-huts with their open sides and central pillars, the chains and manacles that had deprived so many of their freedom still hanging from rusting iron rings. And far ahead, beyond the forges and foundries, was a huge ruin of a building: the Palace of the Furnace Masters.

Once it had been a magnificent edifice with a castellated roof, elegant twisting chimneys and mullioned windows. Like everything else, however, it had been abandoned. Now there were tiles missing from the roof and black cavities where the windows had been; the chimneys were broken and stubby, while the ornately carved Counting House at its western end had collapsed into a ramshackle heap of beams and rubble.

The power of the evil furnace masters had been smashed once and for all after the catastrophic defeat of their giant war-machines during the war for the Free Glades. Hemuel Spume, their leader, had perished when his glade-eater had plunged into the depths of the North Lake in sight of New Undertown, and the slaves of the Foundry Glades had been freed and given a new life in the beautiful Free Glades. Rufus's father, Xanth, had fought in that war along with his best friend, Rook Barkwater, a legendary Freeglade lancer.

'What a terrible place,' whispered Tam, peering over Rufus's shoulder, his face ashen white.

'Gather round, Fifth Splinter,' Sergeant Logglimb ordered in a quiet voice.

Rufus and Tam joined Hudflux, Holt, Lance-Corporal Fledder, Cedifice and Gaddius on the higher branches of the tree, where the sergeant surveyed the scene. The Gyles remained with the nervous, jittery prowlgrins and began camouflaging them carefully with spider-silk nets.

'The prowlgrins are spooked, so we're better off on foot,' said Logglimb, his voice calm and measured. 'Fledder, take the twins and scout out the furnaces to the east. Cedifice, Gaddius and I will search the slave-huts on the western fringe. You two . . .' He turned to Tam and Rufus. 'Think you can handle that tumbledown ruin in the middle?' He nodded towards the Palace of the Furnace Masters.

'Yes, sergeant,' Rufus replied, and nudged his friend.

'Y . . . yes, sergeant,' replied Tam, his face, if anything, even whiter than it had been a moment before.

'Good,' said Logglimb, unsheathing his sword. 'Remember, we're scouting for any sign of recent activity – footprints, churned-up earth, campfire ash . . . Anything. And listen out for Cedifice at *all* times.'

The lancers nodded.

Sergeant Logglimb touched the banderbear badge on his tunic with his fist. 'Freeglader,' he whispered.

'Freeglader,' the lancers of Fifth Splinter replied.

'*Move out!*' Cedifice gave the silent command.

The lancers, their swords unsheathed – except for Hudflux and Holt, who carried their crossbows at the ready – climbed silently down the tree and spread out into the eerie, deserted Foundry Glades.

Rufus and Tam made their way between the mounds of slag and piles of blackened timber that fringed a rough track, beaten flat by countless slave feet and rutted by heavy carts that hauled timber and ore-laden rock. The heavy silence was broken only by the crunch of their footsteps on the polluted earth and a soft wailing sound caused by the light breeze whistling through the black mouths of the open furnaces and out of the rusting chimneys above.

'It's as if the dead are whispering to us, warning us . . .' Tam began, his eyes dark and haunted-looking.

Rufus put a reassuring hand on his shoulder. 'It

doesn't help to think like that, Tam,' he said softly. 'Not in a place like this. We've got a job to do . . .' He nodded towards the Palace of the Furnace Masters up ahead.

As they approached it, they could see that the once magnificent building was even more of a ruin than it had first appeared. The metal-panelled doors at the entrance hung off their hinges, the mullioned windows had all been smashed, while the gaping cracks that ran down the outside walls were so deep that it looked as if the entire building could collapse at any moment.

'Come on,' said Rufus, trying to sound braver than he felt. 'Let's scout it out.'

With Rufus in front and Tam following reluctantly behind, limping slightly as he climbed the steps that led into the main hall, the pair of them went in. There was a pungent smell of damp inside and they had to pick their way carefully through the debris-strewn hallway to avoid falling through the rotting floorboards and ending up with a broken leg, or worse, in the cellars below. Room by room, they checked the ground floor. They were full of ornate furniture, opulent wall-hangings and fine carpets, all rotted and mouldering away to dust.

'All that pain and suffering,' said Rufus, reaching out to a mottled green-tinged tapestry that crumbled like a dry leaf at his touch. 'For this . . .'

They left the ground floor and headed up a creaking staircase to the first floor, which was huge. Carved pillars supported a high ceiling, beneath which row after row of dusty desks with empty inkwells and abandoned quills were neatly arranged. The meticulous columns of expenditure and profit recorded on barkscrolls had rotted to piles of brown mulch beneath each desk.

'Much good it did them,' said Tam, scattering a pile of rotten ledger-scrolls with the toe of his boot.

They carefully climbed another wobbly staircase and, taking the corridor to the left, ended up in an even more opulent part of the palace. They entered a vast hall with rugs on the floors, silver-theaded tapestries on the walls and intricate ceiling mouldings overhead, decorated with gold. Even though the missing tiles meant that rain had got in, rotting the carpets and eating into the plaster, the former grandeur of the place was unmistakable.

'This must be where Hemuel Spume himself lived,' said Rufus, looking around with horrified fascination, 'while his slaves outside died in their hundreds from overwork and foundry croup.'

'What do you think's in there?' wondered Tam, pointing to a small, rounded door at the end of the hall. 'His treasure room perhaps?'

The pair of them crossed the tiled floor, their footfalls echoing round the high ceilings as they went.

Rufus grasped the door-handle, half-expecting the room to be locked. With a soft creak, though, the door opened and they found themselves in a small tiled room. There were shelves set into an alcove, crowded with row upon row of bottled unguents and salves, thick with dust, and in the centre of the room a copper cauldron with pipes, pressure gauges, dials and levers sprouting from its rusting sides.

But that wasn't what made Rufus and Tam recoil in horror . . .

Staring back at them, his knobbly oversized skull just visible over the rim of the cauldron was the skeleton of a waif. Rufus approached and peered inside. The sides of the cauldron were blackened and scorched, and marked with deep scratches from the waif's puny hands as he had fought to climb out. The waif's empty eye-sockets peered up at him, his jaws fixed in a silent scream; his rigid arm-bones reaching out in a desperate pleading gesture.

'What do you suppose happened to him?' Tam wondered, appalled.

'We'll never know,' said Rufus, turning away. 'Come on, Tam, let's get out of here.'

Back outside, they paused for a moment in the gathering gloom. Rufus spotted Hudflux and Holt in the distance, skirting round the looming shapes of the foundries, crossbows in hand. On the other side of the glade, Logglimb, Gaddius and Cedifice emerged from a long slave-hut and entered another.

'Look!' said Tam. 'Round there, behind the palace . . .'

Rufus followed his gaze. Deep ruts – recent, by the look of them – led away behind the ruins. They followed them and found a wide courtyard with stables leading off it on three sides. Several contained ornate carriages, their axles broken, now lurching on their sides like stricken hammelhorns. But the main stable – huge and cavernous as a barn, with great pillars supporting its thatched roof – was empty. Rufus and Tam entered it.

There was thick, fresh straw on the floor and a large bucket of sallowdrop fruit. Heavy chains with manacles at the ends hung down from the roof beams, and there were large metal rings bolted to the floor. There was blood splattered on two of the walls – brown, dried, but clearly recent – and a broken, splintered drinking trough that appeared to have been flung with some force at a third . . .

'Come on, Tam,' said Rufus. 'We'd better report this to the sergeant . . .'

His words were cut short by the sound of Cedifice's voice, whispering inside his head.

'*Fifth Splinter!*' he said. '*Disappear.*'

Rufus turned to Tam who, like all the other lancers in the Foundry Glades, had been alerted by the same warning. Without a word, they followed the waif's order.

Tam rolled into the shadows in the corner of the stables, burying himself in a thin covering of straw. Rufus ran to one of the pillars and shinned up it into the roof rafters where he froze, still as a statue.

Moments later, two figures appeared below him in the stables. One was a tall black-plumed shryke with piercing yellow eyes and long curved beak, gleaming ebony black. Around her feathered neck she wore a necklace of shiny whetstones, worn smooth from honing her razor-sharp talons. Below the necklace, she wore a belt slung over one shoulder, from which four small silvery globes hung on thin silver chains. Her long robe was black and faded and appeared to be made up of a number of tunics stitched together, each bearing the grubby white emblem of a screaming gloamglozer. In her claws she gripped an evil-looking flail, which she cracked impatiently.

'So much for your theory, Squive,' she screeched hoarsely. 'Good riddance, I say.'

The shryke's companion took a step forward into the stables. Rufus looked down from the rafters. The creature was tiny, with blotchy red skin and a round, bloated body supported on thin, spindly legs. His small eyes were set wide apart on either side of a round, low-browed head with a sharp, beaklike nose jutting out over a huge lower jaw. He looked like a cross between a Mire raven and a halitoad – yet the pointed, tufted ears on either side of his head were the sure sign that he was one of the rare, seldom encountered, goblin types; a red dwarf.

So rare in fact were these creatures that Rufus had only ever seen drawings of the tiny goblins in the treatises in his father's library at Lake Landing. Like so many of the strangest, least-known creatures, they came from the Nightwoods, far beyond the thorn forests.

'Pity,' the red dwarf wheezed. His voice had the hooting quality of a nightowl. 'Thought the sallow-drops might tempt it . . .'

The shryke kicked the bucket over and the soft fruit tumbled out across the floor, one rolling towards the corner where Tam lay concealed beneath the straw. Suddenly the light in the stables seemed to dim. Rufus glanced over towards the entrance and almost rolled off the rafter he was clinging to. Behind the shryke and the red dwarf, there was a crowd of silent, sepia-coloured figures. The hairs on the back of Rufus's neck stood on end.

The figures were dressed in a wide variety of clothes of all styles, but all faded and rotting and the same inky brown colour. Some wore old-fashioned sky pirate coats with battered breast-plates and broken parawings. Others had goblin capes of half-rotted animal pelts, or the conical hats of merchants, or tattered traders' aprons. One even wore the rusted armour of an ancient knight academic, hundreds of years old.

But it wasn't so much their clothes that told Rufus where they'd come from, but their faces. They were horrific. Sunken, shrivelled, half rotted away – teeth, noses, ears, sometimes jaw-bones were missing or hanging hideously by a thread . . . They were the faces of those poor sky-cursed souls who had become lost in the Twilight Woods.

Occasionally, a figure might stumble accidentally out of those terrible woods and find their way to the Free Glades, half-crazed and in search of forgotten memories. With their hauntingly blue eyes and silent demeanour, survivors of the treacherous Twilight Woods were known – behind their backs, and in horrified whispers – as death-cheaters.

Few, if any, Freegladers envied them. Rufus's father had spoken of one he'd once met, an old sky pirate who'd spent his remaining days silently in the corner of a tavern in New Undertown. Rufus shuddered. He'd never seen a death-cheater before – and now here were fifty of them standing below him, their dank, rotten odour rising up in the rafters and making him want to gag. He bit his lip and looked away.

'We'd better get back,'

hooted the red dwarf. 'The armourer will be expecting us.'

'You heard him,' screeched the shryke, clacking her flail at the death-cheaters. 'Back to the armoury, you stinking sacks of bones!'

She tossed them hunks of raw meat dipped in phraxdust, the tempting morsels with which she had lured them from the Twilight Woods, and which ensured that their immortality would be prolonged just long enough to do her bidding. With low, moaning sighs, the chewing death-cheaters turned and shuffled out, their weapons – scythes, ancient cutlasses, goblin spears and sling-shots – rattling and clinking like ghostly wind-chimes as they went.

'Come, Squive, best not to keep the armourer waiting,' the black-plumed shryke squawked.

She held out a taloned claw. The tiny figure of the red dwarf leaped up onto it and perched there like a brooding halitoad as the pair of them left the stables.

Up in the rafters, Rufus tensed, waiting for Cedifice's orders. Outside, he could hear the death-cheaters tramping along the track from the Palace of the Furnace Masters, back through the Foundry Glades. Balancing on the roof beam, he gently parted the thatch above his head and peered out. He saw the horrific band making their way towards the forest fringe, the tall figure of the black shryke bringing up the rear.

The shambling figures began disappearing into the darkening forest, only for the shryke to stop suddenly and look about her, beak held high, as if sniffing the air. The red dwarf seemed to lean up and say something and, as Rufus watched, transfixed, the shryke cackled and screeched, 'Better safe than sorry!'

She reached for one of the metal globes hanging from her belt and unhooked it. Then, with a great arcing movement of one feathered arm, she hurled it at the clump of trees at the glade's edge.

Rufus saw a flash of blinding light followed by a loud crack, and to his horror a ball of vivid yellow flames engulfed the trees.

With a cackle of hideous laughter, the shryke disappeared into the forest. For a moment, all Rufus could hear was the sound of blood pumping in his head and his own rapid breathing. Then Cedifice's voice broke through into the shocked blankness of his mind.

'Fifth Splinter! Muster!'

. CHAPTER FOUR .

THE ARMOURER

The lancers of Fifth Splinter stood before the blazing tree, open-mouthed. The diseased foliage fizzed and sparked, blackened tree limbs snapping off and shooting high into the sky as the flames ignited the buoyant sap within. From close by, the high-pitched yelping barks of panicked prowlgrins filled the air, along with the stench of charred wood and burned flesh. Cedifice the waif wrung his hands together, the veins in his paper-thin ears vivid in the hideous yellow light.

'The Gyles,' he whispered. 'They're dead.'

Sergeant Logglimb turned to Rufus and Tam, his face impassive. 'See to the prowlgrins,' he said simply.

Rufus and Tam broke away from the rest of the splinter and dashed towards the yelping, which was coming from a clump of trees to the left of the inferno. Rufus arrived first, bent down and clasped his hands together to give Tam a hoist up to the

lower branches of the closest tree, then scampered up after him. They climbed quickly, neither speaking, until they reached the upper branches of the stunted copperwood where – fur camouflaged against the yellow and orange leaves – there were five cowering prowlgrins.

'Steady, there,' Rufus whispered. 'It's all right. Everything's all right now.'

As he was pulling himself up onto the roost branch one of the prowlgrins leaped forwards, his huge mouth wide open to reveal rows of razor-sharp teeth. Rufus licked his fingers and reached out his hand. The prowlgrin breathed in. Instantly, his mouth closed and the snarls and growls turned to a deep, throaty purr. Beside him, Tam did the same to the terrified prowlgrin next to him.

'That's it,' whispered Rufus in a soothing voice. 'Steady, now. We're here . . .'

He reached out and traced a finger round the flaring nostrils of the third beast, and then the fourth. Tam reached the fifth and turned back to his friend.

'Lyrinx, Nixus . . .' he said, the relief plain in his voice as their own prowlgrins nuzzled against them, purring contentedly.

'Luxus, Dendrix and Dex,' Rufus identified the other prowlgrins on the branch. 'Which means . . .'

'*The other five prowlgrins perished with the Gyles,*'

Cedifice's voice sounded in their heads. *'The splinter has lost half its mounts.'*

Rufus and Tam climbed onto their prowlgrins, gathered the reins of the three others and leaped down the copperwood. As they did so, from over to their right, there came a creaking, splintering sound followed by a loud *whoosh* as the blazing tree – its bubbling sap now buoyant – tore itself out of the ground by the roots and shot up into the darkening sky like a shooting star.

'Sky rest their souls,' muttered Gaddius Felludine, unbuckling his helmet and cupping it in his great hands.

'Listen up,' Sergeant Logglimb barked.

The order went some way to concealing his own sense of loss. The gyle-goblins had been with him ever since they'd enlisted, fresh-faced and honey-fed, straight from their colony. The three of them had turned into the best trackers in Scartree Company and had served the Free Glades well in hundreds of patrols and skirmishes.

There was the occasion at the Battle of Lufwood Mount when he would have lost his life to a blood-frenzied shryke had it not been for the Gyles' deadly lances; and the time the three of them had laid a trap for one of the great lumbering war machines known as glade-eaters, during the Battle of New Undertown, and set it ablaze. He swallowed hard.

And then also to have lost his beloved Pheddix . . .

'Sergeant Logglimb.' The waif's soft voice sounded inside the sergeant's head.

He looked round, momentarily unsettled, to see the rest of the splinter – seven lancers and five prowlgrins – staring back at him.

'We . . . um,' he murmured, gathering his thoughts. 'Yes, we're going to have to double up. On the prowlgrins.'

He turned to the corporal, his eyes glistening, but a stony expression set hard on his face. 'Degg, I'll ride with you on Luxus,' he said gruffly. 'Gaddius and Cedifice, you can ride together on Dendrix. Holt, you take your brother on Dex . . .'

The lancers nodded grimly and climbed onto the prowlgrins, their long ironwood lances clasped firmly in their fists. Sergeant Logglimb turned in the saddle and shook his own lance menacingly.

'We're going after that murdering shryke and her stinking death-cheaters. Whatever that weapon was that killed the Gyles and our brave-hearted prowl-grins, I for one won't rest until I've prised it from the dead claw of the bird-creature . . .' The sergeant turned his glittering eyes on the two young lancers. 'Tam, Rufus,' he said. 'I want you to ride on those prowlgrins of yours, faster than you've ever ridden before. You must get back to the Free Glades, and raise the roost . . .'

'The whole roost?' gasped Rufus.

That was all six companies – over four thousand lancers . . .

'Yes, the whole roost,' said Sergeant Logglimb. 'And as quickly as you can . . .' He paused and smiled grimly. 'Something tells me we're going to need all the help we can get.'

A strong wind had got up in the Foundry Glades. It came hissing through the stunted trees at the fringes of the clearing, whipping up the acrid-smelling dust and soot into angry swirls as it went.

'*Splinter, move out!*' Cedifice's voice sounded. '*Good luck, Tam. Good luck, Rufus.*'

The deep orange and brown prowlgrin, Dendrix, went first, leaping up into the tree-line with Gaddius Felludine and Cedifice on its back. Holt and Hudflux, on the skittish, blue-eyed Dex, followed. Luxus – heavyset and a paler orange – hesitated. Degg Fledder in the saddle was keeping a tight grip on his reins. Behind him, Sergeant Logglimb leaned down and cut a deep notch into the bark of a darkelm tree at the eastern edge of the glade. Then, resheathing his knife, he turned round.

'Tam, Rufus. You're to get back here with the third roost as fast as you can, then follow our tracks.' He tapped the trunk of the darkelm tree. 'I'll make them good and clear.' He touched the banderbear badge on his tunic with his fist. 'Freeglader!'

'Freeglader!' Tam and Rufus replied as Degg twitched Luxus's reins.

The great prowlgrin gave a low whinny and leaped up into the broad low branches of the neighbouring tree. Then the next. And the next. A moment later, the prowlgrin and his two riders were swallowed up in the forest, leaving the young lancers alone in the gloomy Foundry Glades.

Rufus glanced over at the notch the sergeant had carved in the tree; one end wide, the other tapering to a point. It was the simplest and most commonly used of tracking-marks – short, wedge-shaped cuts in the trunks of the smoother barked trees like silver oak and young lufwood. The point of the mark indicated the direction to follow. But there were other ways of leaving tracking-marks. Lots of them – and Rufus had learned them all.

One of the huge, ball-shaped nodules of a lullabee, for instance, could be sliced off in the direction to be followed. Ironwood pines – the lower bark too hard for a knife even to scratch – were often turned into makeshift signposts by embedding carefully pointing twigs into the seeping resin; while a length of a long, frondy branch of the sallowdrop tree could be intricately knotted to give detailed information to those who knew how to read the signs – direction of journey, number of party, rough time of day of passing by . . .

And down on the forest floor itself, there were other signs that could be left. A carefully placed pinecone on a flat stone, for example. A twist of tilder-grass. A re-positioned log . . . Whatever the method, the theory was the same. A lancer of the Free Glades could use tracking-marks to quite literally make the forest talk to his fellow lancers. It was a skill prized even more highly than lancework – and, as he turned away, Rufus remembered with a jolt that the Fifth Splinter had just lost three of its most accomplished 'forest talkers' in this terrible place.

'Come on, Tam,' he called over to his friend. 'Let's get out of here.'

They travelled without easing up for the best part of three hours. It was hard going. Not only was the wind against them, but it was getting stronger with every passing minute. As late afternoon drifted into early evening, the darkening sky began to curdle. Banks of black and violet cloud, heavy with rain, rolled across the sky in waves. Huge raindrops began to drum steadily on the leaves of the forest canopy around them. Rufus pulled his green collar up round his ears and settled down low in the saddle as, beneath him, Lyrinx gave an excited bark and increased the pace of her treetop gallop.

There was nothing a prowlgrin liked more than a rain storm. In the wild, whole herds of prowlgrins would be gripped by the frenzy of the howling wind and driving rain, leave their perches and go galloping off through the storm-lashed forest. They were made for it. Thick oily fur kept them dry, hooded eyelids shielded their eyes, while the spongy pads beneath their feet and the clawed grip of their paws ensured there was no danger of the creatures slipping.

Rufus gripped onto the saddle as tightly as he could, his lance strapped securely behind him like the mast of a skycraft. The rain was blinding and, with the dense black clouds closing overhead, night was falling fast. Behind him, Rufus could hear Nixus panting and blowing as he kept pace, Tam urging his prowlgrin on. Suddenly, in front of them, night turned to dazzling day as a flash of lightning cut down through the sky.

'Sky blast it!' Rufus cursed, reining in Lyrinx, and hastily turning in the saddle to unbuckle his iron-wood lance.

Wind and rain, a lancer could cope with; hail, sleet – snow, even. But lightning . . .

Lightning was a different matter. Lightning was swift, unpredictable and deadly – especially up here, tree-cresting over the forest canopy with a lance sticking up behind you like a lightning rod.

'Rufus!' Tam's voice rang out, just before the crack of thunder broke overhead. 'Forest floor!'

Rufus leaned forward, his face inches from Lyrinx's blowing nostrils, and tugged hard on the reins. In answer, the prowlgrin plunged down into the dark forest below, Rufus feeling the tree's leafy limbs whipping past him like grabbing fingers as the two of them fell. Lyrinx landed on a branch and gripped tight as lightning flashed across the sky high above them. Moments later, Nixus landed on a branch to the left.

Tam winced as he dismounted and pulled the oiled tilder leather blanket from his saddle pack. Rufus watched him. As if reading Rufus's thoughts, Tam shrugged, pulled the blanket over his shoulders and settled down on the branch between his prowlgrin's feet. Great raindrops splattered around them and the thunder – now directly overhead – seemed to make the whole forest tremble.

'Lightning,' Tam said simply. 'Get some sleep while we wait it out.'

Rufus nodded and, neither unbuckling his sword nor unstrapping his helmet so as to be ready to leave at a moment's notice, pulled his own oiled blanket from his pack. He settled himself between Lyrinx's feet, the great round body of his prowlgrin shielding him from the rain which dripped down through the forest canopy. He listened for a while to the sound of the heavy raindrops splashing onto Lyrinx's back, and to her soft rumbling breathing, before falling into a heavy dreamless sleep.

Rufus opened his eyes. He sat bolt upright and looked around. There was nothing. It was like staring at a white woollen blanket. The forest, the tree, even the branch he was sitting on, were enveloped in a thick, impenetrable bank of fog.

'Tree cloud,' murmured Rufus, slamming his fist against the branch in frustration. Above him, Lyrinx awoke with a start, a low growl rumbling in the back of her throat.

'Rufus, are you awake?' Tam's voice sounded through the swirling whiteness.

Rufus got to his feet and stretched with a dispirited groan. Not only was the fog impenetrable, it was also freezing. He felt chilled to the bone and it was all he could do to stop his teeth chattering.

'Yes, I'm awake,' he said miserably. '*Now* what are going to do?'

They both knew the problem they faced. The thunderstorm had drenched the warm forest floor with icy rain, causing great banks of freezing fog to rise up and envelop the trees. This tree cloud could, with a strong prevailing wind, be blown up into the sky in a couple of hours. Alternatively, in the still dank air, tree cloud could smother the forest for days with a blinding blanket of white. This forced even experienced lancers down to the forest floor, where they'd have to inch their way forward through the fog at a slime-mole's pace.

'You heard the sergeant.' Tam loomed up suddenly through the whiteness onto Rufus's branch. He crouched next to his friend, grimacing with pain, the dark circles beneath his eyes made darker by the extreme pallor of his skin. 'We've got to get back to Scartree and raise the other companies – the whole roost – as fast as we can.'

'Are you all right, Tam? Is your leg playing up? Let me take a look . . .' Rufus began, putting a hand on Tam's shoulder – only to have it shrugged off.

'There's no time for that. We have to go on; take our chances tree-cresting . . .'

'In this cloud?' Rufus was shocked. 'But Tam, haven't you noticed? There's not a breath of wind. If we tree-crest in this, we won't be able to steer the prowlgrins. They'll be jumping blind to whatever branch is within reach.' He shook his head. 'We could end up miles off course . . .'

'Do you think I don't know that?' said Tam irritably. Rufus could tell he was in pain. 'But we have no choice. You said it yourself, Rufus, there's not a breath of wind. This tree cloud could last for days. We've got to try to run through it.'

Rufus nodded. 'You're right, of course,' he said, trying to sound cheerful. 'We'll have to take a chance. The sergeant's depending on us.'

'Let's move out. And we'd better use tethers or we'll lose each other.' Tam smiled, handing Rufus one end of a long length of barkrope, before disappearing back into the fog.

There was a rustling of leaves, followed by Nixus's bark. Rufus climbed onto Lyrinx's back and fastened the rope to the saddle.

'Ready?' Tam called through the blanket of white.

'Ready,' replied Rufus.

He heard Tam's prowlgrin kick off from the branch above, and urged Lyrinx on with a twitch of the reins. The prowlgrin flexed her powerful legs and flared her nostrils, both eyes swivelling upwards, trying to see through the cloud to the canopy above. With a grunt of effort, they took off, Rufus hunched over, covering his head as they crashed through branches.

Suddenly they were up and galloping, the tether tied to the saddle slackening then going taut with each bound. Looking ahead, Rufus could see nothing but the white blanket of fog. Beside him, the grey forms of Tam and Nixus – almost close enough to touch, but indistinct and blurred – kept pace with Lyrinx, bounding over the treetops. Beneath him, the prowlgrin swerved this way and that as she felt her way forward from branch to branch with incredible speed.

With no sun and no horizon visible, it was impossible to tell in what direction they were travelling – but whatever it was, they were travelling fast. With a bit of luck, they would outrun the tree cloud and be able to get their bearings. If not, they risked galloping in circles all day, getting nowhere. Rufus bit his lip, and checked his equipment.

'Good girl,' he whispered, patting Lyrinx's side. 'You'll get us out of here, won't you, girl?'

Two, three, or was it four hours later? Rufus couldn't tell; they were still tree-cresting blindly in the endless cloud. Rufus had tried to keep their spirits up, calling across to Tam, reminding him of the training-cradles back at Scartree where they'd both dreamed, one day, of tree-cresting on their very own prowlgrins . . .

But Tam was clearly in pain. His replies short and terse, he needed to concentrate all his effort in staying in the saddle and balancing as Nixus lurched and swayed, Rufus realized. Finally, as the light began to fade towards the end of that freezing dispiriting day, Rufus knew they had to call a halt. He was about to shout across to Tam when he noticed something. Ahead to their left, there was a curious golden glow, faint but just discernible through the white blankness.

'Do you see that?' called out Rufus.

'Yes,' groaned Tam, with effort. 'We'd better head towards it. At least that way, we'll know we're not going round in circles.'

They tree-crested for another hour, until the glow was unmistakable in the sky ahead of them and the icy white cloud actually seemed to be thinning a bit.

'That's it,' said Tam, hoarsely. Rufus could see him quite clearly now, doubled up in his saddle. '. . . Can't go on. Must . . . rest.'

Rufus and Lyrinx followed Tam and Nixus down into the mid-branches, landing – to the prowlgrins' pleasure – in a spreading darkelm. Rufus dismounted and helped his friend out of the saddle, shocked to see how exhausted and ashen-faced he looked. Tam slumped down on the branch, leaning back against Nixus's soft heaving side.

'I'm going to take a look at that leg,' said Rufus firmly, unstrapping a saddlebag and kneeling next to his friend.

This time, Tam didn't protest, but merely groaned when Rufus eased his boot off. The wound wasn't infected, Rufus was glad to see, but had clearly been rubbed raw against the inside of his boot as Tam rode. He must have been in agony. Rufus shook his head as he applied a thick layer of hyleberry salve and gently bandaged the leg.

'That should do for now,' he said, 'but you'll need to rest. We'll set off again at dawn . . .'

But Tam didn't reply. He was snoring gently beneath the protective bulk of Nixus.

Rufus stood up and turned to Lyrinx, loosening the saddle strap a notch and feeding her a handful of dried thousandfoot grubs from his pack. Looking up he could see the evening sky through the branches of the trees.

'Well done, girl.' He patted the prowlgrin. 'We've outrun the tree cloud. But as to where we are, your guess is as good as mine.'

Although it was now dark, the forest round them was bathed in the golden glow, the source of which, it seemed to Rufus, was just a little way ahead to the east. Curious, he left the prowlgrins gently purring over the sleeping Tam, and climbed down the dark-elm to the forest floor. Stooping at the base of the tree, he drew his knife and cut a wedge before setting off, careful to keep his bearings.

A notch in a green birch and a copperthorn later, Rufus found himself on the edge of a new clearing. Ahead of him, the stumps of recently felled trees stretched away towards a solitary furnace, its lone chimney crooked and twisted like an arthritic finger pointing up at the sky. Around it were huge pieces of rusting metal, the remains of bellows, giant cogs, treadles, truncated metal tubes and unattached pistons. Rufus had seen pieces of metal just like them in the ruins of the evil Foundry Glades. Around the furnace, the crooked chimney belching a thin line of smoke up into the glowing sky, a ghostly army was at work.

Death-cheaters – hundreds of them – fed the massive furnace, passing log after log, one to the other, in a long chain that stretched from the vast heaps of timber piled in the corner of the glade to the roaring mouth of the furnace at its centre. Others operated two giant cauldrons to one side; lowering huge pieces of rusting metal into one, pouring white hot metal into long moulds from the other. Still more of the shuffling half-dead creatures were carefully knocking the cooled metal from the moulds, before stringing up the small globes on long racks that stretched from the furnace to a rough timber cabin on the far side of the glade.

Thousands of metal globes twinkling in the glow, lined up in rows . . .

Rufus shuddered. Just like the rusting metal, he'd seen globes like these before, back in the Foundry Glades, strung from the belt of the black-plumed shryke. It was one of these globes – or rather what it contained – that had killed the three Gyles. Now here he was, crouched behind an ironwood tree, staring at thousands of them in this strange new glade.

This must have been how the old Foundry Glades began, he thought, with one furnace consuming the forest around it like a cancer. One chimney becoming two, then ten, then twenty; all belching out evil-smelling smoke – and weapons of war. And now it was beginning all over again. This new foundry, feeding off the scrap metal of the first, dragged here through the forest by . . .

Just then, on the far side of the stockade, there was a disturbance in the trees. A moment later a vast creature emerged, its misshapen head curved into giant tusks on either side of small stalk-like eyes. It was immense, with huge legs supporting a shallow ribcage and stunted-looking arms. Angry welts and weals covered its thick neck and bony back. It was followed a moment later by a second, as big as the first, but with a narrow head fringed by two crests, one above each of its sunken eyes, and a fang-studded mouth that hung exhaustedly open. As Rufus stared, a third came after it, its head embedded between its massive shoulders and a single tusk rising from a carapace-like brow.

The three of them were shackled together by a stiff leather harness that was strapped over their shoulders and round the vast girth of their chests. Taut ropes stretched back into the forest; ropes which, as the creatures lurched forwards – their backs bent and faces straining – revealed themselves to be attached to a huge, flat, and clearly immensely heavy timber cart.

'Nameless ones,' gasped Rufus.

As they came closer, he saw that the creatures were not alone. Hopping from the broad shoulders of one, to the stooped back of another, and onto the horned skull of the third, was the red dwarf. He was clutching a pair of vicious-looking pincer-spikes in one hand, which he wielded with malicious ferocity. He pinched the first creature's ear and stabbed at the lolling tongue of the second, which screwed its eyes up with pain and redoubled its efforts. The third threw back its shoulders, its tusked head bellowing with exertion, only to be rewarded by a vicious stab in the back from the red dwarf.

Slowly, the heavy timber cart emerged from the shadow of the trees and cast a brilliant glow over the tree-stumps around it. Rufus shielded his eyes against the glare. Strapped securely on the back of the cart was a huge, jagged shard of solidified lightning. Rufus could hardly believe the evidence of his own eyes. The timber cart contained the most precious substance in all the Edgelands.

'Sacred stormphrax,' he breathed.

Rufus had lost count of the times he'd pored over the barkscrolls in the library at Lake Landing, reading of the legendary quests mounted by the knights academic of Old Sanctaphrax. How they'd trained for years. How they'd learned to ride and sail and storm-chase . . . And how they'd set off in their sky ships for the Twilight Woods, chasing those storms that disgorged their lightning into the golden depths – lightning which, the moment it entered the eternal twilight, solidified into a glowing jagged shard.

Hurtling down and striking the forest floor, only the very tip of the lightning bolt would penetrate the ground. But it was enough. Though of normal weight in twilight, in the absolute darkness of the earth, the tip would become heavier than a thousand ironwood pines and begin to sink, ever deeper, below the ground. Slowly at first, but rapidly speeding up as more and more of the lightning bolt entered the darkness, the huge jagged shard would bury itself in the earth. Finally, with a sharp crack, the entire lightning bolt of pure stormphrax would, after a few minutes, disappear below the Twilight Woods, leaving only a thin powder of sepia dust on the forest floor.

A thousand times it must have happened down the centuries. Ten thousand . . . Who could say? The Twilight Woods had swallowed each and every bolt of stormphrax into its dark earth. The questing knight academics' only hope of recovering any of the

507

precious substance had been to be there when the lightning struck, then breaking what shards they could from the jagged bolt before it disappeared. No wonder it was so rare and precious a substance.

But Rufus knew that all this had happened during the First Age of Flight. The ancient knights and their sky ships were no more. Nobody had successfully chased a storm over the Twilight Woods for nearly a hundred years, had they?

The heavy cart, dragged by the poor tormented creatures, came to a creaking halt before the rough log cabin on the far side of the glade. The red dwarf scrambled down from the shoulders of one of the nameless ones and rapped on the thick, copperwood door. In answer, the door was thrown open and the light from what seemed like a dozen lamps flooded out from the cabin's interior.

A tall thin figure, slightly stooped and dressed from head to foot in protective hood, apron, gauntlets and boots, stepped out. He was followed by the black-plumed shryke and at least twelve hulking hammerhead goblins. With their large neck-rings, elaborate tattoos and glittering array of serrated axes, swords and spears, Rufus could tell in an instant that these were savage Deepwoods goblins, raised far from the civilized settlements of the Goblin Nations. The figure in the heavy apron pulled off the tall conical forge-hood he wore, and leered down at the shard of stormphrax, his face illuminated by its glow.

Rufus gasped.

'Getting heavier by the minute,' hooted the red dwarf, complainingly.

The black-feathered shryke reached out and grabbed a group of death-cheaters who were stumbling past in the neverending log-line to feed the furnace.

'Drop those!' she screeched, knocking the logs they were clutching to the ground with her flail. 'And take the lightning inside . . . *Careful!*' she shrieked once more, as the six death-cheaters – two skeletal mob-gnomes and four stooped figures in ragged sky-pirate greatcoats – eased the stormphrax off the cart and stumbled beneath its weight. 'Quickly, before the light goes, or we'll never shift it!'

The shryke cracked her flail over their heads. As they hauled the lightning into the stream of light from the cabin's open door, they straightened up and carried it carefully inside.

Rufus forced himself to look at the face of the figure in the apron. It had been horribly disfigured in some sort of fire or explosion, the features blasted away, leaving a fleshy mass of melted skin and scar-tissue. Only the eyes, piercingly blue, seemed to have escaped, ringed by unburned skin where goggles with eye-pieces of some sort had protected them.

'Do we have a deal?' the figure rasped through the

crooked gash that served as a mouth. 'The contents of the grain stores of the first three villages you raid come to me, plus half of any gold you find.'

'All that! Just for these?' growled the largest of the hammerhead goblins, examining the clutch of metal globes in his powerful fist. 'Sister Blackbeak said your weapons were powerful, but still . . .'

The figure turned his hideously scarred face towards the shryke. 'I paid for my discovery with my face,' he rasped. 'A few trinkets and victuals is a small price by comparison. Show our friend, Gutgurn, here . . .'

'My pleasure, armourer,' replied the shryke, bowing low.

She cracked her flail and set the six death-cheaters

who'd just emerged from the cabin stumbling out across the glade. They tripped clumsily over the tree-stumps as they went.

'Further!' she screeched. 'Further! That's right, keep going . . .'

The shryke took a metal globe from the belt at her shoulder and, closing one eye, took aim. Rufus knew what was coming next, yet couldn't tear his eyes away. The shryke swung her taloned claw in a wide arc round her head and let go. The globe flashed through the air and landed in the midst of the retreating death-cheaters. A moment later there was a flash, a loud *crack*, and all six figures were engulfed in white flames. In moments, the desiccated, half-dead creatures were reduced to ash.

'We have a deal,' said the hammerhead, and motioned to his comrades. They each took four globes and strung them from their belts. 'We'll be back for more,' he growled, 'when we've raided the Goblin Nations.'

The armourer permitted himself what, on his tortured face, passed for a smile.

'Return with the grain and the gold and I'll have some more of my phraxfires waiting for you.'

The goblins set off across the glade at a loping half-run, pausing only to look down at the remains of the death-cheaters before disappearing into the forest. Rufus turned to go. His heart was hammering away

in his chest and his mouth was dry. After a day galloping through freezing tree cloud, all he wanted to
do was curl up beneath Lyrinx in the protective
branches of the darkelm tree and forget all about the
horror he'd just witnessed.

But he knew he couldn't. Now, more than ever, he
knew he had to get back to the Free Glades and raise
the alarm.

'*Rufus? Rufus, is that you?*'

Rufus stumbled and almost cried out – but managed to stifle his yelp of surprise. It was Cedifice the
waif's voice in his head.

Cedifice? Where are you? Rufus reached out to the
waif with his thoughts as he followed his tracks back
to the darkelm.

'*We're in a bad way, Rufus,*' Cedifice's voice sounded
again in his head. '*Ran into a war-party of hammerheads,
fifty strong. They got Gaddius, but not before he took ten or
so with him. Went down fighting . . .*'

And the others? Rufus reached the notch on the
green birch tree and paused.

'*Holt and Hudflux were injured when Dex was killed,
and we lost Lance-Corporal Fledder when we rescued them.
Sergeant Logglimb has a barbed arrow in his arm, and I've
got a few cuts and scrapes – but we'll survive. Left half of
the hammerheads dead in return, and shook off the rest.
We're holed up in an ironwood pine on the edge of this
infernal glade. I've been reading the thoughts of the*

armourer down there for a day now. They're not good,
Rufus. And now he's armed the hammerheads. They've
just passed by below . . .'

Hold on there! Rufus arrived back at the darkelm
and began to climb. Tam and I'll come and get you.
We got lost in tree cloud. Lucky we did, Cedifice, or
you'd be . . .'

'No.' Cedifice's voice was calm but firm. '*You must*
leave us now. Go back to the Free Glades and return as soon
as you can with the rest of the roost. There isn't a moment
to lose. The woods round here aren't safe, Rufus. They're
patrolled . . .'

Patrolled?

Rufus reached the branch and shook Tam awake.

'Is that Cedifice?' said Tam blearily. 'Or am I dreaming?'

Rufus was about to reply – but stopped, his mouth
open in horror, as he stared past Tam at the treetops
just beyond.

CHAPTER FIVE

PURSUIT

There, hunched over in their saddles, staring out of the black slits of their rusting visored helmets, twisted pipes and dials encrusting their sepia-stained breast-plates, sat seven ancient knights academic on prowlgrinback. As Rufus gripped Tam's chequerboard collar in a trembling fist and pulled him to his feet, the knights spread out into the trees in a semi-circle around them. Slowly, hardly daring to breathe, Rufus eased himself up into his prowlgrin's saddle. Tam, ashen-faced, did the same.

Lyrinx's nostrils were wide and quivering, and she kept snorting with unease. Both she and Nixus beside her could smell the strange musty odour of decay which was emanating from the half-dead figures in the trees surrounding them.

'What are they waiting for?' whispered Tam, his dark-ringed eyes wide with fear.

As if in answer, the knight in the centre rose in his

saddle and stretched out a skeletal arm, his bony finger pointing directly at them. The prowlgrin he rode was all skin and bone, with wild, swivelling eyes embedded deep in his bony eye-sockets. Yet the creature still wore the distinctive bridle, emblazoned with a nameplate, which had been fashioned centuries before in the armouries of the Knights Academy.

Quederix, it read, in antique letters.

Quederix's rider was in an equally pitiful state. He was dressed in armour of a design not seen in the Edgelands for three centuries – high-crested shoulder guards, a broad 'clamshell' helmet and an ornately tooled breast-plate covered in a tiny filigree of pipes and levers, all corroded and pitted. Everything was encrusted with sepia dust. The knight was missing an arm below the elbow and the jagged remains of a splintered tree branch protruded from one shoulder. Whatever his injuries, they were clearly not fatal though, for like his fellow death-cheaters, the knight had emerged from the Twilight Woods' immortalizing light and lived on.

If, Rufus thought bitterly, you could call the degraded state the once noble knight academic was now in living at all.

One thing the terrible Twilight Woods had claimed for ever and could never be restored, was the knight's mind. His fellow riders had fared no better. Battered, withered and injured, they all sat slumped forwards on their once magnificent prowlgrins, craning their visored faces towards the two young lancers like a flock of starved vulpoons.

'Behold, fine knights of Sanctaphrax! Robbers! Raiders! Thieves!' The ancient knight's quavery voice rose to a high-pitched scream as he shook his bony finger accusingly at Tam and Rufus. 'They seek to steal the sacred stormphrax we have quested so long to find! Geraldius, sound the alarm! The Most High Academe must be warned!'

The knight on the far left of the semi-circle, his ragged prowlgrin perched in the quivering branches of a sallowdrop tree, raised a curved hammelhorn trumpet of antique design and lifted his visor. A skeletal face, half eaten away, stared back at Rufus as the knight put the trumpet to his shrivelled lips.

A sad and mournful note, deep and sonorous, rose into the night air. In the distance, the piercing shriek of the black-plumed shryke sounded in reply.

'Death to the phrax thieves!' screamed the ancient knight, to the hiss and grind of rusty swords being unsheathed.

'Death! Death! Death!' screamed his six companions, digging their heels into the sides of their emaciated prowlgrins.

'Forest floor!' Tam shouted across to Rufus, and the two of them twitched their reins.

Lyrinx and Nixus didn't need telling twice. They dropped like ironwood pinecones down from the great spreading branch and hit the ground running. Above them, the ancient knights' prowlgrins landed on the branch with a clatter of rusting armour and a cloud of sepia dust. One of their number – a bald prowlgrin with skin like bleached barkscrolls and one eye hanging from an empty socket on a glistening thread – misjudged his leap and came crashing down to earth.

As he hit the ground, his ribcage shattered like the timbers of a storm-wrecked sky ship. His rider, a knight in the piped-armour and heavy dials favoured at the academy during the reign of Linius Pallitax, was thrown high in the air. With a ghostly shriek, the knight jabbed at a lever on his breastplate and activated his parawings.

Rufus glanced back to see the knight, his black wings spread wide behind him, swooping down through the air. Like a hungry rotsucker, he landed on Tam's shoulders and clung fast. With a loud yelp of alarm, Nixus leaped high in the air, over Rufus's head. As they sped past in a blur of movement, Rufus glimpsed the gauntleted hand of the sinister knight closing round Tam's throat. Urging Lyrinx on, Rufus swerved through the trees after them and took aim with his iron-wood lance at the terrified prowlgrin just in front.

'Go on, girl. That's it,' Rufus muttered encouragingly, as Lyrinx brought her bounding leaps into time with Nixus. 'Just a little bit faster . . .'

A moment later, with a grunt of effort, Rufus lunged forward and felt his lance jolt with the impact. The knight gave a strange gurgling scream as the lance passed through his chest and lifted him from Tam's back. Rufus drew back the lance and the knight – parawings wildly flapping – crashed to the earth and disintegrated in a cloud of bone splinters and rusting metal. Tam was slumped forward in the saddle, a deep crimson stain spreading across his shoulder telling Rufus that his lance had not only skewered the knight but had also wounded his friend in the process.

'Mid-branch!' Rufus shouted to Tam as he sped past, twitching at Lyrinx's reins.

The prowlgrin leaped into the next tree in their path. And behind him, to his relief, Rufus heard Nixus land on the same branch moments later. He pulled Lyrinx up abruptly and, unstrapping the grappling-hook from his saddle, threw it at the branch above his head. Nixus – with Tam slumped in the saddle – edged along the branch and nuzzled against Lyrinx, while Rufus reached up and tugged on the rope attached to the grappling-hook. The tree branch above them bent down, completely covering them with a thick curtain of leaves.

Rufus secured the rope to his saddle. Then, leaning forwards, he gently laid a hand just above their nostrils to quieten the panting of the two prowlgrins, one after the others. There was nothing to do but wait – and hope they wouldn't be spotted. He peered through the leafy green darkness at his friend. Tam was looking back at him, hunched up and in pain, but clearly aware of their situation. In one fist he clutched his ironwood lance; the other, he pressed against his shoulder. He managed a thin smile, and nodded at Rufus.

Just then, below them, the knights appeared on the forest floor. They were spread out, their prowl-grins trotting through the trees, looking for signs of the two lancers. Stumbling across the desiccated remains of their companion, his parawings still fixed to the empty shell of his armour, they paused and exchanged blank visor-eyed looks.

It was almost, Rufus thought, looking down through the curtain of leaves, as if they envied the ancient knight's death. At last he had been released from the sacred quest for stormphrax to which he, and they, had dedicated their lives centuries earlier.

Rufus shivered. Did their poor twilight-destroyed minds comprehend that the floating city they served was lost; that their quest was at an end and that they were no longer even in the terrible Twilight Woods? He shook his head. What was going through their addled minds, Rufus could only guess at.

The shriek of the black-plumed shryke roused Rufus from his thoughts. Below in the forest, the six ghostly knights turned as the shryke strode into their midst. She raised a glinting taloned claw.

'You sounded the alarm, Centius Thalladix?' the shryke said, addressing the most ancient of the knights.

'Most High Academe of Sanctaphrax,' the old knight replied humbly, bowing his head low. 'Rest assured, the treasury is safe. My knights and I have driven away the thieves. Even as we speak, they'll be drowning in the Mire in their attempts to flee . . .'

In his head, the great knight Centius Thalladix was back in his beloved city, amidst its wonderful floating towers, reporting to the Most High Academe – himself dead for centuries past. The other knights shared his delusion, for all bowed their heads, in turn, to the shryke, though each one of them saw a different, long-dead High Academe standing before them.

'Drowning in the Mire, indeed! You rusting bag of bones!' screeched the shryke, raising her beak in the air and sniffing. 'If that is so, then why can I smell the breath of live prowlgrins above the stench of your decay?'

Rufus swallowed hard as the shryke's piercing yellow eyes turned to the branches of the trees above. They swivelled round until they came to rest on the curtain of leaves shielding Tam and Rufus. Slowly, as Rufus watched in horror, the shryke's taloned claw unhooked a metal globe from the leather strap at her shoulder.

'Tree-crest!' Rufus screamed, releasing the grappling-hook and jerking at Lyrinx's reins.

The two prowlgrins burst through the curtain of leaves that had concealed them, and leaped high into the forest canopy above. Gripping on tight,

Rufus felt the intense heat of the ear-splitting blast as the tree they'd been sitting in burst abruptly into flames. Far below him, the shryke screeched in frustration and hurled another globe.

Lyrinx and Nixus sped over the tops of the trees, leaving the flames and the screeches and the terrible stench of decay far behind. In his saddle, Rufus sat upright, lance in hand, taking in every detail of the surrounding tree-line while Tam slumped forward, holding on grimly as they steered their prowlgrins out across the vast expanse of the Deepwoods. Guided by the light of the full moon, they were riding headlong over the mighty forest in the direction of the Free Glades.

'Tam, how are you?' asked Rufus.

He was standing beside his friend's hammock high up in the top branches of the Scartree.

The pair of them had ridden through the night and most of the next day until – just as Rufus was beginning to fear that Tam could ride no further – they had reached the safety of the Free Glades. Now, an hour later, with the sun low on the horizon, they were on the branch belonging to the Fifth Splinter of the Fourth High-Branch Troop of Scartree Company, Tam's wounds bathed and dressed, and Rufus about to leave.

In the branches all around them, and in the other

five trees that made up the Third Roost, there was a frenzy of activity as lancers checked their equipment, readied their weapons and saddled their prowlgrins. The whole of the Third Roost had been ordered to muster and was preparing for battle.

'I'll be all right.' Tam smiled. 'No thanks to you and your clumsy lancework!'

Rufus returned his smile. 'Sorry about that. I'll try a lighter touch next time!' He patted his friend gently on the shoulder. 'I've got to go, Tam. The company marshal has ordered me to report everything I saw to the roost commander himself . . .'

Tam reached out a hand and grasped Rufus's arm.

'Wait,' he said, his face suddenly serious. 'You remember when I told you about my blooding?' Tam's dark-ringed eyes bored into Rufus's. 'I only told you about it because I didn't want you to think that getting blooded was all battle-cries and glory.'

Rufus nodded. 'Yes, Tam,' he said.

'But now you must do your duty. There's a battle coming, Rufus, both you and I know it,' said Tam quietly. 'A great battle. If my blooding was anything to go by, it will be terrible. War *is* terrible – though sometimes it is the only way to protect these Free Glades of ours. It is necessary. Remember that when you ride into battle, Rufus Filatine.'

Rufus nodded again. Tam's grip increased on his arm.

'And promise me one thing, green neck . . .'

'Anything, old campaigner,' said Rufus, staring down at his friend lying there, his shoulder heavily strapped and his leg swathed in bandages.

'That next time I see you,' said Tam with a smile, 'you'll be wearing a *proper* collar!'

The commander of the Third Roost of the Freeglade Lancers stood beneath the huge ironwood pines, their massive trunks rising up behind him like the columns of a great hall. As the branches of the six trees hummed with frenzied preparations, he stared out across the still dark waters of the Great Lake.

The marshal of Scartree Company emerged from the shadows between the mighty ironwoods, accompanied by a young lancer in the green collar of a cadet. Marshal Holdwood, a grizzled mobgnome, saluted the commander, who remained, back turned, staring out across the lake.

'Freeglader!' he said, touching the crimson banderbear badge on his tunic, and motioned for the cadet to step forward. 'Lance-Cadet Rufus Filatine is here to make his report,' said the marshal.

Rufus approached the commander and cleared his throat. Speak simply and clearly, he reminded himself from his training, presenting all relevant facts without embellishment or speculation . . .

'Fifth Splinter, Fourth High-Branch Troop,

525

Scartree Company set off on deep patrol three days ago . . .' he began.

The roost commander continued to stare out across the lake. 'I'm listening,' he said quietly.

'We tree-crested, then advanced in a mid-branch gallop until we approached the Foundry Glades, which we entered. We found evidence that the nameless ones had been stabled there behind the ruins of the Palace of Furnace Masters, and used to haul dismantled pieces of machinery and forge parts. We were interrupted by a fifty-strong band of death-cheaters led by a black shryke and a red dwarf. The shryke killed three lancers and five prowlgrins of the splinter with a weapon we haven't encountered before – a metal globe that explodes into an intense white fire on contact.'

The commander, still standing motionless, remained silent.

'Sergeant Logglimb and five lancers tracked the death-cheaters, only to be ambushed by a band of hammerheads. Lancer Whytewinter and I were sent back to raise the roost. We got lost in tree cloud and stumbled across a new foundry glade close to the Twilight Woods. An armourer, in league with the shryke and the red dwarf, is producing these weapons – hundreds of them – using stormphrax mined in the Twilight Woods by the enslaved name-less ones. The glade is protected by an army of death-cheaters, and the armourer is selling these weapons to hammerhead goblins and anyone else prepared to pay for them . . .'

'Then this armourer and his accomplices must be stopped,' said the commander, turning round and looking at Rufus for the first time.' He smiled. 'You have done well, Lancer Filatine,' he said. 'Your father is an old friend of mine. Perhaps he's mentioned me?'

Rufus nodded. The commander of the Third Roost had served with the Freeglade Lancers in the War for the Free Glades – but before that he had studied with his father at the Lake Landing Academy. He was a brave, courageous commander, but also private and thoughtful, spending much of his time with the oakelves of Lullabee Island when not on duty.

Rufus noticed the small lufwood disc the commander wore on a leather cord round his neck. On it was a portrait of a young knight academic in armour that reminded Rufus of the ghostly knights he'd encountered back in the forests near the new foundry glade the night before.

'Yes, commander,' he said, looking back at Rook Barkwater. 'My father has often spoken of you.' He looked down, his face flushing. 'It is because of you that I joined the Freeglade Lancers.'

. CHAPTER SIX .

THE BATTLE OF THE PHRAX GLADE

Commander Rook Barkwater sat straight-backed in the saddle of his magnificent skewbald prowlgrin, Chinquix, and raised a gauntleted hand to the red banderbear badge on his tunic.

'Freeglader!' he intoned in a clear, sonorous voice.

From the six ironwood pines that comprised the Third Roost, four thousand five hundred lancers raised their voices in reply.

'Freeglader! Freeglader! Freeglader!'

The battle-cry of the Freeglade Lancers rang round the Ironwood Stands as the Third Roost began to move out. Old Mighty, Great Acorn, Roughbark, Longspear, Silvercone and finally Scartree; the mighty trees were left empty as their companies formed into troops, five splinters strong, and set off in great rippling waves across the southern pastures towards the distant

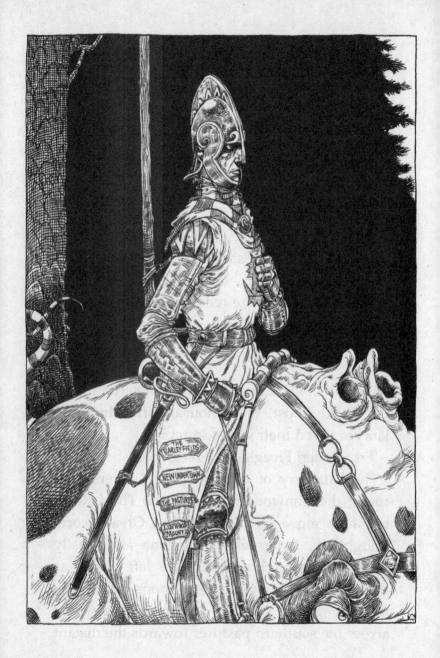

THE BARLEY FIELDS

NEW UNDERTOWN

THE PASTURES

LUFEWOOD MOUNT

tree-line. All around, flocks of woodsquabs and fieldgrouse flapped into the sky, squawking indignantly, while grazing hammelhorns scurried for cover.

Beside the commander, young Lance-Cadet Rufus Filatine felt his prowlgrin, Lyrinx, tense beneath him and snort with impatience as he gripped the reins. She was eager to join her companions in their bounding gallop towards the forest. Rufus leaned forward and traced a finger round her flaring nostrils.

'Easy girl, easy,' he whispered. 'Not long now, we'll soon be off tree-cresting.'

'Indeed we will,' said Commander Barkwater, turning to Rufus with a smile. 'You'll ride with me at the head of the roost. And I trust you've applied yourself to your tracking studies,' he added. 'I'm counting on you to lead us back to that new foundry.'

'I won't let you down,' said Rufus grimly, remembering his comrades in the Fifth Splinter awaiting his return.

'Then follow me,' said the commander, deftly flicking the reins of his prowlgrin.

Rufus did the same, and together commander and cadet emerged from the deep shadows beneath the towering trunks of the six ironwood pines of the Third Roost and set off at a gallop across the sunlit pastures. By the time they'd reached the tree-line and launched themselves up into the forest canopy, the two of them had overtaken the waves of lancers, and were at the front of the column.

'Tree-crest! Open formation!' Hundreds of waif whispers filled the lancers' heads.

Rufus turned to see wave after wave of galloping prowlgrins burst through the lush foliage and spread out over the swaying treetops like wind through glade barley. The sun, still low in the sky, glinted in the creatures' bright, excited eyes while the trees all round resounded to the noise of twanging and thudding as they leaped from branch to branch.

High up in the sky, a lone caterbird flapped sedately as it soared on rising air currents. Behind him, Rufus could hear the cheers of the lancers as they spotted this omen of good luck – and he felt his stomach give a sudden lurch as he wondered how many of them would survive the coming battle.

Would he be among them? Or was this to be the last time he'd gallop across the mighty Deepwoods on prowlgrinback? Rufus swallowed hard and tightened his grip on the ironwood lance.

Far to his left, a couple of slaughterer hammelhorn-herders from the Silver Pastures, the spi-der-silk sails of their skycraft billowing out above them, waved and shouted encouragement. Up ahead, a squadron of librarian knights pulled on their loft-sails, realigned their hanging-weights and brought their ornately carved sky-craft to a hover. As Rufus flashed past, he glimpsed their swords raised in a salute of respect. Soon they were distant specks on the hori-zon as the four thou-sand five hundred lancers of the Third Roost thundered over the treetops.

They tree-crested all through the morning and into the afternoon, head-ing across the vast forest, with Commander Barkwater and Rufus leading the way. Just as his training had taught him, Rufus had noted the forest formations on that desperate gallop back to the Free Glades with Tam the day before.

He remembered the high black peaks of ironwood pines to the west, and then the undulating expanse of copperwood and crimson larch they had crossed for hour after hour. Before that had come the jagged ridges of smoke-ash and lufwood, and then the low hollows of sedgewillow and blackoak. Now he was passing over them once more, signposts in the endless Deepwoods which pointed back to the horror from which he and Tam had fled.

The lancers travelled on through the night, the sounds of hundreds of waif signallers guiding their splinters mingling with the strange hoots and keening cries of the night creatures that they disturbed in their path. All the while, ahead of them, the golden glow of the Twilight Woods grew on the horizon like a false dawn. Rufus urged the panting Lyrinx on, trying not to think too closely of the terrible glade they were approaching. At last, as the moon sank in a sky now glowing with golden twilight, Rufus raised his arm and signalled for the column to halt. From the tree formations around them, he could tell that they were close to the new Foundry Glade.

Sure enough, Lyrinx's nostrils quivered and her brow furrowed as her sensitive nose picked up the faint, almost imperceptible taint of smoke on the breeze. Commander Barkwater joined Rufus in the top of a darkelm as, behind them, the four thousand five hundred lancers dropped silently down into the shadows below like melting tree cloud.

'You've done well, cadet,' the commander congratulated him, noting the low growls and quivering nostrils of both Chinquix and Lyrinx. 'There is a forest foundry at work close by.'

At that moment, the long sonorous clarion call of a hammelhorn trumpet cut through the air just ahead of them. Rufus looked up.

There, like a recurring nightmare, landing on the branches of a copperwood tree, were six skeletal prowlgrins and their ghostly riders. Rufus noticed the commander's hand go instinctively to the painted lufwood miniature he wore round his neck, the muscles in his jaw clenching as his fingers closed round the portrait of the young knight academic.

'Death to the stormphrax thieves!' the quavery voice of an ancient knight sounded from behind a rusted visor, as he and his companions unsheathed their swords. 'Death . . . !'

The six bony prowlgrins abruptly leaped from the branch in a cloud of sepia dust and flew through the air towards Rufus and the commander. Suddenly, from all about them, the ironwood lances of the five splinters of the Low-Branch Troop of Old Mighty Company thrust their points skyward like the quills of a timber-hog.

Rufus instinctively raised his own lance and felt it buck and jar in his hand as the ancient knights and their prowlgrins landed with a sickening crunch. The air filled with a thick musty cloud as the knights' paper-thin armour crumpled, dials and pipes disintegrated and their ancient decaying bodies fell apart like broken puppets, the effects of the shrykes' phraxdust finally spent. They rained down, clattering on the helmets and upraised gauntlets of the lancers, before tumbling down through the foliage and landing in a dusty heap at the foot of the darkelm tree far below.

The commander released his grip on the lufwood portrait and brushed the sepia dust from his shoulders.

'Sky rest their poor tortured spirits,' he said quietly. 'The shryke who misused these noble knights shall pay for this.' He raised his head. 'Forest floor, troop formation. Advance!'

As Rufus followed the commander down through the network of branches, the ground below filled with prowlgrins and their lancers, dropping to the ground like ripe fruit.

'*Advance!*'

The waif signallers spread the command, and the Third Roost set off silently through the trees. After a few minutes, the acrid smell of furnace smoke was unmistakable, and the massed ranks of the lancers came to a halt a few strides from a large forest clearing. Ahead, Rufus could hear the awful screeches of the black-plumed shryke and the papery shuffling and clanking of metal of an army of death-cheaters.

'Invaders!' the bird creature screamed. 'I smell them! Hundreds of them! Defend the glade, you mouldering corpses! They must not take the furnace!'

Dismounting, Commander Barkwater called the company marshals of the six trees to him. He drew a circle in the soft soil at his feet with the tip of his sword.

'Old Mighty and Great Acorn on the left. Longspear and Silvercone on the right. Roughbark skirt the glade and attack from the rear.' He issued his orders in a quiet voice, the waifs beside each marshal nodding, their barbels twitching. 'Scartree Company stays with me. We attack in the centre. The whole roost is to converge here . . .' The commander stabbed at the cross in the middle of the circle. 'At the furnace!'

The marshals nodded and disappeared soundlessly into the trees. Commander Barkwater mounted the great skewbald prowlgrin with his clear blue eyes and patted his side.

'Well, Chinquix, lad, here we go again. You and I, riding into battle – Sky protect us . . .' He turned to Rufus, who stared back at him, white-faced and shaking. 'Ready?' he asked.

'Ready,' said Rufus, trying hard not to let

Lyrinx feel his knees trembling.

The commander buckled his helmet and gripped his ironwood lance under one arm. Behind him, tensed in their saddles, the seven hundred and fifty lancers of Scartree Company clustered amongst the trees. From the glade ahead there came the pounding of feet, the clanking of metal and a low chant-like moaning. Commander Barkwater threw back his head, twitched the reins and roared.

'*Freeglader!*'

Rufus jerked hard on Lyrinx's reins and felt her mighty legs coil, then spring, propelling them both up eighty feet or more into the air. They broke through the branches of the trees on the glade's fringes and sailed out over the glade itself. To his right and to his left were white-tunicked lancers, their ironwood lance points thrust out before them as they reached the high point of their prowlgrins' leap, then hurtled down.

Below him, Rufus saw a sea of ghastly decayed faces with gaping eye-sockets, gap-toothed mouths and grey pock-marked skin stretched over mask-like skulls. With a horrible clanking sound, spears, scythes, jagged spikes and rusting pole-axes were thrust up in the air towards him by a thousand skeletal hands. He bent low in the saddle, braced his lance, shut his eyes and . . .

539

With a sickening crunch and an over-powering smell of decay, Lyrinx landed in the midst of a throng of death-cheaters – before bounding up into the air once more. Rufus pulled his lance back and was shocked to see it encrusted with a severed arm, a breast-plated torso and the gaping head of a withered-looking flat-head goblin, its rings rusted and immoveable in paper-thin ears. With a cry of disgust, he shook his lance free – just in time, as once more Lyrinx came down heavily amongst the foul-smelling crowd.

All over the glade, great swathes opened up – the ground covered with crushed and skewered bodies – where Scartree Company's prowlgrins had landed and taken off. High-, mid- and low-branch troops spread out like the fingers of a giant hand, the waifs' orders ringing in their heads, before turning in again like the clenching of a fist. All about them, the half-dead death-cheaters scattered like dead leaves before a forest fire.

Twitching Lyrinx's reins, Rufus kept up with Commander Barkwater and the white and brown blur of Chinquix, his mighty prowlgrin. Around him, he saw several lancers buckle, then topple from their saddles, rusting jagged spears embedded in their backs and chests. Glancing down, as Lyrinx leaped high once more, Rufus was horrified to see them disappearing into a wild and frenzied scrum of grasping, flailing claw-like hands as the death-cheaters tore them and their hapless prowl-grin mounts apart.

Down into the throng they came once more. This time, Rufus – jaw set and eyes blazing – thrust his ironwood lance down hard as he landed. Heads, torsos and limbs flew up into the air as a thick cloud of dust billowed all round him. Coughing and choking, hardly able to breathe, Rufus pulled Lyrinx up short and shook his lance clean. As the putrid dust cleared, he saw that the death-cheaters had shrunk back into isolated pockets in the glade around him, like tufts of barley-grass in a trampled pasture. Everywhere else, their hideous remains lay strewn about in an obscene jumble.

Commander Barkwater landed in front of him. He turned to his lancers.

'Scartree Company, form lines by the splinter!' he commanded.

Suddenly, Rufus found himself in the centre of a row of lancers, their prowlgrins, like his own, coughing and spluttering and snorting with exertion.

In the distance, a cloud of smoke showed where Longspear and Silvercone companies had trampled the phalanx of death-cheaters who were defending the right-hand edge of the glade. To the left, Old Mighty and Great Acorn companies were regrouping, their lances glittering in the early morning light. Everywhere, the army of death-cheaters lay trampled and broken amongst the tree-stumps along the edges of the glade. Their few survivors – injured and limping – stumbled towards the smoking furnace at the centre of the glade.

As Rufus looked, the figure of the armourer emerged from the rough-hewn log cabin at the centre of the glade, his gloved arms full of glittering metal globes. By his side, the black-plumed shryke opened her beak and spat an arc of green bile high in the air.

'It is easy to kill those who are half-dead already!' she screeched scornfully. 'Now, brave lancers, see how you fare against phraxfire!'

She raised a taloned claw, and fifty hammerhead goblins emerged from the sheds behind the glowing furnace, their leather breast-plates festooned with glittering metal globes. They fanned out in a protective arc round the forge and the log cabin. In reply, on three sides, the clatter of lances being levelled at the hammerheads' chests filled the glade.

Commander Barkwater rode forward on Chinquix.

'Those poor wretches that the shryke harvested from the Twilight Woods have found a grateful death on the ends of our lances,' he announced. 'Close the furnace, release the nameless ones you have enslaved, abandon these weapons and your lives will be spared . . .'

The armourer tore off his hood and glared back at the commander, his disfigured face glistening with sweat.

'You Freegladers make me sick! You expect the whole of the Edgelands to live in peace and harmony just as you do.' He sneered. 'Well, I, Lentil Spume have news for you. As long as I live, I will continue my father's glorious work! The Foundry Glades will rise again and Hemuel Spume's death will be avenged! He saw the future, and so have I, even though it cost me my face . . .'

The armourer shook a gloved fist at the commander, the metal globes he held dancing on the ends of their long thin chains.

'*This* is the future! Phraxfire and war! The strong plundering the weak! The rich enslaving the poor. Just as it has always been!'

Behind him, the shryke threw back her black-plumed head and cackled with laughter. 'Do your worst, Freeglade scum!' she screeched.

Commander Barkwater pulled Chinquix back and returned, stony-faced, to his lancers. A waif signaller's voice sounded in their heads.

'*Roughback Company begs to report, commander. We're in battle order in the tree-fringe, but the red dwarf has the nameless ones harnessed to what looks like an old glade-eater. We'll suffer heavy losses in a frontal attack . . .*'

The commander joined Rufus in the front rank of Scartree Company.

'Hold off until we make our charge,' he whispered to the waif signaller with the marshal of Roughbark Company. 'If we can spare those innocent creatures, we shall.'

Rufus tensed in the saddle. This was it. No longer was he to battle against ancient knights who'd lost their minds, or other demented half-dead creatures from the Twilight Woods. Instead, he was about to charge an army of fierce hammerhead goblin warriors armed with a terrifying new weapon whose terrible effects he knew only too well.

For a moment, Rufus wished he was back in his hammock in the Ironwood Stands; safe, comfortable, with a mild case of bark-croup . . .

No! Rufus gripped his ironwood lance fiercely. He was a Freeglade Lancer, and these merchants of death and misery had to be stopped! He waited for the familiar cry, the sound of which would signal his blooding . . .

'Freeglader!'

The prowlgrins of Scartree Company leaped ahead in unison, the riders hunched forward in their saddles with their ironwood lances levelled at the enemy. To the right and to the left, the same battle-cry sounded, as the other four companies did the same.

'Fire!' screeched the black-plumed shryke, and a hail of metal globes shot out from the ranks of the hammerhead goblins.

In his saddle, Rook gasped as the air around him erupted in a flash of blinding light and blast of intense heat. He was torn from Lyrinx's back and thrown through the air.

The ground came racing up to meet him . . .

When he opened his eyes, Rufus's mouth and nostrils were full of the pungent stench of burned hair and roasted flesh. His head rang with a strange roaring, as if a raging wind was blowing directly past his ears, drowning out all other sound. Around him, figures were staggering and stumbling through the acrid white smoke that billowed up from small black craters in the ground like rising banks of tree cloud.

To one side, five hammerhead goblins half stood, half slumped, skewered by a single ironwood lance that had embedded itself in the earth. Just ahead, a prowlgrin lay burned and charred beside the blackened body of its rider. More goblins lay dead around it, beheaded by a lancer's sabre.

Rufus's eyes stung with tears, but he couldn't look away from the horror. Suddenly, right in front of him, a crazed hammerhead loomed up – only to collapse, clawing at its throat as a crossbow bolt embedded itself between its neck rings. Rufus staggered to his feet. He felt light-headed and giddy – but all around him a desperate battle still raged.

The first volley of the phraxfire globes had wreaked terrible havoc on the Freeglade Lancers. Whole splinters had been incinerated in mid-charge, blackened mounds of ash marking the spot where they died. Enough of the lancers had broken through, however, to take their revenge on the fifty hammerheads.

Rufus could now see – something he'd only known before in theory – the unique carnage a well-aimed ironwood lance could inflict. Everywhere, dead goblins lay slumped in heaps. Having thrown the deadly phraxfire globes, their serrated swords and stabbing spears had proved no match for the deadly lances. And, as Rufus watched, the lancers made short work of the few hammerheads who resisted.

Finally, the last survivors turned tail and fled, and the lancers of the Third Roost regrouped around the figure of their commander, standing high in the saddle of his skewbald prowlgrin, sword in one hand, lance in the other. Behind him, the furnace's heavy door had been slammed shut and its valves closed tight. The lancers' grappling-hooks were already clanging against the crooked chimney as they gripped firmly.

Rufus gazed up at the chimney, which tottered then abruptly crashed to earth. Plumes of black soot rose up in a cloud. And at Commander Barkwater's feet lay the bedraggled figure of the shryke; her head separated from her body, her yellow lifeless eyes staring at the noonday sky.

The roaring in his ears cleared and Rufus felt a

gentle shove in the back. Turning, he stared into the eyes of his prowlgrin, Lyrinx, her harness blackened and fur singed, but otherwise unhurt.

'Lyrinx!' Rufus cried, and wrapped his arms round the great neck of the creature. 'Brave girl. Brave, brave girl . . .'

'Open up!' Commander Barkwater's voice sounded from across the glade. He had dismounted and was standing in front of the heavy door to the cabin. 'The battle is lost,' he bellowed. 'Surrender your workshop and what's left of your weapons!'

Suddenly a glint caught Rufus's eye and, looking down, he saw round the neck of the dead hammerhead goblin at his feet a metal globe. Stooping down, he carefully unhooked it and slipped it into the leather pouch on his belt.

All at once, a terrible roar sounded from behind the cabin. Rufus swung round.

'*Stop them!*' sounded the voice of Roughbark Company's waif signaller.

Without a second thought, Rufus grabbed the nearest ironwood lance and leaped into Lyrinx's saddle. He flicked her reins and the two of them sped round the side of the cabin and into the glade behind it. There, trundling full-pelt towards the log cabin, was a great metal plough with a curved spike protruding from its shovel-shaped front, being pushed by the three nameless ones.

Harnessed into place, the creatures were being tormented by the tiny flailing figure of the red dwarf. In its churned-up wake came the battered remains of Roughbark Company who, by the look of their shattered lances and exhausted prowlgrins, had thrown themselves relentlessly against the great contraption.

The muddy path through the glades showed where the red dwarf had forced the nameless ones to propel the plough towards the lancers, while the hideous little creature had devastated their ranks with phraxfire globes. Now, missiles spent, the dwarf was beating a retreat back towards the cabin – though by the speed at which he was forcing the poor creatures to push the machine, he had no intention of stopping.

Rufus could see, in an instant, that if it wasn't halted, the plough would destroy the armourer's workshop – and take Commander Barkwater and most of the remaining lancers of the Third Roost with it. He urged Lyrinx on and took aim with his ironwood lance. Closer and closer they came to the huge plough and its deadly spike.

'Go on, girl. Go on!' Rufus shouted. 'Now, Lyrinx! Now!'

The prowlgrin leaped high in the air just as the plough's spike was about to run her through. Rufus jabbed down with his lance as they sailed past and landed in the rutted tracks of the contraption.

He raised the lance. On its tip, pierced through his tiny heart, was the red dwarf, his small eyes bulging and his beaked mouth open wide. Behind him, the plough ground to a halt strides from the cabin as the great hunched shoulders of the nameless ones slouched forward and the poor tormented creatures slumped to their knees, panting hoarsely.

Thick tendrils of black smoke began curling up from between the roughly-hewn logs of the cabin and, as Rufus watched, the heavy timbers of the roof burst into crackling white flame. Then, from within the inferno the workshop had suddenly become, the deranged voice of the armourer sounded.

'Nobody shall have my secrets!' he screamed, as the flames that had destroyed his face now claimed the rest of his body. 'Nobody shall learn the secrets of phraxfire!'

Rufus's hand reached for the metal globe in his pocket . . .

Rufus stood before the huge ornately-carved door of the Great Lecture Theatre of the Academy at Lake Landing. He carefully adjusted the fine green and white chequerboard collar he wore before pushing the heavy door open and stepping inside.

'Well, well, if it isn't Corporal Filatine of the Freeglade Lancers,' came his father's gently teasing voice, 'promoted in the field at the Battle of the Phrax Glade by my good friend, Commander Barkwater . . .'

'Yes, yes,' said Rufus, blushing proudly. 'You wanted to see me, Father?'

Xanth Filatine, High Master of the Knights Academy, crossed the wooden floor and clapped a hand on his son's shoulder.

'Indeed I did, corporal. Indeed I did. I have something to show you.'

It had been three weeks since Rufus's blooding and promotion, and only now were things getting back to normal in the Ironwood Stands. The strange creatures known as nameless ones had had their wounds treated and had been taken far out into the Deepwoods and released – but not before the librarians had studied them closely and made many notes.

As for the Third Roost, it had suffered badly at the Battle of the Phrax Glade, but already its ranks were being restored by new young recruits attracted by the tales of its heroic exploits. From Fifth Splinter, Fourth High-Branch Troop, Scarface Company, Cedifice the waif, the twins Holt and Hudflux, and Sergeant Logglimb had survived the deep patrol and joined Rufus on the battlefield. Back at the Scartree, they spoke little of their exploits, as was the way with seasoned lancers.

Tam's wounds had mended, and Rufus had found that his own blooding had forged a new and even stronger bond with his friend. So now it was back to the routine of patrols and lance-drill – and the occasional visit to the academy at Lake Landing.

Rufus strode across the vast empty hall with his father, their footsteps echoing round the vaulted ceiling. The pair of them stopped at a small heavy darkwood desk situated in an alcove on the far side of the lecture theatre. Laid out on a tray, and bathed in light, was an array of tiny, intricately tooled metal pieces.

'Remember this?' asked his father, with a smile. 'Tweezel and I have done quite a bit of work on it.'

'Of course,' said Rufus. 'It's the phraxfire globe – but it's in bits . . .'

'Well,' said Xanth Filatine thoughtfully, examining the intricate mechanism of the globe with the tiny crystal of stormphrax at its heart, so dazzlingly bright it was hard to look at, 'sometimes one has to destroy something to reveal the secrets locked inside . . .'

He shook his head and his grip on his son's shoulder tightened for a moment.

'Secrets that you saved and brought back to the Free Glades, Rufus, my boy. Secrets which mean . . .' He turned to his son, his eyes twinkling with excitement. 'Life on the Edge might never be the same again . . .'

THE END

THE EDGE CHRONICLES

Have you read them all?

THE QUINT SAGA

The Curse of the Gloamglozer
Deep inside Sanctaphrax, an ancient curse has
been invoked . . .

The Winter Knights
Quint struggles to survive the icy cold of a
never-ending winter.

Clash Of The Sky Galleons
Quint is caught up in a fight for revenge against
the man who killed his family.

THE TWIG SAGA

Beyond the Deepwoods
Abandoned at birth in the Deepwoods, Twig
does what he has always been warned not to do,
and strays from the path . . .

Stormchaser
Twig must risk all to collect valuable stormphrax
from the heart of a Great Storm.

Midnight Over Sanctaphrax
Far out in Open Sky, a ferocious storm is heading
towards the city of Sanctaphrax . . .